Book I Iof The Chosen

# RUNNER

Book II of The Chosen

# RUNNER

ROH MORGON

RUNNER: BOOK II OF THE CHOSEN



Published by Dark Dreams Publishing
Cover design by Deranged Doctor Design
Interior design by Roh Morgon

PUBLISHER'S NOTE

This book is a work of fiction. Any references to historical events, real people, or real locales are used fictitiously. Other names, characters, places, or incidents are the product of the author's imagination, and any resemblance to actual events, locales, or persons, living or dead, are purely coincidental.



DARK DREAMS PUBLISHING
darkdreamspublishing.com

ISBN-13: 978-0-9981581-1-2 - ISBN-10: 0-9981581-1-2

First paperback edition October 2017

Printed in the United States of America

*Dedicated to*

*all of the readers*

*whose faith in this story*

*helped bring it*

*to life*

*and, as always,*

*to*

*my one love*

# PROLOGUE

## ΛⲰ⊃†MH⊃↑ ⊃ꟼΛ⊃↑†⊃

## IIV⁎

**J**úniusz 9., hétfő

*Five hundred years has not been enough. Not nearly enough.*

*Not enough to prepare me for this agony that is beginning to split every molecule in my body. The cells scream as they come apart, matching the wail ripping away my vocal cords. Fire races up and down my veins, and my skin smolders, preparing to ignite.*

*I have driven her away yet again. And this time, I know it is forever.*

*She will not come back to me.*

*Not ever.*

*For she has truly seen the evil within me, the evil I was cursed to bear, the evil from which I can never be free.*

*With each mile she puts between us, I descend farther into the pits of hell, embraced by its flames and whispers of promised tortures.*

*And I welcome it, all of it.*

*Because without her, there is nothing else.*

*There is no reason to go on.*

*I am finished with this life.*

# PART I

# THE HITCHHIKER

# MONDAY

## CHAPTER 1

My mind races along with the black BMW through the Wyoming darkness as the car screams northward away from Colorado. I try to direct my thoughts to the future, to anything that lies ahead of me. Because what lies behind me is a nightmare, and yet the most wonderful dream ever imagined.

A dream that ended only hours ago with the death of a man and the near-birth of a monster.

For that is what I nearly became.

A monster.

A true monster. One who kills for blood. One who kills *humans* for their blood.

The horror of what I've done is spiked with my last images of that room—the gore-smeared wall, the crumpled body beneath it, the love of my life standing white-eyed and radiating waves of unfathomable power.

And rage. Incredible rage.

His cruel words echo in my head, inflicting punishment with every breath.

"*You killed him . . .*

"*And now, you will have to kill again.*"

A green highway sign flashes by in the dark, its color reminding me of his piercing emerald eyes as they regained their normal hue, filled with anguish and regret and heartbroken love. They watched me back away from him, step by step, my hands smothering the horrified scream tearing from my throat.

"*No . . . ,*" I cried as I reached behind me for the door.

"*No!*" Nicolas roared as I ran for my car.

But the fury with which he chased me was woven with devastating feelings of loss, of need, of desire that I will never forget.

Nor will I forget how the last little bit of *him* in me shattered into nothingness, leaving me empty and all alone.

An eternity of all alone.

I can feel myself begin to tear apart again, and visualize the two halves of my body ripping away from one another, ragged and bloody. I don't know how I can even drive when I'm torn in two, with one hand steering forward and the other trying to turn the car around and go back.

Back to *him*.

Glancing down, I expect to see blood pouring from the divide running through me, and am surprised my torso appears intact. But that must be only on the outside, as the gap on the inside feels as though it's widening with every mile. It's only a matter of time before my skin splits apart, and then maybe I will die so I no longer have to bear this pain.

The tires thump, thump, thump, and I yank the steering wheel and bring the car back into the center of the lane. White dashes against black asphalt flicker past in a mesmerizing stream. I focus on it in an attempt to keep from thinking, from thinking anything at all.

White, black. White, black. White . . .

Something moves out of the darkness and onto the road ahead of me.

Alarmed, I yank the wheel again, just in time to avoid hitting it.

Was that a person?

Pulling the car over to the side of the highway, I stop and look back.

Was someone really there, or has my imagination truly gotten away from me?

Or was it Nicolas?

Panic shoots up my spine and I shift the BMW back into gear.

Shuffling footsteps approach from the shoulder of the road behind me.

Human footsteps.

A bit of the tension drains away and I turn and look back to see a teenage girl nearing the car, holding her side. When she reaches the passenger door, she tries to open it, but it's locked. Bending down, she peers into the window, her face painted in fear and hope. I push the unlock button.

She pulls on the handle and carefully climbs in, slamming the door behind her.

"Wow. Thanks for stopping. I thought you were gonna hit me back there."

I almost did.

She grimaces as she settles into the seat, then offers me a tentative smile.

I want to ask if she's okay. But of course she's not. She was in the middle of the highway in the middle of the night, and from the looks of her, it wasn't by choice.

"My name's Sandy. How far you goin'?" She tries to smooth her kinky blondish hair, a nervous movement she repeats several times. She's petite, young, no more than eighteen or nineteen, but looks like she's lived twice that.

I know the feeling. My last five years seem like an entire lifetime.

Her question still hangs in the air, unanswered. I force myself to respond.

"Casper."

"Cool. That's where I'm headed." She smiles again, her freckles dancing across her cheeks, along with smears of dirt and what looks to be a bruise developing under one eye.

Thank goodness I don't smell any blood, at least on the outside. The beast slumbers inside me, safely drugged with the lifeblood of the man I murdered only a few hours before.

The rest of her isn't in any better shape than her face. Her arms are covered in more bruises. Her stained T-shirt is torn at the neck, and she's probably been wearing those jeans for weeks. Or months. No jacket either. She must be freezing.

Flipping on the heater, I glance in the mirror and pull back onto the road.

"Nice car." There's a tremble in her voice that she bravely tries to hide with a shallow cough.

"What happened? Are you okay?"

"Oh, you know. Same old thing. A ride I took ended up costing a little more than I was willing to pay."

I look over at her, eyebrows raised.

"I'm all right, other than the shiner I'm probably gonna have. But I left that trucker with a bruised set of balls. It'll be awhile before he wants to use them again." Her laugh chokes off with a gasp and she clenches her teeth, wincing as she massages her left side.

Alarmed, I pull over to the shoulder and bring the car to a stop.

"You don't look 'all right' to me."

"No, I'm fine. Really. Must've bruised my ribs on the gear shift. They're not broken. Just sore."

"Are you sure? Maybe you need go to a hospital."

"Naw. It's nothing serious. Been through worse." Her hand tugs on a curl. "It sucks, though. I didn't have time to grab my backpack. It's still in his truck."

I glance down at my black nightclub dress, the only clothing I currently own. I left everything else behind when I ran.

She notices and a small frown creases her face as she takes in the partially torn straps and the dark splashes down the front.

Her scrutiny sends a prickle across my skin. I check the mirror and hit the gas.

Sure glad I cleaned up the blood smeared across my face and upper body at the last filling station.

"Looks like you had a rough night, too." Her mumbled words reach out, as though she's seeking a connection, her voice underscored by loneliness and need. It's the voice of an outsider.

Like me.

"A rough night?" I choke back a laugh. "Yeah, you could say that."

"Well, I hope you left whoever it was in worse shape than I left that jerkoff in his truck."

My jaw clenches. Her jerkoff was at least still breathing.

"So . . . what's your name?" she asks. "I mean, since we're traveling partners, at least for a little while."

I take a deep breath, not really willing to give it, but then relent.

"Sunny."

"Sunny? Huh. That's worse than Sandy. Were your parents hippies or something?"

Chuckling at the timeworn question, I experience a strange moment of candor with this kid.

"Yeah. They actually named me Sunshine. Thank God they decided I didn't need a middle name."

Sandy laughs, then grimaces. "Yeah, that could've been bad. Something like Rae or, oh, what about that one chick, Moon Beam, or something like that? Her dad was some rock star."

I glance at her, surprised that someone her age would know of Zappa.

"Moon Unit Zappa. Her dad was Frank Zappa. He was pretty edgy for his time." I'd grown up listening to my parents' extensive music collection, which included every album that Frank Zappa had made. Moon was born in 1967, two years before me.

"Moon . . . Unit? I mean, how could you do that to your kid? I had a bad enough time being called 'Beach' or 'Dirt.' I 'spose you had some stupid nicknames, too, huh?"

Faint childhood memories rise to the surface, only to float away on a sea of red.

"Not so much nicknames. But I did get hassled whenever it was raining or cloudy. Or when I was in a bad mood." I grimly smile at the recollection of growing up with everyone always expecting me to be bright and happy, or asking why my hair was dark brown instead of yellow like the sun. If only they could see me now.

"Sunny . . . yeah, I can imagine. Names are weird. People get these stupid ideas about you just based on your name."

Or find your name ironic, and their amusement is the first light you've found in five years of darkness. Bright emerald eyes suddenly flicker in the night sky above the road, and the realization I'll never see them again crushes the air from my chest.

Fighting back the bloodtears, I stare at the streaming lines on the asphalt and concentrate on the hunter's cold stillness within me. When I once again feel dead inside, I drag my attention back to the girl.

"Well, Sandy who is not a beach, why don't you try to get some sleep? We're still a couple hours from Casper, and a rest might do you good."

And I no longer have anything to say, especially to a human.

"I dunno, I'm still a little amped. Besides, couldn't you use someone to help you stay awake while you drive?"

"No. I'm kind of a night owl. Go ahead, at least close your eyes. I'll be all right. I'll let you know when we get close to town."

"Well . . . okay. Maybe for a few minutes. But promise you'll wake me up if you get sleepy, okay?"

"Sure."

"All right. Just for a little while . . ." Sandy closes her eyes, and is sound asleep within a minute.

Poor thing. She probably doesn't feel safe enough to sleep around strangers very often.

And I'm not exactly the safest thing for her to be with. How absurd.

But she's definitely good for me. At least for the time being. Focusing on her gives my mind an escape route from that other black and dangerous road it was following. The road to my own personal hell of loneliness. The road that threatened to make a U-turn at any moment.

I look at her again. She's cute, with a wide freckled nose and full lips, and a round face framed by that kinky, almost golden hair. Asleep, her peaceful expression makes her look even younger. She might as well have a target painted on her chest out here on the road.

Her helplessness triggers something, and for once it's not the hunter or the beast. A vague protective feeling trickles through me, an almost motherly feeling—something I'd nearly forgotten.

Hopefully it will last long enough for me to see her safely on her way—before the beast awakens.

And before its relentless hunger begins once again.

# CHAPTER 2

We're approaching the outskirts of Casper and I glance over at Sandy. Other than breathing very deeply, she hasn't moved since she closed her eyes.

"Sandy." I keep my voice just above a whisper, hoping not to startle her too much.

She jerks her head up, her body tense as she checks her surroundings.

"What? Where are we?" She blinks her eyes several times, looking out at the brightly lit billboards flashing by.

"We're coming into Casper. Where did you need to go?"

"Oh, well, uh, you can just drop me off at the next truck stop. I'll catch another ride there."

Stunned, I look at her.

"You've got to be kidding me. This time of night?" Anger edges into my voice. "Do you want a replay of your last ride?"

She grits her teeth and, frowning, stares straight ahead.

"Seriously. You don't have any friends or family here to stay with?" I try to gentle my tone.

"Just take me to a truck stop, okay?"

"No, I don't think so. I'm going to find a motel and we can talk about it in the morning."

"I'm not willing to *trade* for a warm bed, if you catch my drift." She crosses her arms and glares at me.

Unable to help myself, I laugh. Warm, I am not. And I can't tell her that I'm not attracted to her body, only what's *in* it.

"Look. I'm extremely private. You'll have your own room. No strings attached."

She's quiet for a moment.

"For real? I mean, I can't pay you back, at least for a while."

"You don't have to pay me back at all. Consider it a donation to . . . to freedom."

"Freedom?"

"Yeah. Yours. To make choices. To make the best ones you can without having to give up too much of yourself."

She says nothing as she studies my face.

"Ya know, you're pretty cool. Thanks."

"You're welcome."

"But I do have one favor to ask." Hope lights up her face, matching that in her voice.

"Okay."

"Would you mind, I mean, could we just go by the truck stop that's at the next off-ramp? I just wanna see if that guy's truck is there. I'd really like to get my backpack."

"What, do you think he'll actually give it to you? After what happened?"

"No. I was just gonna take it."

The exit sign looms out of the darkness. I swerve and get off the freeway.

Sandy points to the truck parking and I slowly cruise by the first row. Reaching the end, I turn and drive along the next one.

"There it is. The green one with the yellow trailer," she says quietly.

I pull past it, put the BMW in neutral and set the parking brake. Turning off the headlights, I leave the engine running.

"Stay here. Let me check it out first. Okay?" I look pointedly at her.

"Okay."

I get out and leave my door open with the interior lights off.

Walking around to the driver's side of the truck, I climb up the step, then pause and listen. There's no sound of breathing inside. Grabbing the door handle, I give it a couple good yanks and break it off. The door swings open and I slip inside the cab.

Her scent is everywhere, along with the grimy one of the truck's owner. Crawling into the sleeping compartment, I sniff the rancid air and try to pinpoint her backpack, and finally find it stuffed between the mattress and the side wall of the compartment.

I jerk it free and turn to crawl back into the cab. Sandy is staring in through the passenger window, and gives me a grin and a thumb's up when she sees her pack.

Frowning, I climb out the driver's side. She meets me there, grinning and clapping her hands.

"What part of 'stay here' did you not understand?" I say through my teeth as she takes the backpack.

"Aw, this is so cool. Thank you. But . . . but how did you break off the door handle?" Eyes shining, she kicks it across the asphalt.

"Hey! What do you think you're doing? Get away from my truck!" A short guy with a big belly is running toward us, his gait awkward and stilted.

"Oh, shit! Run!" Sandy takes off for the BMW.

I'm right behind her, and then another guy dashes out from between the trucks.

His breath explodes with a loud grunt as I smash into him and send him flying through the air. He tumbles in the dirt, forcing me to leap over him before springing into the car. Sandy jumps in a second later. Throwing the BMW into gear, I hit the gas, my door slamming shut with the acceleration.

We speed out of the parking lot accompanied by angry shouts. Sandy turns and watches behind us as we race up the freeway on-ramp. The beast inside me whines, begging to be loosed.

"Whoa. That was awesome! You just took that guy right out! Like he was nothing! How the hell'd you do that? Are you a spy, or FBI, or something? That was way cool!" She's practically dancing in her seat as she prattles on.

I ignore her and check the rearview mirror for lights.

Passing a few more off-ramps, I take one that has a sign posted with symbols for motels and food. Sandy continues to ramble with her wild speculations.

"Hey. Sandy." I pause, but she doesn't stop. "Sandy. Enough. Shut up, okay?"

"Okay." Her eyes glow with excitement.

Sheesh.

"You hungry? You want to get something to eat before we check into a motel?" I figure it's probably been awhile since she's had a good meal.

"Uh, yeah, sure. That . . . that'd be great!"

"Well, what do you want? There's a twenty-four-hour diner right here, or we could look for something else. Whatever you like."

"I don't care. What do you feel like eating?"

Right now? After the crap at the truck stop? Something red, hot, and liquid. But I doubt they'd willingly serve that at the diner.

"I'm not really hungry. I had something just a little while before I picked you up." A twisted laugh escapes, and I manage to strangle it into a cough.

"Oh. Okay. Well, then . . . this is fine with me."

Turning into the driveway, I find a space near the entrance and back into it for a quick getaway if needed. Sandy gets out with her backpack and an odd look crosses her face, which is suddenly more pale than before. She wobbles a moment, hanging on to the door.

"Hey, are you okay?" I ask.

"Yeah. I'm fine. Just stood up a little too fast." She smiles and hoists her backpack over her shoulder, then makes her way to the sidewalk. I usher her ahead and follow her slender form inside.

The reek of cooking food hits me like a shockwave and my stomach somersaults. It's been a long time—I'd forgotten how nasty it smells.

A middle-aged waitress walks up holding menus, and I tightly leash the still-agitated beast when it shows a keen interest in her. She leads us to a booth and I follow Sandy, keeping her between the waitress and the restless killer inside me, which, strangely enough, shows no interest in the girl.

Before we take our seats, Sandy asks where the restroom is and leaves. I avoid looking at the waitress and order a cup of hot tea.

When she comes back, I stare out the window and focus on keeping the beast quiet. The ceramic cup rattles on its saucer as she sets the tea on the table, then she quickly walks away.

Picking up the cup, I take a sip, and abruptly recall the last time I had hot tea. And with whom I had it. The grief starts to creep in again.

I look up into green eyes as Sandy sits back down.

Green eyes. I hadn't realized that her eyes were that color. *His* color.

"Hey," she says softly.

I take a breath and look into my tea, then take another drink.

"He must've been something else, huh?"

"Who?" I ask sharply, frowning as I glance up into those green eyes.

"Whoever makes you look like that."

Blinking, I stare back down into my cup. Breathe in. Breathe out.

"Do you know what you're ordering?" In a flash of irritation, it comes out a little harsher than I intend.

"Uh, no. I haven't looked yet."

Glancing at the menus lying on the table, I pick one up and hand it to her. She takes it without another word, and I watch her as she flips through the plastic pages.

She's washed her face, and changed her dirty and torn T-shirt for one that is only slightly less ragged, but cleaner. She's also put on a zippered sweatshirt, and looks decidedly happier and more comfortable, in spite of the bruising that has spread across her face.

"Get whatever you want, Sandy. I'm buying. No argument."

Sandy nods and scans the room for the waitress.

Watching her eat is going to be strange. The heavy smells of frying fat and burnt toast and slopped coffee bubbling on the warmer nearly gag me, making the situation even worse.

I'm outta here.

Fishing a twenty out of the emergency pouch I'd brought in from the BMW, I stand and put it on the table.

"I'm going outside to make some calls and find us a motel. Take as long as you want to eat—there's no need to rush. I'll be waiting in the car."

"O . . . kay. Are you sure you don't want something? I could order it to go for later if you want." Sandy looks up at me, wide-eyed.

"No, I don't want anything. I'll see you in the car."

The waitress walks up just as I step out of the booth. The beast, still on edge, tenses at the scent of human blood coursing beneath her skin. With my jaw clenched, I head out the door.

Damn you, Nicolas. Is this going to happen every time I'm around people now?

I'm so screwed.

How am I going to do this? How am I going to live without you? I don't even know that I want to. I don't even know what I'm doing here.

Opening the car door, I get in and slam it shut. The black hole in my core, the place where I used to feel his essence, begins to swallow me. I grip the steering wheel, seeking an anchor in the dark maelstrom of regret, trying vainly to hold on to my sense of self.

It would be so easy. All I have to do is start the car and get on the freeway heading south. If I drive fast enough, I can make it back to Colorado Springs before dawn, before the sun puts me to sleep.

And then what? How long before he sets me up again? How long before he asks me to kill? How long will it take for me to *want* to do it, without any encouragement?

How long can I remain *me*, before I surrender and lose myself completely?

# CHAPTER 3

A light tapping on the passenger window startles me and I'm pulled away from my internal battles. I look up to see Sandy waiting there, her eyebrows raised in question. As I hit the unlock button, I notice the car is running.

Damn, that was close. Wonder how far I would've gotten before realizing that I was driving. No doubt the direction would've been south, my body making the decision my mind cannot.

"Hey, you okay? Were you sleeping with your eyes open or something?" Sandy asks as she gets in and closes the door.

The Styrofoam takeout container she's carrying reeks, and the nausea and irritation it triggers brings me another step closer to reality.

"Didja find a motel? I saw signs for a couple when we got off the freeway." She sets the food and her backpack by her feet.

Motel. Right.

I glance at the clock. Still have a little while before dawn.

Taking off the emergency brake, I put the car in gear and pull out to the edge of the driveway. I look south first, tighten my fists, and turn north.

"How was dinner?"

"It was good. Thanks. They had a special on steak and mashed potatoes with gravy. The green beans were kinda soggy, though. And I wasn't as hungry as I'd thought. But I did eat the apple pie. I love apple pie."

Ugh. I can't remember when any of that sounded good. And whatever's in that container is about to make me hurl.

Sandy watches me and starts to say more, then stops. We head up the street and I spot a sign for a motel a block away.

Turning in, I park next to the entrance and get out. The lobby door is locked, so I push the after-hours button and stare through the dirty window at the tiles on the floor, their red and white alternating pattern triggering blood images in my head.

I push the button again, holding it for several seconds this time.

They better answer, because if they don't, I'm going to get back into the car and drive.

And I will no longer be able to resist heading south.

An inner door opens. A paunchy grey-haired guy, rubbing sleep from his eyes, shuffles across the lobby.

"Whaddya want?" he mutters through the door, glaring at me.

"I need two rooms."

"All I have left is smoking."

"I'll take them."

He digs into his pocket, pulls out a set of keys, and unlocks the door. When he opens it, his unwashed odor floods over me like a tidal wave. A corresponding surge of disgust rises up my throat and, jaw clenched, I slip through the doorway as far from him as possible. He shambles back through the inner door and appears behind the registration counter.

I quickly fill out the necessary paperwork and hand him cash for the rooms. He mumbles something about a credit card and I shake my head no, and he gives me two key cards anyway. I can barely keep to a human speed on my way out of the stinking lobby.

"This one's yours." I climb back into the car, pass one of the keys to Sandy, and start the engine.

"Cool." She takes it and holds out a fistful of bills in exchange. "Hey, thanks again for dinner. Here's your change."

"Keep it."

She nods and pockets the money, muttering another thanks.

Pulling into an empty space outside one of the rooms, I shut off the engine. Sandy opens her door and stands, slinging her backpack over her shoulder.

The color drains from her face and she clutches at the door as she collapses.

"Sandy!" I leap from the car and sprint around it to find her in a crumpled heap on the dirty asphalt.

But at least she's moving. With a soft groan, she pushes herself to a sitting position. Her hand flies to her nose and she tilts her head back, pinching her nostrils.

Blood seeps past her fingers.

"Aw, shit," she mutters, closing her eyes and leaning on her other hand.

Holy crap.

Fighting off my sudden panic, I back away and brace myself for the beast's reaction.

The taste of blood hangs in the air.

And the beast rumbles, but does nothing else.

Amazed, yet grateful for the reprieve from its incessant lust, I slowly ease down beside her, ready to bolt if necessary.

"Sandy—are you all right?" I reach out, wanting to smooth back her hair, but stop. Despite the beast's calm, I don't trust myself.

The only humans I've touched in a long while have been the donors upon whom I've fed. And the man I killed earlier tonight.

"Sandy."

"I'm fine," she says nasally through her pinched nose. "Just clumsy."

"Sit here a moment. Don't try to get up yet." I rise and reach through the open door to press the trunk button on my keys in the ignition.

I never go anywhere without a blood cleanup kit.

Handing her a folded paper towel from the trunk, I hesitate, still unwilling to touch her.

But the girl needs help, and I'm all she's got right now.

She waits a moment, the paper towel pressed against her nose, then gathers herself to stand. I reach down and Sandy grabs my hand. I slowly pull her to her feet and steady her, still baffled over the beast's lack of reaction to the human nectar mere inches away.

But my inner musings vanish when she straightens and winces, releasing my hand to cradle her side.

The side she was holding when she first got into my car.

"Are you sure you're okay? Maybe we should take you to the hospital to get that looked at." I gesture to her side.

"I keep telling you I'm fine!" Her defensive tone makes me think otherwise, but before I can argue further, she smiles. "Sorry. I've just been on my own awhile and I'm not used to anyone giving a shit. I'm really okay. Just banged my ribs. Nothing's broken."

She shifts the blood-soaked paper towel to a clean spot, then reaches down for her backpack. Tearing my gaze away from the blood on her face and fingers, I get to the pack first and hold it out to her.

"Thanks." She takes it. "And . . . thank you for everything. I don't know why . . . why you're being so nice to me, but thanks anyway." Her green eyes bright with unshed tears, she quickly turns away and heads for her room. I wait until she's inside, then head to my own.

The acrid stench of old cigarettes rolls out when I enter, underscored by the chemical reek of cleaning solutions and a myriad of human odors, all of which are pretty disgusting. My lip curls in revulsion.

I'd almost rather sleep in the trunk of my car. Wouldn't be the first time.

But this will be the first time in a long while that I've slept without Nicolas's comforting presence somewhere nearby—and without it *inside* me, coursing through my body as his blood coursed through my veins.

The black pit in my center yawns, threatening to take me down into it. My eyes ache with bloodtears and I call the hunter, using her to reinforce the stillness before they overflow down my face.

With a grimace, I take a deep breath of foul motel air, open the window, and turn the ancient fan on high.

Focus. Just need to focus on surviving, because I *can* do this.

I head back out to my car to do an inventory, hoping to find a spare set of clothes.

No such luck. The paper towels, trash bags, and water are all that remain in my cleanup kit, further evidence of how much things have changed since I settled in Colorado. I make a mental note of missing items, such as a comb and a mirror. And, of course, clothes. And shoes.

A dismal laugh escapes me. I need a whole friggin' new wardrobe.

Damn.

Shopping is the first priority tomorrow. Hopefully I can get it done and get out of Casper before Nicolas traces me here.

Because as much as my body yearns to go back to him, my *self*—what's left of it—does not. To do so will mean its loss entirely, and I'm not willing to give it up. To give *me* up. Not now, not ever.

Slamming the trunk, I open the car door to retrieve my emergency pouch and recoil from the pungent leftovers still sitting on the passenger floorboard.

That stinky crap's not staying in *my* car overnight.

I lean in, grab the container, and head to Sandy's door.

She answers holding a fresh wad of bloodied tissue to her nose.

Alarm flickers through me, but the beast shows no reaction other than mild interest. My bewilderment quickly shifts to concern.

"Your nose is still bleeding?"

A rueful grin brightens her face.

"Welcome to *my* world."

"What, you falling and hitting your face?"

She laughs and takes the leftovers I'm holding out to her.

"No. Nosebleeds. Doesn't take much of a bump."

"Do they always take this long to stop?"

"Yeah, they can."

And, of course, *I* had to be the one to pick her up. Me, who feeds only on blood. She couldn't have found a worse savior.

"I'm just surprised I didn't get a bleed when I kicked that trucker's ass. Or should I say his balls. He was sure running funny at the truck stop." She giggles and steps back. "Wanna come in?"

Not a good idea. No telling when the beast is going to wake up.

"No, I need to get to bed. I tend to sleep in, so you'll at least have your leftovers if you wake early."

"Okay."

Turning away to leave, I stop and gaze out at the stars dotting the black sky.

"I have to do some shopping tomorrow. If you need anything . . ."

"Really? That . . . that would be awesome. I could use a few things."

Good. That means she might stick around so I can make sure she's all right before I hit the road.

"Okay. See you tomorrow."

Just before she closes the door, her quiet words drift through the cold night air.

"Goodnight, Sunny. Sleep tight."

~

A glance at the clock tells me I have about an hour 'til dawn. Not long enough to go for a run, but too long to sit here with my thoughts. I turn on the TV and flip through the channels.

It's all crap. I haven't been able to watch TV since I came into this life. Not only are most of the programs mindless and absurd, but they make me feel even more alien and outside of the world.

I continue to change channels, using the flashing images as a distraction. Anything to keep from thinking.

But the dark chasm threatens my sanity yet again, and tears begin to well up in my eyes. I desperately grip the stillness to block the rising anguish, but I'm having trouble holding on to it. Every cell in my body is filled with yearning.

Yearning for his laughter, his love, his arms, his fangs.

His blood.

Nicolas . . .

I glance at my car keys on the nightstand.

A knock sounds at the door, tentative, quiet.

I take a breath and debate answering.

"Sunny? You still awake? Can I talk to you?" The hope in Sandy's voice tugs at me.

Oh, hell.

"Just a minute." I turn off the TV.

Going into the bathroom, I wipe the blood from my eyes, being sure to get every trace.

How ironic. Sandy bleeds from her nose, and I bleed from my eyes.

I look one more time in the mirror and am frightened by what's looking back at me. I don't even recognize this haunted thing, her dark blue eyes full of pain and despair.

"Sunny?" She knocks again.

"Yeah. Be right there." Once again I try to embrace the stillness, and thankfully feel its calm take hold.

I walk out and crack open the door.

Sandy is standing there, one nostril packed with what looks to be white cotton.

"I got it stopped." With relief evident in her voice, still sounding somewhat nasally, she smiles.

I feel relief as well. At least now I don't have to contend with her blood glittering in front of my face, dreading the moment the beast decides to raise its ugly head.

"Can I come in?"

Staring past her at my car, then at the faint hint of dawn in the eastern sky, I abandon the last clinging thought of racing southward and glance at the girl.

"I guess. But only for a few minutes. I need to get some sleep." Stepping back, I open the door wide and gesture her in.

She walks in and plops down into the chair next to the dresser and TV.

Since there is nowhere else to sit, I push the pillows upright against the headboard and climb onto the bed.

The distant hum of the highway forms a backdrop for the silence within the room as I wait for her to speak. She seems to have something to say, but is having trouble getting started. I look at her pale face and note that the bruising now covers half of it.

"So? What's up?" I finally ask.

"Nothing in particular. I just . . . I just thought maybe *you* needed to talk. That's all." Her green eyes stare at me with concern.

"Me? Why?"

"Well, um, you know, you're all strong and tough on the outside. I mean, look at the way you got my backpack and handled those truckers. Even the waitresses in the restaurant seemed scared of you. You're pretty badass." The admiration shining from her eyes startles me.

"So what's your point?" Irritation ripples across my skin. Her misplaced hero worship is not something I even remotely deserve, nor desire.

"Well . . . I know that's only on the outside. And what you have goin' on inside is, well . . . I think you're hurting, a lot, and I just wanna let you know that you can talk about it with me. If you want."

Still a prisoner to my instinctive need for privacy, I stare at her as resentment over her invasion into my business bubbles to the surface.

"You know *nothing* of me." I stand, my fists clenched. "You don't have any idea who you're talking to or what I'm feeling." I walk toward the door, intending to ask her to leave.

"But I do. I have this . . . this weird thing inside that tells me what people are feeling. And I mean, it's really strong, and sometimes I have trouble being around people because their feelings are so overpowering. I'm not . . . a . . . *normal* person," she finishes in a whisper.

Turning, I study her, and begin to think that she sees me as more than just a rescuer. She sees another soul outside the normal human world, whether she recognizes that's what it is or not.

I calm myself.

"So why do you think you're not normal? There've always been people who have a greater amount of empathy for others. They usually become therapists and counselors, and use their gift to help them understand their patients."

"Now you sound like everyone else." Her eyes narrow. "They're always trying to tell me that I'm okay, that I'm just imagining things, that it's just a phase. And it's all bullshit! Because I *know* that I'm different. I always have been. And nothing anyone says will change that." She crosses her arms and stares at me, anger shining from her green eyes. Eyes that are also filling with tears.

I take a deep breath, then walk back over to the bed and sit down.

"Okay. Then tell me more about it. And just for the record, I'm certainly not like everyone else."

"I know. I can sense it. It's more than whatever has you so sad and hurting. You're different, too. I'm not sure why, but that doesn't really matter to me." She looks down into her lap.

Despite being taken aback by what she's just said, I'm willing to listen, if that will help her.

"So tell me about it." I keep my expression neutral. "This . . . thing you say you have."

"Well, it's hard to describe. I know what people are feeling. A normal person could see it if they opened their eyes, but most of them prefer to keep them shut. But I don't just *see*. I can *feel* it, too." She glances away, then looks at me, her eyes brimming as she continues.

"Like you, for example. I think you're running from something, or someone, and it's messing you up big time. It's not only all over your face. It's inside, too, and I think it will be very bad for you if you don't go back." Her voice trembles and the tears run down her cheeks.

Oh God. This it too much. My own tears well up, and leaping from the bed, I race for the bathroom and slam the door.

"Sunny? Sunny? I'm sorry, I just want to help. Please. Talking about it might help you."

I lean against the wall, then sink to the floor, hugging myself tight, blood carving wet trails down my face.

"You need to go, Sandy," I manage to choke out.

"This is about a guy, isn't it? I just know it. What's his name? Please, talk to me."

Nicolas. His name is Nicolas. I gave up my world for him. And though he lied to me and betrayed me, I don't think I can live without him.

But the words die in my throat, unable to claw their way out.

"Why'd you leave him?" There is real pain in her voice, as though she actually feels mine.

Her question echoes in my head, over and over.

Why *did* I leave him?

My body feels as though it's about to explode.

"I, uh . . . had to make a choice," I rasp out through my tears, not caring if she can hear me or not. "And . . . I wasn't ready to make it. I don't know that I ever will be."

"Between him and who? Or what?" Her voices catches.

Between him and my humanity? The humanity I don't really have anymore?

My mind shrinks away from this thought, but it's too late. The thought that I left for no reason. That I left to keep from becoming a murderer, yet that is exactly what I am. What was the point of leaving then? What was done was done.

The lid on the black box cracks open. The black box I keep in the corner of my mind, where I shove the memories I wish not to remember, and *she* peeks out. That tiny human part of myself. I thought I killed her too, back there in the Springs.

She says, *I'm still here. I'm still part of you. You left . . . to protect* me.

And then I feel myself begin to fade into the black oblivion of the coming dawn. I try to fight it, but, as always, my struggle is useless. Sandy's voice through the door grows faint and I mutter something about going to sleep, and then the darkness takes me.

# TUESDAY

## CHAPTER 4

Cold, hard tile is the first thing I'm aware of. The second is Sandy's scent, and the sound of her breathing, and the feel of her warm soft body curled around mine beneath a blanket.

Shit.

I raise my head up and look at the floor. Dried blood is crusted where my cheek had lain, and I reach up and rub it off my eyes and skin.

Sandy moves, then slowly shifts back and sits up. I push away the blanket and do the same, keeping my face averted, then stand and step over to the sink. When I'm done washing up, I check the mirror and see her still sitting on the floor, watching my reflection. Her nose has stopped bleeding—there's no sign of the cotton in her nostril. I take a deep breath and her rich human scent fills the air in the tiny room. I close my eyes a moment, then open them and turn around.

"Morning," I say, because there is nothing else I can say.

"Good morning," she replies softly as she uses the wall to stand up. The bruise on her pale face is a mosaic of purples.

Turning to leave the bathroom, I pause when I see the broken doorframe, then continue on out. Sandy follows.

"You didn't answer. I couldn't hear you and . . . I thought maybe you'd gone out the window. But when I checked it outside, it didn't look like the kind that could be opened."

Ignoring her, I sit on the bed to put on my high heels.

"You know, you don't breathe when you sleep. I thought at first you were dead," she says quietly.

I am, sort of.

"And you're cold, but not icy cold or stiff, like someone really dead. I touched someone who was dead once, and you didn't feel like that. So I decided you weren't really dead. Just in some kind of weird trance-like sleep."

I stop. This should be freaking me out. But I don't really care anymore.

Fastening the last strap on my shoe, I stand and straighten my dress, then check the clock. It's 10:08 AM. She probably needs to eat.

"It's a form of meditation in which . . . in which we slow our breathing and lower our body temperature to concentrate better. It helps calm me." I look over at her. "Now, do you want some breakfast? I noticed a café next door, or we could go back to the diner. Whatever you like."

"Yeah, I guess so, if you're gonna get something."

"No, I'm not really hungry right now. I don't usually eat when I first get up. Maybe later. But you should eat." I inwardly wince at the parental tone that just came out of my mouth.

She shrugs, unoffended.

"I'm not really that hungry either. Anyway, I've got my leftovers."

"You don't have to eat your leftovers for breakfast. Wouldn't you like some . . . pancakes, or eggs or something?"

"No, I'm fine for a little while."

Though I'm not so sure about that, I don't feel like arguing with her.

"Well, since food isn't a priority right now, how about you and I get out of this dump and go do a little shopping. I don't know about you, but I could certainly use something else to wear besides this ruined dress."

"Okay." Sandy visibly brightens and walks toward the door. I grab my keys and pouch, then pause a moment before following her outside.

It's a good thing the sun doesn't fry my skin anymore. Otherwise, getting around today would be a whole lot more complicated. Though I'm relieved to be free from my fear of the sun, a new fear has taken its place. The fear that Nicolas's blood has irrevocably altered my system in other ways, pushing me further into the Change and toward becoming a full Chosen who can no longer be satisfied with the blood of animals. One who *must* feed on humans.

Suppressing a twinge of anxiety, I wait by the car while Sandy retrieves her backpack from her room, then we get in and drive around to the front. I ask about shopping while checking out and the clerk gives me directions to a nearby mall.

We're driving up the street toward the mall and Sandy clears her throat.

"So you're a bleeder, too, huh?" she asks.

Say what?

I frown, not sure how to answer.

"I mean, I saw the blood under your face. Sometimes I wake up like that, cuz I've had a nosebleed while I'm asleep."

"Bleeder?" I doubt my definition will match hers.

"You know, you bleed easily. And bruise easily. A lot of people are bleeders."

I stay silent, trying to process her words.

"I mean, it's no big deal. I've had to get transfusions before. And I was on some medication for a while. But I got better as I got older. I don't need that stuff anymore." Yet there is uncertainty in her voice, and I glance again at the bruise on her face.

"Sandy, if you don't mind me asking, how old are you?" I try to sound nonchalant.

"Oh, I'm twenty-one. Old enough to drink, and do anything else I want." She laughs, but it rings false.

"Sandy. I'm not stupid, and as you've mentioned, not quite like everyone else. How old are you really?"

"I'll be eighteen next month," she mumbles.

Shit.

Seventeen. She's the age *I* was when my daughter was born. She's the age my daughter was when I . . . when I was ripped through my car window and into this hellish existence.

My gut twists as I inwardly cringe from the horror of that night five years ago and the evil creature who stole me away from my Andrea to turn me into this *thing* that I am.

"Okay." I take a deep breath, struggling to keep my voice neutral. "Well, since you seem to know so much about me, how about telling me a little more about you. What are you running from? Where are your parents?"

"My mom died when I was born, and my dad left a little while later. I grew up in foster homes. This last one was a real loser." She snorts and stares out her side window.

An orphan. Like Andrea.

I focus on the road ahead.

Sandy smooths back her hair as she glances at me.

"Yeah, so I decided I could take way better care of myself than the state's been doing."

"What . . . what state is that?"

"The state of none of your business," Sandy snaps.

"Fair enough."

I say nothing further. I can't. I can't talk about this anymore. I don't need to add to my pain. I have more than enough already, both old and new.

The road leading to the mall thankfully appears and we cruise the parking lot, checking out the various stores. As we pass the entrance to Macy's, I turn and pull into a parking space.

"Macy's? Awesome!" Excitement erases the pout on her face.

As I get out, I watch her slowly stand and my earlier concerns for her resurface. She looks paler than she did last night. No telling how much blood she might've lost from her nosebleed.

"Are you feeling okay, Sandy?"

"Yeah, I'm fine." She flashes me a quick smile and picks up her backpack, then closes the door.

"You don't need to take that in. Just leave it here. I'll lock it in the trunk." I walk to the rear of the car.

"No, that's okay. I'd rather keep it with me." She slings it over one shoulder and heads toward the store entrance.

Fear lurches through me as I consider what lies on the other side of that door.

People. Lots of them.

Though uncomfortable with crowds, I'm usually able to maintain control around people long enough to shop and take care of any business I might have.

But now? After draining someone to the point of death last night?

I have no idea what'll happen.

With a deep breath, I tightly leash the hunter and the beast inside me and follow Sandy into the mall.

My new cell phone reads 12:51 when we leave the mall and walk to the car loaded down with packages. In spite of Sandy's excitement over her updated wardrobe, she looks tired, and I'd ended our little adventure earlier than I'd intended. She hadn't eaten much of the meal I'd bought her at the food court, claiming she just wasn't hungry. She'd drunk a lot of water, though.

Aside from my worries about Sandy, the day hadn't been the ordeal I'd feared it would be. I didn't know how I'd react to being surrounded by so many humans, but something about Sandy seems to help me keep the beast in check. I'm not sure what it is. Maybe it's that she reminds me of Andrea. Not in looks. A little in personality, perhaps. But mostly I think it's her age and the silliness that can go along with it. And she seems, for all her toughness, somehow fragile, and it makes me want to take care of her.

Opening the trunk, we pile in the bags and boxes. Sandy utters a cryptic comment about our haul, and I can't help but smile. I've been doing that a lot today, more than I would've expected under the circumstances. It occurs to me once again that her intrusion into my life couldn't have come at a better time.

We get into the car and Sandy takes out her new cell phone. Mine rings from somewhere within the leather shoulder bag I'd bought, and I dig through its depths, grumbling about too many pockets. Finally locating the persistent phone, I glance over at her and answer it.

"Yeah?"

"Hi!" She flashes me a quiet grin.

"Hi."

"Thank you for taking me shopping and for my new phone."

I didn't just do it for her. I did it for my own peace of mind. She needs to be on her own as soon as possible. Just in case something happens and I need to leave in a hurry.

Something like me getting hungry.

"You're welcome." I end the call and start the car.

An idea pops into my head, and before I can change my mind, I throw it out there.

"Sandy, what do you think about getting a hotel for one more night? That way you'll have a good night's sleep before you get back on the road." And I'll have a little more time to make sure she's really okay before I hit the road as well.

Sandy looks down at her lap, then nods as she puts away her phone.

"That sounds good." She looks over at me and smiles. "Hopefully it'll be a little better than the one we had last night. That one was kind of a dive. Their floor was too hard, and pretty dirty, too." She snickers.

Glancing sidelong at her, I shake my head. I still can't believe a human slept with me and lived to joke about it.

Her smile fades and the exhaustion creeps back into her face. She leans against the door and closes her eyes.

Poor kid. She had rough night and not much sleep. It's no wonder she's tired.

The Hampton Inn is just a few miles down the road. Sandy doesn't move as I park and quietly get out. I head toward the lobby to get us registered.

She's still asleep when I return. I open my door and slip in.

"Sandy . . . Sandy." I reach out and gently touch her shoulder.

She bolts upright, her eyes wide.

"What?!" Those green eyes dart around, alarm ringing in her voice.

"It's okay. We're here at the hotel. I thought maybe you would rather sleep in a soft warm bed."

"Oh, yeah. That sounds pretty good, I guess." With a big sigh, she grabs her backpack and slowly gets out of the car.

She still looks pale. Even though she'll probably argue, I think she should see a doctor after we get settled. Something just doesn't seem right.

Opening the trunk, I begin collecting the packages to carry to our rooms. Sandy joins me, and we start walking across the parking lot. Our trek quickly turns into a pathetic juggling act, and we laugh as boxes fall out of bags and handles rip. But we finally make it to the lobby where I commandeer a baggage cart.

We steer it into the elevator and I'm glad to see that her nap seems to have energized her some. Her bruise is not the sharp contrast to her pale skin that it was, but then again that might be due to the makeup we bought.

When we reach our rooms, I help Sandy unload her stuff. Whatever bit of energy she'd found is gone by the time we're finished.

"Thanks, Sunny." She offers me a brief smile and sits down on the bed.

"Hey, even though it's kind of early, are you hungry for dinner? You haven't eaten much today."

"No, maybe later. I think I'm gonna lie down for a little while. I'm pretty tired."

"All right. I'll check back with you in a bit. Get some rest."

That'll give me time to find a doctor. But hopefully a nap is all she really needs.

Once inside my own room, I take a deep breath and feel the tension in my body begin to release a little. Even with Sandy's calming presence, I still find it difficult to be with people for any length of time. Including her.

Funny how quickly I got used to being with my own kind, when I didn't have to hide what I am.

Just *who* I am.

Putting my packages on one of the beds, I glance around before taking the cart back downstairs. This will do for one more night. But it makes me nervous to be in Casper for so long. It's too close to the Springs, just barely five hours away, and I worry that Nicolas may trace me here.

And I don't know why. As ready as I feel to run back to him, I also fear him finding me.

Regardless of what I end up doing, I need to get this girl situated, because I can't take her with me, wherever I go. It's too dangerous—on so many levels. Yet the thought of leaving her disturbs me. I can't believe I've gotten so attached in such a short time.

To a human. To someone I could potentially kill at any moment.

That disturbs me more than anything else.

# CHAPTER 5

"Sandy." I knock on her door. She's been sleeping about two hours now, and I want to get her to the urgent care clinic before they close.

No answer.

I knock louder. The only response from within is a faint groan.

Shit.

I pull the spare key for her room from my back pocket.

She's on the floor next to the bed, lying on her side. Her nose is bleeding again, and there's blood everywhere—on the carpet, on her bathrobe, on her.

"Sandy!" Ignoring it, I rush to her side.

"I fell," she whispers.

I grab towels from the bathroom. Terrified that my body will betray me at any moment, I try to staunch the flow.

Bleeder. She said she was a bleeder. As in a hemophiliac?

Oh God.

"Can you sit up?" I shift to help her.

Her weak attempt fails and I become even more alarmed. As I lift her, she winces and groans, and her bathrobe falls open.

Sandy's left side from her ribs down—the side she's been favoring—is a mass of angry purples.

This isn't just a nosebleed.

Examining her more closely, I realize she's panting, her breaths shallow. Rapid, weak pulse, skin cold and clammy—she's in real trouble.

Instinct tells me there's no time to wait for an ambulance.

I prop her door open and rush to my room to grab car keys and purse, then race back.

"Sandy, I'm taking you to emergency." She groans as I scoop her up like a baby and stand.

"My backpack . . . ," she gasps. I balance her against me and grab it, then head to the elevator. When we reach the bottom floor, I hurry up to the front desk.

The clerk's eyes widen as she notes the girl in my arms and the bloody towel at her face.

"Where's the nearest hospital?" I demand.

She quickly babbles out directions. "Don't you want me to call an ambulance?"

"Not enough time," I snarl as I shove through the doors.

Sandy's heart is beating too fast and my blood sense tells me she's in grave danger. I nearly run across the parking lot, cradling her as gently as possible, then carefully load her into the back seat. Her eyes are closed. I can't tell if she's still conscious or not.

"Hang in there, Sandy. We'll be there in just a minute."

I slide into the driver's seat and tear off across the parking lot.

The hospital's only two miles away, but that might not be close enough.

The BMW races down the street, ignoring the speed limit.

Stopping outside the emergency room, I leap out and open the rear door, then reach in and carefully pick up Sandy's limp body and walk into the ER.

"I need help here! She has some sort of blood disorder and I think she's bleeding internally. She needs to be seen—*now!*"

Within seconds, a nurse comes into the waiting room.

"Open her robe," I order.

The nurse's eyes widen as the bruising on Sandy's side is revealed.

"The blood is from her nose—I think she hit her face when she fell."

"Follow me," she says, closing the robe.

We head through a door and into a curtained treatment room. I ease Sandy down onto the bed and step back out of the way as another nurse comes in.

"What's her name? How old is she?" One of them starts sticking little pads all over Sandy with lines that lead to a monitor while the other cleans the blood from her face.

"Sandy. She's . . . she's eighteen."

I don't know how they'll react if they find out she's a minor and I'm not her guardian.

"Hello, Sandy. Sandy, can you hear me?" The nurse gently shakes her.

"Yeah," Sandy mutters.

"Sandy, my name is Janeane and this is Zelle. Can you tell us what happened, honey?"

"My side hurts. And I'm really, really tired." Sandy's voice is barely above a whisper.

"Well, stay awake if you can. We're hooking you up to a monitor to watch your vital signs."

Janeane turns to me.

"Are you a relative?"

"No, just a friend."

"I'm sorry, only family members can be back here. You can wait in the waiting room."

"No. Can't she stay?" Sandy struggles to sit up. "Please?"

"Easy, hon. Just lie back and rest." Janeane glances at me. "Yes, she can stay."

Another nurse comes into the room with a clipboard and begins asking Sandy questions. Her responses fade in and out, but she manages to remain awake long enough to sign the forms. The pen slips from her fingers as she tries to give it back to the nurse, then her eyes close.

"Okay, Sandy, I need to draw some blood and set up an I.V. You might feel a little sting in your arm." Zelle says something about low blood pressure, but finally the tube begins to fill with red. She finishes with the remaining tubes, then hooks up an I.V. line. Clear fluid begins running into Sandy's arm.

The nurses continue talking to Sandy as they work on her, even though she makes no indication that she hears them. Janeane is typing on a small computer near the bed when a doctor steps inside the room.

"All right. What do we have here?"

One of the nurses quickly fills him in and he requests they do an abdominal ultrasound. He spends a moment examining Sandy, but she doesn't respond to his questions. He then turns to me.

"And you are?"

"Sunny. A friend."

"I'm Dr. Graystone. Do you know what happened?"

"Not really. I picked her up hitchhiking last night, sometime after midnight. She said she'd had a fight with a truck driver."

He turns back to Sandy and peers at the bruising on her face.

"And what's this about a blood disorder? There's no mention of it on her paperwork."

"She called herself a *bleeder*, said something about transfusions in the past and medication. She had a nosebleed last night that lasted awhile. Her nose was bleeding again when I found her on the floor in her hotel room, just before coming here."

The doctor nods and starts typing on the computer.

One of the nurses comes back with the ultrasound machine and I step into the hall to give them more space to work. The other nurse—Zelle—directs me to a sink where I can wash Sandy's blood off my hands and arms.

On my way back to the treatment room, I remember the backpack.

Maybe there's something in it that will help—Sandy's insistence on bringing it might be more than just a fear of losing her stuff.

The doctor is leaving as I walk up. A nurse wheels Sandy's bed out through the curtains while Zelle trails along with the I.V. bag.

"Where are you taking her?" I try to keep the panic from my voice.

"Over to radiology." He stops in the middle of the hall. "We're still waiting on the lab results, but based on the ultrasound, I've ordered a CT scan. It appears she may have some internal bleeding, but we need to determine the source and extent of it before choosing a course of action. You're welcome to wait here."

"I . . . I just remembered her backpack. She insisted I bring it—it's in the car. I'll go get it."

"Good. If she does have an underlying medical condition, it might contain her emergency info."

The car is still running where I left it, and I quickly pull it out of the loading zone and into a parking space. Grabbing Sandy's pack, I walk back to the room, set it on the chair, and start pulling out her things. Clothes, a sketchbook, a photo album, a few trinkets. I unzip one of the smaller compartments and take out a charm bracelet. Looped and fastened through the bracelet is another one, a simple medical I.D.

bracelet like kids in school used to wear. The name *Sandy Miller* is engraved on the underside, along with an Ohio address and a phone number. Below that are words that might help the doctor.

"Von Willebrand. This says she has von Willebrand disease." I hand it to Janeane. She reads it, thanks me, and heads out into the hall.

Zelle and the other nurse roll Sandy's bed back into the room. The girl's still unconscious, and I can do nothing but stand there and stare at her pale, bruised face.

Ohio. She's just a young, sweet kid from the Midwest who should be hanging out with friends, going to school, and enjoying life, and not lying beaten in a hospital bed surrounded by strangers.

The doctor re-enters the room, followed by Janeane. She gives me the bracelet and I tuck it into Sandy's backpack.

"Any word from the lab?" he asks.

"Not yet," Janeane says as she enters more info into the computer.

"Were you able to reach her family?"

"The number's been disconnected."

"Well, let's try to wake her again."

He leans over Sandy and calls her name several times, then gently pushes up one of her eyelids and points a penlight at her pupil.

Sandy jerks her head away and squints up at him.

"Hi, Sandy. I'm Dr. Graystone. Can you hear me okay?"

"Yeah."

"Sandy, do you have von Willebrand?"

"Yeah."

"Are you taking any medication?"

"No."

"Okay. Well, you're bleeding internally and we may have to do surgery to stop it. Do you understand?"

"Yeah."

He continues to explain the risks of surgery—and the risks of not having surgery.

Like death.

Oh shit.

I watch, horrified, as Sandy signs another form. The phone on the wall rings and Zelle answers it, then passes it to the doctor. He listens a moment, nodding, then hands it back and tells her to call Dr. Wilson.

Everything begins to happen very fast.

His expression grave, the doctor rattles off orders to the two nurses. I catch words like "hemoglobin," "factor," and "two units of type O negative" in his instructions, and both nurses fly into high gear.

At some point in the flurry of motion, the phone rings again. The doctor picks it up, and after a brief conversation, barks out a quick "Thanks, Bill," and hangs up.

"All right. Let's finish up—they have an O.R. team standing by upstairs."

He heads over to the computer and I stare at the bag of blood hanging from Sandy's I.V. stand. Red life flows down the tube into the girl's arm.

I can't help but compare her need for blood to mine. It's as vital to her as it is to me. She will die if she does not get it, as will I, though it will take me much, much longer.

That she could die from its loss while in *my* care, even though I've neither desired nor taken a single drop of it, is beyond cruel.

The doctor finishes at the computer and turns to me.

"It's a good thing you found that bracelet."

"What is von Willebrand disease?"

"It's a blood-clotting disorder, similar to hemophilia, but usually not as severe. She appears to have been beaten, as you said, which explains the extensive bruising and nosebleeds. But her more serious injuries are internal. The CT scan revealed she may have a small tear in her spleen. Under normal conditions, it would heal on its own. But with the uncontrolled bleeding from the von Willebrand, we need to evaluate it surgically and perform any necessary repairs."

This is sounding worse by the minute.

"You said this happened a little after midnight?" he asks, looking closely at me now.

His scrutiny makes me nervous, as I'm sure his medical training enables him to pick up the subtle differences in my physiology. The beast inside me takes notice.

I bend down and start putting Sandy's things back into her pack.

"It was around two a.m. when I picked her up outside of Wheatland. I'm not sure how long she'd been walking. She said that a trucker who gave her a ride tried to rape her and that all he did was push her around and slap her before she kicked him and got away. She did mention banging her side on the gear shift."

"Hmm. Well, we'll need to examine her for evidence of rape or any other trauma. Why did you wait so long to have her seen?" His accusing tone triggers the beast, and I clench my jaw as I slap it back down.

I zip the pack closed, stand up, and look the doctor directly in the eye.

"Because she claimed to be fine. She had bruises and was favoring her side, but nothing seemed life threatening. She refused to see a doctor. It wasn't until this afternoon when we were shopping that I realized something more might be wrong."

He flinches, then stutters something to the effect that it was a good thing I brought her in.

"How long will she be in surgery? Where can I wait for her? I mean, she doesn't have anyone else."

"Depending on the extent of the splenic tear, or any other injuries, it could be anywhere from four to six hours. You're welcome to stay. The O.R. waiting room is up on the third floor." He leaves and I step over to Sandy's bed.

"Hey, kid." I squeeze her hand and her eyes flutter open. "Hang in there, okay? I'll see you when you get out."

She offers a weak smile and I step aside as the nurses push her bed out and down the hall. My insides knotted with worry, I shoulder the backpack, look at the time on my phone, and start walking. 4:23 PM. Sure hope the routine surgeries are done for the day and that the hospital's having a quiet evening.

I'd hate to turn the O.R. waiting room into its own trauma site.

# CHAPTER 6

The crowded waiting area turns out to be more than the killers in me can handle. Since there's nowhere close to go for a real run, I have to content myself with jogging countless laps along the poorly lit streets surrounding the hospital, stalked by memories—memories that threaten to rob me of my dwindling resistance to the siren call of Nicolas only a few short hours away.

The emptiness in my core aches as I remember the first time I saw him, *felt* him, staring at me from across the street when I stepped out from the little shop in Colorado Springs just a few short months ago. How his emerald eyes peered into my soul, demanding to know who I was, and the little nod and smile he gave me as he vanished into thin air, too fast for even me to track.

The emotions he stirred up by his very existence—fear, fascination, uncertainty—were only amplified later that night, rippling across my skin when I found him waiting outside the bar where I worked. I'll never forget our first conversation over tea in the little coffee shop down the street, how his sophistication and mystery began to seduce me even then.

And I'll never forget how I felt as he unveiled his world to me, bit by bit, and my realization that I was no longer alone. That there were others like me, who lived on blood, yet were not the monsters of movies and books.

Or so I thought.

But I was too blind to see it at first—blinded by love and lust and the thrill of being swept off my feet by an elegant prince whose true darkness he kept hidden from me.

Until it all came crashing down in a rain of blood and betrayal.

Anger surges through me at how he set me up to commit murder, at his broken promise to allow me to make the Choice on my own terms, at the rage and cruelty he speared me with as I refused to be manipulated yet again.

And at myself, for succumbing to the deadliest drug of all—love—and for learning too late that its price among The Chosen is more than one's freedom.

The price is one's soul.

~

It's midnight when I stop by for the umpteenth time to check on Sandy. She's out of recovery—finally—and has been moved into a room on another floor. Though it's past visiting hours, one of the nurses at the station gives in when I insist on seeing the girl and leads me to the room.

Sandy's still unconscious, pale, the I.V. line still in her arm. The bright tracks running across her monitor screen bounce up and down, each with their own rhythm, accompanied by soft beeps.

"How long before she wakes up?" I ask, watching the shallow rise and fall of her chest.

"She woke in recovery. She'll probably sleep the rest of the night now."

"Is she going to be okay?"

"There weren't any complications in surgery that I'm aware of, so her prognosis should be good. I'll be back to check on her in an hour or so. You can stay 'til then."

"Thanks." I drag a chair over and set it next to the bed as she leaves.

I don't know why I'm still here. I should be on the road, running north, putting as much distance between me and the Springs as possible, eliminating any chance I'll surrender to Nicolas's irresistible hold on me.

Yet, as I look at the girl on the bed, frail and so, so young, I realize a new hold has taken over.

But it isn't really new. It's some of the same feelings I have for Andrea—parental, protective—and they bring the memories of my daughter to life once again.

It's been months since I last saw her, and the bright blue eyes of *her* daughter. My granddaughter. Cherub cheeks and black curls and that beautiful little baby smile.

My chest aches at the memory of that last stolen sight of them as Andrea paid for her groceries, unaware that her dead mother stood only a few feet away. And I'll never forget that tiny face peering at me over Andrea's shoulder, nor how her expression flickered with curiosity at the sight of the woman who looked so much like her own mother.

I would die to protect them, which is why I am half a continent away.

Because the thing I need to protect them from is *me*, and the ugly things living inside me.

Sandy whimpers in her sleep and I rub her hand to offer what little comfort I can.

I just want to help this poor girl, at least until she recovers. I can't bear the thought of her being out there on the road again, a ready victim for the next monster who crosses her path.

I only hope that monster isn't the one standing over her bed right now.

~

Dawn is not far off when I'm finally forced to leave. But not by the nurse, who graciously let me stay by Sandy's side the rest of the night. It takes the threat of the rising sun to hasten my retreat from the hospital and flee for the privacy of the hotel room.

As I drive, thoughts of Nicolas shove their way back to the surface. I'd fought them off all night, focusing on the quiet beeps and lights of Sandy's monitor any time the longing for him threatened to take over. But now, alone in the car, the urge to keep driving all the way back to the Springs hammers at my fragile resolve.

My nails dig into the steering wheel as the emptiness claws through me, followed by indecision. The freeway sign looms ahead, beckoning me south.

But it's the sight of the sun's glow peeking over the eastern horizon that finally gives me the strength to pass the on-ramp and speed toward the hotel.

I collapse into bed, skin crawling with the sick fear that I'm losing the battle to save what's left of *me*. That it's too late, that I've given too much of myself to Nicolas to ever completely win my freedom from him.

The black sleep descends over me, bringing an image of his red-laced emerald eyes, staring at me through the darkness.

# WEDNESDAY

## CHAPTER 7

His voice whispers words of love, and his blood within me echoes their sweet song. I reach for him and the empty space beside me in the bed shocks me awake.

My mind is flooded with memories of him—of those last days before our dream of an eternity together was reduced to nothing more than a pile of smoldering ashes. It feels as though it was just yesterday . . .

*We stand next to his car on top of Pikes Peak, watching the sun slowly sinking through the scattered clouds toward the western horizon. It won't be long until that bright sphere succumbs to the jagged teeth of the Rocky Mountains in the distance, their raw edges sharp and hungry.*

*I wait for that first touch of heaven and earth, my camera momentarily at rest. Nicolas's arm lays lightly across my shoulders as he waits with me.*

*"Are you happy?" he asks, his Hungarian-accented voice low as he nuzzles my hair.*

*"Yes."*

*Our shared blood pulses warmly within my veins, radiating love and passion and joy throughout my body.*

*"I know how much you miss your life out there." Nicolas gestures toward the landscape falling away from the Peak's edge, a complex tapestry of forested slopes and green meadows and shimmering lakes stretching as far as the eye can see.*

*"When I fled my Maker and his cruel ways, I headed east. I did not stop until I was somewhere deep in the wilds of the Asiatic mountains, far beyond his influence, his manipulations, and all the temptations with which he tormented me." He takes a long breath. "This mountain, these views—they remind me of my time in those lofty peaks. It was a time of great introspection . . .*

*"My hard-won freedom was not without cost, though. I had thought my greatest challenge would be adapting to an animal diet, and though difficult at first, I succeeded in proving to myself that it is possible to survive without killing people—something that was very important to me, and still is.*

*"What I had not expected was the profound loneliness that accompanied my voluntary exile, that being alone brought an ache to my soul surpassing any loss or pain I had so far endured . . ."*

*Remnants of that loneliness flicker within me, calling up my own days of feeling so lonely I thought I would die. My love for him surges, and I turn to him, and he takes me into his arms, holding me as though he will never let go.*

*"It was the endless isolation that finally drove me back to face my Maker and assert my position in The Chosen world. For as I learned, Chosen cannot thrive in seclusion."*

*He eases back, his emerald gaze glittering as he stares into my eyes.*

*"I understand your connection to the mountain forests and your desire to live a carefree life. Perhaps someday we can return to that life—together.*

*"But I do not want you to ever feel alone again, for I understand that all too well."*

*He embraces me once more, and our passions rise beneath the fiery Colorado sky, and we give ourselves over to the sharing of blood and emotions and the rapture of being one.*

~

The black emptiness where I used to feel him gapes open and I bolt out of bed to keep from getting sucked down into it. I quickly dress, grab my bag and keys, and race from the room.

It's past noon when I get to the hospital, irritated that I didn't wake earlier. The warm scents of the medical personnel and other visitors brush past me as I move through the hallways, and the beast awakens, rumbling with need. The hunger begins to smolder deep in my belly. Alarm rushes through me as I realize it's only been two nights since I fed.

On a human. A human who died.

Hunting tonight is an absolute necessity if I am to maintain control.

Bypassing the elevators, I head for the hopefully empty stairway.

Sandy's asleep when I ease into her room. She's still hooked up to the monitor and I.V. Other than the bruise covering half her face, her skin is as pale as mine, though without the translucence that marks my kind.

Stupid kid. Her toughness nearly caused her to die.

Just like me, when I was foolish enough to take on a hungry bear.

Shaking my head, I move her backpack from the chair I'd left it in earlier and sit down. I watch her soft breathing and marvel over the connections we seem to have. I'm puzzled that the beast has had no desire for her blood, not even when I was wearing it.

After a little while, I remember her photo album and get it out of the pack. I open it and slowly turn the pages of her life.

It seems every few years there's a new family in the photos—a total of nine different groups of people. That's an average of two years with each one. No wonder she feels estranged, like she doesn't belong. I can see how her disease would make her feel even more different.

And the whole empathy thing. It kind of seems like it's real. She sure had me pegged.

I look at the last few photos and Sandy's alone in them. I can see the alienation in her expressions and the loneliness shining from her green eyes.

Poor kid.

"Hey. You're back," her voice whispers from the bed. "The nurses said you were here all night."

"How are you feeling?" I ask, shoving the album into her backpack.

"More like I was hit by a truck than a trucker."

I smile and shake my head, glad her sense of humor's intact. But she still sounds a little groggy, probably from the anesthesia.

"I'm really thirsty." Sandy clears her throat. "Can I have some water?"

She watches while I grab the pitcher from her bedside tray and fill the empty cup, then hand it to her.

"Thank you." After taking a small sip through the straw, she sets the cup on the tray. "This really blows," she mutters, scratching at the I.V. tape on the back of her hand.

"Yeah, it does. Why didn't you say something? You gave me quite a scare."

She stares at her hand.

"I'm sorry. You've been so nice to me. I . . . I didn't want to cause you any hassles. I thought maybe I'd just cracked a rib or something, and all I needed to do was tough it out." Sandy frowns. "Guess I was wrong."

"Almost dead wrong."

"Maybe so," she whispers. "Wouldn't be the first time."

I don't know what to say to that, so I don't say anything.

"Thanks for bringing in my backpack. I'm glad you found my med bracelet."

"Why weren't you wearing it?"

A shrug is all she gives me as her gaze shifts back to her hand.

"People always want to know what it is, what's wrong with me. They look at me like I'm a freak. It's none of their damn business."

That's a pretty foolish stance when you can bleed to death from a simple injury.

My struggle for an appropriate response that doesn't sound like a reprimand is interrupted by the sound of footsteps entering the room. The nurse glances at me as she stops next to Sandy's bed.

She's way too close for my liking and I scramble out of the chair and step across the room.

But the beast does nothing. Just silently watches.

Its lack of reaction to her is very strange considering its earlier behavior.

"How are you feeling this afternoon, Sandy?" She checks the monitor, then types on the computer next to it.

"Sore."

"It's about time for your pain med. I'll be back with it in ten minutes or so, which is also when you're due for another walk. Okay?"

"Ugh. Okay."

The nurse smiles at Sandy, then moves past me and out the door.

"Oh, Sunny! Can you catch her? I'd like some ice for my water. It's gross when it's warm."

I hurry after the nurse, and I'm just a few yards from her when all hell breaks loose inside me.

The beast roars, preparing to pounce. Caught off guard, I slam to a halt, then crush myself against the wall and turn my face toward the floor, my vision shaded in pink.

Holy crap.

My body's strung tight, ready to leap upon anything that moves. Choking back the fires of hunger, I compel myself to take long, deep breaths and slowly regain control over the maddened creature. The coiled fibers in my muscles grudgingly relax.

What the hell?

The nurse is long gone by the time I feel brave enough to move. I make my way back to Sandy's room, shaken by the sudden unpredictability of the beast.

"You'll . . . you'll have to ask her for the ice when she comes back."

"No biggie . . ." Sandy peers more closely at me. "Hey, are you okay?"

"Yeah, I'm fine."

"You don't look fine. What's wrong?"

"Nothing."

Which is actually the truth. The last of the tension melts away and the beast quietly curls up and goes to sleep.

This is too weird.

I force a smile and change the subject.

"So, what's this about a walk? They let you out of bed already?"

Sandy giggles.

"Yeah. Guess they shot air in my gut to do the surgery, and now I have to fart it out. By walking. It really stinks, too."

I can't help but chuckle.

"Hey, wanna see my incisions?" She lifts up her gown.

Three small bandages trace a curve along the bottom of her ribcage. A fourth covers her belly button. She peels this one back.

Just below her navel, a small, pink cut is held together with several neatly tied sutures.

"This is where they pumped in the gas, like blowing up a balloon. Look how bloated I am! I feel like I swallowed a basketball! Freaky, huh? My doctor—he's pretty hot for an old guy—told me this morning that they did a lapascopy or leperscopy or something like that and used a tiny camera to look around in there. I don't remember what the other holes were for. Fixing my bleed, I guess."

"Do they hurt?"

"Naw, not much. But my whole belly's really sore. And my shoulder's *killing* me. The nurse said that's from the gas, too. That's just weird."

"How long do you have to stay in the hospital?"

"Doc said a couple days, mostly cuz of my VWD."

"VWD?"

"Von Willebrand disease. He just wants to be sure I don't get any more bleeds."

I nod, then tense as footsteps once again enter the room. Panic shoots through me at the sight of the nurse walking back in.

But the beast just calmly watches her, bearing no sign of its earlier aggression.

"Hi, Sandy. Ready for your walk?"

"Not really."

That's my cue to exit. Need to get out of here before my inner Jekyll morphs into Hyde again.

"I'm going to take off. I'll be back in a little while. Can I bring you anything?"

"A book would be great. I'm not picky, but I do like horror."

Ugh. Horror is my *life*. That's the last thing I'd want to read.

"I'll see what I can find." I grab my bag from the table.

"Bye." Her plaintive tone makes me feel like I should give her a hug or something, but that's more than I can deal with at the moment.

Instead, I reach out and give her hand a gentle squeeze, then hightail it out of the room for the familiar safety of my self-imposed solitude.

~

Back at the hotel, I call the desk clerk to let him know I'll be keeping my room for a few more days, but will be checking out of Sandy's later today.

But first I have a little cleanup to do.

I head back upstairs and open her door. The smell of dried blood floats through the air as I walk into the bathroom.

Yet again, the beast is strangely quiet. I pick up a bloody towel from the bathtub and, bringing it close to my nose, breathe in slowly. Still no reaction. I sniff again, and notice something odd about the way it smells. It's somehow different from other human blood I've smelled. Not that I've spent any time just *smelling* human blood, but I'm always aware of its delicious scent, both in and out of the body.

I search through the bloody pile and find one on the bottom that's still damp. Same thing. The oddness of the scent is more pronounced now, or maybe I'm becoming more attuned to it.

Very interesting.

It's also interesting that there's still no response from the beast, in spite of how it reacted to the nurse earlier.

I'm tempted to taste the blood, to see if it tastes as different as it smells. But that would probably be pushing things a little too far. That could not only trigger the hunger, but could trigger it for *her* blood.

Not a good thing for either one of us.

Collecting the red-stained towels, I put them in a plastic bag from the garbage and tie it shut. I set it by the door, then gather up the bags and packages from our shopping spree.

Regret lances through me as I acknowledge my selfishness. I had encouraged her to shop, feeding off her delight as she freely spent money like she never had before. Instead I should have been noticing that things weren't quite right with her. I should have insisted on taking her to the doctor sooner.

I could've . . . I could've even given her some of my blood. Maybe it would've healed her, like Nicolas's did for me after the bear attack.

But part of me shrinks back from that idea in horror, remembering that's how The Chosen control their human donors.

I would not want that, and neither would she. It would be better to die.

# CHAPTER 8

With flowers and my bag in hand, I keep my gaze fastened to the floor ahead of me on the way to Sandy's room. Thankfully, the beast had remained quiet—though vigilant—while I was in the store. I'm starting to think being in the hospital, where blood molecules float freely in the air, is making the beast more psychotic than usual.

I walk into Sandy's room. It takes me a second to realize the patient in the bed is not her.

Oh no.

Fear flashes down my spine as I turn and nearly run to the nurse's station.

"Sandy. The girl with von Willebrand's. What happened to her?"

The nurse shrinks back and stutters, "Uh, calm down, ma'am. She's just been moved to another room."

I realize I'm staring at her through a crimson haze, the beast raging to escape.

Oh shit.

Snapping my eyes shut, I sharply inhale and turn my face away. I pause, then slowly open them as my vision clears.

"Uh, I'm sorry. Can you tell me where she is?" I fish a paper and pen out of my bag and make a big show of writing down Sandy's new room number. Anything to keep from looking up at the nurse again.

Mumbling "thanks," I turn and walk back up the hall.

When I find her room, I'm disappointed to discover she's no longer in a private one. I take a deep breath and cross the floor to her bed beneath the window, ignoring the elderly woman asleep in the other bed near the door. Sandy's asleep as well, her monitor and drip quietly doing their jobs.

Her eyes open when I stop next to her bed and set the flowers on the nightstand.

"Sorry. Didn't mean to wake you." I keep my voice low as I settle into the chair.

She smiles. "You could sneak up on a cat. I didn't hear a sound. I just sorta knew you were here."

Hmm.

"Thank you for the flowers. They're really pretty. I love all the different colors."

"You're welcome. How are you feeling?"

"All right. Still sore, but not as much. Moving around helps. You know the old saying, 'Two farts in the wind are better than one in the belly!'" She giggles quietly.

"I haven't heard that one."

"That's cuz I just made it up." Sandy grins.

She must be feeling better. She's sounding more and more like a normal teenager.

"Here. Brought you something." I fish the book from my bag and hand it to her.

"Stephen King?" she says loudly. The sleeping patient in the other bed groans. Sandy claps her hand over her mouth and lowers her voice. "I love Stephen King!"

"Hope you haven't read this one." It was the least creepy one I could find.

"*The Gunslinger*. No, I haven't. Oh, wait, it's part of The Dark Tower series? Awesome. I've been wanting to read this. Thanks!"

She flips through the book while I take out the Casper area map I'd bought. I unfold it and lay it across Sandy's bed.

"Do I look like a table?"

"You're not doing anything else, are you?" I study the roads leading into the mountains directly south of town.

"Whatcha looking for?"

"Someplace to hike. Thought I'd check out the area around Casper Mountain."

"Hiking? You don't strike me as the outdoorsy tree-hugger type." Sandy snorts.

Glancing sidelong at her, I shake my head.

I can't resist.

"I've hugged . . . a lot . . . of trees." Climbing them. And sleeping in them.

"Never would've guessed," she replies, eyebrows raised.

"And you thought you knew everything about me."

"I know a lot more than you think."

My jaw clenches at the old fear of discovery creeping up my spine.

"Don't be too sure of that." I fold the map and put it in my bag, then stand and offer her a tight smile.

"What, are you leaving now? You just got here."

"I'll be back tomorrow after lunch. You've had a long day and should get some rest."

Her expression makes me feel guilty as hell. If I didn't need to hunt so badly, I'd stay longer.

"You've got a book to read." I reach out and squeeze her hand. "And I've got things to take care of this evening."

Sandy frowns and turns her head to stare out the window.

"Are you *really* coming back?"

"I said I would."

"Yeah. I've heard *that* one before." She jerks her hand away.

"If I say I'm going to do something, I do it."

"Whatever." Sandy picks up the book and opens it, her scowl directed firmly at the page.

Yep. Teenager.

I leave the room without another word.

~

Driving across town toward Casper Mountain, it's all I can do to keep the frenzied creatures inside me from completely losing it.

It's bad enough just trying to manage the emotional fallout from my disastrous relationship with Nicolas, how I fear that I may yet give in and go back to him. Or deal with the gut-wrench I feel every time I think about my daughter and her baby in California.

But now I've let myself get attached to this girl, and worse, she's apparently become attached to me. Her sudden dependence on me scares me to death, because I'm only going to do what it seems like everyone else in her life has done.

Abandon her.

And I can't help that. My life is too dangerous, too volatile, to risk sharing it with a human. If it was that easy, I never would've left California. I would've found a way to re-enter Andrea's life and be a part of the family she's building.

But violence is my life now, and it's always just a matter of time before it shatters everything around me and I have to move on.

The old despairs sink their talons in deeper, joined by all of my new ones.

And I only know one way to make them all stop.

ಌ

Hot blood fills my mouth as it pumps from the buck's torn throat. I drink deeply, savoring the sensation of it as it washes through my system and replenishes my veins. The taste is foul, not what I want, not what I *really* want. But the chase and the kill satisfy both hunter and beast, and the hunger is kept at bay by literally drowning it in several gallons of deer blood.

Draining the last of it, I sit there a moment, the deer's body still cradled in my arms, and bask in the red warmth, almost too bloated to move. The faint rustle of leaves being compressed into the ground catches my attention and I turn my head to see a bobcat warily approaching about ninety feet away. He stops, and his golden eyes stare at me through the crimson veil of mine. His stubby tail lashes as he debates whether to hold his ground or run.

I slide the deer to the ground and slowly stand, then walk quietly away in the opposite direction. I prefer that he get the carcass, rather than any of the other creatures that live here. I find that I'm especially partial to cats these days.

From the other side of the clearing, I watch as he approaches the deer. His soft spotted coat triggers the anguish in my gut as I recall a beautiful snow leopard and the princely Chosen who was fond of her.

I remember the living sculpture Nicolas made of us in the center of his topiary garden. Two big leopards, one spotted, one dark, embracing in eternal conflict. The forms bore the careful attention he applied to his craft, to his music, to his collections, to me.

And to his donors. His gentle concern for them made him unique among The Chosen, even those within his own lineage, and I still cannot believe the Nicolas I left standing in that bloody room was the Nicolas I fell in love with.

Longing for him surges through me, for his arms around my body, his fangs in my throat, his blood running through my veins, and the endless ecstasy of The Chosen union.

The black chasm in my core gapes open, threatening to devour my sanity.

Oh God, Nicolas, how did this turn out so badly?

But I know the answer. It was me. It was my unwillingness to change, my unwillingness to Change. To no longer be this half human, half monster thing that I am, riddled with insecurity and the decaying moralities of my former life. To become full Chosen and accept everything that it means.

To no longer be alone.

Wrenching my gaze away from the spotted cat, I flee deeper into the mountains, running as hard and as fast as I can.

# THURSDAY

## CHAPTER 9

Pulling into the hospital parking lot, I steel myself for another long day with people. I took down two good-sized bucks last night, but after my time with Nicolas feeding on human blood, deer tasted thin, bitter and gamey, and I could barely gag it down. But gag it down I did, until I thought I would explode, in the hope that flooding my veins would help make the beast and its hunger more manageable.

I walk silently through the hospital halls to Sandy's room. I don't know how long I can continue to visit. I've alarmed several of the staff members over the last couple days, and I'm sure that I've become a topic of discussion by now. Being around medical personnel who observe physical conditions for a living makes me very nervous, and I'm anxious to quit this place for good.

As for Sandy, I've decided how best to help her, yet keep her safe from me and whoever or whatever may come after me. I don't know if she'll go for it, but it's the only option I can see for now that will give her an opportunity for a good life and give me a little peace of mind.

Her nose is buried between the pages of the book when I walk into her room. The I.V. is gone, but she's still attached to the monitor. The other patient is elsewhere, thankfully.

Sandy looks up.

"Hi," she says, almost in a whisper.

"Hi." I hand her the little purple stuffed dragon I'd picked up on the way over.

"I'm sorry." Her eyes fill with tears as she takes it.

"It's okay."

"I don't know what's wrong with me. One minute I'm pissed off, the next I'm crying . . ." She strokes the dragon's shimmery wing, then wipes away her tears, now spilling over.

"Hey, it's understandable. You've been through a lot the last couple days. Some creep tried to rape you, you almost died, and now you're stuck here sick and feeling all alone."

Both hands fly to her eyes, her body shudders, and the sounds tearing from her throat pierce through all my defenses.

I hesitate, then wrap my arms around her, arms that only a few short hours ago held a struggling deer as I drained away his precious life.

She latches on to me, crying in earnest now. My jaw clamped tight, I hold her and fight to keep my own warring emotions from pouring crimson rivers down my face.

"Hey, Sandy. I have a plan. I want you to think about it. Okay?"

Sandy nods and, sniffling, slowly releases me.

"I found an apartment, not too far from Casper College. I'd like you to think about living there, and maybe trying to go to school."

"Are you going to live there, too?" She looks up at me, hope shining through her wet lashes.

"Just long enough to help you get settled. I do a lot of traveling and would appreciate you taking care of it for me while I'm on the road."

She drops her gaze and fusses with the dragon.

I wait, letting her consider my offer. Ideally, she'll settle in, go to school, make friends, make a life. One that I'll drop in on less and less as time goes by.

Sandy sniffles and yanks a tissue from the box on the bedside stand.

"The nurse told me anesthesia can make a person pretty looney for a couple days afterward," she says.

"I've heard that. I've also heard that just being a teenager can make you a little looney, too."

She laughs and wipes her face.

"Yeah."

Taking a deep breath, Sandy picks up the dragon.

"Thank you. This is really cute. I love dragons."

The sketchbook I'd found in her backpack had been filled with them.

"You're welcome. I got one, too." I pull it out of my bag and she grins.

But as I put it back, I don't tell her it's to help me remember her on lonely nights once I've hit the road again. I have a whole collection of stuffed animals, each one guarding a memory of someone I'd known or somewhere I'd been since becoming the thing that I am.

It's only one of the many bits and pieces of my life that I left behind at Nicolas's estate.

Fighting back the emptiness suddenly twisting my gut, I zip my bag and look back up at Sandy.

"Okay," she says. "I'll do it. I'll . . . take care of your apartment for you."

"What about school?"

"Do you think they have art classes? I really like to draw."

"I'm sure they do. I'll pick up a college catalog and you can see what they offer."

She nods, then her face brightens.

"Hey, guess what? I made a friend."

"Great. Here in the hospital?"

"Yeah. Her name is Cara. We met in the hall. She's like you and me—she has a blood problem, too."

I highly doubt it's anything like mine.

"Wanna meet her?"

Not really. The best way to keep the beast manageable is to not give it any reason to be otherwise. And that means staying as far away from people as possible.

Except for Sandy. I still can't figure out why she has such a calming influence over it, but it's become pretty obvious that she does.

"Come on. I need to go for a walk anyway. It's the only way I can get these farts out." Reaching under her gown, she disconnects the monitor leads, then throws back the bedcovers and slides from the bed. She stuffs her feet into a pair of white hospital slippers, flashes me a conspiratorial grin, and steps gingerly toward the door.

With a sigh, I follow close behind. If I stay near her, maybe the beast won't react to the people we encounter.

I hope.

It's erratic behavior has me completely on edge, not unlike when I first left my mountain refuge and re-joined human civilization.

But I learned how to restrain it then, learned the vigilance and the preparation that it takes, and I can do it again. I've just become so used to being the master of them both—beast and hunter—that this sudden rebellion has totally shattered my confidence.

My skin crawling with self-doubt, I closely trail Sandy through the hallways.

ᴥ

We stop outside of another room, its door cracked open a few inches. Sandy lightly knocks, then grins at the subdued response from within the room.

"Good. She's awake. Here, you need to wear this stuff." She grabs a couple pale yellow hospital masks from a wall-mounted dispenser and hands me one, then follows that with a matching paper gown and booties. After donning hers and rubbing her hands with disinfectant, she eases the door open.

"Hey, Cara. It's me, Sandy. Want some company?"

I follow Sandy into the dimly lit room. A young, frail-looking woman occupies the single bed in the center, hooked up to an I.V. and accompanying monitor.

"How're you feeling?" Sandy settles into a chair next to the bed. I stay back, unwilling to test my hold on the beast.

The girl, who appears to be not much older than Sandy, clicks off the TV and offers a wan smile. Her pallor is underscored by dark circles beneath her brown eyes, her head covered by a bright pink-and-yellow knit beanie. I try to imagine her as a brunette, then as a blonde. She would've been pretty either way. Her beauty now is that of someone valiantly fighting for her life.

They talk, though Sandy dominates the conversation despite being muffled by the surgical mask. The girl's heartbeat is weak and the smell of her blood odd, but different from Sandy's. The beast shows no interest in her, but I still don't trust it.

"Oh, Sunny. I forgot you were here! Come on over. Cara would like to meet you."

Taking a deep breath, I approach the bed.

"Hi. I'm Cara. Sandy's told me a lot about you." She smiles.

I glance over at Sandy. "Has she now?"

"Yeah, she said that you were really nice to her and took her shopping." Cara tugs her beanie down over one ear. "I love shopping. I haven't been for a long time. Been too sick, and I can't be around crowds because I might catch something and get even worse."

Nodding, I try keep my expression neutral beneath the mask. Life is so damned unfair.

Sandy reaches out and pats Cara's arm.

"But that's okay, cuz I told you I'd give you some of my stuff. I got too much anyways. It won't all fit in my backpack. And I figure since we're about the same size, you might as well have some of it. That way we can both have something new." Sandy laughs. "If you can't go to the shopping, we'll just bring the shopping to you!"

"Sure, Sandy. That'll be great. It'll be fun trying on everything you told me about."

I look down at the thin frame of the ailing girl, and her return smile seems wise and beyond her years. She will be gone soon, this one. I can sense it, and only hope that Sandy gets out of here before that happens.

"It's nice to meet you, Cara. I'm glad Sandy has someone closer to her age to talk to."

"It was just luck that we met out in the hall when I was on one of my fart walks." Sandy grins.

Cara giggles. "I can't believe you call them that."

Sandy shrugs, her masked smile shining from her eyes.

"Oh, hey. I have something to show you. Sunny brought me a dragon! Well, not a *live* dragon. Remember how I was telling you I'm really into dragons? I'll go get it. Be right back."

And before I can react, she's gone.

Leaving me in the room alone with Cara.

I brace myself for the beast's explosion, but it never comes. All it does is quietly raise its head, then goes back to sleep.

More puzzled than ever, I can't help looking back at Cara, wondering about the odd smell of her blood.

"So you really picked her up hitchhiking?" she asks.

"I did. I still can't believe anyone in this day and age, especially a girl, would be foolish enough to hitchhike."

"I think it's awesome. She's been all over the country. I've been stuck here in Casper my whole life." Cara shakes her head. "But hitchhiking does sound kinda scary. She was telling me about some of the run-ins she's had with the people who've picked her up. And not just guys, either. But she said most of them have been nice, and usually give her a little money to help her out or buy her food. I think it's cool. But I'd never be brave enough to do it." She sighs. "Not that I could, even if I wanted to."

"Did she say how long she'd been on the road?"

"No, but it sounded like at least a few months."

I inwardly shudder. It's only a matter of time before she takes a ride that turns out to be her last.

Sandy shuffles back into the room, the purple dragon nestled under one arm and her sketchbook in hand.

There's no way I can let this kid go back out there on the highway again.

Since it looks like we're going to be here awhile, I move the other chair over and settle in next to Sandy as she launches into an enthusiastic discussion about dragons and her art.

It's going to be a long afternoon.

# FRIDAY

## CHAPTER 10

Folding the lease agreement, I stuff it in my bag as I leave the manager's office. The furnished, two-bedroom apartment is fairly close to Casper College, my next stop. Sandy seemed willing to give it a try—maybe all she needs is someone to help her find her place in this world.

Anything's got to be better than being fodder for some asshole's groping in the cab of his truck.

It's tempting to stick around for a while to help her get on her feet. But being only a few short hours from the Springs is adding an edge to the tension I can't seem to shake. It's been four nights since I fled the club. As soon as Nicolas realizes there's no sign of me in the mountains west of the Springs—if he hasn't already—he'll start searching elsewhere. He knows me too well, and knows the first place I'll run will be into the wilderness, as far from him as I can get. One look at a map and he'll see the I-25 heading north into Montana and Canada, same as I did. And if he comes through Casper while I'm still here, he'll sense me, like he always has, and there will be no escape.

And as much as I would love for him to find me, would die for him to find me, that prospect is absolutely terrifying.

Because this time, I *will* give myself to him and his world. Completely. One hundred percent. I will forever lose the me that was, forever lose that tiny part of myself that is able to see humans as people, not *food*. Forever lose my daughter and my final connection to humanity. And that is what terrifies me the most.

~

The traffic in the hospital hallways is thankfully light as I pass through with Sandy's bags of new clothes gripped in both hands. She'd asked me to bring them to share with Cara, and her request had made me cringe at my growing attachment to this resilient, warmhearted little nomad.

As I enter her room, I notice her roommate and all her belongings are gone, the bed neatly made up for its next occupant.

Sandy's curled up beneath her blankets, her back to me. I tread quietly, not wishing to disturb her from her nap. But then I realize her body's shaking, and a heart-wrenching sob from her breaks the silence in the room.

"Sandy?" I drop the bags and gently touch her shoulder through the covers. She turns toward me, her green eyes spilling tears across her freckled cheeks.

"She's gone! She . . . she died . . ." Her words fade into a long wail that rips through me.

"Your roommate?"

They never said two words to one another while I was here.

"No! *Cara*." Sandy rips the blankets away and sits up, then buries her face into her hands, sobbing.

My throat tightens in sorrow for her and I gather her into my arms. Her body convulses as she clings to me and weeps and I make no attempt to calm her—her tears seem to be for more than just losing Cara. They are the tears accumulated through a lifetime of loss and rejection, and my own press heavy against my eyes.

Her sorrow gradually becomes quieter, less violent. Reduced to shuddering whimpers, she eventually grows still.

I move one arm from around her and stroke her hair. Sandy finally releases me and I breathe a sigh of relief. In spite of the fact that her blood holds no interest for the beast, the hunter inside me is tense from being embraced by what she considers to be potential prey.

"I'm sorry about Cara." I tuck a golden ringlet behind her ear.

"It's okay. I didn't know her very long. But I really wanted her to get well." She sniffles and reaches through the neck of her gown to unhook the monitor wires from her chest. "I'm gonna go wash my face."

Settling into the chair next to the bed, I take out the Casper College catalog and thumb through it. Sandy finishes in the bathroom and shuffles back across the room.

"Screw these." She flings the monitor wires off the bed. "The nurses are used to me unhooking them. I don't know why I still have to wear all this junk."

"So has the doctor said anything about when you can be released?"

"Tomorrow. I was so excited when he told me. As soon as he left, I went to Cara's room to tell her, and that's when I found out she'd . . ." She frowns, then wipes her eyes.

"Hey. I brought you something." I hand her the college catalog, hoping to give her something positive to think about. "And I signed the lease today for a two-bedroom apartment just down the street from the college."

Sandy stares at the catalog, but doesn't open it.

"Why are you doing this? Why are you being so nice to me? What do you want?"

"I just want you to . . . to have a chance."

"Why? What do you care? I'm nothing to you. Just some dumb girl you picked up hitchhiking."

"You . . ." I take a deep breath. "You remind me of someone."

"Who?"

It takes all the strength I have to choke out my answer. I haven't talked about her to anyone in this life, ever.

"My . . . my daughter."

Sandy says nothing. Her questions hang in the air, unasked.

"She, uh . . . she was your age the last time we spoke."

That's when I was ripped away from her, never again to be part of her life.

"How long ago was that?"

"Over five years ago," I whisper.

"Did she die?" Sandy's tone softens.

"No."

I did.

She stares down at the catalog for a long moment, then chucks it across the room.

"So, what—did you just decide one day you didn't want to talk to her anymore? Didn't *want* her anymore? You think you can make up for it with *me*?" Her accusations, laced with old buried resentments, cut me to the bone.

Rage flashes through me, and it's not from the hunter, nor the beast. It's all mine, and I've been lugging it around since the night I woke up as a monster.

I jerk myself out of the chair, snatch up my bag, and head out the door.

Stupid me, getting involved with this girl. There's just too much pain here in both of us.

"So you're running away? Is that what you *always* do? *Run*?" Sandy screams from her room.

*She's right*, says the little voice from the black box, the black box holding the tiny piece of me that's still human.

I stop in the middle of the hall and clamp my eyes shut.

Damn you. I ran because of *you*. If it wasn't for your weak human sniveling, I'd be with Nicolas right now, alive and whole, a true Chosen, instead of this dead and broken half *thing*.

I *despise* you.

*But I am part of you, the part that still has a daughter. Remember her.* The lid to the box opens a crack farther.

Remember her? For what reason? I can never speak to her, touch her, hold my granddaughter. What's the point? I'm better off with my own kind. I'm tired of this shadowy half life, skulking around the edges of society, watching but never belonging.

"Sunny! I'm sorry! Don't leave. Please come back."

The fury still boiling through me, I spin around and head into her room. I shove the door shut and leap to the side of her bed before she even realizes I'm back.

Glaring down at her through a crimson haze, I growl, "You want to know why I haven't spoken to my daughter? You want to know why I ran? Why I *still* run?"

She pales, but shows no other reaction to the blazing red eyes, the hands arched like claws, low at my sides and ready to strike, the bared teeth of an accomplished killer.

"What am I supposed to say to her? 'Hi, hon, Mommy the Monster is home? Can I have a hug? Can I hold your baby?'" I snarl.

Sandy swallows and says nothing.

"Yeah, so . . . now you know. I am definitely *not* normal. And the one who is looking for me? He is much, much worse."

She continues to watch me, her green irises framed in red from her tears.

Green eyes turning red. They remind me too much of Nicolas.

Oh God.

The grief for what *I've* lost wells upward, choking me. I feel myself being sucked into a bottomless pit of longing, fear, love, hate, regret . . . and I am drowning in it.

My family. My love. My *life*.

All gone, washed away in a cruel, violent sea of red.

The bloodtears erupt from my blood-colored eyes. Horrified by what I've just done, I shield my face and turn away, shaking, struggling to regain control. Sandy's gasp tells me I'm too late, that she saw what kind of bleeder *I* am.

But the tears won't stop, and I no longer care.

I can never go back to my daughter, to the life we had, the life we shared. And now I've thrown away my only chance to share what little life is left to me with someone who understands my needs, someone who loves me as I love him, and without whom I don't think I can survive.

I can't take this anymore. I have to go back to Nicolas. I will die of loneliness if I don't.

Sandy's arms wrap around mine from behind as she presses against me, murmuring quiet reassurances. There is something serene about her presence, and the tension running through my veins begins to drain out. I steady myself and use the hunter to find the stillness within me, to help kill these human emotions that make me so vulnerable, so exposed. The ache in my eyes recedes and I take a breath as the tears stop flowing and my vision begins to clear.

The hunter protests against this human wrapped around us, and as my awareness returns I shrug Sandy's arms aside and head to the bathroom, my face and hands sticky with blood.

The creature in the mirror sickens me. I look like something out of a Hollywood slasher movie. And I really liked this silk blouse. Should've known better than to buy something in pale blue, or any other light color.

I strip it off and stuff it into the trash, then wash up. Wrapping a towel around me, I walk out and across the room to the shopping bags I'd left on the floor.

"Mind if I borrow one of those tops I bought you?"

"No, go right ahead."

As I'm rummaging around in the bags, I hear her sudden intake of air.

"Oh my God, what happened to your back? Did *he* do that to you?"

I can only imagine her face as she looks at the spider's web of thin silvery scars running down the length of my back.

"Who?"

"You know, *him*. The one you're running from." There's a note of anger in her voice.

"Nicolas? No, he didn't do that. A bear did."

The bear whose attack a few months ago nearly killed me, changing my life yet again.

"A bear? I mean, you look like you were whipped with a, well, a whip."

I snort. That wouldn't even faze me. Tick me off pretty bad, though.

"It was a bear. Let's just say I bit off a little more than I could chew."

"Is that where the scars on your arm and face came from?"

"Yep. Same bear. He's dead now." A black T-shirt with skull and rose designs on it spills from the shopping bag. Perfect.

"You killed him?"

"Yes I did." I yank the shirt down over my head and shrug into it, then turn around.

"You really are badass." Sandy's staring at me, admiration lighting up her face.

"Knock it off. There's nothing badass about killing."

Sandy looks down and nods, then peers at the floor. She's standing next to several fat drops of my blood.

Before I can react, she grabs a tissue from the bedside tray, then eases into a crouch and wipes up the mess.

"Thanks." I glance around for any more stray spots as I reach out for the tissue and head to the bathroom.

"Sure. I, uh, do have a little experience with cleaning up blood."

Unable to help myself, I let loose a short laugh.

"Yeah, I guess you would. Seems like you and I do have a few things in common."

Cleaning up blood is a nightly regimen for me. It's usually not my own, though.

I flush the tissue down the toilet, then grab the garbage bag containing my ruined blouse and head back into the room. I set it by my purse in the corner to add to the collection of blood-stained clothing in my trunk.

All of my instincts urge me to destroy anything with my blood on it, and I have from day one—usually by burning. It goes along with that whole fear-of-discovery thing that constantly shadows me.

Sandy watches me with intense fascination etched all over her face.

"Well, what now? Do you still want the apartment?" I ask.

"Are you going to be staying there?" she replies, sounding hopeful.

"Only for a few days. But I can stay at the hotel if you'd rather."

"No, no. You can stay at the apartment. I mean, it's *your* apartment."

"No, actually it's yours. I rented it for you. I've become a little . . . fond of you, and you've had some tough breaks. So I thought I would help you get a fresh start. Or at least someplace safe 'til you sort out what you want to do."

Tears fill her eyes and she stands there hugging herself.

Shit. We can't keep doing this crying stuff. We both need to get a grip.

I walk over and gently take hold of her shoulders.

"Sandy. Stop. Maybe this is something that was meant to be. Why else was *I* the one to pick you up from the middle of the highway?" I shake my head. "I haven't figured it out. Maybe it was to help each other. So just accept it and let's move on. We both have a lot to do, and frankly I can't handle any more meltdowns, either yours or mine. Enough's enough. Okay?"

She nods and I release her as she reaches up to wipe away her tears.

A knock sounds at the door and I glance at the clock. Must be dinnertime, which is confirmed when Sandy opens the door and I get a whiff of whatever stuff they've cooked up for her. Blech.

She looks at me and I nod for her to let the nurse in. I walk up along the far side of Sandy's bed and stare out the window at the fading light. It's about dinnertime for me, too.

I can feel the nurse glancing at me uneasily while she's getting Sandy situated with her meal. She quickly leaves and I turn around to see Sandy staring at me.

"What?"

"You sure had her spooked. What's been going on with you and the nurses?" she asks, in between bites of bread.

"I, uh . . . I'm just not comfortable with people, and sometimes they pick up on that."

"Oh. So they haven't seen you freak out, or your eyes turn red or anything, right?" She pokes her fork at the spinach on her plate and wrinkles her nose in disgust.

I give her a wry smile.

"Oh, great. Maybe that's why the doctor suddenly decided I could leave. Which makes me happy, cuz the food here really sucks."

It smells bad, too. I've got to get out of here. I need to hunt, badly. My emotional crack-up consumed all my reserves and I'm dreading trying to get from here to the car.

If the nurses were spooked before, they really will be now if any of them run into me in the hallway tonight. It would be kind of nice to have Sandy escort me outside.

I laugh quietly. That's hilarious. She's like a reverse bodyguard. She protects people from me, instead of the other way around.

How crazy is that?

"Look, I need to go. Call me later tonight if you get bored. I'll be up."

"Okay. I'll look at the college catalog. Maybe you can help me pick out some classes?"

"Sure. We'll see what we can figure out."

I grab my bag and head for the door.

"See ya later," Sandy calls as I wave.

With a tight hold on the beast, I enter the gauntlet of the hospital hallways and hope for the best.

# CHAPTER 11

I pull the car over and park in a turnout along the dirt road. After managing to get through the hospital and twice through the hotel lobby without killing anyone, this might be a lucky night for me to try pronghorn antelope. Though smaller than mule deer, their top speed of nearly fifty-five miles per hour—the second fastest land animal in the world—will offer a fresh challenge to the hunter whose eagerness for the chase is vibrating through every cell in my body.

Her impatience is rivaled by both the beast's need to tear something apart and the hunger burning deep within, sparked by my earlier emotional breakdown.

My appalling weakness this afternoon disgusts me. Losing control like that, becoming incoherent, brings a high risk of exposure that could be fatal, or worse.

Lab rat. I shudder at the thought.

Getting out, I stretch, then start walking along the road, casting for the musky antelope scent. The road is bordered by a sparse forest on my left, but to my right is rolling grassy plains.

Pronghorn country.

I cut up into the hills at a steady jog. There's no wind tonight, unusual for this area, so I'll need to be practically on top of them before I can catch their scent.

It feels so good to be out here, away from the pressures of constantly trying to maintain control. Here, in the wild, sleeping in trees doesn't sound so bad. In fact, after today, it sounds pretty damn good. The hunter, tense with anticipation, nearly purrs in agreement.

A stray breeze carries a hint of my prey and I veer off to follow it. Topping a rise, I slowly sink to a crouch as I spot the herd grazing along a draw below me. They're about six hundred feet or so away, and several, sensing movement, raise their heads and look in my direction.

The area is dotted with sagebrush and I pause behind a clump before slipping along the ground to the next one. I continue to work my way down the side of the hill, bush to bush, until I'm about sixty feet from the edge of the herd. They're nervous and keep looking up the hillside, but seem to be unable to spot me.

Counter to my normal hunting browns and blacks, tonight I've dressed in khaki colors to better blend with the grasses. I'm able to move very quietly and can instantly freeze to a statue. I'm a little closer now and, crouching behind the brush, begin looking for a suitable target.

An older buck is slowly grazing his way along with the herd, but positioned a little to the outside in a guard position. I shouldn't take on such a mature and experienced animal for my first encounter with a new species, but he is too tempting.

Shifting to come in directly at his shoulder, I wait until he is nearly even with me. Inch by inch I creep out from behind the bush so that it doesn't obstruct my launch.

I spring, and landing about thirty feet out, spring again. I hit the ground a few feet from him and he's already starting to spin away as I ram into him, just behind the shoulder. He staggers and goes down, and I grab his horns and try to twist his head. But his horns are shorter than a deer's antlers and I don't have much leverage. His neck is much shorter and stiffer, too, and suddenly I'm hanging on, my body flying, as he lunges to his feet and begins to buck and plunge.

He then stops, twists and tries to skewer me, and as my feet plant back on the ground I yank sideways on his horns and he goes down again, taking me with him. I scramble on top of him, bending his head as far back as it'll go. He kicks and struggles, trying to get up. I pin his head with my body, and reaching down with one hand to open his throat, I feel a stabbing pain pierce my belly.

But it's too late for him, and as the red river from his jugular begins to flow, I bury my teeth in the wound and begin to gulp in the lifeblood as it pumps out.

The hot sagey taste is wildly exotic compared to deer and elk, and I gladly succumb to the power the blood has over me. It traces its way through my system and into my veins, and a sense of relief washes through me, leaving me re-energized.

I continue to drink, but before the lethargy begins signaling that I've had my fill, there is no more. The beast growls in frustration and hunger still burns in my gut.

But that's not the only thing burning. I slowly regain my feet and lift up my shirt.

Damn. About halfway between my belly button and my side is a long, ragged wound weeping blood. It looks deep and is beginning to really hurt.

Looking at his horns, I can see from the blood on one that it was a front prong that got me. It's three or four inches long—enough to cause some real damage.

I'm going to need more blood for healing, lots more, and I'm not in the best shape to get it.

As the pain in my belly starts to increase, so does the hunger, and I am instantly transported back to my fight with the bear, and the twin agonies that had me near the point of death.

But there is no Nicolas to rescue me this time, and no human blood that I am willing to take to speed the healing.

And I can't hole up here in the wilderness to heal. I have to pick Sandy up from the hospital tomorrow.

That's going to be interesting. Going into a building full of humans and blood while I'm fighting the healing hunger. I don't think that's going to work.

Shit.

I start walking in the direction of the car and the nearby woods. I need to find something a little easier to kill. A lot of something easier.

My gut burns with the dual fires of pain and hunger, and the flames are beginning to lick up into my veins. I lift up my shirt and look again at the wound. It's no longer seeping, so apparently the buck's blood was enough to begin the healing process. I think about Sandy and wonder how much I'm bleeding internally. Nicolas had told me after the bear attack that our injuries heal on the outside first to prevent further blood loss and, more importantly, restore our ability to fight.

The pain surges and I tense in preparation for the flare of hunger that always follows. And it does. I grit my teeth and wait for both to ease.

Clamping my arms around my middle, I struggle up the hill as wave after wave of pain and hunger burn through me. It's nothing like the injuries from the bear, but it still hurts like hell.

Finally I reach the car and decide to drive farther up the mountain to an area I hunted the first night. There were plenty of deer up there, and I might luck out and find a small buck. Or even a doe, as much as I object to killing females. But I don't need any more injuries right now. What I need is blood, lots of blood, and I will take anything I come across.

Hopefully it won't be something on two legs.

# SATURDAY

## CHAPTER 12

I crack open my eyes and peer at the sun that is blazing through the branches. The one beneath me is hard, rough, and bumpy. Groaning, I now remember why I don't like to sleep in trees. To use an expression of Sandy's, this sucks.

Sitting up, I clench my jaw against the inevitable pain and hunger that movement always generates when I'm injured. But it's not too bad right now.

It shouldn't be, as I took both a doe and a half-grown buck last night. In fact, it was stumbling across the buck's trail that kept me from reaching the car in time to return to the hotel before sunrise.

I raise my shirt and look at the healing wound. The outside has closed up and is a fiery welt a little over two inches long and forked in the shape of a tree branch. Or an antelope horn. Weird.

The strange crawling sensation deep in my belly where the flesh is slowly knitting together reminds me of what it feels like to hold fishing worms as they wiggle and squirm.

Ugh.

But it's interesting that I seem to be healing fairly quickly. It supports the theory I had when I was recovering from the bear injuries. Because I was accustomed to a diet of deer and elk, their blood would have been far more healing for me than the horse blood Nicolas gave me.

As for the human blood? There's no denying how fast my healing accelerated when he gave me that, something I sincerely wish he'd never done.

It would probably heal me just as fast now, but that's not an option. Not now. Not ever.

I climb down out of the tree, being careful not to jar the knitting flesh inside. Again the pain flares, but it's muted and bearable. The fiery hunger, however, is another matter. And it will continue to be a problem as long as I am healing, even after the pain is gone.

Squinting up at the sun, I'm guessing it's about noon. Roughly six hours since my last kill, as though I needed the sun to tell me that. The flames beginning to race up my veins are plenty of proof that I need to feed again, and soon.

Sandy. I shake my head as I think about Sandy waiting impatiently for me to pick her up from the hospital.

My options are limited.

I could pick her up now, drop her off at the hotel, and come back. It would be close to two hours before I could be back out here, and I have no idea how long it will take me to locate suitable game, which is likely all bedded down for the day.

Three hours from now I could be curled up in a ball of agony, burning from the inside out as my healing cells scream for more blood. Not good.

I don't have any choice. I need to hunt and I can't delay much longer.

But the least I can do is drive partway back into town and call to let her know that I haven't forgotten. That might take an hour, maybe a little less.

I think I can handle that. I hope.

Hiking back to the car, I mull over how to care for her and get her situated while dealing with my own problem.

A wave of mild pain passes through my belly, and the hunger answers with a roar, sending tendrils of fire throughout my system.

Gritting my teeth, I hunch over and hug myself and wait for it to subside.

Hell with it. She's on her own until I'm recovered.

Finally reaching the car, I waste no time turning around to head back to town. The BMW flies along the dirt road, leaving a trail of khaki-colored dust, not unlike the color of the hunting clothes I'm still wearing. Except what I'm wearing is drenched in blood.

As I reach the asphalt, I try the cell, but still no signal. Growling in frustration, I barrel down the road, punching SEND every thirty seconds or so. I don't get through until I'm nearly back into town. It's been twenty-seven minutes since I left. I pull over onto the shoulder, shift into neutral, and jam on the parking brake.

The hunger flames through me again, surging up my throat and out into my veins, and I hear Sandy answer.

"Hey, where are you? I tried to call you last night, and you never called back. They released me early this morning and I'm packed and ready to go."

But I can't speak yet. I hold my breath waiting for the fires to die down.

"Sunny? What's up? Are you there? Damn cell phones." And she hangs up.

I focus on breathing, and finally the hunger quiets enough that I may be able to actually talk. But I don't have long, as these waves of fire will keep increasing in frequency until they are continuous.

I've traveled this road before, and I dread what is coming around the next bend.

Pressing SEND again, I put the phone up to my ear and listen to it ring. As it stops, I say, "Sandy. Listen to me. I don't have much time. You understand?"

"Yes," she says quietly. Sharp girl.

"Good. I've had a . . . a slight setback, and won't be able to pick you up until probably this evening. I'm sorry, but it can't be helped. I would be there if I could, but it's just not possible right now."

"Are you okay? You sound like . . . like you're in pain or something."

Too sharp.

"I'm fine. I'll see you this evening. I need to go now."

"Okay . . ."

Pushing END, I whip the still-running car around and head back up the mountain.

# CHAPTER 13

It's near sunset when I get back to the car. As I haul my cleanup kit out of the trunk, revulsion rolls through me at what I'd done to the little deer family I'd found. Once again, I had to trample on my own moral boundaries. However, I can handle the regret a lot better than the inferno that was threatening to engulf me and push me into uncontrollable insanity.

Insanity that could drive me toward easier prey. Accessible, unaware. Two-legged.

I slap down the beast and force my thoughts away from the uncomfortable craving now tormenting me. The hunger fires are momentarily quenched, which has allowed the craving to make itself known.

And the craving is for the one thing I refuse to give it.

*Human* blood.

Damn it. Damn the bear and Nicolas and everything that's happened to bring me to this point. If I'd stayed in California, I never would have known the sweet song of human blood as it caresses my mouth and fills my veins.

And I never would have known Nicolas . . .

The black hole in my core strains at its bonds, but I pull the stillness tight around it and refuse to let it open.

Stuffing my bloody clothes into the bag in the trunk, I slam the lid down, yank the driver's door open, and get in. The BMW repeats its earlier dusty slide as I whip it into a U-turn and head back down the road.

Sandy's probably terrorizing the nurses with her impatience. Guess I'll be adding to their terror when I show up in this mood.

As I hit the paved road, I start calling. The signal finally goes through.

"Hi," Sandy answers quietly.

"You ready to go? All checked out?" I can't keep the irritation out of my voice.

"Yeeaah . . . Everything okay?"

"Just fine. Be waiting out front," I snap.

"Okay."

Ending the call, I try to shrug off the tension that has me feeling like a compressed spring. But it's no good. My agitation is connected to the craving, and Sandy is just going to have to deal with it.

Alarm pours through me as I think about her.

What if the healing hunger is unaffected by Sandy's . . . block, or whatever it is that keeps me from reacting to her blood?

What if the craving overrides everything that protects her from me?

Oh shit.

She doesn't even have money for a cab.

~

Turning into the hospital parking lot, I see Sandy waving from a wheelchair outside the door, her backpack and shopping bags on the sidewalk beside her. A nurse is standing behind the chair.

Damn.

I pull up to the curb and get out. As I'm walking around the back of the car, the beast growls and stares hard at the nurse. I freeze next to the trunk, afraid to get any closer. The nurse helps Sandy into the car, then with a curious glance at me, takes the wheelchair and heads back to the hospital doors. Once she's safely inside, I grab Sandy's stuff and shove it into the back seat, then walk around to the driver's door.

The sight of Sandy through the window, the thought of being in the car with her, sends fear rippling across my skin.

With my breath held tight, I open the door and get in.

"So . . . are you okay?" she asks hesitantly.

"I told you. I'm fine." I struggle to sound civil, but it's difficult.

She's quiet for a moment, then replies, "You know, you can't lie to me any better than I can to you."

"Drop it."

She doesn't say anything more, and I'm glad, because I'm not in the mood for her babbling tonight.

So far, so good. The craving is still there, although weaker, but the beast is showing no reaction to Sandy in such close quarters and my tension eases a bit more as we drive to the hotel.

The loading area in front of the hotel is clear. I park at the curb, get out, and start gathering her things. Her door opens, and I glance over to see her struggling to stand. I reach out and she grabs my hand. I almost pull her to her feet, but remembering how fragile she is, I wait and let her stand at her own speed.

With a tentative smile, Sandy steps onto the curb and I shut the door. I grab her pack and shopping bags, then gesture with my chin to go ahead. She frowns and walks toward the doors and I follow her into the lobby.

She glances at me when we reach the elevator.

"Sunny—"

"We only have one room now, but it has two beds. I'll be leaving again shortly and won't be back until tomorrow, so you'll have the room to yourself."

"But—"

"How are you feeling, by the way?" I haven't even asked her. Been too wrapped up in my own crap.

She stares at the floor a moment, then answers.

"Still a little tired and sore. But better, I guess."

"Good."

The elevator doors open and we start to walk in. But someone is in there waiting to come out, and as he walks past me, the beast lunges with a roar. I quickly turn and step to the side, keeping my face averted as I try to control both the beast and the craving that is suddenly clawing at my throat. I blink several times, but my vision stays red.

Shit.

"Sunny! The elevator."

I can hear the machinery trying to close the doors, and with a quick glance behind me, turn and duck into the car. Sandy steps back inside and lets the doors close.

Apparently her protection, or whatever the hell it is, doesn't extend beyond her when I'm in a healing crisis.

"Sunny, what's going on? You seem really upset and hostile and, I dunno—are you mad at me? Have you changed your mind? I told you I can take care of myself. You don't need to do this." The anguish in her voice nearly chokes me with guilt as the beast slowly calms and my vision begins to clear.

"I'm sorry, Sandy. This has nothing to do with you. I'm just dealing with some . . ." I glance at her through a pink haze, then look away again. "Some stuff that came up."

The whir of the elevator machinery is the only sound in the car for a long moment.

"Can I do anything to help?" she asks.

"No. This is something I need to handle myself. All I want you to do is rest and get better. Okay?"

"Okay." She releases a long sigh.

The elevator stops on our floor and the doors open. I cautiously stick my head out and glance up and down the hall before stepping out. Sandy follows me to the room and waits while I pull the key card out and open the door. I can feel her studying me, and the hunter growls, disliking the scrutiny from this human.

Funny. The hunter reacts the same to Sandy as it does to any human. So why is Sandy able to mute the beast, the bloodthirsty killer? I just don't get this.

We walk in and I set her backpack on the bed nearest to the door and her packages in the corner.

"You can have this bed. I've been using the one by the window."

"Okay."

"Tomorrow we can officially move into the apartment. It's furnished, but I don't know what else we're going to need." I pause, trying to get my words together. "The problem is, I don't really know what my . . . schedule is going to be for the next few days, and we may need to continue to stay here."

"Okay. Whatever you want or need to do is fine with me. I'm just grateful to have a place to stay." Her face softens and her eyes begin to shine.

"Don't. Remember what I said. No more crying. It doesn't do any good and only delays what needs to be done."

She sniffs a couple times and nods.

"Good." I walk over to my bag, take out my wallet, and pull out several bills. "Here's money for food. There's a restaurant next to the lobby. This should cover you for the next couple days in case I can't get back. The room is taken care of, so you don't need to worry about that." I walk over and hand it to her.

"Ninety dollars?! I could eat for a month on this, maybe longer. I don't need this much."

"You haven't seen the prices on the menu downstairs."

"Well, I could always walk to someplace cheaper. There's got to be fast food joints around here." She starts taking stuff out of her backpack, apparently looking for something.

"I'd rather you not leave the hotel. What if something tears loose or you have a relapse or something? Who's going to get you to the hospital?"

"I was doing fine taking care of myself before you . . . came . . . along." She stops as she sees my face. "Okay. Fine. I won't leave. But what am I supposed to do if I have to be *stuck* here all day and night? At least at the hospital I had nurses to talk to." She sits on the bed and crosses her arms.

She has a point. I would go crazy if I was cooped up in this room for half a day, let alone several.

I glance at the clock. 9:36. I have time.

"What about the book I bought you?"

"I finished it."

"Well, we could run to the grocery store and see if they have anything else you'd like."

"Could I get some snacks, and maybe some sodas or something to drink?" she asks hopefully.

"Aren't you on some sort of restricted diet for a while?"

"Not really. There's a few things they said I shouldn't eat for now. But mostly I can have what I want."

"All right then." I hand her the pad of paper and pen from the desk. "Make a list."

"Okay."

"And we'll go on one condition."

"Yeah?"

"That when we get back, you'll stay here in the hotel after I leave. No going out when I'm not here. Deal?" I stare directly at her.

"Uh, yeah. Deal. No problem." Her eyes go wide as she stammers her answer.

Hiding my smile, I turn to get my bag. I do enjoy the effect my stare has on people. It usually gets me exactly what I want.

I watch from the car as she weakly shuffles up and down the grocery aisles, my frustration mounting.

Damn it.

She should be the one sitting in the car, resting, and I should be the one in there, shopping.

But I can hear it now. "Cleanup on aisle four. Make that five as well, and six . . ."

The beast jumps up hungrily at the bloody images that are suddenly traipsing through my head.

Snarling, I fold my arms and slump down in the car, watching as Sandy goes through the checkout. When she finally hands over the cash, I get out and wait by the side of the car. A young guy bags her groceries, talking animatedly with her as she laughs and nods. He sets the bags in the cart and pushes it toward the door as she walks alongside.

I debate whether or not to go help her and decide I'm probably better off staying here at the car. I watch as they approach, hammering down the beast that is eagerly watching as well.

"Would you like me to put these in the trunk, ma'am?" His warm spicy scent radiates toward me and a short strawberry-blond curl flips onto his forehead as he speaks.

*No, cuz I'll probably stuff you in there, too, right alongside the bloody hunting clothes.*

"No. I'll take them. Thanks." My tone is clipped as I barely restrain a growl.

Sandy's eyebrows raise in surprise as I grab the front of the cart and tug it sharply out of the boy's grasp.

"Well, okay, then. Have a nice night." His expression puzzled and a little alarmed, he smiles briefly at Sandy and quickly walks back to the store.

"That was pretty rude . . . ," she begins.

"Save it. Get in the car." I grab the bags from the cart and put them in the back seat.

She hesitates, then, her back stiff with indignation, settles carefully into the front seat.

Getting in, I slam the door and, without looking at her, start the car. I don't waste any time getting out onto the street.

"What is *wrong* with you?"

I bite my tongue, literally, to keep from snapping at her. The pain distracts me momentarily from the agitation that is threatening to boil out of my veins. Until it triggers a new rush of hunger.

That was stupid.

Staring straight ahead, I focus on driving somewhat legally. That's all I need. Wouldn't want to be the cop pulling me over tonight.

"Is it something I did?" she asks.

I take a deep breath and try to calm down.

"I'm sorry. This is not about you. But I don't want to talk about it, and I'd like you to stop asking me questions right now."

"Okaaay." Out of the corner of my eye I see her turn and face straight ahead.

The rest of the ride back to the hotel is thankfully silent.

~

11:07. I still have a couple hours before the hunger starts to become a real concern, but I don't want to let it get to that point. Folding the empty grocery bags, I look over at Sandy in her bed as she readjusts the pillows behind her back.

The explosive tension I've been trying to contain has faded now that I'm away from other people. Even the idea of being in close quarters with them had me on edge. I stuff the bags in the crack between the mini-fridge and the wall, then standing, lean back against the dresser and fold my arms.

"Sandy."

She looks up at me, the questions and the hurt shining in her green eyes.

"I'm sorry about . . . earlier, and the fact that I can't stay to help you out and keep you company. I can't explain what's going on, but please believe me when I say that it has nothing to do with you."

"I get it. I know something happened, and I wish you would talk to me about it. But I think part of it is that you feel like you can't leave me to go back to . . . wherever you came from. Where you should be heading right now. I just feel bad that I'm keeping you here when we both know you should go."

My insides writhe as I concentrate on the stillness that is the only thing holding me together.

Because she's right. I would be back in the Springs by now. Which only reaffirms my belief that we were supposed to meet. That there is some reason why we did and for everything that's happened since I picked her up in the middle of the road.

"I'm not quite ready to go back. I need to figure some things out and make some firm decisions before I do. Your situation has nothing to do with it," I say carefully.

"Well, then, maybe it has something to do with your daughter."

My chest tightens. She's too astute, and now I'm done with this conversation. I push off from the dresser and grab my bag.

"I need to go. Call if you need anything. Leave a voicemail—I'll check periodically for messages."

"Will you be back in the morning?"

"I don't know. Probably not. I'll call you when I wake up."

"Okay."

I head for the door. As I'm closing it, I hear her say, "Sunny, I'm sorry."

Me, too.

~

Images swirl around in my head like the dust the BMW is raising as we fly up the dirt road. A baby's face framed in black curls, bright blue eyes shining with innocence. A daughter's face, the same blue eyes gazing at her child with motherly love.

And the one who overshadows them both. Emerald eyes flashing red with desire, his sensuous lips curled to give me his sharp caress.

Other faces spin into view. A boy balancing on the knife-edge of danger, slips and becomes a broken, twisted ragdoll drenched in blood. A pleasure-seeking girl, addicted to her impending death, her life draining from her drop by drop. An arrogant and cruel young man, screaming in agony as first one monster, then another, drinks the very life from him.

The maelstrom speeds up, the faces flashing by faster and faster, and I feel its force begin to tear away at the bindings that hold the black emptiness closed. Pain flashes through me, and the rip in my gut from which it flares is not from the stab of a horn.

Oh God, no! Please, no . . . I can't take this anymore . . .

Wrenching the wheel to the side, I slam on the brakes and yank the key from the ignition. I'm out the door before the car comes to a full stop.

I run.

# SUNDAY

## CHAPTER 14

The sun is beating down on my face, and I crack open an eye and snarl at the unwelcome intrusion of searing light.

Go away. I don't want to wake up. Ever.

Shifting on the hard knobby limb under me, I realize the pain in my rib is from the stub of a broken branch.

Screw it.

I jump down from the tree, landing awkwardly off-balance, and realize I'm hungover from the orgy I drowned myself in last night. My clothes are stiff with dried blood and reek from the potpourri of dying animal stink that permeates them. I reach up and feel my hair—it's the same as my clothes, crunching as I pull a section away from my blouse where it was stuck.

Shit. I rub at an itchy spot on my face, and crusted blood flakes off, the rust-colored sprinkles drifting away on the slight breeze.

I shake my head, trying to clear it. I let the beast run amok last night, killing everything the hunter could find for it. It didn't matter what it was. If it breathed, it died.

Stupid. Waste of life. And I'm sure the whole area is now ruined for hunting. It's a dead zone and will likely be avoided for quite some time into the future.

But that doesn't matter anymore. Because I'm leaving. And I won't be back.

~

I finish scrubbing my hair, face, and arms in the icy snowmelt that is rushing down the little creek. The rest, filthy with the blood that soaked through my clothing, will have to wait until I find the car and fresh clothes.

Standing, I look around, trying to figure out where the hell I am. I tried backtracking along my trail, but it ran so randomly up and down the mountainsides that after several hours I gave up and just started heading north.

The peak to my right seems a little familiar and I head up to its top at a brisk jog. When the view below me reveals several stretches of a dirt road, I start making my way downhill toward it, hoping it's the right one.

The sun's still fairly high in the sky when I round a bend on the road and the BMW finally comes into view. I've been pretty worried that it had been stolen or towed—I'd be totally screwed. Most everything I have is in that car. Normally I would've set up stashes in the area as a backup, but I had no intention of staying this long.

Pressing the trunk button, I fish out a fresh set of clothes and strip, then take a quick sponge bath using the water from my cleanup kit. When I examine the scar from the antelope, I'm pleased to see that it's finally lost the pink tinge and is becoming the silver of my other scars. It's still ragged and a little thick, though, and the pulling I felt when arching my back tells me the healing inside isn't quite done.

But it's a definite improvement over yesterday. The injuries from the bear took several days to heal. Of course, they were much, much worse. I just hope the wild game will be enough, and that I don't need human blood to finish healing.

Dressing, I chuckle as I think of the reaction some rancher would have if he came around the bend and saw me standing here naked with bloody clothes lying on the ground. He'd sure have something to talk about—if he was smart enough to keep on driving.

Yeah.

The mood I'm in, Nicolas isn't going to have to convince me to finish the Change. I'll be able to walk right up to him and announce, "*Well, you bastard, you wanted a murderer for a mate? You got one now.*"

Right.

Disgusted with myself, I stuff the ruined clothes into a plastic bag. At this rate, without access to a washing machine, I'm going to have to go shopping again. I slam the trunk, get in the car, and head down the road.

Other than being irritable, the hunger still seems to be sated, even though it's been close to eight hours since I fed. Mass quantities of blood last night probably has something to do with it.

But the craving for *human* blood is still there. It somehow feels different than the hunger.

Crap. Looks like I'll need to keep avoiding people for a while longer. This ought to be interesting.

The clock reads 2:07, and I try to recall what day it is. Sunday, maybe.

Sunday. The eighteenth. Move-in day.

Good. The sooner I get Sandy settled, the sooner I can leave. The guilt I've been feeling over abandoning her pales in significance when compared to the insanity that consumes me whenever I let my thoughts drift to what I left behind in Colorado.

I rouse the hunter and take hold of her stillness in preparation for the afternoon with Sandy and whatever humans I might encounter. As I pull into the hotel parking lot, I realize I probably should've called her when I got into cell range. Oh well.

Sticking my key card into the lock, I open the door and walk in.

Yeah, I should've called. Because she's not alone.

As his rich spicy scent hits me, I recognize the boy from the grocery store. The beast jumps up, watching intently, and I struggle to stay calm.

"Oh, hi. I didn't expect you back . . . so . . . soon." Sandy's voice trails off as she sees my face.

They're sitting side by side on her bed, leaning back against the pillow-cushioned headboard, a bowl of chips between them. I glance at the TV they were obviously watching and regret interrupting what is probably a rare teenage moment for Sandy.

"Uh, I . . . I was just leaving." The boy's strawberry hair falls over his eyes, and he jerks his head to flip it out of the way. He quickly stands and I can smell the fear that is suddenly emanating from him.

"No problem. I'll come back later." I turn around to leave.

"Wait, Sunny. I can explain." Her words slide out, smooth and practiced. She's probably had to say that a lot in her transient life. Poor kid.

Opening the door, I stop. I take a breath of the hallway air, air that isn't laden with the boy's attractive scent, and the scent of his fear calling out to the hunter.

"Sandy, there's nothing to explain. You're not doing anything wrong. You have a friend over. Big deal. I'm going over to the apartment to get situated. I'll pick you up later." I try to keep the strain out of my voice, but I don't think I'm very successful.

"But wait . . ." Her voice cuts off as the door closes. I head quickly down the hall past the elevator to the stairwell.

The room door opens. "Sunny!" she calls.

I stop at the stairwell door, turn around, and wait as she makes her way along the hall. I can see that she is still weak, and concern suddenly replaces the tension that is rippling through me.

"Sunny, what's wrong? I just wanted to introduce you to Danny. He's very nice. I just wanted him to see that you're really cool, ya know, once someone gets to know you. You kinda . . . freak him out." Her green eyes search mine, and I glance away, considering my answer, then look back at her.

"Sandy, I told you that being around people was difficult for me sometimes. Well, I lied. It's difficult for me most of the time, and lately, *all* of the time. Except for you. I don't know why that is—it just is. So I really have no interest in meeting Danny, and right now, it would be best for all of us if I don't. So let it go." I watch as she nods in surrender. "Call me to pick you up when you're done with your movie—preferably before dark."

"No, I want to come with you now. I'll just tell Danny that I need to go and will call him later."

"Well, it's up to you." I pause, giving her one more chance to change her mind.

"It'll just take me a few minutes to pack up my stuff. Do you mind waiting?" She looks at me hopefully.

"No. I'll be back in a little while, no rush." I turn, open the stairwell door, and head down, ending the conversation.

~

I watch from the car as Danny comes through the lobby doors and walks across the parking lot to a beat-up white Toyota Corolla. Huh. Not even a pickup truck. In cowboy country, that definitely makes him a misfit. No wonder they hit it off so well.

Hell, I'd probably like him if I didn't want his blood so badly. There's just something about it that makes him extra attractive. Remembering red-haired Terry from the club, I wonder if it's because Danny's a strawberry blond. Maybe it's like Terry said, that it has something to do with the red gene making their blood so spicy and desirable.

As he pulls out of the parking lot, I breathe a sigh of relief, head into the hotel, and back up the stairwell.

# CHAPTER 15

"Wow. This is my room?" Sandy stands at the doorway, staring at the surprisingly large bedroom. The bed is a queen and a five-drawer dresser stands against the wall next to the sliding closet doors.

"Yeah. All yours." I walk in and put her backpack on the bed, then set her bags of clothing from our shopping trip on the floor. Opening the closet door, I count the hangers.

"This should be enough, but if you need more, there're some in the coat closet."

"Oh, this is so cool—I can't believe it!" She walks in and plops on the bed, running her hand over the mattress.

"Looks like we need to pick up bedding, towels, soap . . ." And a sturdy lock for my bedroom door, even though I don't plan to stay long.

"Can we go shopping? I'll make a list!" Sandy looks up, eyes shining.

This is worth it. Seeing her happy over such *human* things makes me feel, well, more human myself.

"Sure. You make the list. I'll buy."

"Awesome!" She claps her hands like a little girl.

It is awesome.

~

The sun is starting to go down as I take the sheets out of the dryer. I throw the wet towels in and bundle up the sheets to take back to the apartment.

Sandy is humming to the song playing on her new portable stereo as I walk up to her doorway. I watch as she fusses with the little dragon figurines I let her buy, turning them this way and that on her dresser.

I tap on her open door. She jumps and turns around.

"Shit. I wish you wouldn't sneak up on me like that."

"I thought you could . . . feel . . . people." I try to keep from smirking.

"No. It doesn't work like that. It's only when people are really super emotional, and mostly just when they're upset or pissed off. But sometimes I'll be near someone who is really happy, and I like that cuz it makes me happy, too."

Well, she probably won't get much of that from me. I snort to myself and walk in with the sheets. I set the bundle on the chair I brought in from the dining room and pull out the bottom sheet. As I start to put it on her bed, she steps over to help.

"No. I'll do this. You need to take it easy. I think we stayed out a bit longer than we should've."

Her eyes have lost their earlier brightness and the dark circles beneath them show me she's more tired than she'll admit. I'm hoping I didn't jeopardize her health with our shopping trip—again.

Sandy frowns, but says nothing more. She's learning that it's useless to argue with me.

She hands me the other sheet and, as I finish making the bed, brings over her new comforter. I open it up and spread it on the bed, smiling at the neon-colored flowers and butterflies that cover it. I don't know about her taste, but she loves it, and that's all that matters.

Smoothing out the final wrinkle, I look up at her slightly crooked grin, and grin back.

Yeah. Definitely worth it.

"Thanks!"

"No problem. The towels are in the dryer and should be done in another half hour, maybe forty minutes or so. You're clear on where the laundry room is, right?"

"Yeah, yeah. Across the parking lot and around the corner, first door on the right." Sandy rolls her eyes as she repeats my earlier directions.

I raise my eyebrows at her flippant tone.

"Sorry." She offers me a wrinkle-nosed, toothy grin, and I instantly forgive her.

"Yeah, well, I need to go now. I don't know if I'll be back before morning. If not, I'll see you sometime in the afternoon. We can go over your classes then if you want."

"Danny said he'd help me. He's enrolling for the fall semester, too."

“That’s good. I’m glad you’ve found a friend.”

I just wish it was one that I didn’t want to sink my teeth into.

As I turn to leave, Sandy says, “Uh, Sunny? Can I ask you a question?”

“Depends on the question.”

“Well, where do you sleep when you’re not . . . here, or home, or whatever.”

Recalling her comment that I don’t seem the “tree-hugger” type, I smile.

“Trees.”

“What? Trees?”

I quietly laugh and head for the front door, grabbing my bag and keys on the way out.

# MONDAY

## CHAPTER 16

Despite my comment about trees to Sandy yesterday evening, I really do love the billowy softness of a bed, and am grateful to have beaten the rising sun back to the apartment earlier this morning after last night's run on the mountain.

I flip back the covers and lazily stretch, then sit up and raise my shirt to look again at the pronghorn scar. It's finally smoothed out and looks more like my other scars. The beast is calm and I haven't felt the flames of hunger scorching my veins since my killing spree the night before last. The craving for human blood seems to be fading, and I can only hope that it will soon cease altogether as the last internal remnants of my wound finish healing.

Relieved that I seem to be regaining some control over my body, I glance at the clock. 11:07. Early enough that I should be able to finish getting Sandy settled in by the end of today.

Then I'll be free to leave.

I quickly dress, anxious to get the day started. Just as I unlock the door, I remember my to-do list sitting on the nightstand and start back across the room.

And then I feel it.

A . . . pressure . . . in the air. Power. Energy.

Nicolas.

*Nicolas.*

He's here.

Somewhere close by.

*He's here.*

But he feels . . . different. And angry. Very angry.

A lightning bolt of fear strikes through me, and then the emptiness in my core rips through its bonds, seeking that which will fill it. I stagger as the pain and loneliness overwhelm me and a ragged gasp escapes my chest.

Oh God.

My door flies open and I spin in horror, the dread of him warring with the need of him.

"Sunny! What's happening?!" Sandy's voice reflects the anguish I'm feeling.

Sandy. Not Nicolas.

I look past her through the open door, but he is not there.

Yet I feel him so strongly.

And there is definitely something off about him.

"Sunny, are you all right?" Her voice trembles.

Sandy. *Sandy*.

I need to get away from here, from *her*. Lead him away from her.

The possibility that Sandy may be in danger galvanizes me into action. I release the hunter, who is tensely standing by, and grab her stillness, her coldness, her calculating action.

Glancing at Sandy, I walk past her into the living room to peer through the windows, but there's no sign of him or his car. She follows me, then moves out of the way as I head back to the bedroom. I can feel her watching me from the doorway as I snap the latches on my suitcase and pick it up.

"You're leaving."

"Yes. Something's come up and I need to go." I grab my bag and keys and turn to go out the door.

Sandy's blocking my way and I glare at her to move. She reluctantly steps back and I brush past her on my way to the front door.

"That's it? We're done? No goodbyes?"

The hurt in her voice penetrates the hunter's detachment. I stop, and setting down the suitcase, turn to her.

"I'm sorry. I . . . didn't intend to leave so abruptly. I hoped to spend at least another day with you to make sure you have everything you need and to prepare you to be on your own." I watch as tears spill from her eyes and run down her cheeks.

"Oh . . . Sandy. Come here."

She rushes across the room and throws her arms around me, sobbing. I give her a quick hug, then touching her shoulders, gently push her back.

Brushing kinky strands of hair from her wet eyes, I try to smile.

"This isn't about you. In fact, I'm leaving because me being here may be putting you in danger. You'll be fine. We'll stay in touch by phone, but I don't know when I'll be back. It may not be for quite a while. The lease is paid up for the next six months and I can renew it if you want to continue to stay here."

"But . . . can't I come with you?" Tears are still streaming down her face.

"No, that's not possible. It's not safe right now. Besides, you need to start a new life for yourself. Go to college, get to know Danny, fall in love." I can feel my own tears threatening, and focus once again on the stillness.

"But I really have to go now." The power that I sense seems to be getting stronger, which means he is getting nearer.

Turning, I pick up my suitcase and head to the door.

"Oh, by the way, I put some money in the cookie jar for you. It should last you awhile if you don't go 'shopping' too often." Two thousand should hold her for a time. I can always wire her more.

I open the door and stop, checking the air. I don't detect his scent anywhere. Hopefully I can get out of here before he can zero in on me.

Sandy starts to follow me out and, listening to her rapid heartbeats, I stop again.

"Sandy. Go back inside. No questions, just do as I ask. And please, stay inside for the rest of the day. For me."

She doesn't answer, but she does stop. I hear her step back into the doorway.

"If you'll do something for me. Just one more thing." The sorrow in her voice makes me cringe.

"What?"

"Go visit your daughter. Talk to her. Let her get to know you again. You're not the . . . the monster you believe yourself to be."

Oh, you have no idea.

Fighting to stay in control, I head to the car.

"Sunny! Please! For me. Do it for me!"

I keep walking and don't look back.

# CHAPTER 17

Pulling onto the street, I head in Nicolas's direction, which seems to be somewhere near the highway. I stop several times and step out of the car, trying to focus on exactly where he is. Finally it seems like I'm getting nearer and my next stop confirms it. His energy is definitely stronger now. My breath catches as I feel my body respond to it.

Soon. Very soon . . .

I stay outside the car for several minutes, hoping he'll get a fix on my location. As I concentrate on him, I sense him drawing closer, which means he's pinpointed me. Getting back in the car, I turn south, heading toward the mountains. I stop several times, get out and wait, and feel him getting closer and closer.

Too soon . . .

Satisfied that he's now tracking me, I keep a steady pace as I leave the paved road and start up the mountain. I stop one more time and watch the dirt road behind me, fighting to keep my inner turmoil at bay. When I see the dust rising from his car, I jump back in mine and race up the road.

Whipping the car around the turn for one of my hunting areas, I slow a bit to be sure he makes the turn as well. The black car hesitates, then follows my dust. I hit the gas and race for the pullout. Sliding in, I jerk the car to a stop and bail out into a dead run for higher terrain and the trees.

Because whatever happens, I intend to meet him on ground of *my* choosing. The increasing anger I feel from him is spurring my own, and I don't think our reunion is going to be a very peaceful one.

Halfway up the steep hillside, I leap into a tree and quickly scramble to the top. I turn and watch as his car pulls in behind mine. I wait.

But he doesn't get out and my temper begins to succumb to my curiosity.

The door finally opens, and a slim leg steps out, followed by a slender shape. The fury emanating toward me is laced with a bewilderment that comes nowhere close to mine.

It's not Nicolas.

It's Éva.

Huh.

She feels just like him. Yet now that she's nearby, I can detect the subtle differences that mark her own energy signature, which is somehow more powerful than it was before.

Maybe that's it. Maybe it's her power that's fooling my senses.

But something else has changed as well, and I can't quite put my finger on it.

"Sunny! Where the hell are you?" she bellows in rage. My own flares in response.

"Why don't you come up here and find out?" I doubt Nicolas would actually kill me, but I don't hold any such beliefs about her.

I can see her bristle as she steps across the road. She stops at the edge, her eyes searching upward for my location.

Hmm. I remember what Nicolas said about The Chosen being unwilling to "soil their clothing or muss their hair." I'm suddenly very glad that I brought us up here. I might actually have a chance.

"What do you want, Éva?" I yell down the hill to her.

"We need to talk." Her anger is edged with her typical impatience.

"Is that *all* you want? Because I'm pretty sure you want to do a lot more to me than just talk."

"That's quite astute for you. Bravo. I was beginning to wonder if you were ever going to learn *anything* about The Chosen." The scorn drips from her voice.

Bitch. The red veil drops over my vision as the beast roars its defiance.

But I won't let her bait me. I have the advantage out here and we both know it. I stay in my tree.

"So. Did Nicolas send you, his little messenger girl?"

I watch her go very still. Score.

"You have no idea what you've done." Her voice is icy, and beneath her anger, I catch a glimmer of hatred that was never there before.

"I'm sorry about Dominic. Things just . . ." I don't know what else to say. She was his sponsor, and I killed him.

"Yes, that was a complete waste. I don't think I'll be able to forgive you for that." She pauses. "But not for what you did. It's what you *didn't* do."

I didn't take his lifespark. I didn't complete the Change.

Her regret can't be anywhere near mine.

"So what now?" I yell down at her.

"Come down here so we can talk. I promise not to kill you. Yet."

I think about it for a moment, then silently climb down the tree. Working my way across the slope, I drop down into a deep ravine and quietly move downstream along the creek bed. When I reach the road, about six hundred feet from where the cars are parked, I peek out around the embankment. Éva is still standing at the road edge, her head slowly pivoting as she tries to locate me.

Smiling, I slip across the road and circle around through the trees to the cars. I creep up to the passenger side of the BMW and watch her a moment longer on the other side of the road.

"I'm here. What do you want to talk about?"

She whirls in my direction, unable to hide her surprise.

I smile, and both the hunter and the beast smile with me.

"Well. Nicolas said you had adapted quite well to this rather . . . *barbaric* type of life. I will be sure not to underestimate you again."

Then she is gone.

And she whispers in my ear, "But don't underestimate me either."

I swallow and look at her as she steps back, her smile no less deathly than mine had been.

"So. Here we are. Each ready to tear the other apart over the next insult. I hope you harbor no illusions about who would win." She stiffens as her smile fades and the red blossoms in her eyes.

"No, I do not. I don't even know if you keep your promises. Yet, here I am."

"So you are." Her eyes shift back to a dark amber and some of her tension eases.

She takes a deep breath, crosses her arms, and turns to stare back up the hill.

Her silence is matched by that of the forest around us as everything stops to watch our Game unfold.

"I don't understand how you could choose *that*," she gestures toward the slope, "that wild existence, over *him*." She turns back to face me. Her eyes are filled with unshed blood.

My own fill as well. I clench my jaw as the empty chasm inside me yawns and threatens to swallow me down. Thoughts spinning, I try to figure out how to respond to her accusation, but fail to find words that will make any difference to her.

"Do you realize that you have utterly *destroyed* him?" Her lip curls. "And by destroying him, you've almost destroyed *all of us*? We've been nearly incapacitated with his pain since the night you left. And that leaves us vulnerable to our enemies at a time when tensions between the lineages are the highest in three centuries."

I don't even know what to say. But I understand the pain. I live and breathe that pain on a level she will never comprehend.

"I should kill you where you stand, because of what you did to us, what you did to *him*. But I promised not to . . . for now. Whether or not I do so in the future is up to you."

There is nothing I can say in my defense. The last thing any of The Chosen, including Nicolas, can know is that I have a human family. Because once they understand the source of my reluctance to Change, they will swiftly eliminate that which is most precious to me.

"I tracked you down to deliver a warning. And I do this not as Nicolas's second-in-command, or his 'messenger girl,' as you so eloquently put it, but as the *head* of our lineage."

Head of the lineage?

As she registers the shock on my face, she nods.

"Yes. Though I did not wish to, I had to take over the lineage to ensure our survival. Nicolas did not fight much. In fact, I believe he was relieved to give up his responsibilities. You really did not leave us any other option when you chose to abandon him."

Took his lineage? He didn't fight much?

Oh God, Nicolas, what have they done to you? What have *I* done to you?

My chest tightens, but the black emptiness is quickly overshadowed by burning red rage. I scream inside as I struggle to maintain my sanity.

Nicolas . . .

The bloodtears spill over and begin streaming down my face. Éva looks at me, shaking her head, and continues.

"Because Nicolas has led us so well over the centuries, and, until meeting you, had spoken of retiring, I did not kill him as is customary. And I doubt I could do it anyway. Our histories are too . . . intertwined." Anguish flits across her face, but is quickly erased by frozen calm. She continues.

"Unfortunately, with you gone and his rule overthrown, he has nothing left but his regrets. In retrospect, it might have been kinder to end him."

My sanity explodes, and the beast and the hunter take over. I launch at her, thrusting one dagger-nailed hand at her face, the other at her throat. We go down in a snarling, whirling frenzy, nails and teeth flashing. I feel my skin ripping in dozens of places as I try to slice her throat open.

But she is too fast and too strong. I suddenly find myself on my stomach, one arm wrenched behind my back, her cold breath below my ear.

"Stupid little fool." And she sinks her fangs into my neck, and draws. Hard. And again, and again.

Icy terror races through my veins as they feel the life being drained from them. I struggle, trying to twist out of her sharp hold, but she just growls and draws again. I lie there helpless as she steals away my blood, the growing lassitude in my body matched only by my escalating fear.

She releases my throat, but not her grip on the rest of me. Not that it matters—I can no longer summon the strength to move.

"I should re-Make you, right here and now. You would be completely obedient to my every wish, including killing any human I so desired. And I know how you hate even the thought." She rakes her fangs across the side of my face. "But I don't want you and your defects anywhere near my lineage, let alone part of it. I'd rather you suffer the isolation of an outsider and the eternal loneliness that goes with it."

My back and arm are abruptly free of her weight and painful grasp. I fight to move, to get up, but my empty body refuses to respond.

Surprise pierces my stupor as she retches, again and again, and my precious blood splatters onto the ground.

"You can keep that cesspool of pathetic emotions to yourself—I had enough of them through Nicolas." She spits, and a red, sticky glob slides down my face. "Stay away from Colorado—and stay away from *him*. We are done with you. Have a nice, long, lonely life."

Her heels grind against the hard-packed dirt as she walks to her car, gets in, and drives off.

A firestorm of deep hunger blasts through me, engulfing every cell, and my whole body screams in agony.

And I cannot move.

~

The sound of crickets slowly penetrates the fog in my brain. I try to ignore the inferno that seems to be turning me to ash, seeking the strength to roll over. I summon the hunter and the beast, but they are trapped behind flames and do not respond.

Nicolas . . .

Nicolas. What did they do to you? How could Éva . . .

*Éva.*

And the beast growls.

Éva. I'm going to hunt you down and rip out your heart for what you did to Nicolas.

As the heat of rage begins to join the flames of starvation, the beast and the hunter break through the wall of fire.

You bitch. I'm going to kill you.

Pushing off from my hands, I rock back onto my knees, then reach out to the top of the tire and use it to pull myself upright. I grab the fender and force myself to stand. The torch that is my body flares anew with the effort.

You better be watching for me, Éva, because I'm coming for you.

I get myself into the car, start it up, and turn around, leaving the lights off. When I get to the main dirt road, I turn right and head farther up the mountain.

The house is set back, up a long driveway, its barbed-wire fence butting up to the road. Thankfully its dim porchlight doesn't extend past the small lawn.

And there they are, bunched up in the corner of the pasture, oblivious to the death that will soon be among them. I ease the car to a stop and quietly get out. They watch as I climb through the fence, but they're used to people, and most of them continue to lie there, chewing their cud.

The one I choose doesn't even have time to moo.

# WEDNESDAY

## CHAPTER 18

It's a little after nine p.m. when I enter the outskirts of Colorado Springs. Thoughts cartwheel through my brain and I'm unable to slow them down long enough to formulate a solid plan. All I can think about is finding Nicolas and killing Éva, and I'm not even sure in what order those things are happening.

I'm running on pure instinct and I hope it's enough to keep me alive.

That, and the loaded .357 sitting in my leather bag on the passenger seat.

The gun came with the BMW several years ago, both gifts from an unusual bar owner in California whose past I'd decided was straight out of a spy novel. He'd also been my employer and took me under his wing when I'd first ventured back into civilization from my solitary life in the Sierra Nevada mountains.

I smile as I recall Joe's insistence on teaching me how to shoot after he'd seen me toss a guy—literally—out of the bar. He said anyone who could handle themselves like me in close quarters better know how to do it from a distance, too.

But I never thought I might actually need that skill. And need it I do. Because the only way I'm going to slow down Éva long enough to kill her—before she kills me—is to empty that big gun into her face.

~

The drive to Nicolas's estate is surreal. I did not expect to see the raven-crested gates again so soon. It's only been a week since I left, and yet, once again, it feels like a lifetime.

I punch in the code and the ebony steel flashes as the gates open, forbidding in the moonless night. The macabre topiary creatures in the garden stare as the BMW creeps up the driveway, curious as to what horrors may be unfolding this hour.

The house is dark, its black windows watching as I stop in front of the stairway and quietly get out. I pause for a moment next to the car, searching for the familiar vibration of power that signals Nicolas's presence. But he does not seem to be here—I can feel no trace of him.

Or of any Chosen, for that matter. Including Éva.

Huh.

Well, maybe they're at the club. That changes things.

Not wishing to disturb the housekeeper, Marie, I get back into the car and head down the driveway. The gates open as the car approaches and I shake off a ripple of fear as I go through them.

Thoughts tumbling, I drive across town to the club and pull into the parking lot. A black Ferrari is parked in Nicolas's spot with a license plate that reads LEANDRO. I don't think it's one of Nicolas's cars. The car Éva was driving yesterday doesn't appear to be here either. But that doesn't necessarily mean *they* aren't here, even though I don't feel their specific signatures among the multitude of Chosen energies emanating from the club. I really don't have any choice but to check it out.

Both parking lots are full—must be a busy night—so I park on a side street near the front of the building. Any of the other exits have too many keypads to deal with, and I may need to leave in a hurry. And entering through the front door is my only option since I don't have keys to the others.

I grab my bag with the .357 and get out, then pop open the trunk and contemplate its contents.

It was during the long drive south from Casper that I recalled my last fight with a Chosen. Katarina, like Éva, had quickly demonstrated I was no match for an Elder. But Nicolas had just as quickly demonstrated how to actually kill another Chosen. I might not have the necessary strength to tear off Éva's head, but I've got the next best thing.

A really sharp machete.

I'd picked it up in Denver, along with a sheath and a long coat to conceal it. Strapping the sheathed blade to my hip, I slip into the coat and quietly shut the trunk. I unleash the hunter and loosen the bounds on the beast, but not all the way. Vigilance and focus are what I need right now, but a bit of savagery just below the surface won't hurt.

This should be very interesting. I steel myself and walk across the street to the entrance. As full as the parking lots are, there's no line outside tonight. Wednesdays do tend to be quieter, catering more to the regulars of both species. But there are definitely Chosen inside. I can feel them. I open the front door and slip inside to the jarring thunder of heavy metal.

Standing in the entryway is a tall, broad figure dressed in black. Chosen energy hits me as he looks over, his expression quickly shifting from curiosity to animosity. His snarl is matched by my own.

Before I can react further, a second huge Chosen is there, every bit as hostile as the first. As their red eyes bore into my own, electric tension prickles across my skin.

"I'm here to see Nicolas," I growl, holding their gazes.

"What business do you have with him?" The first one, hair as black as his clothes, steps forward menacingly.

Holding my ground, I open my mouth to reply.

A masculine, silken-smooth voice bearing an unidentifiable European accent cuts me off.

"She is welcome here. Steven, Michael, please." The black curtain across from the front doors ruffles briefly, and the Chosen who walks through it is the tall, blond male I'd seen here before. The one Nicolas threatened to kill for just looking at me.

Instantly submissive, the two Chosen bow their heads and step out of the entryway. The volume of the pounding music rises briefly as they move through the heavy black draperies and into the dance area.

Powerfully built and devastatingly handsome, the blond stands a moment looking at me, then slowly smiles. His blue eyes tinged with pink, he walks forward, arms open in welcome.

"Come in, come in. I apologize for the misunderstanding." He stops a few feet from me, halted perhaps by the wariness I can't help but project, and lowers his arms.

"My name is Leandro. And you are Sunny, correct?" His gaze slowly rakes me up and down, the pink flaring in his eyes again.

Alarm lances through me. I've been so focused on Nicolas and Éva, I haven't given much thought to the other Chosen I might encounter.

Smiling, he steps closer. I freeze when he reaches out and lifts a lock of my hair. He leans toward me, taking in its scent, and with a low growl, I shift away from him—just as his other hand brushes against my breast. With a roar, I slash out at his face, nails fully extended. He traps my wrist in an iron grip, laughing as his other hand slides beneath my coat to relieve me of the machete.

"Nicolas is a fool to have let *you* get away. But his loss could be my gain, perhaps?" His eyebrows raise as he curls one side of his lip, exposing a gleaming fang.

"Not in a million years." The venom drips from my voice as the beast and the hunter howl their outrage. I yank my arm back and he releases me.

Leandro laughs again.

"We shall see. I have everything else here that was his, why not you?"

Fear rips through me again, but not for myself.

Nicolas. What have they done to you?

"Where is he?"

"I don't know." He examines the sharp edge of the machete, then raises his long lashes to look at me.

"Is Éva here?"

"Now you're looking for Éva?"

"She and I have some unfinished business."

"She's not here either. But I have her number in my office." Leandro slowly smiles, and tendrils of fear crawl through my veins.

"Come." He turns and walks to the curtain, parting it with the tip of the machete.

"I'm not going anywhere with you," I growl, stepping back.

"Stray kittens bold enough to walk into the lion's den shouldn't be surprised when they get pawed." His eyebrows arch suggestively. "Unless that's what they really came for."

Asshole. I'm done here.

I turn toward the door. His hand is suddenly on my shoulder and his breath on my neck.

"Don't be so hasty. Éva was quite adamant that I give you her number if you showed up," he whispers, his voice husky. He noses my hair and softly groans.

I duck out of his grasp and, turning, aim again for his face. This time my nails hit home, leaving thin red streaks on his cheek that vanish within seconds. The beast howls for more.

Eyes glittering, he steps back, the machete held loosely at his side.

"Do you want her number or not? It doesn't matter to me." He rubs his cheek. "I won't harm you. Éva was quite specific about that. She said you belong to her."

Like hell I do. *She* belongs to *me*.

Leandro pulls the drapery back. The high-pitched whines of guitars are drowned out only by the guttural screams of the vocalist. Heavy drums reverberate off the walls.

Hesitant, I look through the opening into the main room, then glance at Leandro again. He remains still, his face impassive. The crashing noise vibrates uncomfortably through my body, ratcheting up my tension, and the beast and hunter shriek in warning.

Gritting my teeth, I go through the curtain.

The stage where the DJ is normally set up is a frenzy of black leather, instruments, and screeching sound. I can't tell if the band members are human or Chosen, because Chosen energy is pulsating throughout the whole room. The area in front of the stage is a mosh pit, with rabid fans running, crashing, and throwing themselves into each other and the mob surrounding it.

As we wade through the pierced and tattooed crowd, I'm able to spot Chosen sprinkled throughout. The humans, eyes fastened on the stage, jump and slam fists in the air as they rage along with the band. The Chosen, eyes fastened on the humans, are for the most part still, with only their heads turning as they avidly survey the banquet before them.

The whole mood of the club is dark and sinister, much like I expected it would be the first time I visited it with Nicolas. But what I'd found then in the upscale dance club had been lighthearted seduction and mutual satisfaction between Chosen and donors. The absence of violence had changed my perceptions of The Chosen. With the exception of Katarina, I'd begun to believe they were not the monsters I'd thought them to be.

Until my last visit, that is.

Tonight the danger permeating the air is tangible, as solid as a living entity. The Chosen feel far more predatory and the humans far more innocent, in spite of their black clothes and makeup and death metal music. I'm not sure how many of these "donors" will make it out of here alive.

"Like what I've done with the place?" Leandro leans in, too close, whispering in my ear.

"Not really." Flinching, I swerve to avoid any further contact with him.

He laughs and strides on ahead, his body cutting a swath through the metal-mad crowd. He is rather striking, his blond good looks set off by the black leather blazer, black jeans, and biker boots. All eyes follow him as he passes. I trail him to the dark draperies at the rear of the room, where another large Chosen holds them open for us. We weave through the stacked liquor cases and stop at the door.

I try to see the code Leandro taps into the keypad, wondering if it's changed, but his fingers are too fast. He opens the heavy soundproof door and holds it for me as I step into the hallway. The tumultuous din from the stage abruptly shuts off as the door closes. We walk in silence to Nicolas's office where Leandro quickly enters the code and opens the door.

As I walk into the room, Nicolas's scent wraps itself around my body. I inhale deeply, trying to capture as much of him as I can. The black emptiness in me—where he is supposed to be—gapes open, roaring like an animal in pain. But I refuse to give in to it and use my anger to slam it shut, my instincts screaming to keep this weakness for Nicolas hidden from the big blond Chosen.

Turning to face Leandro, that anger surges at the pink-tinged desire shining in his eyes.

"So where is Nicolas?" I demand again. Though his scent is strong, it's old. He hasn't been here for at least a week. Probably not since the night I ran.

"As I said before, I don't know. It's not my turn to watch him."

"What happened to him? What did you do to him?" My voice, thick with anxiety and rage, sounds shrill even to my ears.

"Temper, temper, little kitten. I did nothing. As for what happened to him, I don't know, and it's really not my concern." He sets the machete down onto the desk.

"He's your Maker! How can you say it's not your concern?" Both baffled and outraged at his indifference, I glare at him.

"He isn't my Maker anymore. I hold no allegiance to him."

Shock floods through me. Just like that? Their loyalties shift that fast?

Leandro looks at me intently, his mood darkening.

"So tell me, who is *your* Maker? What lineage are *you* from?" The threat in his voice only aggravates me further.

"It's none of your damn business."

"But it is. When a foreign lineage waltzes into our territory and seduces our Maker, it tends to raise questions. But when that seductress unmans our Maker and causes a power shift the way you have, we want answers." His tone turns dangerous.

I slide my hand into my bag and wrap my fingers around the grip, but don't take the gun out yet.

"Don't bother. I can smell the steel and gunpowder, and nothing short of a cannon's going to stop me. And we already know that I'm much faster than you." He quietly laughs.

Shit. Didn't think about The Chosen sense of smell.

"You know, you're very cute. You come in here all teeth and claws, but underneath you're really quite fragile, like a suckling still on her mama's teat. I completely understand Nicolas's attraction to you."

Leandro is suddenly standing inches from me, his eyes flashing red. I leap back, and like we're in some kind of strange dance, he follows, then grabs my arms and smashes me into the wall. Pinned there, I struggle as he presses himself against me, and then his mouth is on my neck.

"Don't move, or I won't be responsible for what happens next," he growls, his voice hoarse. "Understand?"

I freeze, then slowly nod. This is the dance of predator and prey, fueled by pure instinct. Any sudden movement on my part could trigger him. I should've known better, because I'm usually the other partner in the deadly tango.

He lips my neck and presses closer as panic races through me, everything telling me to fight, to run. But the hunter knows this game and waits, tightly coiled, ready for her moment.

Leandro snarls a curse and abruptly releases me. He steps back, looking at me curiously.

"Éva knows you're here, and apparently disapproves of my intentions, so it seems you will not get to experience the pleasure of sharing blood with me. That is unfortunate for you. Perhaps another time."

As the red in his eyes fades, so does his tension and his guard.

I launch past him for the door to the outside, dragging my nails across his throat as I pass.

But instead of retaliating, Leandro turns to face me, wiping off the blood with his fingers as the deep wound seals shut.

He licks his fingertips and smiles.

"That's twice you've blooded me. Should I consider that foreplay?" He smirks, eyebrows arched.

"Consider it a warning," I growl as I punch the code.

But the light doesn't flash green and the door doesn't open.

Crap. I was afraid of that.

Turning back to face him, I give myself to the beast and the hunter, prepared to fight to the death. I whip out the .357 and point it at his face.

Leandro laughs. "Relax. I'm done. I just wanted to play a little and see what you're made of."

But I don't believe him and I don't relax.

He turns, picks up a pen and a notepad from Nicolas's desk, and writes on it. Tearing the sheet off of the pad, he starts to walk toward me, the paper pinched between the fingers of his outstretched hand.

Cornered, with nowhere to run, the beast rips a growl from my throat and I pull back the hammer.

Leandro stops and smiles, then sets the paper on the corner of the desk.

"You really are quite adorable. I think you could keep me entertained for a long time."

"I'd rather die."

"I said a long time, not forever." He smiles again, then walks behind the desk and reaches into a drawer. I hear the electronic hum of a button being pressed.

"Now, where was I before you decided to crash my party?" He steps out to the center of the room.

The hallway door opens and a dark-haired young woman enters, followed closely by the first Chosen who'd met me at the club entrance. His large hand engulfs her slender arm as he ushers her in.

"Oh, yes. Dinner time. Come here, tender one." Leandro reaches out toward her.

Eyes big, she glances first at her escort then at Leandro. She doesn't even seem to notice me standing there with my hands wrapped around the revolver. The Chosen gently pushes her forward and releases her arm. She tentatively walks up to Leandro.

His eyes crimson, he arches his eyebrows and looks at me as he reaches out to gather her to him. Still watching me, he strokes her hair, then bends to nuzzle it.

"Are you ready for me?" he whispers to her as he smiles at me.

She nods. He snugs her up to his waist and turns for the bedroom door.

"Steven will see you out. And don't forget the phone number."

The one he didn't even have to look up before he wrote it down.

~

The BMW races along its familiar route up the Ute Pass, but I drive right on past my old house. It holds too many memories that haven't even had time to dull. I shut off the longing for that simple life I'd tasted and continue up the highway.

The dirt road to the lake is muted in the darkness that seems to be celebrating the absence of the moon. I pull off onto the shoulder, park, and open the trunk.

Once in my hunting clothes, I feel an overwhelming sense of relief. I've had enough of The Chosen world and am more than ready for the one I know best.

The hunter inside me whines, eager for the wind in her hair and the smell of the pines, and the uncomplicated life of stalk, chase, kill, sleep. I close my eyes and remember my time in the mountains, and part of me wishes I'd never come back from the wild. Then I would've been spared.

Spared from the shrapnel of a dream exploding into a million pieces, a dream I thought I'd finally embraced, as it embraced me. As *he* . . . embraced me.

I gratefully hand control over to the hunter and the beast. Moving into the trees, I break into a run.

# CHAPTER 19

The early afternoon sun is beating down, warming the steps I'm standing on. The sound of the doorbell reaches my ears for the second time as I stare at the ornate raven crest on the door. Finally hearing soft footfalls crossing the foyer, I step back as the front door opens.

"Mademoiselle!" Marie's blue eyes light up, then dim with disappointment as she peers past me.

The beast takes in her scent and begs to be set loose, craving this blood it's had before.

But another scent drifts out the door. *His* scent. I step back again as I steady myself not to fall apart.

"Hello, Marie," I manage to say, genuinely glad to see her. She's always been gracious and kind to me, and besides Alfonso, the only acquaintance of Nicolas's who's never felt threatening.

Of course, the fact that Marie and Alfonso are human has a lot to do with that.

"Mademoiselle, I'm so glad to see you, if you don't mind me saying so." Her polite French accent is accompanied by a shy bow and curtsy.

My wonder at where on earth Nicolas found this pretty, innocent creature is surpassed by my amazement that she's managed to stay this way, in spite of her employer and his circle of deadly friends.

"Marie, it's good to see you. Is Nicolas here?" I ask, though I can feel he's not.

Her eyes fill with tears and she turns her head as she wipes them away.

"No, mademoiselle. He is . . . gone." Her voice breaks as she looks back at me with sorrow etched across her face. "I had hoped he was with you."

Unprepared for her reaction, I look away, fighting the building pressure in my eyes with everything I've got. It finally eases, and I turn back to face Marie.

"When did he leave?" The tremble in my voice is something I can't hide.

"Sometime between midnight Sunday and Monday morning when I arose and . . . and discovered that he was no longer here . . ."

Today's Wednesday. Two-and-a-half days. That's all I missed him by.

Nicolas . . .

Clenching my jaw, I brace myself for the answer to my next question.

"Can you tell me what happened when he left?" I can only hope that Éva's assault on Nicolas happened at the club. I can't imagine the trauma Marie must have endured if it happened here. She's very fond of her employer.

"Ah." She pauses as she wars against her strict servant training. I can see her struggling with what to tell me. I patiently wait.

"Yes, as much as I know. Please, come in," she says, nodding.

Marie opens the door wider and I step inside. She closes it behind me and I follow her to the library door, leashing the beast tightly as her scent drifts behind her. She stops and turns to me.

"Would mademoiselle like some hot tea?" she asks, sticking to her comfortable role as servant.

"Only if you'll have some with me."

She smiles and curtsies, then heads down the hall to the kitchen.

Relieved by her absence, at least for the moment, I slowly savor the smell of *him* that is woven tightly through his house. A dim echo of his blood, it fills me as his essence once filled me. I fight to keep the emptiness in my core from ripping open.

But shock tears a gaping hole in it—in the deepest part of me—when I walk into the library.

Everything in here is draped in white sheets—the books in their floor-to-ceiling cases as well as all the furniture. The room is dark, almost black, hidden from the sun by thick burgundy draperies.

Gone . . . Marie said he was gone, but that word didn't mean much until now.

Walking through the ghosts of the room, in my mind's eye I can see the ghosts of those who lived and visited here. Ghosts of my life.

I'm startled as everything brightens from the light of the overhead chandelier, then realize that Marie has come into the room. She looks at me, eyes filled with grief, one that likely mirrors my own. Walking over to a table, she sets down the tea tray.

"I am sorry, mademoiselle. I should have prepared the room first." She steps over to the windows and draws back the drapes. Sunlight bounces in, breaking the morose darkness.

The mythical creatures in the garden beckon me to the window, their leaves and vines softly waving in the mild breeze. But their mood seems somber as they consider their fate without their master. I find myself fighting back tears once again as I watch them.

I listen as Marie removes the sheets from the upholstered chairs and their table behind me. She pours the tea and the scent of fresh-brewed Darjeeling wafts through the air. The porcelain cups softly clink as she sets them on the table. She then goes still, apparently waiting for me.

Breaking my own stillness, I turn and flash a grim smile at her, then sit in one of the chairs. She hesitates and I gesture to the one on the other side of the table. She gingerly sits down on its edge and looks up at me, her blue eyes wide.

Pushing one of the cups closer to her, I pick up the other and sip the steaming tea. She takes her cup and saucer and holds them as she turns her gaze out the window.

"The last night that I saw you, Mr. Ambrus came home very upset. I do not believe I have ever seen him so, uh, how do you say, *distraught*. I heard him upstairs in his bedroom. He, ah, was . . . I've never heard such sounds from someone. I could hear him pacing back and forth, and things breaking, and the sounds he was making . . ."

Horrified, I set down my tea, get up, and walk to the window.

Oh, Nicolas, how could I have done this to you, to us? Is one life truly worth the destruction of so many others?

The unstoppable tears course down my face as I stare out at the garden.

"Mr. Ambrus left a little while later. He came back after dawn and went back up to his room. I did not hear anything more from him. That evening I asked him through the door if he needed anything. He told me that he did not wish to be disturbed and that it would be best if I stayed in my quarters. He did not leave his room for the next few days that I know of." Marie's voice sounds distant as she continues.

"I believe it was early Thursday when Mesdemoiselles Basarab and Dăneşti and Monsieur Williams arrived. I think the others must have arrived throughout the day. I'm not sure, because Johan told me that Mr. Ambrus requested I stay in my quarters with the door locked and not to come out until I was told. I was very worried for Mr. Ambrus and wished to check on him, but I stayed in my room."

I listen as she picks up her cup and takes a sip, then another. Setting the cup back onto the saucer, she takes a big breath and starts again. There is now a distinct tremble in her voice.

"That evening I became more worried when I heard shouting and crashing sounds from upstairs. It sounded like several of them were up there. I could hear Mr. Ambrus yelling at them to leave, and a little while later they all came downstairs. They went into the main dining hall and started arguing again very loudly. Mr. Ambrus was with them because I could hear his voice, too."

Marie pauses and a sob escapes. My chest tightens and I clench my jaw to keep from echoing it.

"I started to unlock my door, but Johan was outside and told me not to unlock it under any circumstances. I asked if I should call the police, even though Mr. Ambrus has strict instructions never to do so. He said no. He sounded very upset and said he would go check on Mr. Ambrus.

"It was quiet for a few minutes, but then the fighting started. It sounded like a pack of wild dogs, and I could hear furniture breaking, and shouting, and Mr. Ambrus . . ."

Her voice breaks and she starts weeping quietly. I hug myself as I silently cry with her.

"After a while the fighting stopped. I could hear someone crying, one of the women I think. It was quiet after that, though sometimes I could hear their voices." She pauses.

"They were here for three days. Most of the time they stayed in the dining hall, but I did hear the front door open occasionally. I listened for Mr. Ambrus, but I never heard him. I was so worried for him. And I was very frightened for myself." Marie finishes in a whisper.

Poor thing. She must've been terrified, expecting one of those monsters to come through her door at any moment.

"It must have been around midnight Sunday when I heard them leave. I waited awhile to be sure they were all gone, then came out of my room. I started to open the door to the dining hall, but Mr. Ambrus yelled at me from inside the room not to. I asked him if he was all right, if there was anything he needed me to do. He said he was fine and that I was to go back to my quarters and stay there until morning. I did as he asked.

"But, mademoiselle, he did not sound fine. He sounded tired and . . . old. I don't know what they did to him, but it was . . . bad."

Though her story is tearing me apart, I breathe a small sigh of relief to hear that Éva hadn't lied and Nicolas did survive having his lineage stripped from him.

"The next morning, I checked the dining hall to see if Mr. Ambrus was still there. It looked like a . . . battleground. Most of the furniture, including the banquet table, was broken and smashed. And there was blood everywhere. I then went upstairs and knocked on Mr. Ambrus's door. He didn't answer."

Marie stops speaking and takes several breaths. Her voice cracks when she begins again.

"When I went into the kitchen, I found an envelope for me. It contained instructions to close up the main part of the house. Mr. Ambrus said that he would no longer need my services, but that I was welcome to continue to live here. He left a similar letter for Alfonso. And he left one for you. I'll put it on the table."

A letter for me?

She stands and I can feel her looking at me. I don't dare turn my blood-streaked face to her, so I continue to stare out the window. She waits a moment, then leaves the room and closes the door.

Sobs rip out of my throat and I wrap my arms tightly around myself, terrified of the letter and what it might or might not contain. Moments pass, one after another, and the letter behind me begins to loom larger and larger, like some monstrosity waiting to pounce. If I don't look at it, then maybe it doesn't exist and all possibilities will still be possible. But once I read it, I can't unread it, and my future will be limited by what it says.

With crimson tears streaming down my face, I turn to the table and pick up the envelope. My name is on the front in his elegant handwriting, and I hug this small shred of him against my breast. Fingers trembling, I then turn it over, carefully open it, and unfold the letter.

*My dearest Sunshine,*

*The fact that you are reading this confirms that it was indeed necessary for me to write it.*

*It seems I am forever apologizing to you for my actions, as my judgment regarding you appears to be eternally impaired.*

*But this will be the final time.*

*I need to explain our last evening together. I do not expect forgiveness, but wish only that you forgive yourself.*

*As you may have surmised, Dominic was being groomed to join The Chosen. He was quite promising at first and we were eagerly anticipating his Change. His talents and assets would have been a valuable addition to our lineage.*

*But as his education progressed, we began to see his darker side, one that was quite sadistic. I will not tolerate mistreatment of the donors who sustain us, so he was deemed to be unsuitable.*

*Unfortunately, he knew too much of us and was proving to be difficult to manage. His potential exposure of our society, combined with the possibility of defecting to our enemies, left us with only one option.*

*As head of the lineage, it is my responsibility to carry out such decisions. However, I delayed doing so, and the problem escalated.*

*Desperation with the circumstances between you and me drove me to make one of the worst decisions of my existence. I knew Dominic's brutality would emerge when faced with a strong female, so it seemed he was the perfect candidate for you to complete your Change. I felt that you would bear little regret over the destruction of one who was so callous and cruel.*

*But once again I underestimated you. Your commitment to your humanity and the value you place on life is beyond anything I seem able to comprehend.*

*I have deeply wronged you by placing you in such a situation. That you stopped at the point you did demonstrates your uncanny will and advanced evolution.*

*You did not kill Dominic. That was my doing, and mine alone.*

*You are one of the strongest beings I have ever encountered, and I feel humbled to have known you.*

*But I am also ashamed. Ashamed that I attempted to force you to compromise your beliefs.*

*Worse yet, I violated the sacrosanct rule of my lineage. I took away your Choice.*

*I am not worthy of one such as you.*

*Your last memory of me, of the monster that I truly am, should tell you how right you were to run, to get as far from me as possible.*

*Your only mistake in this was coming back here.*

*As my last gesture of goodwill to you, I am protecting you from the consequences of that poor decision.*

*It is with great regret that I must say goodbye.*

*Do not attempt to find me. In this, I promise, you will not succeed.*

*-Nicolas-*

Panic begins pummeling every cell in my body, and the black abyss in my core tears open wider and starts to engulf me, swallowing me from the inside out. My veins burst into flame as I slowly sink into a fiery hell of loss and regret.

Oh, Nicolas . . . Nicolas, what have I done?

*Nicolas . . .*

# CHAPTER 20

Pikes Peak towers in the night sky above, and the black lake below is a dim reflection of the bottomless one inside me. The one that has devoured my soul, leaving me nothing more than an empty shell.

The breezes up here at the top of the rocky outcrop try to lure me from my catatonic state, sending tendrils of scent to tease and tempt the huntress. But she has disappeared deep within, hiding as she mourns the loss of her mate. I am left with only the maniacal beast and my own desolate thoughts under the dark moonless sky.

I think back to the night Nicolas and I sat here watching the moon sparkle on the lake's surface of water and ice. The Peak, silently watching us, reminded me so much of *him* as the moonlight danced across its snow-covered flanks, like it danced across his pale skin.

It was the night I discovered another spirit who understood me, who I could share my darkest secrets with. It was the night I got my first glimpse into The Chosen world, one to which I thought I could belong. Nicolas's description of the Change, of how it's offered only to those who want it, and how they are cared for during and after, led me to believe I had finally found my place in the world. For if blood-drinking creatures were capable of that kind of compassion, then perhaps I wasn't the monster I believed I was, that there was still hope for me.

But it all proved to be a lie. Or was it? Was I only seeing what I wanted to see and ignoring the obvious—that these are creatures who feed on people, who view human beings as nothing more than pleasure toys and cattle?

As for my gentlemanly, kind and caring Nicolas, who treated his servants almost as his children, who cared for the well-being of his donors . . . that he would turn out to be the biggest monster of all as he ripped the veil of illusion from my eyes has been the most difficult part of this to comprehend.

The Chosen. Their world that I thought I could be part of is even more removed from me now than the human one. My apparent foreignness triggers an instinctive hostility in them that I was completely unprepared for. I'm still having trouble grasping how weak and vulnerable I am among them. Without Nicolas's protection, I stand little chance of survival in their competitive society. Éva and Leandro demonstrated that perfectly well. And Leandro . . . I doubt that he would've let me leave without Éva's decree otherwise. I shudder as I contemplate how long he would've kept me around until he grew bored and ended me. A "long time" has an altogether different meaning when spoken by an immortal.

And what of my fate now? I don't seem to age as I did when human, yet as we discovered on the fateful morning when Nicolas almost killed me with his passion, I am not quite immortal.

But I am alone. And I have a feeling I will be for a very, very long time.

The cold, black depths swallow me down. I feel myself sinking as though I'm immersed in the dark waters that lie in the shadow of Pikes Peak.

*Nicolas . . .*

# FRIDAY

## CHAPTER 21

Steeling myself to remain calm, I hit SEND on the cell phone. After several rings, Éva answers.

"Hello?" The irritation in her voice tells me I've probably interrupted something important. Good.

"Éva."

"Sunny. Such a surprise. I truly did not believe you would have the guts to call."

"Where's Nicolas?" I demand. I refuse to play her stupid Game.

"So . . . *now* you are concerned about him? It's a little late, don't you think?"

Her voice and her words cut me like a knife.

"Just tell me where he is."

"I recall telling you to stay away from him."

"Is that what he would want? For you to keep me from him?"

"Nicolas has proved himself incapable of sound judgment where you're concerned."

He'd said as much in his letter to me.

"Éva." I grit my teeth. "Please."

She takes a deep breath.

"When I returned from our little visit and found Nicolas gone, I realized I should have just killed you, and I deeply regretted not doing so. Because *you* did this. This is all *your* fault."

Perhaps most of it. But *you* were the one who stole his lineage, you back-stabbing bitch.

Growling, I bite my tongue to keep from speaking. Right now, I need info, not a fight.

"I am possibly the last one on earth who would tell you where he is . . ." Éva pauses. "If I knew. But I don't. He has vanished. We suspect he has Chosen to follow the path of the Old Ones. And if that's the case, then none of us will hear of him again. That is their way."

*Nicolas . . .*

"As for you," Éva continues. "The only reason you are still alive is I *know* how much you are suffering. Your blood is toxic with grief, and I can't think of a better punishment than living with that for the rest of your days. And trust me, you will. The pain of losing him will *never* leave you."

No . . .

My gut clenches as I press END.

~

Marie answers the doorbell on the second ring. She opens the door only a crack.

"Mademoiselle." Her tone is polite but cool.

She probably blames me, too. Rightfully so. She's had more time to think about my role in Nicolas's disappearance.

"Marie, I'm sorry I left without thanking you yesterday. I was . . . quite upset." My own tone is distant as well. That's how dead people sound.

Because that is what I really am now. The real me has drowned in black sorrow, and all that's left is the beast and its unceasing hunger for blood. The tether holding it back has worn thin, and I don't have much time here.

Marie nods, but doesn't say anything.

"Is Johan here?" At least I can talk to him without wanting to attack him.

"No, mademoiselle. I have not seen or heard him since he left my door that night to check on Mr. Ambrus." Her voice quavers.

Oh God. They killed him. He was just a young Chosen, a servant trying to protect his master. And they killed him.

"I'm sorry, Marie. Perhaps he's—" But the words die in my throat at her pained expression.

She's not stupid. She knows.

"I . . . I left some things here. Is it all right if I get them?"

Marie nods and, stepping back, opens the door to let me in.

I quickly head upstairs to the bedroom that was mine before I started sharing Nicolas's.

When I open my box of books and trinkets from my days in California, and the one containing my stuffed animal collection, I realize they mean nothing to me now. They're just anchors to my past, a past I no longer feel a connection to, a past I wish to leave behind. I seal the boxes closed and put them back in the closet without taking a single item.

One side of the closet is home to aristocratic evening gowns, silk blouses, tailored slacks, Italian high-heeled shoes—an expensive, sophisticated wardrobe, fit for a queen.

A wardrobe I have no use for now.

I sort through my remaining clothing, selecting rugged jeans, sweaters, and boots, and start filling my suitcase. Where I'm going, I won't need much, so only the basics get packed. I almost leave the laptop behind, but stuff it into its carrying case at the last minute.

The final item is one I've been avoiding, unable to even look at it.

But I can't just walk away from it. It contains too many memories to ignore, and I need to open it to know whether or not I want to hold on to them.

The ebony jewelry box, inlaid with a pair of ivory- and onyx-spotted snow leopards, is one that Nicolas had made for me. I remember trying to hold back my tears when he gave it to me, his whispered words of love as he held me.

I trace the outlines of the two leopards standing side by side on the top, one slightly larger than the other, then take a deep breath and open the box.

Nestled in a black velvet compartment is the necklace he gave me to wear the night of my presentation to his Chosen council. The centerpiece, a large round sapphire in sparkling royal blue, is suspended in a chain of small black diamonds. Its matching earrings lie in an adjacent compartment.

He told me the jewels paled in comparison to my eyes and were nothing more than weak imitations whose brilliance could never match mine.

But it's the bracelet that breaks my heart.

It's one I broke that night in a rage, sending glittering gems bouncing across the floor.

It's the same one he had repaired, with different stones, stones that reflected our sapphire and emerald eyes. The same one that he planned to give me on our bonding night.

The bonding night we never had.

I pick it up, my chest tight, then quickly place it into a satin jewelry bag and tuck it into the suitcase.

Though the necklace and earrings are probably worth millions, I close the box. Perhaps they will help ease some of Marie's pain.

A final glance around the room reveals nothing more that I need to take with me. I shut the suitcase, grab the laptop, and head back downstairs.

Marie is waiting for me at the foot of the winding staircase. She moves back into the hall as I descend, but her warm, delicious scent lingers in the air. The taste of her blood leaps from my memory as though it was only yesterday that it caressed my tongue.

Hers was the first human blood to cross my lips. It was after the bear attack that nearly killed me. Nicolas gave it to me without warning, without my permission. Though it was mixed with that of a horse, and I drank it from a cup, the attraction I feel for it is undeniable.

I was so focused on Nicolas when I came by yesterday that Marie had no real effect on me.

But it's a different story today, and I need to get out of here before she sees the beast peering from my eyes. I open the door and step outside.

"Thank you, Marie. One more thing—I'd like to leave you my cell phone number, just in case you hear from . . . Mr. Ambrus."

Reaching out, I hand her the piece of paper I'd written it on. She takes it, nodding.

"Thanks again, Marie, for all your kindness to me. I truly wish things had gone differently."

"So do I, mademoiselle, so do I," she whispers.

I turn to leave, but remember something I've always wanted to ask her.

"Marie."

She stops closing the door and cracks it back open.

"Yes, mademoiselle?"

"How long have you been with Mr. Ambrus?"

"Since I was a little girl," she breathes.

"How long?" I persist.

"Fifty-four years, mademoiselle."

Shock penetrates the numbness in my brain. She doesn't look a day over twenty.

"Goodbye, mademoiselle." And Marie closes the door.

~

The BMW screams north, following the asphalt trail. I have nowhere else to go, nowhere that I fit in, except in the wild. Far from humans to tempt me, far from Chosen to hunt me down and kill me.

Far from the memories of love that haunt me.

Run and hunt and swim and sleep. Maybe that will bring the hunter back. I do miss her.

But, Éva, don't rest too easy. I will come for you some day.

Just not this day. I need to regroup, to plan. I need to get stronger.

I glance at the sign as it flashes past my window. There should be plenty of wild here.

WELCOME TO MONTANA.

I doubt they would welcome me if they knew what I truly am.

Without You

*The wind*
*Whispers your name*
*A song drifting through the air*

*I cannot listen without you*

*The sun*
*Kisses my skin*
*Like the heat of your touch*

*I cannot feel without you*

*The sky*
*Echoes the blue of your eyes*
*Their image peering into my soul*

*I cannot see without you*

*You live*

*Wild and free*

*Without me*

*I cannot live*

*Trapped and broken*

*Without you*

*~ CN*

# PART II

# THE CATALYST

# WEDNESDAY

## CHAPTER 22

His sightless eyes stare accusingly at me, but I feel no remorse. He was like all the others before him, rash and overconfident in his ability to subdue me. I'd chosen him for his youth and inexperience, using both to my advantage. His young male pride had interfered with his common sense, and he'd realized too late that my smaller size and apparent helplessness were just a cover for a bloodthirsty killer.

But thirsty no longer. His sweet blood now courses through my veins, and my only regret is that I can't take in any more. I close my eyes and wallow a few moments longer in the red warmth that bathes my insides, and nearly convince myself that this is enough, that I do not need or want anything else.

But it's a lie, the same lie that I tell myself over and over.

Taking a deep breath, I open my eyes and pull the dagger from its sheath on my belt. I pick up a massive paw and cut off the largest claw to add to my collection back at the cabin.

No matter how many bear claws I take, no matter how much bear blood I drink, I cannot forget.

I cannot forget that there is something out there that is infinitely sweeter, more satisfying, and truly what my body craves.

What I crave, what my kind evolved to live on, is not the blood of animals.

It is human blood.

And it will never stop calling me.

~

Approaching the darkened log cabin, I taste the air for any sign of visitors. There's a male bear that seems to have taken an interest in my cabin lately, though I have no idea why. Usually cabin lurkers are attracted by the food and garbage around the summertime rentals. But I'm not the typical hiker or tourist. My cabin has no food and I don't generate any odorous garbage. And I certainly don't smell like the average inhabitant either. So I can only assume it may be a territory issue, which makes him that much more dangerous.

But thankfully I don't detect any sign that he's been here. It's been nearly a week or so since his last visit and it's possible he's moved on.

Normally I would welcome my dinner coming to me, but in this case I don't really know what I'm dealing with—except that his tracks are big. The black bears that I target tend to be smaller and inexperienced, so there's less chance of injury. But the risk is worth it. I've come to prefer bear over the deer and elk I normally hunt. Like people, they're omnivores, and their blood is the closest to human.

But human blood is infinitely richer, a multidimensional tapestry of taste and smell and feel. My veins twitch at the memory.

I abruptly shut off thoughts of blood as I unfasten the padlock from the hasp, thumb the rusty latch, and walk into the dark room. Grabbing the butane fire-starter, I light the oil lamps that are scattered around the tiny one-room cabin. The wood-burning stove is next, and the kindling and newspaper I stuff into it catch fire after a moment with the lighter.

This place is far back in the mountains, so primitive it doesn't even have running water. But at least there's a well with a hand pump. I head back outside with the bucket to fill it for my tea and bath.

I've thought about buying a used bathtub so I can bathe the old-fashioned way with water heated from the stove, but the thought of lugging it on foot through the mountains sounds like too much hassle. So I content myself with icy lake plunges and warm sponge baths. Sometimes I rent a motel room in town for one night, then stand under the hot shower for hours, getting out only when I'm yanked back to reality by a concerned call from the front desk about the running water.

But I don't do the motel thing very often. That requires me to be around people more than I can handle. Without the hunter—who vanished the day I read Nicolas's letter—to help me focus, the beast is nearly unmanageable. It's best to stay out here where I have little chance of human encounters. In the two months I've been here, my reaction to people doesn't seem to have eased much at all.

Speaking of people, tomorrow is Thursday, my town day. That's when I hike out to pick up my car and drive down to Kalispell to call Sandy. I usually spend a half hour, or longer if I let her, listening to her talk about the previous week and the latest developments with Danny. I'm glad she has him and it sounds like she's made some other friends as well. She'll be starting school soon and hopefully will get busy enough that she won't have time to fret about me.

And she won't have time to nag me either. At one point she became so insistent I visit my daughter that I threatened to quit calling her if she didn't knock it off. She stopped badgering me about it, but it's always there in her undertones.

I'll be glad when her attention shifts elsewhere and I can fade away. She's the last reminder of my former life, the one I had before I became truly dead. As it is, I have trouble keeping track of the days, and sometimes I don't notice that Thursday has come and gone. Of course then I get the lecture when I do call about how worried she's been, that I'm the only one who really "gets" her, and on and on.

I don't know why I don't just cut it off. But when I think about doing so, all I see is her scared and bruised face staring hopefully through my car window, and her photo album of loneliness, and I just can't do that to her.

The sturdy cabin is warm and cozy now, and I can feel the dawn approaching. I quickly bathe with the hot water from the pan on the stove, crawl into bed, and gratefully sink into darkness.

# THURSDAY

## CHAPTER 23

Cruising through the outskirts of Kalispell, I start checking my cell phone for signal. Coverage in the Montana town that's ringed by the Rocky Mountains is spotty at best. My weekly phone calls to Sandy are seldom in the same location as the week before. But at least I've narrowed down which parts of town have the best reception.

Driving into the grocery store parking lot, a glance at the phone shows full bars. I park and shut off the car.

My voicemail has three messages from Sandy.

Hmm. She's usually more patient than that. She knows I don't have reception at my cabin.

Frowning, I listen to the first two messages. Her words are punctuated with sobbing then cursing as she describes a fight and subsequent breakup with Danny.

Crap. I don't want her here. It's been almost more than I can take just to talk to her over the phone once a week and try to sound somewhat normal.

Hitting END in the middle of her third message telling me that she's *in* Kalispell, I stare out the window at the soaring peaks.

I could just head back up there and pretend I never got her messages. I could call in a week or so and tell her I lost track of time. Maybe she would've gone home by then.

Shit. I press 3 and hit SEND.

"Hello? Sunny?"

"Hi, Sandy."

"Oh man, I was getting worried. I've been here since early this morning. I was afraid you weren't going to call."

"Where are you?" I try to hide the impatience in my voice.

"Are you okay? You're not upset or anything, are you? I just thought you might like some company. Have I come at a bad time? I . . ."

"Sandy. Stop. Where are you?" I remember a time when her babbling was somewhat amusing. But not now. Nothing is amusing anymore.

"I'm at the truck stop on Highway 2 across from Albertson's, west of 93."

Truck stop? She didn't . . .

"How did you get here?" I demand, knowing the answer.

"Hitched." Her quiet answer carries a hint of defiance.

Damn it. Stupid girl.

"I'll be there in about fifteen minutes." I snap the cell phone closed.

Heading south down Highway 2, I start looking for motels. My cabin really isn't suitable for visitors. There's no refrigerator and only one bed. Not to mention the cabin's about three miles from where I leave the car. It just isn't possible for her to stay with me.

I make note of several, then see the truck stop. I pull in, slowly cruise through the parking lot, and spot her leaning against the front of the building. She has white iPod earphones plugged into her ears, a sweatshirt tied around her waist, and is holding a book she's deeply engrossed in.

I smile in spite of myself. Maybe I did miss her a little.

The wind blows her kinky hair across her face, and as she raises her hand to push it back, she looks up and sees me. Grinning, she bends and stuffs the book into her backpack, swings it up onto her shoulder, and starts toward the car.

She looks much healthier than when I last saw her. Her hair is sun-bleached, almost blonde now. Her skin carries a summer glow under her freckles, a vast improvement over the pasty white she was a couple months ago after she almost bled to death.

Blood. Concern suddenly whips through me. Whatever it is about her that mutes the beast, I certainly hope it's still working or this will be a very short visit.

She stops by my side of the car a moment, looking at me quizzically. I raise my eyebrows at her, not sure what she wants. She frowns, shakes her head, and walks around to the passenger side. After dumping her pack in the back seat, she climbs into the front.

"Hi," she says, faint traces of the frown wrinkling her forehead.

"Hi." I carefully take a shallow breath. No reaction from the beast.

Good.

Shifting the car into gear, I turn and head for the exit.

"What's wrong? Are you *that* pissed off that I'm here?"

"What are you talking about?" I glance at her, puzzled.

"I haven't seen you in two months, not since the day you rushed off, and you couldn't even get out of the car to give me a hug?"

Oh.

"Sandy, do you recall me being much of a hugger? Cuz, *I* don't. And I'm not."

Especially if I think I might kill you.

"Yeah. Okay. Whatever."

I slam on the brakes and look at her.

"All right. I'm . . . sorry. I forgot." Her tone softens.

"Forgot what?" I frown.

"Forgot that you're not . . . like everyone else." She pauses.

Damn right I'm not.

"Can we just start over?" She looks at me hopefully.

"Okay." Easing the car out of the driveway, we head down the street.

"So how've you been? Anything exciting going on in your life?" she asks lightheartedly.

We talk every week on the phone and I always tell her the same thing.

"Fine. Nothing in particular."

Shaking my head, I pull into a driveway half a block from the truck stop.

"Hampton Inn?" Sandy asks, puzzled.

"Sure. Thought it would be a treat. They're usually nice."

"But what about the cabin? Can't we stay there?"

"It's pretty rustic. I don't think you'd like it." Parking the car, I shut it off and look at her.

"But it sounds so cool, out there in the forest and the mountains. I was really looking forward to a change in scenery."

"Sandy, it's actually more than rustic. It's primitive. There's no heating, no electricity, no running water. And the bathroom is an outhouse behind the cabin."

"Cool! That sounds awesome. You didn't tell me that you were doing the pioneer thing! What a fun way to live!" She grins at me.

"I don't think you'll like it. There's no TV, radio, or internet. I'm afraid it'll be pretty boring."

"Well, what do *you* do?"

Besides hunting, killing, and drinking blood? Not much.

"I read and hike a lot."

"That sounds like a perfect vacation to me. I really don't want to stay in some stuffy ol' hotel."

Neither do I, but at least I'd have my own room and privacy.

"It's a three-mile hike from the cabin to the car and an hour drive into town. So we really can't run to the store if you need something."

"Then I'll just have to do without. Wouldn't be the first time."

No, probably not.

"Come on. It'll be fun. It'll give me a chance to figure out what to do about Danny."

Good luck with that. Hasn't helped my situation at all.

I take a big breath—one last check on the beast. It doesn't bat an eye at her scent. I suppose this could work. But the food thing will be a little awkward, both hers and mine.

"We'll have to do some shopping then. I don't really have anything to eat. And as I mentioned, there's no electricity, so there's no refrigerator and no microwave. You'll have to make everything from scratch and cook it on a wood stove." Hopefully this will discourage her.

"Great! Sounds just like camping, only with a roof over our heads. It does have a roof, doesn't it?"

"Yes, it has a roof, and four walls and a door. And that's about it. So, yeah, it's a lot like camping."

"Well, let's go. We can stop at the Albertson's across from the truck stop." She grins.

Shaking my head, I start the car and head back the way we came.

"Can I ask how long you were planning on staying?" I try to suppress my irritation.

"About a week. School starts on Monday the twenty-seventh."

A week? Cooped up in one room with her? Well, if the beast doesn't want to now, it'll likely be ready to kill her by the end of the week. And if it doesn't, I probably will.

ꟷ

Our last stop is the sporting goods store to get a large pack so I can haul her food to the cabin. The sleeping bag she brought looks warm enough for our chilly nights, but she'll need a thick sleeping mat to insulate her from the cold floor.

Her enthusiasm hasn't dampened at all. If anything, it's only increased, and I can tell that I'll need to take a run once she gets settled in the cabin.

We make the long drive back into the mountains to the sounds of her exclamations at the scenery along the way. I really start looking at it for the first time since arriving here. She's right. Flathead National Forest and Glacier National Park are quite breathtaking. Guess I just hadn't lifted the veil of death long enough to notice them before.

Arriving at the lodge where I leave the car, we park and get out. After lashing Sandy's sleeping mat to her backpack, I fill mine with the food and supplies we bought. I tie the saucepan and the small frying pan to the outside of my pack, then glance over at Sandy.

She's staring up at the small peak that overlooks the lodge, a look of wonder brightening her face.

"You ready?" I ask as I close the trunk and lock the car.

"Oh yeah. This is going to be *so* fun." She turns to me smiling, then leans down to my pack. "Here, I'll help you put this on. I think we bought too much stuff, as usual."

"No, that's fine. I don't need any help."

But I'm too late.

She grabs the frame with both hands and can barely get the pack off the ground.

"Holy shit! You can't carry this three miles. I can't even lift it."

Giving her a sidelong glance, I pick it up with one hand, slip my arm into the strap and sling it around onto my back, then slide my other arm through. With a big shrug, I settle it into place and fasten the buckle across my chest.

"Oh my God, you did not just pick that up like that. That's some crazy shit!" Her green eyes are as big as silver dollars.

Snorting, I turn and head up the trail.

# CHAPTER 24

Sandy surprises me with her lack of complaints as we make our way up steep slopes and through dense brush. I forgot how tough she is.

It's nearly dark when we reach the cabin. I've been testing the air for the last mile or so, checking for any sign of bear, but all seems to be okay. I've cleared out most of the bears within a few miles of the cabin, partially from dietary preference, but also for territorial reasons. I really don't want them hanging out anywhere close to where I sleep.

"Here we are. Home sweet home."

"Wow . . . this is awesome! A real log cabin!" She pauses as she looks it over. "Well, I'm glad we finally made it. I was starting to wonder if you were lost or something."

Not likely. That only happens when I've let the beast run amok in a feeding frenzy. Then I wake up in the morning not knowing where the hell I am or how I got there. Kinda like a drunk having a blackout. Fortunately, that doesn't happen very often.

Unlocking the padlock, I open the door and walk in, Sandy right behind me.

"Stay here. I'll light the lamps."

"Good, cuz it's frickin' dark in here. I don't know how you can see anything."

Unfastening the cross straps, I ease the pack to the floor next to the cupboard. I walk back across the room and take down the bear-claw necklace hanging on the wall above the headboard, then slide a box out from under the bed and drop it in there. I don't feel like answering her questions about it.

Picking up the lighter, I quickly go around the room and light all the lamps. A soft amber glow brightens the room.

"Wow, this is really . . . cozy. It's not much bigger than my bedroom." She surveys the room as she slips her own backpack off and sets it on the tiny two-person table that shares the wall with the cupboard.

I walk over and, opening the wood-burning stove, stuff it with newspaper and kindling, then light it.

"You can hang your backpack on that." I point to the large nail in the wall that's next to the little free-standing closet at the foot of the bed, then continue.

"You have your choice. You can either sleep in the bed or in the sleeping bag on the floor in front of the stove. You'll be much warmer there, but the bed will be softer. It's up to you."

I start to remind her of my odd hours, then frown as I realize she's going to be right here with me every morning while I'm dead to the world. I can't handle that. Looks like I'll be spending the week sleeping in trees. Crap.

She looks at me funny and I realize she's had the same thought about my strange sleep.

"I'll just take the spot on the floor. That'll be fine," she says somewhat awkwardly.

This is going to be a weird week.

Shaking my head, I add a couple chunks of wood to the stove. I'm going to be doing a lot of wood chopping over the next few days. I don't usually run the stove except for right before I go to bed. She's going to need it all night.

"You can unpack the food and put it in that cupboard. I'm going outside to get more firewood."

As I shove the last few logs against the wall to make room for more, I hear her open the cupboard door and take a sharp breath. Glancing up, I see her staring at the empty shelves.

Shit. I didn't think about that.

"Uh, Sunny?"

"Don't ask," I snap. "Just put everything away except what you want for dinner."

I walk across the room and out the door.

Damn it. She probably thought I was just low on food when we were shopping, and that I was getting disposable dishes and utensils because I only had enough for myself. Can't imagine what's going through her head right now.

Picking up the axe, I grab a log and set it on the stump to split it into smaller pieces.

THUNK!

I toss the chunks into a pile and pick up the next log.

THUNK!

When the pile has become a small mountain and I feel I can no longer delay going back inside, I grab an armful of wood and walk through the door.

Sandy is stirring what must be soup in the saucepan that's on top of the stove, and the smell triggers faint rumblings of nausea. She steps aside as I come in and set the wood down. Wrinkling my nose, I open the stove door, stir the coals, and add a couple more logs.

Without looking at her, I walk across to the table to put the battery in the new lantern I bought for her. Flickering lamp light doesn't cause me any problems when I read, but I wasn't sure how well it would work for her. Yet, when I pick up the lantern, its weight indicates she's already put the battery in. She's done the same with both the big and small flashlights.

Good. She needs to be self-sufficient while she's here, because I don't think I'm going to be able to stick around much. I really don't want to be under the microscope, even hers.

I feel her eyes on me as I walk back over to the other side of the room. Opening my closet, I pull out a dark turtleneck and a pair of black jeans, then keeping my back to her, quickly change. I turn around as I'm adjusting the collar and see that she has two bowls with spoons on the table.

"I'm going out for a while, but first I need to show you the outhouse. Bring a flashlight and a roll of toilet paper with you."

Setting the hot pan on a folded dishtowel in the center of the table, she nods.

"Let me get my coat," she says quietly.

I nod and wait for her by the door.

She shrugs into her jacket and grabs the toilet paper and flashlight. Opening the door, I go outside and she follows me out. As I automatically test the air, I become aware of another complication.

Shit. This is turning into a real pain in the ass.

If Sandy comes out here in the middle of the night to use the outhouse, what if that bear is nearby, and I'm not?

Gritting my teeth, I walk behind the cabin to the outhouse, Sandy shining the light ahead of me. I open the door and step back so she can see in.

I brushed all the webs and dirt out of it earlier when I came out here to chop wood, but it's still creepy and gross. She may have no problem heeding the warning I'm about to give her.

"Wow. Real pioneer style. Maybe I'll just use the woods." Sandy peers inside, grimacing.

"Not where I might step in it." Of course, I'd smell it first, but the idea is revolting. That's one thing I don't miss about being human.

"Not for that. I'll . . . I'll get used to the outhouse. It just looks . . . scary at night."

"Well, that leads me to an important point. There are bears out here, and you need to be very careful when you're outside, especially if I'm not here. And I would strongly suggest that you not step out of the cabin at night—at all—unless I'm with you. Understand?"

"Bears? Yeah, no problem. I can't imagine coming out here at night by myself. If it wasn't bears, I'd be waiting for Jason or Freddy or someone to get me."

"Who? What are you talking about?"

"They're serial killers from horror movies." She laughs. "You know, *Friday the 13th*, *Nightmare on Elm Street*?"

"Oh. Well, I don't go to the movies much anymore, and when I did, I didn't like horror."

And now I am one.

Holding my hand out, I glance at the toilet paper and she hands it to me. I quickly string it onto the little rope and hook the looped end back over the bent nail.

Pointing to the large nail protruding halfway up the wall, I put my hand out for the flashlight. It takes her a second to understand, then she hands it to me. I slide the short lanyard hanging from it onto the nail.

"Oh, okay. Got it." She nods as I hand her back the flashlight.

I turn to walk back to the cabin.

"Uh, Sunny? Do you . . . mind waiting out here for a few minutes?" Embarrassment deepens the color of her cheeks.

"No problem. I'll be right over there." I point to a tree a short distance away, then head in that direction to give her as much privacy as possible.

"Thanks." She disappears inside, then closes and latches the door. The flashlight clanks against the wall as she hangs it.

This is . . . much more difficult than I imagined. I realize that we only spent a couple days together while settling her into the apartment. I was gone much of the time and could claim that I'd eaten elsewhere without question. I didn't have to worry about *her* being eaten by a bear. And the lock on the bedroom door secured my privacy as well as my belongings.

The door creaks open and Sandy steps out, the beam of the flashlight bouncing on the ground ahead of her. She shines it in my direction as I push off the tree and start walking back to the cabin. Pulling open the cabin door, I follow her as she walks inside.

"Sandy."

Unzipping her jacket, she turns to look at me.

"I need to leave for a while. You should bolt the door after I'm gone."

The look of disbelief and hurt on her face forces me to hesitate a second as it registers in my dead brain. Shaking my head, I reach for the door.

"Wait," she says with a catch in her voice.

Taking a deep breath, I turn to face her.

"Can't you wait a little while? I mean, I just got here. I thought we could talk and spend the evening together. I even made soup for dinner."

"I'm not hungry. Knock yourself out." As soon as the words escape my lips, I realize how harsh and unfeeling they sound.

Tears begin to fill her green eyes.

"I'm sorry. I didn't mean it to sound like that. Thanks for making dinner. I'll . . . I'll stay and have some soup."

Sandy nods, wiping away the tears, then takes off her jacket and hangs it on the peg next to the door. She walks over to the table and scoops up a ladleful of soup from the pan.

"That's enough for me," I tell her after she pours it into a paper bowl.

She tightens her mouth and fills the second bowl, then sets the bowls, plastic spoons, and napkins at either end of the tiny table.

This is going to be really weird. I walk over and sit down as she takes her place in the other chair.

"It's minestrone. You said you like minestrone when we were picking stuff out at the store."

I nod. I probably did say that, not expecting that I might actually have to eat it.

"Oh, I forgot the bread. Do you want some?" She bounces up and turns around to the cupboard.

"No thanks. I'm not much of a bread eater."

She gets a slice out and puts the rest back. There's not even enough room on the table for the loaf.

Sandy sits back down and takes a spoonful.

"Ooh, it's really hot," she says as she blows on it.

I study the reeking bowl in front of me. I'm not sure how to handle this. I guess the best way is to get it down all at once and hold it for as long as I can before heading outside to the "bathroom."

Sandy takes a bite of the bread and smiles.

"How cool. Our first real meal together." She pauses and frowns. "Ever."

Yeah, and it'll be our last. I can't fake this every night. The smell of the soup under my nose has me ready to hurl and I haven't even taken a bite.

Might as well get it over with. I pick up my spoon and take in a mouthful. Between the chunks of food and the taste, I nearly gag as I chew. I force myself to swallow and quickly get another spoonful. The beast growls at the insult to my system.

Looking up, I notice that Sandy is watching me curiously. I glare at her and she drops her gaze to her bowl.

Finishing my token amount of soup, I sit back and fight to keep it from coming up. My stomach roiling, I swallow several times. This isn't working.

"Wow, for someone who's not hungry you sure finished that in a hurry. Want more?" She reaches for the saucepan.

"No." I swallow again. "Uh, excuse me for a moment." I get up and head out the door.

Running far enough away that she won't hear me, I lose the soup. The greasy acid flavor lingers while the beast throws a temper tantrum, insistent on washing away the filthy feel and taste with proper food.

I finish retching, sprint back to the well and, pumping the handle, wash out my mouth the best I can while trying to keep from getting soaked. I swallow some of the water, then instantly throw it back up in an effort to rinse my insides. It helps some, but the beast's outrage is going to be difficult to resist for long.

Wiping my face off with my sleeves, I walk back into the cabin.

Sandy gives me a hard look.

"So that's how you stay so slender? Purging? That's really unhealthy. Girls die from that."

"Must be allergic to something in the soup," I mutter as I grab my bowl and take it over to the wood-burning stove. The flames flare green as they feed on the coated paper.

"Whatever. I get it. It makes sense now. You have an eating disorder, though you don't really show it. Most girls are either really fat cuz they eat all the time or really thin and pale cuz they never do and they . . . Oh. Never mind." She shuts up, embarrassed.

But she's seen me naked, at least from the back. Pale and slender yes, but muscular and fit, not skinny and wasted. Distraction should keep her from thinking too hard about it.

"Yeah, well. There it is. So please don't get your feelings hurt if I choose not to eat. It would be best if you just make food for yourself. I'll eat when I'm ready."

"Okay." She seems to accept this and I breathe a small sigh of relief.

I've had all the socializing for one day that I can handle, and the beast is becoming difficult to manage. But it's not lusting after Sandy's blood, which I still find interesting. In fact, it seems to almost have an aversion to it.

Well, at least I don't have to worry about the beast taking over and killing her. I, on the other hand, may run out of patience with her.

“Sandy, we’ll have to talk tomorrow. I really need to go. Do you need to use the outhouse before I leave?”

“No,” she says, disappointed. “You go ahead.”

“Remember to bolt the door.” I slip outside and close it firmly behind me. When I hear the bolt slam home, I slam into a dead run.

# FRIDAY

## CHAPTER 25

My eyes pop open to the late morning sun and I instantly scent the air in the direction of the cabin. All I smell is smoke from the chimney. No bears, no Sandy.

Good. I was worried when I fell asleep that she would go wandering in the woods looking for me. At least I know she didn't come this way and see me sleeping up here.

Scrambling down the trunk of the tree that was my not-too-comfortable bed, I circle the area around the cabin before returning to it. It seems she stayed inside. There's not even fresh scent on the path leading from the cabin to the outhouse. Guess she took my warning to heart.

Frowning, I realize that she probably needs to pee pretty badly. After trying the latch, I knock on the door and step back to wait for her to open it.

The bolt thumps, door swings outward, and Sandy bursts past me in a fast walk to the outhouse. My frown shifts to a smile as I step into the cabin. The smile fades as I see what she's done.

She found the spare blanket in my closet and, using cord and safety pins from I don't know where, has rigged up a drapery to separate my bed from the rest of the room.

Sweet, lonely girl. She's finally starting to grasp what an intrusion her visit is.

The door opens and she stomps her feet on the mat before coming in.

"Hi. I'm glad you finally came back. I've been thinking about making a run for the head for the last hour." She grins as she closes the door.

"Sorry," I manage to remember to say.

Following my glance toward the drapery, Sandy blushes.

"I hope you don't mind. I feel bad that you're too uncomfortable to sleep in your own bed with me here. I promise I won't peek through the curtain. Please don't feel like you have to sleep somewhere else, wherever that is out here. For what it's worth, I sleep really heavy and don't wake up much before ten. Kinda like you."

No, sweet girl. You're nothing like me.

Glancing at her, I grab the bucket and go outside. I'm pumping the handle, watching the water gush out of the pipe in waves, and hear her come back outside. She says nothing, and my skin ripples in irritation beneath the weight of her gaze upon me.

"Sunny, can I ask you some questions?"

"Depends on what they are."

"What really happened when you left the apartment?"

Before I learned what The Chosen council had done to *him*, or after?

"Next."

"Uhh . . . okay. What about what's his name, Nicolas? I thought you were going back to him. You've avoided talking about him every time I bring it up."

Don't say his name. The name of the one I loved, the one I . . . destroyed, and lost forever.

"Stop. No more." I yank the bucket from the ground, water sloshing out, and go back inside. I suddenly don't feel like having that cup of tea. I set the bucket on the table and turn to leave. Sandy has followed me back in. Her green, tear-laden eyes reflect my pain and guilt.

"Sorry . . . I mean it. I'm *really* sorry. It's my fault you didn't go back sooner," she says quietly.

Yeah, kinda. But it was my Choice. One I'll regret for the rest of my existence.

Beast, where are you? I need you, your mindlessness, your savagery. We need to run.

Unable to respond, I open the door and flee for the mountaintops, far from the reminders of my past.

~

It's after dark when I get back to the cabin. I try the latch, then knock.

At least Sandy understands the need to keep the door bolted. I step back as she unbolts and opens it, then slip in past her. Instantly I regret coming inside where the overpowering smell of her dinner permeates every molecule of air. My stomach heaves and I clench my jaw.

I look over to see regret flickering in those green eyes. Our visit has not been what she expected, what she hoped for. *I* regret her disappointment, but that's all I'm capable of. Changing the reasons for it is beyond me now.

"Even the *smell* of the food bothers you, huh?"

Nodding, I tell her, "I think it's best if I wait outside until you're done. I won't go anywhere."

"Okay," she says quietly as I go back out the door.

Stretching out on the large flat boulder that sits off to the side of the cabin, I trace the outlines of the constellations with my eyes. I've been studying astronomy lately and find the familiarity of the star formations somehow reassuring.

As I pick out the stars belonging to Cygnus, a stray breeze brushes past my face. On it is the scent of bear, and it's strong.

I launch for the cabin and rip the door open.

"Bolt this. NOW." I slam it shut as I glimpse her shocked face.

"What about you?" she yells from inside.

"I'll be fine. You stay inside until I come back. Understand?"

Without waiting for her answer, I move in the direction of the bear, intending to draw it away from the cabin.

I spot a large bulk through the underbrush and listen as he sniffs and paws at a log. His full size is obscured, but I can see enough to know he's huge and probably the same one that's been cruising through here for the past few weeks.

The breeze shifts in the opposite direction. Sudden movement and a deep growl tell me he's caught my scent. As he bursts through the brush, my fears are confirmed.

Grizzly. A big son of a bitch, too. Shit.

Turning, I break into a dead run. Grizzlies are quite fast, as fast as an average-sized horse, capable of thirty-five to forty miles per hour in short bursts. I manage to put some distance between us, though, enough to keep him from catching me, yet still keep him interested.

Careful not to taunt him too much, I lead him several miles away from the cabin. I don't really want to antagonize him, because then he might make a point of hunting me. Black bears are one thing, but a grizzly's a lot bigger and far more dangerous. They're extremely territorial, too, which is why I've been a little concerned about his visits. And now that I know he *is* a grizzly, I'll need to be doubly careful.

Circling down the backside of the ridgetop to which I've led him, I sprint for the creek in the bottom of the valley, hoping to lose most of my scent in the water. After several miles, I cut across another ridge and make my way back to the cabin.

Sandy shoves open the door in response to my knock, her eyes wide with fear. I slip inside and step to the closet behind the blanket curtain to change out of my wet clothes.

"Are you okay? I've been so worried! Was that a bear chasing you? I could hear growling and something big run past the cabin when you left."

Listening to her pacing around the room as she talks, I strip and get into dry clothes, then grab a couple hangers and hang up my wet stuff. I come out from behind the curtain and slide the hangers onto nails high on the wall behind the stove.

"Sunny? Will you *please* talk to me?"

"Yes, I'm okay. Yes, that was a bear, the same one that's been hanging around here for the last several weeks."

"But why didn't you come inside where it was safe? I don't understand."

"Because I needed to lead him away from the cabin. I didn't want him to try to break in here."

"So you put yourself in danger and let a *bear* chase you? What if he'd caught you? Didn't you learn anything when you got those scars?"

That strikes a nerve. I turn away and clamp my jaw to keep from responding as the crimson veil drops over my vision.

Hell yeah, I learned something. I learned what human blood tastes like, learned how fulfilling it is to drink from human veins, learned what a monster truly is. Don't you *dare* lecture me.

Turning back to her, I glare at her through the red haze. Her eyes widen in alarm.

"Yes, I did. I learned how to handle damn bears. All *you* need to worry about is doing what I tell you and keeping the door bolted when I'm not here. Got it?"

She stands there, staring open-mouthed at me, bewilderment creating lines on her face.

"Sunny, what's happened to you? You're not the same person who picked me up and took care of me when I was sick, who laughed at my stupid jokes. You can't hardly even look at me, or talk to me." Tears spill down her cheeks. "I know it's my fault for keeping you from going back. You have every right to be angry with me."

"No, it's not your fault," I whisper. "And I'm not angry with you." I pause, struggling with what to say next.

"I'm angry with *me*. I'm angry because the Choice I made turned out to be the wrong one. The cost of that decision was far greater than the sacrifice I thought I was avoiding." Pausing, I take a deep breath as echoes of pain begin to resonate through me.

"The reason I can't talk is because it hurts too much to think, to let myself feel *anything*. And in many ways, you remind me of what I lost. I'm . . . finding that difficult to handle."

Sandy starts in my direction, her arms rising to hug me.

"I'm sorry. I . . . can't." I slip out the door into the darkness.

A darkness that doesn't come close to the one within me.

# SATURDAY

## CHAPTER 26

THUNK!

Peeling my eyes open, I taste the air in the direction of the cabin.

THUNK!

Sandy's scent floats in it, and I listen to her chopping wood from my perch in the tree a few hundred feet from the cabin. I'd spent the rest of the night patrolling a mile-wide radius around the cabin, not daring to go any farther.

Stretching the kinks out of my back, I crack my neck and climb down the tree.

A scream of pain shatters the quiet forest morning.

Already halfway down the trunk, I launch off in the direction of the cabin, casting for the bear's scent as I hit the ground in a dead run.

As I enter the small clearing in front of the cabin, the first thing that registers is the blood. It's running, no, pumping, from the slice in Sandy's calf that I can see through the ragged tear in her sweats. She's sitting on the ground, her hands tightly gripped around her leg, tears coursing through the alarm in her face.

Noting the blood-smeared axe lying on the ground next to her, I realize what happened.

Goddamn it. We're too far from any kind of medical facility.

Dashing inside the cabin, I grab the long tail of cord hanging down from the curtain where she'd tied it to a nail. I yank it down, slash off several feet, and head back outside.

Panic starts running through me as I watch her blood running onto the ground.

"I screwed up, Sunny," she sobs as I tie the cord tightly below her knee over her sweatpants, then slice off the blood-soaked fabric below the tourniquet so I can see what I'm dealing with.

This is bad. Very bad.

She's going to bleed to death. There's no way I can get her anywhere in time to get help.

Sandy looks up at me, gasping in pain, those green eyes wide in fear, then stares back down at her leg. A six-inch piece of skin and flesh gapes open, held on only at the bottom, blood pulsing and pooling on the raw surfaces.

Pulling my arm out of its sleeve, I slice the fabric at the top seam and pull the sleeve free.

"This'll probably hurt," I warn her.

She nods, bracing.

Pushing the flap of muscle and skin back up against her calf, I wrap her leg with the piece from her sweats, then tie the sleeve around it. The knit fabrics are instantly saturated in crimson.

She sharply inhales and cries out as I finish tying the knot.

I look at Sandy's paling face, the blood soaking the bandage, the blood-soaked ground.

She sees the doom in my eyes and bravely smiles.

"It's okay. I always knew this was how it was going to end. Can't help but think that when you're a bleeder."

I won't let this happen. I won't let her die without doing everything possible to stop it.

I can't lose someone else I love.

"Sandy. I, uh, I don't know if this will work. I don't know what will happen, or what the . . . risks are. There is one thing I can try, and it will require you to be very open-minded." The blood tears begin running down my cheeks as I finish speaking. I can't believe I'm doing this.

She nods, her wide-eyed gaze innocent, trusting.

Standing, I turn and look up at the surrounding peaks.

Nicolas. I had so much to learn from you. You had so much to teach me. We had all the time in the world to explore knowledge and work through our differences and love one another.

And I threw it all away. All because I refused to accept what I am, to become what I am.

I don't know what I'm doing. Please help me.

Lifting my right wrist, I pierce it along the vein with my nails. The four arcs of blood quickly join one another. I turn, step to Sandy's side, and crouch down.

"You need to drink this." My voice cracks as I cradle her shoulders and hold my bloody wrist out.

"I *knew* it," she says as she takes my arm and raises it to her mouth.

"You know nothing," I whisper.

~

The sensation of her drawing my blood is surreal. It feels so different than when Nicolas took it with love, or Éva took it with hatred. It's more like giving. There's no arousal, no fear. Just a warm feeling of benevolence, as though my system knows this is a gift of life. Her pull is so weak compared to a Chosen pull that it seems like my veins open up to help her.

Then abruptly, I somehow know she's had enough. Before I can even move my arm, my veins weirdly clamp down and the flow shuts off. As I gently pull my wrist away from her mouth, she looks up at me with wonder in her eyes. A wonder that mirrors my own. I reach out and hug her to me. She's now part of me. I can *feel* it, and I know she can as well.

My arms wrapped around her, I drink in her warm, human scent. Is this how a Maker feels when they make a Chosen? This . . . connectedness? It's different from the sharing with a mate. The link is familial rather than passionate, more like with a sibling, though not as strong as with a child.

Yet there's another sensation woven in. It's a sense of . . . ownership. She is not only part of me, she now *belongs* to me.

Nicolas's response to my question about the humans in his life suddenly makes sense.

"How do you feel?" I quietly ask, wondering if she can perceive whatever effects my blood might be having on her. I ease her to the ground, then loosen the makeshift bandage to peer at her wound. The bleeding has stopped.

"Like . . . like we're joined or something," she says sleepily. "I can *feel* you more than ever, and I get it now. I get your secrecy and why you keep everything to yourself. You're scared people will find out what you are." She pauses, then looks up at me. "And all I want to do now is protect you and keep you safe."

Huh. It's as though her emotions are an echo of mine.

And though I've felt protective and even motherly toward Sandy since the night she climbed in my car, the feeling is now intensified several times over, with a distinct possessive edge to it.

Is this what's going on with The Chosen and the donors? Nicolas said the humans were controlled with Chosen blood that was in the special liqueur the donors were required to drink.

Mild shock fills me as I finally understand. I understand that Chosen control over their donors is based on mutual connection, an instinctive need for all to protect all within their blood circle. Though Chosen are the primary beneficiaries in this symbiotic relationship, the humans also gain from it. Besides the pleasure they receive during feeding, they attain a sense of community which may be lacking in the lives of those who are drawn to this . . . lifestyle.

I look back down at Sandy, now peacefully sleeping against my bent knee, her skin a healthy pink as she breathes in and out.

Sandy said she's always felt like an outsider. With no true family of her own, she would make a perfect donor.

That is, if she didn't have such a tendency to bleed to death.

~

Returning from a quick afternoon patrol around the cabin, I open the door and walk into the dimly lit room. Sandy's wrapped up in her sleeping bag in front of the stove, asleep in one of the wooden chairs with her leg propped up on the other. She stirs and opens her eyes.

"Hey," she says with a yawn.

"Hey. How are you feeling? How's your leg?" I set the wood down in its box beside the stove, then crouch next to her makeshift bed.

"It's sore. Guess that's what happens when you try to chop off part of your body."

"Let's take a look at it."

She tugs the sleeping bag aside and doesn't say anything as I untie the sleeve binding her wound. I gently unwrap the blood-stiffened fabric from her leg, careful to ease it from the injury so it doesn't pull apart.

The wound is still seeping slightly. But the raw edges appear to be adhering to one another, showing early signs of healing. I softly prod the area to see if blood is pooling anywhere inside.

"Ouch! That hurts!"

"How bad?"

"Not like before. It's just . . . real sore."

This is so weird. My blood apparently sealed Sandy's injury, yet *I* need outside blood to heal my own. I just don't get it.

"You should probably have stitches, but I want to see if the wound heals any further on its own. Besides, there's no way to transport you the three miles to the car without jostling your leg, and I'd hate to have it tear open and start bleeding again."

Especially in the middle of a forest teeming with bears.

"Ugh. I don't want stitches."

"Well, you should be seen by a doctor. Maybe tomorrow, when it's had more time to heal, I'll take you in. We need proper bandages anyway."

Or, if we're lucky, my blood will continue to do its magic and she won't need to see a doctor at all. Just the *idea* of spending time with her in a hospital sets me on edge. Between being surrounded by humans, fear of discovery, and a chance encounter with someone else bleeding, the environment is ripe for an incident that could allow the beast to get away from me.

When the hunter disappeared, she took her calculating patience and cold stillness with her, along with much of my control over the beast. My struggles with the impulsive creature are now constant and, frequently, a hair's breadth from failure. Not only is hunting more difficult and dangerous, but any kind of stress could tip the balance in the wrong direction.

Which has me extremely puzzled. Confronted with Sandy's blood pumping furiously from her leg, I expected *something*, some reaction, from the volatile beast. But it did nothing. I could feel it watching, but it was dispassionate, even disinterested. I'm clueless as to why.

Shaking my head, I grab the water bucket and head outside to fill it.

# CHAPTER 27

"Can I ask you something?" Sandy's tone is soft, tentative.

Smiling, I glance up from her leg that I'm carefully sponging.

"Sure. I might even answer this time."

She takes a breath, but I can still feel her tension. Poor kid. I don't have much of a track record answering her questions.

"Am I going to become like you now?" Her voice holds a combination of hope and fear.

"No, you're not. The process is complicated and takes many days." That's all I really ever got from Nicolas. And I have little recollection of my own incomplete Change, except of blood and fear and horror at what I'd become.

"What will happen to me then?"

I think about the donors in the club and wonder if their addiction was to the liqueur containing Chosen blood, as well as to the pleasure of being fed upon.

And I think about Marie in her fifties looking like she's twenty.

"I'm not really sure." Looking down at the hours-old wound that's already halfway healed, I shake my head.

"Are there others like you?"

Sandy knows there's at least one, yet avoids mentioning his name, like she understands the pain it causes.

"Yes." But not quite like me. I'm the outsider in the community of outsiders.

"Do you drink blood?"

I grit my teeth a moment before answering.

"Yes."

"Human blood?"

"I have. I don't anymore."

"Do you want to?"

"Yes," I whisper.

"That's why you don't want to be around people, huh?"

"That's why."

"Do you want mine?"

"No, surprisingly not. And I haven't been able to figure that out."

Sandy visibly relaxes.

"I didn't think so. I mean, you've never looked at me the way you look at other people. I think it has to do with my blood being screwed up."

"Possibly." She might have something there. She's pretty perceptive.

Sandy's quiet as I finish bandaging her leg with strips torn from the bedsheet.

"So if you don't drink human blood, what do you drink?"

Smiling, I look up into her curious eyes.

"Bear."

"Bear? You're shittin' me."

I get up and walk over to the bed, pull out the box, and take the bear claw necklace out.

"And deer and elk," I say as I walk back and hand it to her.

"Holy shit. These are bear claws? Are they all from one bear?" She starts counting.

"There's one claw from each bear."

"You've killed eight bears?"

"Nine, actually. I didn't take one from the bastard who gave me my scars. Wish I had."

"You must really hate bears."

"Yeah. But they don't like me much either. They attack me anytime I come across one."

"Like blood enemies or something."

"Something like that."

"So is that where you go at night? Hunting?"

"And running. It helps to keep me . . . relaxed."

She grows quiet as she contemplates our discussion. I take the opportunity to shift the topic.

"Are you hungry? You haven't eaten at all this afternoon," I ask. Rosy color has gradually replaced her earlier paleness and she looks like herself again.

"Well, I wasn't, but now that you mention it, yeah, I am." She starts to get up.

"Sit tight. I don't want to disrupt the healing in your leg."

"But . . ."

I cross the room and open the cupboard.

"There's stew, cream of potato, clam chowder . . ."

"What stinks the least?"

Laughing, I answer, "It doesn't matter. They all stink."

"Clam chowder then."

Grabbing the soup and the can opener, I quickly spoon it into the saucepan and set it on top of the stove. Adding water from the pitcher, I stir it as Sandy watches.

"You said there are others like you."

"Yes."

"Why are you out here by yourself then? I know you're lonely. How come you aren't with them?"

Taking a breath, I try to piece together the simplest answer.

"I'm not exactly like them. I'm a little . . . different." I don't even know how to explain it.

"Different how?"

"I'm still . . . partially human. I don't fit in with them very well."

"Partially human? You mean, cuz you look like a regular person? Except for being pale. Oh yeah, and your eyes, of course."

"Actually, I look just like the others. But they're faster and stronger than I am."

I leave out the immortal part.

"Seriously? I thought you were pretty fast and strong."

"Well, they're more so." I decide not to mention their fangs either. That sounds too much like it's straight out of a horror movie.

"So how come you're partially human?"

"Because I've never . . . really killed anyone."

Except for Dominic, though I didn't do it alone. And it wasn't intentional.

"Why not?"

I stare at her, horrified by her nonchalance.

"Because I don't *want* to. Because it's wrong. Because I don't want to tear apart a family the way mine was."

Sandy's quiet for a moment.

"Because of your daughter."

"Because of my daughter."

The silence between us stretches taut.

Yet once again, Sandy avoids going further with it, as though she senses I don't want to talk about it.

This is weird. The old Sandy would've just blurted it out, along with her opinion.

"So how does killing someone make you . . . you know, one of *them*?"

"Each living thing has an energy, a life force, that makes them unique. *They* call it lifespark. When a . . . changeling feeds on a human and the human dies, they consume the human lifespark and it finalizes the Change."

"So is that all you need to be like the others? A lifespark?"

That, and a callous disregard for human life.

"Yes."

Sandy's quiet as I hand her the bowl of soup.

"Is that all you need to be with him? With Nicolas?"

Icy pain and regret flashes through me and the beast goes wild.

The force of the door slamming behind me shakes the cabin. I give myself to the beast and I run.

# CHAPTER 28

The sun is slipping below the western peaks as I knock on the cabin door. I listen as Sandy hobbles to the door, unbolts it, and pushes it open. I hesitate at her sharp intake of breath. She hops back from the doorway as I walk in, grab the bucket, and head outside to get water.

Carrying the full bucket back inside, I pour it into the large pot and set the pot on the stove. Sandy opens the stove door as I bend to grab a couple pieces of wood, then settles into her chair and props her leg up on the seat of the other.

"Are you sure you don't know Freddy or Jason?" Hearing humor in her voice, I turn to look at her, frowning.

"What?"

She gestures up and down at my clothes. My *bloody* clothes.

I stumbled across a buck in my mad run to stave off insanity. The chase, along with his blood, had been a welcome distraction from the torment exploding within me.

Chuckling, I add the wood to the glowing coals, close the stove door, and walk around her chair to the middle of the room.

"Well . . ." I dart to the cupboard.

"Do you think . . . ," I say as her eyes widen, then turn to focus on me.

My leap lands me on the bed.

"That they could . . ." Sandy's head whips around to locate my new position.

Laughing, I dash back to stand next to her chair.

"Keep up with me?" Smiling, I look down at her.

Her head snaps up to stare at me open-mouthed.

"Uh . . . no. In fact, I think you'd kick their asses."

"Damn right I would." Laughing, I walk around the other chair and glance at her leg.

"Let's see what it looks like now."

Sandy obediently pulls up the leg of her pajamas.

Untying the strip of sheet, I unwind it from her leg and remove the folded material that covers the wound. The edges of the skin flap are scabbed over and there's no sign of redness. Looks pretty good for a leg that had a chunk carved out of it barely six hours ago.

"Wow, that's pretty cool." Sandy reaches down and traces the outline of the injury.

"Well, it seems to have worked. Looks like you won't need stitches. We'll just have to watch for infection."

"Do you think I'll have a scar like yours? All silvery and stuff?"

"I have no idea. This is new for me, too."

After refolding the pad of fabric, I cover the wound, wrap the sheet strip back around her leg, and tie it. I pull her pajama pant leg back down and look at her.

"Can I get you anything? Do you need to use the outhouse?"

"Yeah, I could use some help getting to the head."

As she eases herself out of the chair, I walk over and grab her jacket and hand it to her. She puts it on and fishes a flashlight out of a pocket.

"Ready?"

She nods, and I help her hobble out the door.

It's funny. I don't even mind helping her. All traces of my earlier irritation with her visit have completely vanished, ever since I gave her my blood.

Interesting.

~

"Out." Sandy grins triumphantly as she lays down her cards.

"You know, it really isn't much fun playing against someone who wins *every* time and is so damn gloating about it." I count up my points. "Well, that's it. You won this round. Do you want to play another?"

"Naw, I'm kinda tired. I think I'm ready for bed." Sandy gathers up the cards and yawns, moving her leg from the pillow on the stump I'd brought in to use as a leg rest. She stands and hobbles out of the way while I return the chairs and table to their space against the wall. I walk over and grab her mat and sleeping bag from the foot of my bed and arrange them in front of the stove.

"Need a last trip to the outhouse?" I ask as I check to see if the clothes I washed earlier are dry yet. They're not. I turn the hangers around on the nails above the stove.

"No. I should be okay for the rest of the night. Are you going back out?"

"No. Think I'll stay in and do some reading tonight." I feel the need to stick close. Besides, I'm tired of sleeping in trees.

"Cool. See you in the morning then." Sandy eases herself to the floor and gets into her bag.

"Goodnight." I blow out all the lamps and take the reading light to the nightstand. Already in my sweats, I get in bed and snuggle down into the covers.

Oh, this feels much better than a damn knobby branch.

Picking up my book from the nightstand, I settle in for a night of reading.

# SUNDAY

## CHAPTER 29

A distant cacophony resolves itself into frantic roaring and yowling in my head. Through an inky molasses I can feel the beast and the hunter slamming against my sluggish consciousness in a whirling frenzy. As I fight through the immobilizing chains of sleep, I realize there's a third sound, separate from those within me.

It's Sandy, and she's screaming my name. From outside the cabin.

MOVE, BODY, MOVE!

My arms struggle to respond, and I shove myself out of the bed and fall onto the cold wooden floor.

COME ON, WAKE UP, GODDAMN IT!

The beast and the hunter take over, clearing the way through the leaden fog that keeps trying to suck me back down. I push myself up off the floor, stagger to the door and open it to the grey of early morning.

"Sunny! Sunny!" The terror in her voice strikes terror in my veins as I swing my head in her direction.

I see her just as the bear charges.

Pushing off the doorframe, I scream in fury as I clumsily run across the clearing. The bear reaches Sandy and stops, then rears up on his hind legs. My movement catches his attention, and as his eyes fix on me, he roars and swings his fistful of daggers against Sandy, batting her out of his way. Her body flies over the ground until its impact against a boulder lands it in a crumpled heap.

I look back up at him as he barrels toward me. Still fighting my nonresponsive body, I can do nothing but dive to the side. I go into a roll and he's right behind me. I roll again and as my feet touch the ground, I push into a leap. His claws catch the leg of my sweatpants and jerk me to the ground. Hot breath pours down the back of my neck and I slam myself upward against the bottom of his jaw. His teeth snap together, and grunting in pain, he hesitates and I launch myself forward. Landing on my hands, I spring again. One more leap gets me to the big pine that stands at the corner of the cabin.

His claws puncture the trunk inches below my heels as I race up the tree. I swing myself to the other side of the trunk, but he has no trouble reaching around and nearly nails my foot.

Taking the only choice open to me, I launch out from the tree, hoping the cabin roof doesn't collapse when I hit it. I land, jump down to the ground and run to Sandy, and carefully scoop her up. We make it inside the cabin and I bolt the door just as he reaches it. The planks creak beneath his weight, and he slams into the door several times, his furious roars adding to the deep thunder of his body hitting the stout wood.

Sandy groans as I set her limp body on the bed. She's bleeding on her side from the gouges his claws made when he hit her, but my instincts tell me there are worse injuries.

"Sandy! Sandy! Can you hear me!?" Crimson tears blur my vision as I move her kinky hair from her dirt-smeared face.

"Sunny, I'm so sorry," she whispers.

"Ssshh. It's not your fault. I never should've brought you out here."

"'S okay. Glad I came." She swallows. "I got to know the real you . . ." Her voice fades into a soft moan and she closes her eyes.

They open again as I unzip her jacket

"Sunny. I . . . I can't move." Tears run down her cheeks. "I can't move."

Oh God . . . I was afraid of that. Her back must be broken.

Pulling up her torn pajama shirt, I look at her side and the sea of blood soaking the bed.

I don't think I can heal all of this. There's too much damage.

Sliding up my sleeve anyway, I grab my wrist.

"Sunny, no. It won't help. I'm too . . . busted up. And I'm really tired . . . ," she whispers.

I raise my eyes to look into her tear-filled green ones, framed by her stark-white face. Slicing open my vein, I place my wrist against her mouth. She clamps her lips in refusal.

"Sandy . . ."

Blood is starting to run from her nose, joining mine on her lips. I wipe it off with my sleeve.

"Sunny. You have to promise me something. Please." Her voice cracks.

"Okay," I breathe.

"Go see your daughter." She pauses as she struggles for breath. "You think she's over you, but I know she's not. And you're not over her."

My chest tightens all the way up to my jaw.

"Promise me."

"I promise."

She coughs, and new blood froths her lips. I bite back the sobs that threaten to tear out my throat.

"No, don't go." I hold out my wrist once again. "I . . . need you, and you need me. Please stay. Please take this."

"No. Sunny. You have to do something else. You have to. For me. Promise." Her voice is demanding, fed by that inner strength she's shown time after time.

"Okay."

"Take it. Take my life thing, my . . . spark."

"NO!" I recoil in horror, shaking my head.

"Yes. That way I can still live. In you. Please."

No . . .

"You need it to be whole, and I don't want to leave you. Please."

No . . .

"Do it now, cuz everything's getting hazy. There isn't much time. Please."

No. I can't do this.

"Sunny, I don't want to leave you . . ." Her voice fades.

Oh God, help me. Please let this be the right thing.

I gently pick up her arm. A weak smile lights up her paling face.

But I just can't do it, and she sees this in my eyes.

"Hurry," she whispers as her eyelids begin to flicker. "Please . . ."

Grief squeezing my chest, I pierce the vein in her wrist, raise it to my mouth, and begin to draw.

The taste of human blood triggers a horrifying rapture I cannot help but succumb to. That it's *her* blood—someone I love—and that her vibrant life is draining away with every swallow, sickens me. And yet, I'm unable to stop.

Sandy's green eyes snap back open and she smiles again.

"Thank you . . ." Her voice falters as she watches me.

I try to ignore the ecstasy building within me as her veins empty. My tears fall to join the blood on her clothes and I inwardly scream at the injustice of it all as she fights to keep her eyes open.

"I love you," she sighs, her breath trailing away.

A warm vibration pulses in the blood filling my mouth. Her eyes widen in wonder, then the light within them dims, and the smile fades from her lips.

Bright energy bursts against my tongue and follows her blood as it traces its way into my system. I gasp as it hits my veins and the tissues in my body begin to electrify. As in my long-ago blooddream of killing Marie, the power suddenly permeating every cell in my body works its way into my core and into my *self*—like I've injected a nuclear blast straight into my soul. Everything flares into bright, blinding white and I stand, feeling as though my whole body is going to explode in euphoria. I can see the atoms as they spin through their molecules in the air, in the blood-drenched body before me, in my very hand.

And I can feel *her*. In me, throughout me, completing me. Her precious gift is beyond my comprehension, beyond my wildest imaginings.

Thank you, Sandy. I love you, too.

Needles of pain suddenly stab the warm white glow as every fiber in my body detonates in a flash of crimson. Soul-crushing agony envelops me and, collapsing to the floor, I scream and sink into blackness.

# CHAPTER 30

Ahhh . . .

My body twists yet again—

—muscle writhing against bone

—joints screeching as they pull apart

—acid surging through every cell

Release.

Breathe.

Again it starts—

Again I scream.

The sound fades, its echo ringing in my head.

Awareness slowly returns, accompanied by waves of molten pain pulsating through me. I can do nothing but lie here gasping as each one passes, giving me only a second to recover before the next one rips through. Time becomes condensed down to brief pauses of lucidity bracketed by mindless torment.

The lucid periods begin to grow longer and longer, until the torture is reduced to shuddering flashes every few minutes. And as those wane, I realize that now my whole body *aches*, every muscle and joint, and the fires of hunger are roaring in my gut.

My mouth throbs and when I reach up to rub it, a stinging pain lances through my lip. I taste blood at the same time I realize my whole mouth is swollen.

But it's not just swelling that I feel. There's a tooth where one didn't used to be. I trace its length and sharp point with my tongue, then feel the matching one on the other side.

Fangs. I have fangs.

Why do I have fangs? What . . . what's happened to me?

Slowly pushing my sore body off the floor, I stagger to my feet and look around. It's pitch black, yet I can see perfectly.

I'm in some sort of log cabin. It looks familiar . . .

As I turn to survey the tiny room, my gaze falls across a bed against the far wall.

Someone is lying in it.

Blood soaks the sheets, blood that's permeating the surrounding air. My gums spasm and hunger twists through my belly and out into my veins.

I move closer.

A young girl, no more than seventeen or eighteen, lies blood-smeared and motionless in the bed.

She's dead.

Golden, kinky hair frames an innocent face dotted with the freckles of youth. I shudder at the vacant stare of death in her dull green eyes, eyes that tug at something within me.

I think I know her . . .

*Sandy*. Her name is Sandy.

And with her name, jumbled memories come flooding back. A tidal wave of heartache and loss and disbelief slams into me and I nearly throw up.

Oh God. How could I have let this happen?

Sandy . . .

Oh, no, no. *No*.

I hug myself and turn away as my mind tries to sort out the events that led to her lying lifeless on my bed, framed in blood.

Events that led to me standing next to her, a fully fanged Chosen.

The horror at what I've done begins to fade as the puzzle pieces slide into place, and I realize there was no other path for us. That her fate was sealed the night I picked her up on the side of the highway.

The only thing easing the bitter taste of remorse is the echo of her final words.

*I love you*.

And the only thing I can do now is embrace her gift and be who I'm supposed to be.

ϰ

The clock on the nightstand reads 9:00. when hunger finally rouses me from my stupor of regret. I try to recall when the attack happened, but my memory is still blurry.

Was it early morning? This morning?

If so, that's nearly fifteen hours. Fifteen hours of mind-bending torture. No wonder my body hurts so much.

My gums spasm and I cup my mouth, only to slice the inside of my lip. I make my way to the closet, open the door, and, peering into the mirror hanging inside, bare my teeth.

Son of a bitch.

Those suckers are huge.

And it seems like my jaw opens wider than it did before, like the hinge stretches or something.

Holding my lip up with my fingers, I look at where the toothy daggers emerge from my gums.

Just like Nicolas said, there's a special groove between the eyetooth and the incisor. Those two teeth seemed to have moved apart slightly to allow the fang to slide down almost between them.

Closing my mouth, I wince as the points catch on my lower lip. I open it again, and practice pushing my bottom lip out so that I can close without pinching it.

I grimace into the mirror.

Yep. Full-blown monster now. No doubt about it.

Even with my mouth closed, the bumps under my lips make me look even scarier than before.

But Nicolas retracts his. In fact, all The Chosen do.

I concentrate on them, visualizing them going up, but nothing happens.

Huh.

As I push on one, trying to force it back up, my belly knots in hunger. The gums above my fangs throb, and a primal *need* surges through me. Deep, raw, animal. The yearning to sink my teeth into something warm is nearly as demanding as the craving for blood.

This I know, and I know what to do about it.

Shutting the closet, I realize something else feels different. Like I'm missing something.

And then it hits me.

I'm all alone in my head. No hunter, no beast. *No beast*. Only me.

Either they died when the remaining part of my human self died, or we are now one.

A shudder ripples across my skin, and I don't know if it's fear or elation.

My actions are my own now. I have only myself to control, only myself to blame.

I never realized how fractured I was before.

But now I feel complete. A sense of peace settles over me, along with acceptance and an inner strength I've not felt before.

I turn to head out the door and spot the still form lying on the bed.

*Sandy.*

It was her lifespark that made me whole.

I walk over and look down at her pale face, suppressing the grief that threatens to unmake me. I'll have time for it later. But right now, my newly made Chosen body needs to feed.

Smoothing back her golden curls, I lean down and kiss her cold forehead.

Thank you, sweet child. You live in me now. You're truly part of me, and I promise not to waste your gift.

With a last look at her lying motionless on the bed, I head outside to kill a bear.

~

Exhausted from the last several hours of catch-me-if-you-can, the grizzly stops again, his head hanging low as he pants. Blood trails from numerous wounds all across his body. I sidle up to him, slash him across the face, and jump back as he rears. Waiting until he's fully upright, I launch and slam hard against his chest. He grunts, staggers and falls back on his rump, then keeps going over backward. As I leap off him, I drag my nails across his throat yet again. He lies there, then rolls onto his side, panting.

The bloodlust urges me on, my fangs aching to bury themselves in his flesh. I run up a tree and tear off a branch, and landing on the ground beside him, shove it at his front paws. He grabs it, sinking claws and teeth into the bark as he snarls in fury. Darting to the back of his neck, I reach around and drive my nails into his windpipe. I squeeze, crushing it, then release and leap back as his claws wave uselessly at me one last time.

It's over now. I circle him, growling as he slowly quits struggling for air. Leaping onto his shoulder, I shove his muzzle upward and plunge my fangs into his throat. I bite, and bite again, reveling in the sensation of his flesh giving way as the blood pumps into my mouth. His lifespark then flows into me, a dim shadow of Sandy's before him. But I feel it, and I hope Sandy does too.

I drink until I can take no more, my first blood as a true Chosen.

~

Walking through the cool night air to the cabin, I'm amazed at the change in my senses. I didn't pay much attention earlier when I was so focused on the bear. But now I really notice it.

When I was attacked five years ago, I was confused by my heightened vision, hearing, and sense of smell. I didn't understand what had happened to me and had difficulty adapting to my new state of being.

But it's different this time. I know *exactly* what's happened and relish the improved sharpness of my perceptions. I'm a little surprised, because, other than strength and speed, I had no idea there was this much difference between Chosen physiology and my own. But not anymore. Though the waning moon is hidden behind the peaks, everything appears crisper, like it was freshly polished in a gentle rain.

Grains of sand jump out in sharp relief as I look at the ground, and not just the ground beneath my feet. The ground tens of feet ahead of me is pebbled in sand grains light and dark. The air is full of tiny motes of dust and pollen that drift with the night breezes. Turning around, I watch them swirl and eddy with the wind of my passing, a wind I can actually hear when I focus on it.

And the smells. Oh, the *smells*. I've lived by my nose for the last five years, using it to find food, to warn me of danger, to give me a picture of my surroundings. But now . . . now the bouquet of scents has another depth to it. The only way I can describe it is to compare it to the difference between 2D and 3D, like a map of the world drawn on paper versus a bas-relief globe.

Remembering the fight with the bear, I chuckle about my surprise at how much stronger and faster I am now. I probably could've killed the bear a little sooner if I wasn't experimenting with my newfound abilities.

A chill runs through me as I also remember the physical satisfaction I felt when I sank my fangs into his throat. It was ecstatic. It's daunting to think that I now have another urge that must be fought and managed.

Running my tongue across my teeth, I'm grateful that the damn things retracted after I fed. I used to feel like I was missing out on something when I discovered The Chosen had them. But like the bloodtears, this is a part of Chosen physiology with complications I hadn't expected. I just hope I can learn to restrain my fangs better than I have the tears.

Contemplating my new self, I realize that I'm not upset by the changes like I was the first time, nor frightened. And it's not just because I've been through something similar, though I have little memory of the event five years ago, other than horror.

It's because this time it was *my* Choice, and I made it knowing full well what it meant.

The clearing around the cabin is dark and quiet as I approach, as though the surrounding forest is mourning the tragedy it witnessed in the grey of last dawn. I purposely avoid looking at the boulder and ground splashed with Sandy's blood and walk to the side of the cabin.

Grabbing a shovel and a couple pieces of wood, I head back out into the forest.

# MONDAY

## CHAPTER 31

My eyes open to the sounds of birds singing, then squint at the sunlight streaming in through the crack beneath the door, a bright stripe illuminating the base of the stove and the floor next to me where I slept. Instinct kicks in and I edge away from the light. The clock shows 3:06.

At least I can still wake up during the day, though today it's hours later than normal.

Wondering what else in my physiology has changed, I unzip Sandy's sleeping bag and tentatively stretch out my arm, allowing my fingertips to brush the sun's foray into my dark refuge.

Nothing. No burning. I reach a little farther and gather the beam into my palm.

Thank God. Losing my recently developed ability to withstand the sun was a price I'd feared might be part of my conversion to full Chosen.

Sorrow clutches at my chest as I stare at the body wrapped up in the blankets on my bed. I'd waited until daylight to bury her. She's a child of the light, and should be put to rest under the sun—the sun that shone in her curls and danced across her face, leaving its freckled kisses behind.

Last night I read her journal, wanting to learn all I could about this sweet girl. My heart, or what remains of it, felt as though it was being torn into pieces as I read her comments about me. About how much she looked up to me, in spite of her speculations about my true nature. But when I read how she felt I was more of a mother to her than anyone in her past, guilt nearly made me retch, and I had to stop reading.

If it wasn't for me—if I'd left her standing there on the highway—she wouldn't be lying there on that bed, cold and lifeless.

I climb out of the sleeping bag and look again at the items I'd taken from her backpack, debating whether she would want me to keep them, or place them with her. After making one more pass through her photo album, I stop on a recent picture of her. It's one of the few in which she's not wearing that haunted lonely look. I take it out of its sleeve, set it on the table, and put everything else into her pack.

Slipping my arms through the straps, I shrug it onto my back and walk over to the bed. I pick up Sandy's shrouded body, cradling it like a baby, grab the sleeping bag, and head out the door into the afternoon sun.

It takes about an hour to get to her gravesite. I'd chosen a place on the south side of a peak that has a magnificent view of the surrounding mountains and forest. Stopping at the base of the grave I dug last night, I lay her down beside it and spread the sleeping bag out in the bottom of the hole. I gently place her inside, then slip out of the backpack and open it.

The first thing I take out is her sketchbook. Kneeling down, I tuck it next to her blanket-wrapped body. I then place the little purple stuffed dragon I gave her in the hospital on her other side.

Its twin is tucked away in the dresser back at the cabin. I'm wishing I'd brought it now, because I'm not sure I can handle looking at it when I get back.

Crimson tears blur my vision as I set the pack at her feet and kneel by the side of the hole.

"Beautiful child, I told you when we met that it was for a reason. That this would be it was something I could have never foreseen." I fight back the sobs choking me as the tears run down and splash red upon the bare ground.

"If I had known, if I'd had any idea that meeting me would result in your death, I never would've picked you up." A ragged moan rips through me as her image crystallizes in my head, that of her bruised and freckled face peering hopefully into my window on a dark and violent night.

"And yet, you've been one of the best things that's happened to me in these last five years. I can't imagine not knowing you. I just wish you knowing *me* didn't cost you your life."

My body shudders as I take in and release a deep breath.

"I . . . I never thought I could have another child. Because that's what you've been to me—a daughter. I just wish I'd told you . . ." My chest collapses as the sobs finally break free. The mountains mourn with me, echoing my sorrow, its sound bouncing from cliff to cliff.

And my sorrow isn't just for my sandy-haired daughter.

She wasn't the only one who died.

For I'm not only burying her, I'm burying the last little piece of my humanity.

ϰ

The golden orb is sliding behind the western peaks as I pound the wooden cross into the ground. My wood carving skills aren't too great, but good enough that I can read the cross arm:

SANDY MILLER MARTIN
JULY 11, 1989 - AUGUST 19, 2007

I look back one last time at the lonely little mound perched on the mountainside, just as it disappears into the shadows cast by the setting sun, and wish her well on her journey into the light.

# TUESDAY

## CHAPTER 32

The cabin door clicks shut and I snap the padlock into place, then step out into the late afternoon sun beaming down into the clearing and take one last look around. After saying my goodbyes to Sandy yesterday evening, I'd spent the rest of the night saying goodbye to yet another mountain forest that my wild side had grown to love.

I don't understand why each time I find what seems to be the ideal place to live, my life turns into a disaster.

My gaze falls to the rock that broke Sandy. Scuffing dirt and grasses over the blood-soaked ground, I shake my head at her needless death, then head down the trail to the car.

It takes much less time than my trips usually take. I guess I'm moving faster without even realizing it. Opening the trunk, I lay my suitcase inside, then set the large backpack next to the entrance of the lodge. I have no further use for it.

The familiar purr of the BMW signals the beginning of another journey. I have a feeling it will be a long time before it ends.

~

The highway sign for my first stop flashes by in the darkness. It's taken me nearly eleven hours to reach Casper, and the sun will be coming up soon.

Unwilling to face my next challenge just yet, I pull off the highway and head for one of the roadside motels that dot the outskirts of town.

As I lie down and stare at the ceiling, waiting for dawn's darkness to rescue me from my thoughts, I wonder how other Chosen deal with their guilt and regrets. Do their emotions and memories fade with time? Or do they accumulate, becoming heavier and heavier until the bearer collapses beneath their weight and seeks the final death.

Perhaps that's what the Old Ones are. Chosen who've tired of their immortality and withdrawn to wither away somewhere alone.

Is that what Nicolas has done? Gone away to die?

Bloodtears trace wet trails down my face as the words in his letter echo in my head.

*Do not attempt to find me. In this, I promise, you will not succeed.*

# WEDNESDAY

## CHAPTER 33

Bracing myself as I walk into Sandy's apartment in Casper, I inhale the air that's saturated with her scent. I smell Danny's as well, though it's old, close to a week.

The rest of the late afternoon passes quickly as I pack Sandy's things. Her set of little dragon figurines she'd bought the day we moved in to the apartment goes into a box. A photo album she'd made, with pictures of her and Danny and other kids their age, joins it. I add to it a framed photo of her with her cute strawberry-blond boy, both of them grinning as they sit together on the back of a patient-looking horse.

Oh, Danny . . .

The bag of clothes I'll take to a homeless shelter somewhere along my route. I'll drop the textbooks off at the college's used-book store. Anything that I don't feel comfortable disposing of in the dumpster will be destroyed or disposed of somewhere far from here.

One more sweep around the apartment to check for anything I missed.

Damn, this packing and moving thing gets old.

But this next part? Not something I've done before, and I've been dreading it all afternoon.

I unplug Sandy's cell phone from the charger and turn it on.

It shows at least a dozen text messages, and a number of voice mails as well. A couple are from girls, but the rest are all from Danny.

Taking a big breath, I scroll to his number and press SEND.

The phone rings twice before he answers.

"Sandy! Sandy, I'm sorry. I shouldn't have said that. I promise never to talk to you like that again."

Tears well up in my eyes for him, for what I'm about to do to him.

"Hello, Danny. This is Sunny."

"Oh . . . hi. Where's . . . where's Sandy?" Innocent concern trickles through his voice as he says her name.

"She, ah . . . she's heading out to California."

"What?" he asks in confused disbelief.

"Danny, I've boxed up some things for you that she wanted you to have. They'll be by the front door of the apartment."

"I don't understand."

"I'm sorry." I hate this.

"But why? Why isn't she telling me herself?"

"She . . . wanted to. But she just couldn't."

"But what about school? It starts Monday." His desperation is painful to hear.

It's time to end this.

"Things change, Danny. People change. I'm sorry."

"But . . ."

I turn off the cell phone, take out the battery and SIM card, snap the card in half, then squeeze the phone until its body crumples within my fist.

I'm sorry, Danny. More than you'll ever know.

~

Once again the highway stretches before me. As I drive into the setting sun, I dwell on all that has occurred in my life since I left California.

I've discovered that I'm not alone, that there are others like me.

The one thing I swore I'd never do, I've done.

It healed me.

I also found love, not once, but twice, though they were different kinds. And I lost both of them in different ways, yet at the very end their goals were the same—to help me Change, to accept and be what I am.

And I do.

So now I head west to keep a final promise to one.

And to break a final promise from the other.

Soulless Ones

*They say we have no souls*
*No life*
*No love*

*But how can soulless ones*
*Live so brightly*
*Love so deeply*
*If we have no souls*

*They say we have no feelings*
*No pity*
*No remorse*

*But how can one empty of feelings*
*Let pity stay the hand*
*Know remorse with every step*
*If we have no feelings*

*They say we are monsters*
*Governed by need*
*Driven by lust*

*But how are we monsters*
*If all have need*
*And all feel lust*
*When all are monsters*
*To another*

*They say we have no souls*

*Then why do soulless ones*
*Feel love so strongly*
*So fully*
*Feel loss so bitterly*
*So utterly*

*If we have no souls?*

*- CN*

# PART III
# THE DEVIL

# TUESDAY

## CHAPTER 34

It's been nine days since I became a full-fledged monster, and nearly six months since I left the west coast. A sick laugh escapes as I remember the trivial events that prompted my flight to Colorado. They pale in comparison now, and seem like something from a child's dream. Nothing like the nightmare I left in the shadow of Pikes Peak.

But it hasn't all been a nightmare. I did find something I'd thought to be impossible in this life.

Inhaling sharply, I slap those memories down and shove them back into the black box. Because those memories, the memories of what I lost, are too full of pain and regret. I grab the stillness and relief flows through me as those emotions, and everything connected with them, smother under the cold detachment.

I pull into the parking lot across the street from where my daughter used to work. Hopefully she still works here, because I don't have the patience anymore to sit outside her house and watch for her. Those days are over.

But I do need to see her, to reassure myself that my human life wasn't just another dream.

Then I'll decide how much of my promise to Sandy I can keep.

Tugging the baseball cap brim lower, I grimace at my reflection in the car window. My disguised self glares back in the form of a punk street kid—pierced, tattooed, and wearing ragged clothes. The piercings will heal as soon as I take out the jewelry, and the fake tattoos, though just hand drawn on my skin, will fade within the hour. The tats aren't very good—I was never much of an artist. But they'll do the job. I put on my sunglasses and head toward the building.

It's late afternoon and the lobby is beginning to fill with people leaving for the day. My jaw clenches as the fragrant chorus of human blood hits me. Even though I gorged on several deer last night, this may be harder than I thought.

Walking past the staircase to the far side of the elevators, I stop and casually lean against the wall as though waiting for the doors to open. Andrea's always preferred stairs and I'm hoping to catch sight of her as she comes down the wide stairway. I watch the other workers as they descend in twos and threes, deep in their conversations.

The elevator next to me opens and people brush past me as they exit. I'm trapped between them and the wall at the end of this short hallway and, without warning, violence coils in my muscles.

I need to get out of here. Coming inside was not only risky, it was stupid.

Waiting until the last of the crowd leaves the elevator, I start to follow them toward the front door.

And then I look up, and she is standing at the bottom of the stairs, not twenty feet away, staring directly at me.

Oh shit.

I dart into the elevator, nowhere else to go. The doors begin to close and I let out my breath. And then a slim hand shoots into the rapidly shrinking gap, followed by a slender arm, and her shoulder wedges into the opening. The doors rebound and she steps inside and stands there facing me, the confusion on her face giving way to recognition.

"Hello, Mom."

My chest constricts as I struggle to stay within the stillness, to not react to the sound of her voice saying "Mom." I hold my breath, terrified of her scent, because to want *her* blood is more than I can take. Somewhere deep inside me I find the icy strength necessary to get through the next several minutes without having a complete breakdown.

Grateful my sunglasses hide the pink veil, I tip my head and face her.

"Hello, Andrea."

The elevator doors shut behind her. I reach over, press 3 and, when the elevator begins to rise, press STOP. The car clanks to a halt.

Turning to face her again, I'm not surprised to see both hurt and anger blazing out of her blue eyes.

"Can you suggest somewhere private that we can talk?" I quietly ask.

Biting her lip, she stares at me a moment, her eyes scanning over me. I see bewilderment creep in as she notes the differences between me and the woman she used to call Mom.

Nodding, she presses L with a shaking hand, then folds her arms and turns her back on me to face the door.

This is going to be very painful.

~

As we cross the street, I'm aware of her glances in my direction, and can sense the alarm growing in her.

"You walk differently," she finally says as we step up on the sidewalk.

Yes, I do. Like a hunter, a predator. A killer.

"Where've you been?" she asks after a long moment.

"I'd rather wait 'til we get to where we're going, okay?"

Out of the corner of my eye I see her nod, then she reaches up and wipes her cheek.

Oh, Andrea. I am so sorry. I never should've come back.

We cross several more streets and enter a parking lot for the beach. Andrea takes out a cell phone from her purse, presses a number, and holds it up to her ear.

"Hello, Cynthia? I have a few stops to make after work. Is it okay if I pick Rhia up a little late?" Her voice trembling, she pauses. "All right. I'll be there by six. Thanks."

*Rhia*. Her daughter. My granddaughter.

My head feels as though it's going to explode.

Andrea puts the phone back in her purse, then folds her arms and hunches over as we continue across the asphalt.

Swallowing, I concentrate on the arctic calm that is the only thing keeping me sane.

When we reach the sidewalk that runs along the edge of the beach, she turns and we follow it, our silence now muffled by the roar of the ocean. She steps off the concrete into the sand and heads toward the scattered picnic tables paralleling the walkway. I trail her, reflecting on what a beautiful woman she's become and how well she wears adulthood.

Andrea stops by a table apart from its neighbors and sets down her bag. My skin tingles beneath her heavy gaze as I walk past her to the far end of the table. Taking a seat upon it, I focus on the horizon where sky meets water and taste the ocean scents traveling in the salt-laden air. Seagulls wheel overhead beneath the late afternoon sun, screeching at one another as the waves pound the shoreline. The churning sand beneath the watery onslaught mimics the emotions roiling deep in my gut.

Andrea sits down on her end of the table, a breeze blowing her dark hair across her face, and stares out toward the sea.

"Why?" she asks, her voice cracking. "Why didn't you come home?"

My throat tight, I whisper, "Because I couldn't."

"Why not? What happened? Everyone thought you were dead."

I am.

"Everyone except me," she croaks. "I knew you weren't. They kept telling me you were and I knew you weren't."

There are no words I can say to explain any of the last five years, or why I didn't come home.

The surf crashes over and over, accenting the mute pain between us.

"So why now? Why did you suddenly decide to come back now?" She turns toward me. Accusation thickens her voice, and I can't bear the thought of seeing it on her face.

My gaze drops to the sand stretching before us.

"I needed . . ." The words catch in my throat. "I needed to know that you were all right."

She jumps off the table and stands in front of me, her fists clenched in fury.

"What's wrong with you? Look at me, dammit! Take off those damn sunglasses and look at me, for God's sake!" Her lips quiver as tears stream down her cheeks.

The icy envelope protecting me nearly shatters, and I choke on the bitter tastes of sorrow and guilt. Fear of losing control triggers something within me, and lightning-quick, my mood shifts. Muscles tense and pink anger hovers on the edge of my sight.

The only way she's going to accept my lack of explanation is to show her.

I slowly reach up and take off my hat and set it on the table, then take off my glasses. My vision has cleared, the pink gone, but it's not going to make any difference. I look up into Andrea's face.

Her sudden intake of breath pierces the frozen detachment and stabs me deep in the chest.

"My God, what happened to your eyes?" Hers glitter like twin sapphires, brimming with fresh tears as she stares into mine.

We used to share the same blue color. But no longer. Today mine are glaciers, with only a hint of palest blue, the price I had to pay for subduing the hunger.

She peers closer and my body turns to stone.

"You're not . . . you're not wearing contacts. Why are they so . . . ?"

Cold? Inhuman?

Because, my sweet daughter, they are the eyes of a monster. And there is nothing I can do to change that.

She reaches out to my face and I pull back to avoid her touching my cool skin. She slowly lowers her arm, then closes her eyes and turns toward the sea.

"You want to know if I'm all right? Well, I am. Perfectly. I'm married now, to a really great guy." She pauses, sniffling. "And I have a . . ." Shuddering gasps rob her of the last word.

"A daughter," I finish, my voice barely above a whisper. "I know."

"You know? You *know*? How do you . . . ?"

Her body trembles as she raises a hand to her mouth. I fight to keep my seat on the table.

"I've been watching you off and on since I found you at City College three years ago."

Her back stiffens and she hugs herself again. Andrea slowly turns around to face me.

"You've been watching . . . ? Why didn't you . . . ?" The grief and shock painting her face only underscore the tragedy of her words.

"Because I couldn't. Because of *this*." I hold my hands out, indicating my face and body. "Because of how you'd react, how you're reacting now." I pause, my fingers curling, their razor sharp nails biting into my palms.

"When I found you, you'd made a new life for yourself and seemed happy. You had school, goals, friends—a life. And it would've ruined everything for you if I came back into it."

"No, it wouldn't—"

"Yes, it would've. Because I couldn't have stayed." I take a deep breath and go on.

"Because I *can't* stay. Because I'm not . . . your mother . . . anymore." My voice trails off as I shift my gaze from her bright blue eyes full of tears to the grey blue of the thundering sea.

I listen to the pounding of her heart, the quiet sobs as they rip from her chest.

This was why I didn't come back, why I shouldn't have come back. We will both spend our lives remembering these moments filled with grief and unanswerable questions.

"Mom . . ." The word tumbles from her lips and I close my eyes to shut it and her out.

"I'm sorry, Andrea. I never meant for you to see me. You were better off believing me dead." Opening my eyes, I glance at her anguished face, then at my hat and glasses as I pick them up.

Before putting them back on, I turn and give her a hard stare. Gut-wrenching pain breaks through the stillness again as I see her flinch at my gaze.

"You need to forget that I was here. It would be best if you tell no one you've seen me, not even your husband."

"But . . ."

"No buts. That's just how it has to be. They all think I'm dead. Do you realize what would happen if it gets out that I'm not? What do you think the media would do? Or the police? Or the insurance company?"

Her eyes widen. But only for a second. Andrea lowers her gaze and her head, then nodding, turns back to face the sea.

She always been smart, since she took her first breath. Since I gave birth to her.

"Will I ever . . . see you again?" She chokes as she fights to get the words out.

I take a deep breath as I fight to get out my own.

"No, I don't think so . . ." My collapsing chest tells me I need to go, and now.

Before the bloodtears start, tears I won't be able to stop.

I step onto the sand behind her. Wrapping my arms around her, I gently squeeze her as I press my lips into her hair.

"I love you, Andrea, forever and ever." Releasing her, I step back and leave.

Very fast.

When I turn back to look at her from down the beach, she is still staring out at the sea.

---

It seems so wrong to regret my promise to a dying girl, but I do.

I wish to God I'd never come here.

I wish *none* of this had ever happened.

My memory is now seared with the anger and disbelief twisting Andrea's features. Her words are indelibly stamped into my mind, words that will echo over and over and over, filled with accusation and pain.

Like a clip from a horror film, our encounter replays in my head and I cannot erase the images and sounds of my daughter as she confronts the monster who was once her mother.

"*Mom . . .*"

The BMW screams up the 101, its speedometer matching the highway's number. It weaves in and out of the crawling cars, chased by the scenes unfolding behind my eyes.

"*Mom . . .*"

Just west of Goleta is a turnoff for Eagle Canyon. Jamming on the brakes, I slide the car around and barely make the double turns, then hit the gas again for the short quarter mile to the end of the road. I pull the car off to the side and bail out.

"*Mom . . .*"

I run.

# WEDNESDAY

## CHAPTER 35

It's late afternoon when I stumble out of bed. I'd made it to a hotel last night with barely enough time to get into a room before the sunrise took me down.

Emotionally hung over, I stare at the blank paper on the desk for what seems like hours. I finally pick up the pen and begin writing.

A dozen paper balls litter the floor when I stop to take a shower. I quickly wash, dress, and pack, then turn back to the desk.

Oh, Sandy. I tried.

But like everything else, I screwed it up.

And I have only myself to blame for letting both you and Andrea down.

I've failed everyone in my life. And not just failed them, I've *destroyed* them.

Jaw tight, I read the letter one more time:

*My sweet Andrea,*

*I wish I could explain, but I can't.*

*I do want you to know that my disappearance from your life was not my choice.*

*But staying out of your life was. It was a decision I made because it was best for you. I know you won't believe me, but trust me on this.*

*My life over the last five years has changed me in ways I can't describe, but I think you saw that. And because of those changes, it isn't possible for us to have a relationship. To be honest with you, it would be very dangerous for you and your family for us to even attempt it.*

*Please believe me. I would be with you if I could. But I can't.*

*My memories of you have been the only thing that's kept me from total insanity these last few years. You've never been far from my mind.*

*I will love you forever.*

Reality sets in with the acknowledgement that I can't really send this to her. I can't leave any physical proof that I exist. From what I'd read after first returning to civilization, my disappearance had caused quite an uproar in the news. If it ever became known that I'm still walking the earth, her life would be dumped completely upside down by the investigation and the publicity it would spawn. The circus would be nonstop. And she would bear the brunt of it because I would have to disappear.

Again.

There is no way I will allow her and her family to share their lives with a monster.

I tear up the note into tiny pieces and watch the scraps flutter to the floor.

~

The passing oaks and vineyards do little to improve my mood as I head north. In fact, everything here looks so dry and brown, and seems lifeless after the rich, damp greens of Colorado and Montana. I miss my mountain near Colorado Springs, and think of returning there someday. But I won't do it alone, for Nicolas is too tightly woven into that landscape, and to return without him would only deepen my sense of loss.

Before beginning my search for him, however, I need to clear my head with some time in the wild. I'm still not used to my new Chosen senses and, as I discovered in Santa Barbara, am easily overwhelmed by the massive amounts of information assaulting my ears and nose. Learning to filter the input and focus on what's critical is mandatory if I'm going to re-enter the worlds of both human and Chosen.

The increased strength still surprises me, nearly double what it was before. And speed—I'm fairly certain that I can now duplicate Nicolas's disappearing act, though I'm unable to confirm it myself.

I'm sure Andrea could, though.

My chest aches with the memory of Andrea staring at the horizon, hugging herself. I can only imagine the emptiness she must've felt when she turned to see that I was gone, and once again hate myself for not trying to work things out with her.

But all I felt at the time was the horror of our situation, and my control slipping by the second, and not knowing what would happen if I lost it.

I no longer trust myself. In some ways, I was better off living with the hunter and the beast in my head. We'd reached a balance of power, yet I still retained the upper hand.

Most of the time.

Now, all that power, the violence and stealth and cunning, is mine and mine alone, and I'm finding it to be even more unpredictable than the creatures who once shared it with me.

And that scares the hell out of me.

I think about how I came into that power, and the sacrifices it demanded, and shove away the glimmer of regret that accompanies the memory. But it doesn't take much effort. And I'm not sure why. It's as though a filter exists between me and my emotions about Sandy, and her loss does not pain me nearly as much as I anticipated. Perhaps because she's now a part of me and, in some way, not truly gone.

Or, perhaps Chosen physiology doesn't permit remorse for one's victims.

Either way, I'd expected that she would continue to haunt my thoughts. But to my surprise, she doesn't. At least not in the way I feared.

Which is a huge relief.

Because between Andrea and Nicolas, I have no more room in my life for ghosts.

# MONDAY

## CHAPTER 36

It's dark when I drive across the Oakland Bridge into San Francisco.

The last month in the Sierra Nevada Mountains has allowed me to get a better handle on my abilities and gain some control over my reactions. But the passage of time has done little to reassure me that reuniting with Nicolas will be any better than the disastrous reunion with Andrea.

I worry now that he may not welcome me back into his life. That between my constant rejection of him and my present state as a full-Chosen, he'll want nothing to do with me. Worse, he may even hold me responsible for his fall as the head of his lineage and will seek only one thing from me—my death.

Yet, I have no choice. I have to find him. And this is the only place I can think of to start.

Black water shimmers beneath the lights dotting the bay. Flashing brakes and the occasional honk accompany the crush of cars around the BMW as I slowly make my way across the bridge toward downtown. The congestion has already set me on edge. My tolerance for the clamor, stink, and manic pace of cities seems to have withered even further after so much time in the wilderness.

The plan is to haunt nightclubs catering to the goth crowd, hoping to pick up info about any underground clubs that might cater to *my* crowd. First, though, I've got to find a motel where I can safely lay up during the day.

And then it's hunting time.

But it's for a far more dangerous prey than I've ever hunted, and I can only hope my new Chosen abilities can keep me from getting killed.

# FRIDAY

## CHAPTER 37

Goths fascinate me. They frequent the clubs in ones and twos, cloaked in black and tattoos and piercings. Charcoal lines encircle their eyes, chrome studs encircle their wrists. Silver-colored chains and safety pins and zippers accent the inky canvas and leather of their clothing. Many favor pale makeup and black-dyed hair. Contacts are popular, featuring reptilian green or feline gold bisected by slit pupils, along with the more common blood red and ice blue.

I fit right in.

The small club tonight seems inhabited by a significant number of social misfits, dancing solo in their own little dark pools of isolation to music by Marilyn Manson, Nine Inch Nails, and other bands I don't recognize. The dance floor filled with gyrating bodies forms a sharp contrast to the booths and tables bracketing it, their motionless squatters watching the activity with a practiced air of indifference.

I'm one of those squatters. The small corner table I've staked out for the night is near the entrance where I can keep an eye on the door. Rings of condensation have formed on the stained tabletop around a glass of ice water and a bottle of Sierra Nevada Pale Ale. The beer to my right is for my nonexistent companion, the water is for me. I pick up the glass and take a sip.

This is my second weekend here at the Cat Club, and so far I've heard no whispers of an underground club, nor sensed the presence of another Chosen. I haven't been able to bring myself to strike up a conversation with anyone and, despite the furtive looks drifting my way, no one's had the nerve to approach me.

Though I slaked the red thirst with a small blacktail buck south of the Bay earlier this evening, I feel wired, like I've had too much caffeine. Memories continually assault me, of human blood and its honeyed ecstasy, as if I'd savored its exquisite taste only yesterday. Its tantalizing scent saturates the room, making it difficult to maintain focus. My mouth aches.

I scan the club again, and a surge of frustration triggers a low growl. I don't understand why The Chosen haven't approached me yet. This is Alina's territory, and it is she whom I've come to find. As one of Nicolas's Elders, I expected she'd sense me, like he did when I first entered Colorado Springs. Her lack of response is puzzling.

A guy standing at the bar across the room stares at me over the rim of his glass. Not quite as gothed-out as many of the other patrons, he's wearing a black Bauhaus T-shirt with black jeans. He seems to be debating whether or not to talk to me. I take a drink of the beer to show him I'm alone.

His decision apparently made, he picks up a leather jacket from the barstool next to him and saunters over. The hunger stirs at the scent of liquid pleasure running beneath human skin and my nails dig into the table.

"Mind if I sit here?"

He's tall, medium build, light brown hair neatly trimmed. Deep-set hazel eyes peer down at me from an angular face. Thin lips, framed by a mustache and goatee, offer a half-smile. He's not bad looking. For a human.

"Go ahead."

He takes the chair across from me and gestures toward the bottle of beer.

"You need another?"

"No, I'm fine."

He nods.

"I'm Ben."

"Sonya." The name still feels strange on my tongue, but instinct tells me it's safer to keep my real one hidden until I find Alina.

"You new in town?" He lounges back in the chair, but his nonchalance seems a little forced. Raising his glass, his eyes narrow as he examines me.

Something tells me he's run into my kind before. I'm not sure what it is. It's almost like I can sense Chosen blood within his veins.

A jolt of electric anticipation surges through my body. I try to stay calm.

"Been here a couple weeks. Do you come here much?"

"Sometimes. On weekends when I don't have anything better to do." He takes a drink. The ice rattles in the glass from a slight tremor in his hand.

I glance over the tattoos lining his arms and bite back a smile at the image of Dracula poised open-mouthed over the neck of a terrified woman.

Then something among the inked figures catches my eye, and as I look closer, a chill ripples across my skin.

Two pinkish scars, small and rounded, a little over an inch apart. Several other pairs lurk among the colorful murals decorating his forearms.

Fang marks.

My gums spasm and my teeth drop into place, anxious to add their own signature.

A cell phone chimes from his leather jacket. He fishes it out of a pocket and taps on the screen, then his face lights up and he grins.

"Hey, I gotta go. Nice meeting you. See you around." He stands and shrugs into his jacket.

"Uh, sure." But before I can gather my thoughts to ask for his number, he's out the front door.

I jump up to follow him. When I step outside, a steel-grey Maserati sedan with blacked-out windows is pulling away from the curb, and the guy is nowhere in sight.

As the car recedes in the distance, I want to scream, to say, "Come back! Please, come back!"

But I don't.

Only one thing would've sparked that light in his eyes when he received the phone call. That light is one I've seen before, up close, intimate.

It's the fevered response from a donor who's about to relish the pleasure of giving himself to a Chosen.

A flood of emotions rolls over me as I recall my own pleasure at both giving and taking blood, and Nicolas's savage embraces when he made Chosen love to me.

Despair slithers through me, molasses-thick, and my body sags beneath its weight. I lean against the side of the building and hug myself, fighting back the bloodtears while the image of bright emerald eyes seeps into my mind.

Oh God, Nicolas. I miss you so much.

"Hey, are you all right?" A male voice just a few feet away breaks through my misery. He's human, and the copper-rich smell of his blood is mouthwatering.

I wave him off without looking at him and push away from the building. Hands in my pockets, I shuffle along the filthy sidewalk toward my car. The night sounds of San Francisco surround me—distant sirens, the constant hum of traffic, sitcom laughter from TVs in cramped apartments. My sense of alienation increases.

It's not just Nicolas I miss. I miss being able to talk with someone without noticing the scent of their blood, without worrying about losing control, without fearing I'll kill them.

As much as I hate to admit it, my need for companionship seems to have grown since I finished the Change. Desperation to end this loneliness fuels my search for The Chosen nearly as much as my longing for Nicolas.

But they are here. I know that now. That tattooed guy's scent is engraved in my mind, and it's only a matter of time and patience before I track him down.

# WEDNESDAY

## CHAPTER 38

The silver filigree locket looks so innocent and delicate nestled on the white cotton in its little white box.

But it, and the ammunition I'm placing inside it, will hopefully prove a powerful deterrent against the one trait of Chosen physiology giving me the most trouble.

It's a trait I'd long envied, admiring its potential effectiveness for my style of hunting. And when I became full Chosen, in spite of my outward horror, I was secretly thrilled to finally possess my own.

Fangs.

Twin daggers of pleasure for me, and piercing death for my prey.

There's nothing so satisfying as sinking them into a soft throat, reveling in that burst of passion as they slip into a hot pulsing vein and release its liquid bliss. I feel complete at that moment, the moment of being truly what I was meant to be. They're more than just deadly weapons in my hunting arsenal. They define what I am in no uncertain terms, and those years of searching for myself and where I fit into the world ended with their aching emergence.

However, right now, they are a complete pain in the ass.

They seem to function independent of me, reacting to any stray scent at the most inopportune moments, and refusing to retract when I most need them to. I feel like a teenage boy whose body—specifically one part—has a mind of its own anytime a pretty girl walks by.

It used to be bad enough trying to control the two creatures in my head. Now I have to deal with the two in my mouth, and they're proving to be the most difficult to contain.

But I think the locket will do the trick.

I found it in one of San Francisco's many shops catering to hippies, goths, and anyone else with an unconventional lifestyle. About three-quarters of an inch in size on a long silver chain, the locket back is solid silver, with a tiny hinge on one side. The open filigree pattern on the front is vaguely Celtic, circling a small red garnet in the center. It's not something I'd normally wear, but if it works like I hope it does, it just might be a lifesaver.

I open it up and insert a tiny piece of the black felt that came with it, then pick up the bottle of essential oil and unscrew the top. My head jerks back as I wave the bottle beneath my nose and the scent of cloves fills my nostrils. I sneeze once, nearly spilling the pungent oil. But a sneeze isn't nearly as bad as the burning from the eucalyptus and camphor oils I'd tested in the store, nor the instant hunger and fang-drop from the patchouli and musk.

And it doesn't reek nearly as bad as the proverbial garlic.

Releasing an amber drop onto the felt from the tiny lid-mounted eyedropper, I load my secret weapon in my war on the fangs, screw the lid back on the bottle, and snap the locket closed. With one last look at my personal silver bullet dangling from its chain, I slip the necklace over my head. The locket settles neatly between my breasts, safely out of the way until I need it. I raise it to my nose for a final test and smile at my involuntary recoil.

~

It's Halloween night. The streets and clubs are filled with witches and zombies and vampires, but no Chosen. If there's any night they'd prowl among the humans, this would be it.

I've spent hours drifting from club to club, searching for the real monsters beneath the elaborate costumes. A silver-sequined mask is my only concession to the holiday, though my hunting blacks and black leather jacket seem to blend in well enough.

Disgusted with my futile quest, I decide to check out the Cat Club for one last look before heading out of the city to hunt.

The place is packed. The pungent clove oil I'd dabbed on my face and throat, reinforced by that in my locket, is doing its job, and though I'm wading through living bodies pulsing with human blood, I'm able to keep my reactions to it at bay.

But I'm having a little more trouble with the mass of flesh pressing against me. Fortunately the music is loud enough to cover the near-constant growl rumbling deep in my chest. My aversion to being touched by humans has increased since I made the Change, and it's taking everything I have not to clear a space around me with fangs and claws.

I spot a gap next to the wall and work my way through the crowd to lay claim to it. A couple to my right dressed as a gothic Raggedy Ann and Andy ease back to give me a little more room and I settle in against the crudely mortared brick.

A black-caped figure to my left turns and regards me with eyes as dark as night. He flashes me a leering grin, his yellowish fangs in sharp contrast to the white of his teeth.

My breath catches, then slowly escapes.

They're fake. His fangs are fake. Plastic.

I'm tempted to show him mine.

Rolling my eyes, I turn away and stare out at the masquerade madness convulsing through the club.

The feel of the air surrounding us abruptly changes. I look toward the door and stop breathing all together.

A stir ripples through the masses as four costumed figures enter, drawing every gaze in the club. Their elegant seventeenth-century garments appear to be the real thing, with details that only my eyes are likely to pick out in the dim light. Two stately females, blonde and auburn curls tumbling to their shoulders beneath wide-brimmed hats, glide into the room, their brocaded gold and ruby gowns sweeping the floor. Two males follow, sporting doublets and matching breeches in indigo and ivory. Their pale faces are bordered with shoulder-length hair, pointed goatees, and wide mustaches, no doubt the fashion of that time.

But it's not the costumes that have stolen my breath.

The air shimmers around each of them in transparent swirls of amber and violet, shot with fine threads of various other colors. I've felt Chosen auras before, but this is the first I've *seen* them. I recognize traces of Nicolas in their feel—these Chosen are of his lineage. *His* lineage. It does not belong to that traitorous bitch, Éva, no matter what she thinks.

I push off from the wall and move toward my quarry.

As one, their haughty gazes shift in my direction and appraise me from across the room. Several lips curl, and the shorter male smiles, and with no further expression, they turn about-face and stroll out of the club.

Elbowing my way through the crowd, I reach the door and shove it open. As I step outside, I run into a broad, black T-shirted chest.

"Excuse me." I start to push past him, but he steps in front of me again.

I look up into golden eyes perched above a hawklike nose and wide cheekbones. Full lips part and tug to one side, allowing me a glimpse of the fang behind them. Crimson flashes in his pupils and I ease back, hands up in surrender.

"Hey, I don't want any trouble." I yank off my mask and let it fall to the sidewalk.

The costumed Chosen behind him slip into a waiting limousine.

But they're no longer necessary—not with this one standing barely three feet away.

I just hope he doesn't intend to kill me.

He's studying me, his arms now folded across his chest. Thick wrists each bear a wide silver cuff, Native American in design. His skin is an odd color, reddish-brown with a dusky undertone, and his black hair is pulled back into a braid. He's tall, about six-five, a little taller than Nicolas. But much broader, more muscular.

An aura dances around his body in shades of deep forest green. It feels strange.

He's not of Nicolas's lineage.

I move out of the doorway and notice a pair of Harleys parked at the curb. One of them holds a beefy, leather-jacketed biker with wild, curly red hair and a matching beard. He grins. His fangs aren't plastic, either. A bright russet aura hovers about him like a glove, bearing no hint of Nicolas.

A chocolate-skinned waif pokes her head out from behind his back, hazel eyes shining above a wide smile, then she scrambles down off the bike. Clad in brown chaps and a dark green leather jacket, she saunters toward us, cleaning her nails with a small dagger. She's no more than four-foot-five, maybe four-six, a petite pixie with a mop of kinky hair the same chocolate color as her skin. Her energy, absent any trace of Nicolas, glimmers a deep purple.

A child? The Chosen would bring someone so young into this life?

Her jacket swings open to reveal a pair of perky breasts beneath a pale green tank top, startling me as I realize this is no child.

My gaze returns to the silent Chosen in front of me. Something about his scent tugs at me, something familiar, but I can't place it. His golden brown eyes bore into mine and red flashes within their depths again, accompanied by a low growl and a masculine desire I can taste as though his blood runs in my veins.

Alarmed, I take another step back.

"So, Taz, has she said anything yet, or is she as tight-lipped as you?" The tiny Chosen's birdlike voice carries a hint of French, or Spanish, or both. She drags the tip of her blade across his massive, denim-covered thigh as she walks past him, and I'm struck again by how big this red-skinned Chosen is.

I tear my gaze from him and look down at the childlike female now standing before me.

Opting for my current alias, I offer a half bow and introduce myself. "My name is Sonya."

"Chia. And this here's Taz. That's Redd." She waves the dagger toward the obvious bearer of that name.

"So, Sonya. What're you doing here?" Chia pricks her fingertip with the dagger. A drop of blood wells and she sticks her finger in her mouth and sucks on it as her green-flecked hazel eyes scrutinize me.

Against my will, I glance back up at Taz. He takes a deep breath and I can't help but notice the size of his biceps. He could crush me with little effort.

"I'm looking for someone."

"I can see that." Her sarcasm breaks the spell and I look back down at her. "But I'm pretty sure this big Indian's out of your league. You're a little too prissy for him. He likes it rough, don't ya, Taz?"

"Shut up, Chi," he growls, glaring at me. "Who you looking for?"

The question, though logical, catches me off guard. I'd expected to deal with Chosen of Nicolas and Alina's lineage. I'm not sure what to reveal to these "foreign" Chosen.

"The Chosen who got in the limo—who were they?" I ask, avoiding his question. My chances of getting to Alina might be better through them.

Taz's large frame suddenly looms over me, reeking with the promise of violence.

"*Who* are you looking for?" he repeats, his menacing tone underscored by red-lit eyes.

Wrong approach, asshole.

"It's none of your business." I glare up at him through a scarlet veil. "We're done here."

I turn to leave and nearly trip over Chia. Her blazing eyes and bared fangs transform the pixie into a diminutive demon from hell. She hisses and crouches as though to spring, nails and dagger ready.

The burly red-haired Chosen materializes behind Chia.

"Come now, lass. Sonya, is it? You surely don't want to piss *her* off." A faint Scottish brogue accents his words as he gestures down at her with his thumb. "She might be just a wee Creole, but she can fight like the Devil himself. I'll not go against her."

Outweighed and outnumbered, I clench my fists and suppress a snarl.

"I'm looking for . . . Alina Dăneşti."

The Scot lets out a booming laugh. Chia relaxes her aggressive posture, but only a little.

"Are ye now? And what business might ye have with her?" He hooks his thumbs into his jeans' pockets and tips his head. His eyes are russet brown, and his freckled skin, though pale, still bears a faint ruddy hue. A broad nose rests above his thick red mustache and beard.

"It's personal." I smile at him, hoping he's the leader of this group.

Taz, standing behind me, snorts. Chia growls and spits on the sidewalk.

The ringing of a cell phone breaks our little standoff. Redd pulls it out of his jacket pocket.

"Yeah?" He pauses, listening. "Yeah, it's under control. We'll wait here." He shoves the phone back in his pocket and looks up past me. "We gotta roll."

"You go on. I'll take her back to the house." Taz grabs my arm.

My other one flashes out with nails extended. I growl and spin out of his grasp, leaving him with four bleeding lines across his cheek. The wounds seal up immediately.

Ignoring the snarls behind me, I stare into those golden eyes. To his credit, he makes no move to touch either his cheek, or me.

"I'm not going anywhere with you."

He grunts.

"Suit yourself." Taz turns and saunters toward the bikes. A long ebony braid swings against his broad back.

I fold my arms and glance at Redd as he passes. Chia skips behind him, then turns and walks backward, grinning at me as she motions with the dagger across her throat.

Taz pulls on a half-shell helmet and a pair of sunglasses, and straddles the sleek black chopper, kicking it to life with one stroke. Its thundering sound echoes off the buildings, reminding me of Nicolas' Cobra. Redd mounts his bike, its twin tanks and fenders gleaming a burnt orange in the moonlight. Chia hands him a half-helmet and puts on her own, then climbs up and vanishes behind his bulk. The big Scot steps down on the kickstarter and his Harley adds its roar to the first one.

A limo slowly cruises by. It looks like the same one the costumed Chosen disappeared into only a moment ago. The window lowers briefly and I catch a glimpse of blonde curls framing a delicate pale face. Redd, sporting dark glasses along with his helmet, salutes the car, turns on his headlight, and shifts the bike into gear. Chia shoots me the middle finger as they take off after the limo.

I look at Taz sitting on his Harley, arms crossed, waiting.

No real choice here. I've been searching too long for any sign of The Chosen to pass this up.

Swallowing my pride, I walk over to the rumbling machine.

"I'll follow you in my car."

Taz pulls off his glasses and gives me a hard stare.

"Not gonna work that way. Get on." He jerks his thumb over his shoulder, pointing to the backless seat behind him.

"What if I'd rather not?"

His harsh laugh indicates I probably don't want to find out.

"Thought you wanted to find Alina."

That I do.

With a deep breath, I nod and climb on behind him.

# CHAPTER 39

Taz jerks the bike into gear and I'm forced to grab onto him to keep from falling off. My body lurches with every shift as we make our way through the steep city streets. Racing up the freeway on-ramp, the Harley's throaty sound is the only thing I can hear over the rushing wind.

I try not to lean too close to his back, but every time he speeds up to cut through the traffic, I have to tighten my grip on his waist or risk becoming pavement splatter. Besides being scared shitless, pressing against so much *male* has me more off-balance than his accelerations, and I curse my rebellious body as it yearns for more.

The lights of San Francisco sparkle in the dark water below as we cross the Golden Gate Bridge north out of the city on the 101. Not knowing where we're headed has me a bit unsettled. But it seemed as though Taz and his friends work with who I assume to be Alina's Chosen, and I can only hope my decision to go with the big Indian wasn't a fatal one.

We haven't been traveling long when Taz takes the off-ramp for Highway 1 and Mill Valley. Streetlights flash by as we rumble through the town, and after we make several turns, we're abandoned to the Harley headlight and occasional bright spots from the porches and windows of the houses strung along the road.

The smell of oak woodlands fills my nostrils and some of the tension drains away, only to be replaced by the twist of hunger.

Wonder how easy it'll be to slip away for a little hunting expedition.

The motorcycle slows, then veers onto a darkened lane. We pass several houses before turning down a tree-lined driveway. An older one-story with a covered porch and peeling white paint flickers in and out of the Harley's bouncing light, and as we approach, the garage door opens. I chuckle at the rusted hulks of several old cars peeking out between dead weeds in the front and side yards.

Not exactly what I expected for a Chosen country manor.

Taz rolls to a stop inside the garage and kills the engine. I climb off and glance around, noting several motorcycles in various stages of assembly, the walls and shelves lined with tool boxes, and even the obligatory biker babe posters and calendars stuck on nails to the unfinished drywall.

Just like any biker garage.

Leaning the Harley onto its kickstand, Taz swings his leg over the seat, takes off his helmet, and hangs it from the handlebar. He drops his sunglasses into the helmet and presses a button near the grip. The garage door creaks to a close.

With a sidelong look, he gestures toward a grease-smudged door bearing a sign in bold letters that state, NOT AN EXIT. Smoothing back my wind-whipped hair, I walk past him.

"Nice tits," he says, his voice low.

I whirl and glare at him.

"You don't need to be looking at them."

Fleeting surprise lights up his face, then his eyes narrow, followed by a one-sided smile.

"Didn't have to. Felt them against my back the whole way here. And now that you mention it, they do look as nice as they feel."

"Screw you." I turn back toward the door.

He chuckles.

"Anytime."

"Don't flatter yourself." I reach for the doorknob, only to discover it's locked. Crossing my arms, I wait while Taz produces a key and opens the door. My blood is boiling and thoughts of ripping that smug look from his face flit through my mind.

"After you," he says, smirking.

The kitchen we walk into hasn't been cleaned in a very long time. A roasting pan filled with black oil and small motor parts sits on the greasy stove, and it's hard to tell what color the ancient linoleum floor used to be. Tools and nuts and bolts litter the dusty counters. But the grime-encrusted sink is empty, and there's not a dirty dish or beer can in sight.

Definitely a Chosen kitchen, in spite of the mess.

"Remind me to get the name of your housekeeper," I mutter.

Taz grunts and ushers me on ahead past the dining area and into the living room, which isn't in any better shape than the kitchen.

A parts-strewn coffee table takes up the center of the room. Several large floor pillows occupy a corner and a big-screen TV uses most of one wall. Two long couches and an upholstered chair, all covered by an assortment of dirty blankets, line the remaining walls. The corner of one blanket on the couch below the window has slipped down, exposing the fabric beneath.

Bloodstained fabric.

An image surges into my mind, an image of Taz entwined about a woman on the couch, his fangs buried in her neck. Electricity ripples across my skin and into my upper jaw. Shocked, I look away, gums aching. I don't know if my reaction is from the idea of feeding on a human, or the unexpected vision of *him* moving against her, but neither is acceptable.

I shake my head to clear it and survey the rest of the room. There's nothing else to indicate that the occupants of this house might be something other than low-class human trash.

These Chosen are certainly nothing like Nicolas and his Elders. Guess you can't escape your roots, no matter what you feed on.

"You still sleep?" His gruff voice startles me and I nearly jump out of my skin. I turn to find him leaning against the small dining room table, its surface behind him covered with repair manuals, biker magazines, and stacks of mail.

"Yeah."

"You can crash on one of the couches. No one will bother you."

I nod.

Taz pushes off from the table and ambles past me to the front door. He opens it and turns to look back at me.

"Stay here. If you leave, I will find you." The cold light in his eyes and hard set of his mouth promises that if he does find me, things might get a little unpleasant between us.

I hate being told what to do.

But rebelling won't get me to Alina, so I just need to bide my time. If it turns out these assholes aren't going to help, I'm outta here. And I guarantee that big bastard won't be able to stop me.

His hawkish stare drills into me a moment longer, then with no further word, he stalks out the front door, slamming it behind him.

# CHAPTER 40

I listen for the garage to open, for the roar of his bike. But the lengthening silence indicates he left on foot.

Maybe he's going to visit a neighbor for a late-night snack.

A glance at my cell phone indicates the sun will be rising soon. Since it seems like no one's here, I decide to have a look around.

The first thing I notice is that, in contrast to the garage, the walls of the rooms I've seen so far are bare, as well as those of the hallway stretching off to my right.

It makes me a little sad. Most homes have at least a few photographs out on display. Guess if you've outlived your family, you wouldn't want those reminders around anymore.

I wander down the hallway and stop at the open doorway on the right. The bathroom. It contains normal toiletry items—towels, soap, combs, toothbrushes. The last makes me laugh as I visualize Redd and Taz brushing their fangs.

The sight of the mirror draws me farther inside. Recalling the colorful auras cloaking The Chosen, I peer at the edges of my reflection, straining to see a glimmer of my own. But no matter how much I stare, or squint, or unfocus my gaze, I cannot see even a hint of one surrounding me. Disappointment deepens into chagrin as my examination settles on the tangled dreadlocks the wind twisted into my hair.

After trying unsuccessfully to pick out the worst of the knots with my fingers, I give up and grab an elastic hair band from a small bowl on the counter. It doesn't look quite so bad in a ponytail, but it's still a mess. Frowning one last time at my auraless image, I continue my exploration.

Across the hall is a narrow laundry room, looking like any laundry room, with a windowed door at the other end leading to the backyard.

The remaining three doors down the hall are closed. I feel guilty snooping, but understanding these Chosen is more important than social politeness. I pause and listen at the first door, then do the same with the two at the end. Sensing no one, I take a chance and turn a doorknob.

A large piece of red-and-green plaid fabric covers the window. Another plaid in green and black, woven with thinner lines of red and white, droops from tacks on the wall, leaving no doubt as to whom this room belongs. Most of it is taken up by an unmade queen-sized bed, its covers spilling to the floor. The laundry piled next to the open closet appears to be migrating across the carpet. A sock and several T-shirts hang from half-open dresser drawers. Biker magazines sliding from stacks against the wall complete the picture.

Redd is a bit of a slob.

Quietly closing the door, I turn to the opposite one.

The large master bedroom is filled with candles and religious icons and wooden masks perched on shelves or hung from the walls. Knives in all sizes accent the displays. A king-sized canopy bed, covered by a deep purple quilt and draped with lavender sheers, occupies the center of an ornate rug. Hanging in the doorway of what must be the bathroom is a lavender-and-purple bead curtain, and next to it a wild rainbow of tiny sleeves peeks from the closet.

Chia. The room has a dark, disturbing feel to it, and I gladly pull the door shut.

My hand starts to turn the doorknob of the last room and stops. Though I peered into the other bedrooms without entering, and felt invasive just doing that, even the thought of opening the door to this one seems like a major trespass.

But this is probably the most important one. Taz, despite a lack of communication skills, appears to be the leader of this little group, and I need to find out what makes him tick.

I ease the door open.

The room is an immaculate island in the clutter and unkempt chaos of this house. A low oak dresser beneath the window and a wooden chair next to the door are the sole pieces of furniture. Neatly laid out in one corner is a huge, shaggy, brown fur. I can only guess that it might be his bed.

In contrast to the stained and filthy carpeting in the rest of the house, the mottled beige carpet in here is clean. Other than a brown quilt covering the window, the walls are bare, devoid of any hint about the occupant's interests, and the closed closet doors offer nothing by which to gauge his wardrobe tastes.

Something on the dresser draws me into the room against my will, and I find myself drifting toward it to get a better look. It's a bundle of silvery sage leaves, its charred end resting in the ashes filling an abalone shell. Beside the shell is an eagle feather fan. The feathers look real, not painted like the ones in the tourist shops.

But what intrigues me most lies next to the fan—a worn copy of an old travel book on Europe. I can't resist picking it up.

The pages are yellowed and dog-eared, and tiny notes scrawl down many of the margins. I carefully flip through the book and, stopping on the page for Paris, begin to read the barely legible handwriting beside the print.

*The City of Love.*

*That's what they call it.*

*Its real name is the City of Pain.*

*I understand now why Angelique was the way she was,*

*and why I'm the way I am.*

*It's in the Blood.*

*And it'll never let me go.*

"Put that down and get the fuck out of my room."

I nearly drop the book. Without looking at Taz, I set it back in its place and walk toward the door. He says nothing as he steps back to let me pass, and my nerves receive another shock, this time from the scent clinging to him, a scent I know all too well.

It's the musky scent of deer blood.

Before I can turn around, the door slams behind me and the deadbolt rams home.

The distant rumble of a Harley brings me back to reality.

I've been curled up on the couch for the last half hour, trying to process what happened in the bedroom. I'm not sure what has me more stunned—that this crude, aggressive Chosen feeds on *deer*, or the glimpse those written words gave me into a tortured soul.

Yet in thinking about the violence that feels as though it will explode from him at any moment, I realize that it hasn't. Not when I slapped him, nor when I initially refused to leave with him, and certainly not when he found me in his room going through his belongings, an offense that might actually merit bodily harm.

The garage door opens and the house vibrates with the thrump-thrump of a Harley engine until the door closes and the motorcycle shuts off. Redd and Chia are laughing as they enter the kitchen.

"Well, look what the cat drug in," Chia says, heading down the hall. "Good. We need a maid around here."

I stare daggers at her retreating back.

Redd pauses at the dining room table, tossing a handful of mail onto the pile in the middle, and shoots me a grin.

"Pay her no mind, lassie. She's harmless. Most of the time." He laughs. "Exceptin', of course, when she's pissed off. Which happens a lot, come to think of it."

"What the fuck!" Her shrill voice echoes through the hallway.

"And I'm guessing she's a wee ticked now. That's my cue to leave." He waves and starts down the hall, only to stop.

"Get outta my way!" Chia shoves past him and storms over to the couch. She glares at me with crimson eyes, her pulsating aura the color of a fresh bruise. "What the fuck were you doing in my room?"

I want to tear out her throat, but force myself to calm down and remain seated. From out of the corner of my eye, I notice Redd slip down the hall.

"I didn't go in."

"Like hell you didn't! Your stink is everywhere!"

"I did not go in. All I did was open the door for a minute. I never went into the room."

"Liar!"

"Easy now, Chi. She's tellin' the truth." Redd crosses the room and places his hands on the tiny shoulders.

"Bullshit. I don't even know why she's up here!"

"Be reasonable, Chi. I checked things out. Her scent isn't anywhere past the doorway."

She snarls at me.

"I still don't want her up here. She should be downstairs. I wanna vote."

Downstairs? Did I miss a door that leads downstairs?

Redd looks at me, shaking his head.

"We only have a few rules around here," he says. "One of them is to stay out of each other's space."

"I'm sorry. I meant no disrespect." I sit up a little straighter. "But I needed to get an idea of my surroundings, and no one was here to explain any rules."

"No one should have to tell you to stay out of people's stuff." Chia looks up at Redd behind her. "I'm serious. Let's vote. *Now*. I want her—"

"She stays up here." Taz's gruff command cuts her off. I didn't even hear him come out of his room.

"Taz—" Chia pleads, turning to him.

"She stays." His face is unreadable. He disappears down the hall and closes his door.

"Redd, that's not fair." Her face screws into a pout and she crosses her arms.

The big Scot shrugs.

And then we all feel it at the same time.

The pull. The inescapable pull into darkness by the rising sun.

"Shit," Chia mutters, then staggers off down the hall, followed by Redd, who waves before stumbling out of view.

Grateful for the interruption, I slip off my jacket, curl back up on the couch, and tug the ratty blanket over me.

Beginning to wish I never got on that damn bike.

# THURSDAY

## CHAPTER 41

Panic jolts me awake and my eyes snap open. I lurch to my feet, growling. Scanning the unfamiliar surroundings, I take in the blanket-covered couches, the engine parts on the coffee table, the big screen TV. Memory clicks into place.

Crap. It wasn't a dream.

Trying to calm my jangled nerves, I listen for sounds of movement. The house is as silent as a tomb, which it kind of is, now that I think about it.

A black quilt over the window blocks out the light well enough that I can't tell what time of day it is. But the hunger in my belly doesn't live by the clock.

And it's informing me that it's time to hunt.

Taz can kiss my ass.

The feel of the three auras hangs in the air, like invisible fog. Cat-footing it to the front door, I quietly unlock it, then ease it open and slip through, snugging it shut behind me. The light of late afternoon greets me as I step off the porch and try to get my bearings.

Mill Valley sits in a cluster of communities strung along the Highway 101 corridor north of the Bay. From what I recall of my internet research, the areas west and north of here are mostly undeveloped, and dotted with state and national parks. They're also filled with a booming population of blacktail deer.

Heading up the driveway, I pick up the pace. At the county road I turn left, traveling in the opposite direction from town and the freeway, and break into a brisk trot. The birds singing and flitting through the brush bring a smile to my face. I savor the scent of oaks and dried grasses lining the roadway, and the tension coiling my muscles begins to unwind. The houses tucked against the road thin, and spotting a promising ravine, I jog up it and into the wooded hills.

ኍ

It's just after dark when I step off the road and start down the driveway. My hunger's feeling pretty satisfied, as much as that's possible with deer. I'd rather have bear, but can't afford to leave their carcasses lying around as I did in the Montana wilderness expecting the carrion eaters to take care of them. There are too many people and not enough big scavengers, and a rash of dead bears would stir up both the rangers and the media.

Taz is leaning against a porch post as the unlit front of the house comes into view, his arms crossed and his expression murderous. He says nothing until I get closer.

"I told you not to leave."

"I don't recall actually agreeing to that."

He straightens and unfolds his arms, hands clenching into fists.

"We need to get a few things straight if you wanna stay healthy."

"Yeah, we do. Like—what *am* I, your prisoner? Cuz I'm not really sure what I'm doing here."

Taz sneers at me.

"You're staying alive, that's what you're doing. And you can keep doing so, as long as you do what you're told."

"Why? Why keep me alive? You still haven't told me why I'm here."

The air whispers and he leans over my face. His eyes, palest gold, glitter with streaks of red in their depths. Surprise creases his brow and he frowns for a split second, his nostrils widening, then his lip curls and an ominous growl rumbles from his chest.

"You waltz into our territory uninvited, a foreigner, prowling our streets, huntin' and leavin' bodies we can't find. And then you have the balls to demand to see the ruling Elder?" His deathly laugh sends a shot of fear up my spine. "You're lucky we didn't take you out the minute you crossed the bridge into the city."

I swallow. And then his words sink in.

"Wait. How long have you known I was here?"

His answering snort tells me just how naïve I was.

Taz eases back.

"Since the night you checked into the motel. Been tracking your every movement for weeks." He shakes his head. "Boy, are you dumb. Pretty. But dumb."

I bristle at the insult.

"So what now? Are you going to take me to see Alina?"

He laughs again.

"No. Not until you tell me why you need to see her so badly."

I'm tempted. But he's not of Nicolas's lineage, and for all I know, might actually be working against Alina. I have no idea if The Chosen in the limo that Redd followed belong to her, or an opposing faction within the lineage.

"Like I said before, my business with her is my own. And as for the bodies you couldn't find, there are none because I didn't leave any. The only hunting I did in the city was for Chosen."

His eyes narrow as he studies me. He takes a breath as though to speak, then stops at the sound of the front door opening.

Light momentarily pierces the surrounding darkness and Chia steps out, wearing an orange tank top beneath her green leather jacket, her kinky chocolate hair surrounding her head like a furry helmet. The moonless night envelops us once again as she shuts the door.

"She came back? Shit. Well, you better put a leash on your pet, Taz, cuz I don't wanna have to look at your mopey face the next time she takes off."

"Shut the hell up, Chi. Give it a rest. Go tell Redd we're gonna jam." He turns and walks toward the garage, long black braid swinging against his leather biker jacket.

Chia wrinkles her nose in a toothy grin, then grabs her crotch and points at me and then Taz, nodding and thrusting her hips. Laughing, she disappears inside the house.

God, she's disgusting.

The garage door machinery hums and clanks and fluorescent light floods the dark driveway. A second later I hear the door to the kitchen open and Redd's laughter. The bikes start, one after another, their twin galloping engines booming from the open garage. Redd rolls out with Chia perched behind him and gives me a thumbs up along with his perpetual grin. Taz follows a second later and gestures me over.

"Get on," he yells over the engine, handing me a black half-helmet that matches the one on his head.

"Where are we going?" I shout back.

"Taking care of 'business.'" He smirks.

I look down at my sweater. Though it's black and I tried to be careful, it's stiff with dried deer blood and it reeks.

"Do you have a shirt I can borrow?"

Taz rolls his eyes, kicks the stand down, and leans the idling bike onto it. Swinging his leg over the seat, he mutters something about "women," and vanishes into the garage. He reappears a few seconds later with a black Metallica T-shirt and my jacket and tosses them to me.

Turning my back on the trio, I'm conscious of their stares as I quickly change. The shirt is huge on me, but at least it doesn't smell of deer. It does smell of him, though, rich and masculine, and triggers all sorts of unwanted feelings, including a flush of desire.

Stupid body.

"Wow, Taz. She's pretty hot. Bet you can't wait to see what the rest of her looks like. I might want some of that myself," Chia hollers, giggling. Redd guns his engine and laughs.

Taz is staring at me curiously when I turn back around, and I remember the silvery scars from the bear—scars that did not disappear when I completed the Change.

I pull my ponytail out from beneath the T-shirt and chuck the sweater into the garage as the door's closing. Shrugging into my jacket, alarm jolts through me and I quickly check my pockets.

They're all empty. No wallet, no cell phone, no keys.

Shit.

Taz is shaking his head when I look up, his mouth tugged into that infuriating half smile. He mouths the word, "Dumb."

Guess he's right. I am dumb.

With a heavy sigh, I step over to the bike, take the helmet from him, and slip it on. Taz settles onto the bike and rocks it upright, nudging the kickstand back into place. I get on behind him as he revs the engine and it answers with a throaty roar.

"Gimme your hands," he yells over his shoulder.

Why do I keep ending up with Chosen males whose only communications with me are in the form of an order? Not that I'm *with* Taz, but he's even worse than Nicolas.

I extend my arms on either side of him, and he grabs them, yanking me forward, and wraps them tightly around his waist.

No way.

But as I start to pull back, he shouts over his shoulder again.

"Stay put. I need you to lean *with* me when I lean, and I don't like your weight jerking this bike all over the road every time I change speed."

That makes sense.

"All right." I squeeze my arms around him to show I get it.

"Good. As long as I can feel those tits in my back, we'll get along fine."

Asshole. I relax my grip a little, but not too much. He might try to dump me off just to prove his point.

Taz turns on the headlight, throws the bike into gear, and we ease up the driveway, tires crunching against the cement. I glance back at Redd, his bike's light weaving back and forth in the darkness as we slowly make our way to the county road.

When we get onto the asphalt, Taz twists the throttle and my body jerks in spite of my hold on his waist. I reluctantly grip him tighter, and he shifts into higher gear again and again, the Harley loudly proclaiming its ownership of the black road stretching before us.

# CHAPTER 42

Taz was right about hanging on. Instead of being scared to death like last night, I feel secure enough I might actually enjoy the ride—if I wasn't also feeling guilty. Embracing his thick, muscular waist feels strange, so different from Nicolas's trim form. But moving and leaning with him in rhythm to the curves has a familiar sensuality to it, and as wonderful as it feels, it also feels wrong to be doing this with *him*.

Bloodtears threaten to well up as I think about Nicolas and holding his powerful, catlike body, and him holding mine, and how well we fit and move together. I miss his sharp kisses, his deep growls of desire, the feel of him taking my blood as I take his, the way his emerald eyes peer into my soul.

I press against the broad, leather-covered back, blindly seeking comfort. God, I have to find Nicolas. Don't know what to do if I don't.

The bike slows and the yellow glare from a stoplight just ahead penetrates my visit to memory hell.

"Everything okay back there?" Taz asks as he brings the bike to a stop.

"Yeah. Fine." I relax my grasp on his waist and ease back to rub the wind-dried bloodtears from my face.

But I'm not fine. I won't be until Nicolas is the one in my arms.

The light turns green and I take hold again as the bike shifts into gear. Buildings from the '40s and '50s line the street of an older downtown area, sheltering businesses closed for the night. We pass one that's not, a corner liquor store with brightly lit windows, then slowly cruise by a row of motorcycles parked rear wheels to the curb in front of a neon-signed bar.

Great. A biker bar. This just gets better and better. Wonder if they're also Chosen.

Taz pulls past an empty space and, stopping, drops his feet to the ground and pushes the bike backward into the spot. Redd backs in beside him, revving his motor before shutting it off. Taz kills his a second later. The sudden silence hurts my ears.

Rock and roll booms through the bar door as it opens. Taz takes off his helmet, then taps the side of my leg.

Though I'm sure he's just signaling me to get off the bike, it feels as if he now thinks he has the right to touch me. I bite back a growl and waste no time dismounting.

Taz dismounts as well and hangs his helmet on the handlebar. I hand him mine and glance over at Redd and Chia as they climb off.

A rough thumb wipes across my temple, startling me. I jerk back and glare at Taz.

"Keep your hands off me." I curl my lip.

"You have blood on your face."

I scrub it with my fingertips.

"Better?" I turn my head side to side.

He puts the tip of his thumb in his mouth and nods, looking thoughtful.

"Couple things before we go in," he says.

"Okay."

"Act human. No fangs. Got it?"

Really? I'm not *that* stupid.

"Yeah. Got it."

"And, unless you want horny scooter trash crawling up your ass all night, you might want to consider acting like you're with me."

"I think I can handle myself."

"That's the problem. When some H.A. grabs your pretty tit and you rip out his throat, it's going to bring us some unwanted attention. We don't want that kind of attention."

Grabs my what? H.A.?

"What's an H.A.?"

"Hells Angel."

Hells Angel? Great. Sounds like we're walking onto some kind of Hollywood movie set.

His mouth tugs to one side as he studies me.

"And try to downplay how much you hate me. Otherwise, it'll just be an advertisement that you're shopping for a new old man."

"I . . . I don't *hate* you."

He snorts.

Redd steps up beside Taz and clears his throat.

"You lovers ready?"

The big Indian frowns and shakes his head, and together they start for the entrance. Chia is already there, waiting. I take a deep breath and follow them.

Taz opens the door and holds it while Chia and Redd pass. He looks at me and I walk on in ahead of him.

A quick glance around the bar reveals everyone is human. Except for us, of course. And the biker garb is real—no Halloween costumes here. My ears, just now recovering from the roar of the motorcycles, are freshly assaulted by the din from dozens of conversations, booming laughter, clacking pool balls, and Lynyrd Skynyrd's "Free Bird" blaring from the jukebox. I pause a moment, overwhelmed, and search the crowd for Redd and Chia. Taz presses against me from behind, and growling under my breath, I quickly step forward. The bar noise lessens to a muted hum, and I can feel the quiet, respectful stares as we walk past.

The little bit of clove oil still clinging to my skin from last night barely mutes the blood scent floating through the air. I focus on staying calm.

Catching sight of Redd's wild hair, I cross the room to a small round table he's claimed against the wall, Taz on my heels. Just as we walk up, Chia plants a kiss on Redd's cheek and heads toward the bar. The conversations around us pick back up again, but at a lower volume than before.

I look at Redd, surprised at her display of affection, the first I've seen, but he ignores me. In fact, his usual jovial expression has been replaced with a scowl that somehow also looks right at home on his bearded face.

Taz, still behind me, puts his hand on my shoulder, but before I can shrug away from him, he leans down and mutters in my ear.

"Try to make it look real."

Frowning, I glance around the room and realize we are still on center stage. My muscles tighten at the sea of human faces, mostly male, looking in our direction, lingering over *me*.

Maybe he's right.

I nod in agreement.

He strolls around in front of me, then reaches into his back pocket and takes out his wallet, its thick chain anchored to a belt loop. He pulls out a twenty.

"Why don't you go get us some beers."

Biting my lip at yet another order, I take the money. As I start to move off, his arm drifts out and he squeezes my ass.

I freeze. As casual as possible, I turn around and reach up as though to hug him. He leans down and I whisper into his ear.

"You do that again and I'll tear off your hand, human witnesses or not. Are we clear?"

I lean back and lift a corner of my lip and stare directly into those golden eyes.

He sucks air in through his teeth, his gaze drifting downward and resting on my chest.

"You want a piece of me, you're gonna have to wait until we get home." A smile flits across his face as he looks back up. "Honey."

Oh, he is such an ass.

I whirl around and stalk to the bar. Spotting a gap between a couple of bikers, I lean in and rest my hand on the bar, the folded bill between my fingers like a raised flag. The barkeep, talking with someone at the other end of the bar, looks over at me. He continues talking.

Great. Recalling my own bartending days, I decide to cut him some slack and settle in to wait.

"Hey, sweetcheeks. Why don't you let me buy your drink."

The voice is from the guy to my left—early twenties, medium height and build, wearing a denim cutoff vest over a white T-shirt. His dark blond hair is to the base of his neck and curled behind his ears. He's kind of cute, in a rogue, puppyish way. But the scar on his face and those on his knuckles reveal his puppyhood was left behind long ago.

The hunger stirs at the blood scent rising from the kid's skin. My gums pulse.

"No, I don't think so. My . . . my old man wouldn't like it." I half-turn and look at Taz, who's staring intently at us. The kid glances over his shoulder, looks back at me, and shrugs. He takes a drink, but not before I notice the alarm flickering in his blue eyes.

"Offer's open if you want to trade up."

His juvenile bravado, though somewhat charming, makes me laugh, and I turn back to the bar in time to see the bartender finally wandering in my direction.

"What'll ya have, sweetheart?" he asks, as though he's doing me a favor by even talking to me.

God, is this how all bikers speak to women? I'd love to show him just how much of a sweetheart I really am, fangs and all.

"Four Coronas."

He steps away without a word, presumably to get the beers.

Jerk.

While I'm waiting, I look down the bar and notice Chia sitting on a stool chatting with some biker chick, a brunette. They laugh, but Chia's eyes hold a predatory glow in them that I recognize.

It's the seductive fire of a Chosen on the hunt.

An aching spasm in my upper jaw releases my fangs and they descend as excitement prickles throughout my body. Everything turns pink.

Shit.

I slam my eyes closed and rub my mouth, trying to retract the damn fangs while fighting to maintain control.

"That'll be eighteen bucks."

I hand the bartender the twenty without looking at him.

"Keep the change," I mutter through my hand. I take a chance and, opening my eyes, stare at the floor. At least my vision is clear now. But I can still feel the sharp points of my hunting teeth. Stupid things.

I look back at Chia, but she's gone. And so is the brunette.

That only makes things worse. I stare at the four bottles of Corona, green wedges of lime poking out of their tall necks, my teeth aching and my mind spinning.

Get your shit together, girl. This is not the place to lose it.

Remembering my necklace, I pull it from beneath the T-shirt and clutch it under my nose. The sharp clove scent sears my nostrils and the tension in my gums eases. The fangs slide back into place.

God, this sucks. Being around these other Chosen who feed on humans is pushing me way too close to the edge.

I wrap my fingers around the bottles, turn, and weave through the crowd back to our table. Taz's golden-eyed stare accompanies me the whole way.

As I set the bottles on the table and let out my breath, I notice Redd is gone.

"You havin' a moment over there? I wasn't sure if you were gonna eat that punk kid or gut the bartender." Taz's low voice doesn't hide its sharp disdain. "We can't afford any problems."

"I'm *fine*."

"Good." Taz picks up a beer and takes a small swig, then grins. "Your old man, huh? There's a nice dark alley out back if you—"

"You need to get over yourself. Where's Redd and Chia?"

"That's not your concern."

But as he answers, I spot Redd standing outside the women's bathroom. I see no sign of Chia. Or the brunette.

A chill runs across my scalp. God, I hope she's not killing that girl.

My gut twisting, I cross the room and grab the bathroom door handle.

"I wouldn't go in there if I was you, lassie."

I ignore Redd and pull the door open.

Chia is sitting on the counter, her arms and legs wrapped around the brunette standing before her, teeth buried in the girl's throat. They're both moaning. Chia's scarlet eyes fly open to glare at me. She releases her bite hold and hisses, her mouth and fangs dripping blood down the girl's leather jacket.

My own fangs drop again and violent hunger surges in my belly. Redd pushes the door shut, mercifully shutting off my reddened view of the tiny Chosen and her prey.

"Just to warn you, she doesn't share. For such a wee thing, she has a monstrous appetite." He grins, pink highlighting his pupils.

"She's not going to kill her, is she?"

"Would it bother you if she did, lass?" The edge in his voice sobers me right up.

I hesitate, searching for the answer least likely to get me dead. As in *really* dead.

"It's . . . it's none of my business." I drop my gaze to the floor in submission, then turn my back on him and head to the table.

Feeling battered by the repeated assaults on my control, I ignore Taz and take a seat. The clamor and bustle of the packed room seem distant, unreal.

Running with killers. Great. Don't know why I'm surprised. Taz was right—I am dumb.

I just want to find Nicolas. And if it means playing this out with Taz and his buddies, so be it.

Welcome to The Game, Sunny.

# CHAPTER 43

I'm still lost in my thoughts, staring across the crowded bar without actually seeing it, when Taz's chair scraping beside mine jolts me back to reality. He stands and I look up as Redd approaches the table. He stops halfway across the room and his beard twitches beneath a fleeting smile.

Taz touches my shoulder.

"Stay here."

I nod without looking at him, and then his lips are against my ear.

"We will hunt you down if you run. That's what we do, and we're very good at it."

Icy fear flashes through me at his chilling words, and it finally sinks in that I might not stand a chance against this seasoned trio.

"Got it." I keep my voice neutral.

"Good."

Taz straightens and walks across the room toward Redd, that black braid swinging against his leather jacket. The gaze of nearly every woman in his path fastens hungrily on him as he passes and I chuckle at the glowering expressions of their male companions.

He is pretty hot, for an asshole. But then, I haven't encountered any Chosen who weren't alluring in some way to humans. Even Redd earns appreciative glances as the two of them make their way through the pool table room in the back and outside to the smoking area.

They disappear and I can almost hear a collective sigh from the women. Shaking my head, I slowly study the room, noting that most of the bikers are in their thirties or older. They orbit around tables dotted with empty glasses and bottles, fresh drinks in hand, deep in conversations both serious and not. Their women shadow the men, sometimes as silent observers; in other circles, they've gravitated together to hold their own private discussions off to the side.

A group in the far corner sparks my curiosity. They wear an intensity about them not unlike that of The Chosen, a mantle of natural power that places them above the rest. One of them leaves the others and heads to the bar, exposing the back of his black leather vest.

Arching red letters on a white background spell out *Hells Angels* over a golden-winged skull and a small *MC*. The logo is cradled by *Oakland* in a reverse-arch at the bottom.

Taz wasn't kidding.

As the Angel walks up to the bar, I notice Chia perched on a stool talking to the young blond biker who'd offered to buy me a drink. My eyes scan the other barstools, and some of my tension drains away at the sight of the brunette from the bathroom. She looks a bit pale after her encounter with the little Chosen, but otherwise healthy. Well, at least alive.

Redd was right about Chia. She's on the hunt again, and the young biker looks to be her next course. She laughs at something he says, and as he leans toward her, she reaches out and rubs his crotch. His eyes widen and he grins as she slides off the barstool. She shoots him a backward glance and struts toward the front door. The puppy's after her in a half second, and they're both laughing as they walk outside. An image of their bodies writhing together, her fangs deep in his throat, leaps unbidden into my mind.

My gums throb. And all around me—

—human nectar pulses beneath fragile skin, beckoning, calling

—dozens of hearts pound, pound, pound in a hypnotic rhythm

—the rich, intoxicating scent of coppery-sweet blood caresses my face, my tongue, my soul

Fiery craving detonates through every cell. Everywhere I look, exposed throats beam an invitation. The room before me turns red as the fangs slam into place, and the driving urge to bite robs me of all thought.

I rush to the bathroom, not knowing where else to go.

Turning on the faucet drowns out the sound, and the stink of bathroom and pungent soap masks the smell. I cram the clove necklace against my nose and try to focus on something, anything, besides the living current of blood on the other side of the door. But it doesn't stop the craving.

Mouth aching, a sense of desperation takes hold. I need to bite . . .

I yank back my jacket sleeve and bury the damn fangs into my trembling forearm.

Pain, along with revulsion at the taste of my own blood, puts an end to that solution. Disgusted with myself, I catch my reflection in the mirror. The red-eyed monster, lips and bared teeth stained with blood, horrifies me. I shove my face under the running water.

The shock of the cold water does the trick. My gums spasm, then relax and the fangs slowly retract. I scrub my face a moment, turn off the water, and grab a paper towel. Drying off, I look back up into the mirror, exhausted. But my vision is clear and my teeth back in place.

Damn. Haven't felt like that—well, I've never felt quite like that. The beast and its violent urges always seemed *separate* from me, something I had to master and control through mental domination. Its rage was never mine.

But this . . . this was all me, and I had no clue how to stop it.

I take a deep breath, still a little shaky. The sharp craving has died down to a dull hunger, but it's nothing I can't manage. I hope.

Examining my reflection again, a laugh tumbles out at the strands of hair that have worked themselves loose from the elastic band. They frame my face, sticking out in every direction like Medusa's snakes. They certainly gave the monster in the mirror a nice finishing touch.

A quick tug on the hair tie frees the rest of my hair. It's hopelessly tangled from the bike ride—no wonder Taz wears his in a tight braid. I smooth it back the best I can, wrap the band back around it, and take one last gulp of bathroom air before heading back out into the bar.

Thank God Taz isn't back at the table yet. Don't feel like explaining anything to him. I settle into my chair to wait, hoping we can get the hell out of here before something else happens. Necklace clutched against my nose, I stare at the floor and focus on the ZZ Top song booming from the jukebox, and long for the carefree nights on my Colorado mountain.

~

A disturbance in the air at the far end of the bar catches my attention. Redd appears from the back room, wiping the beard around his mouth and bearing a satisfied gleam in his eyes. A single spot of blood, no bigger than a pea, stains the front of his denim shirt. Taz strides along behind him, his expression devoid of any emotion.

But as they reach the table, I sense conflict boiling within him. His flickering gaze is hungry, and I wonder why Redd didn't stand guard for him as he obviously did for the big Scot.

Unless he doesn't feed on humans.

The possibility astounds me.

"You seen Chi?" he asks in a clipped tone.

"Yeah. She headed out the front door with that young biker from the bar, the one who was talking to me."

Redd's eyebrows raise as Taz's face creases into a frown. Unspoken concern fills the glances they exchange with one another.

"Let's go. Now." Taz turns and heads for the door, Redd close behind him.

I hustle, catching up with them as they step outside. Several bikers are standing around the entrance, talking in low tones. Taz scents the air, then sets a restrained pace for the corner at the end of the block, Redd and I on his heels. Once we reach it and make the turn onto the side street, away from the view of the bikers, he breaks into a run. Redd and I speed up, but lose him as he veers into a small parking area lining the alley behind the buildings.

Spotting his silhouette near several dumpsters against the stucco wall, I see him, one-handed, pick up a small figure by the jacket. Redd leaps toward them, landing next to Taz.

"Put her down, bro."

The harsh glare from the spotlight mounted high on the wall throws shadows across the carved angles of Taz's face. Blazing red eyes pierce the darkness, and his sharp fangs gleam in the fragmented spotlight beam. Chia squirms in his grip, hissing and scowling at him with the same red-filled eyes, her claws raking the powerful arm holding her.

"I said, put her down. Bro." Redd moves. The slender point of a Scottish dirk presses against Taz's throat.

Taz snarls and gives her a shake, then opens his hand. Chia drops to the asphalt and springs away. She stays a half-dozen feet behind Redd, growling, her fist clenched around her own tiny dagger.

The big Indian shoots Redd an ugly look, then turns and crouches down between the dumpsters.

A still form lies in the shadows. Taz probes the unbitten side of his throat, swearing softly under his breath.

"Is he alive?" asks Redd, peering over Taz's shoulder.

"Barely." He stands and glances over at Chia, who's now pacing, the anger on her face slowly giving way to fear.

Taz looks at me.

"Kill that light," he says, pointing at the spotlight. "Then go stand at the edge of the parking lot. If anyone tries to come back here, stop them. Distract them, fuck them, I don't care what you do. As long as you act human and keep them from coming back here."

Nodding, I scan the ground for something to throw at the spotlight. A large bolt next to the dumpster provides the perfect missile. Fortunately, my body hasn't forgotten its teenage years spent throwing softballs, and I take out the light with the first shot.

I assume my post near the street, listening for approaching footsteps.

Taz turns to Redd.

"You know what to do. He don't have much time."

Redd nods, drops to one knee next to the unconscious biker, and rolls back his sleeves. Shock doesn't begin to describe my reaction when he plunges his nails into his other wrist. He keeps them there, holding the wound apart, and pinches the biker's jaw open with his dripping hand. Placing his wrist against the young man's mouth, Redd massages his arm, forcing out the blood.

"C'mon, ya dumb bastard. Drink up."

The kid suddenly chokes. Redd yanks his arm away as the kid coughs a couple times, then watches as he fades back into unconsciousness. Redd slices his wrist a second time and presses it against the bloody mouth. I can't tell if the kid is swallowing, but when he reaches up to grab the Scot's arm, Redd pulls it away. He leans back on his heels as the young biker passes out again.

Chia leans over to look at the boy, then looks guiltily up at Taz.

"Sorry, Taz. I just got carried away. You know how it is."

"I told you no more."

"I know. I been real good lately." She looks away, her mouth quivering as her eyes fill with bloodtears. "Haven't killed no one for a long time. Too long . . ."

"That's no—"

"Leave her be, Taz. We got bigger problems."

"What now?" He turns back to Redd.

Redd's moved the kid closer to the wall. He rolls the unconscious biker onto his stomach.

On the back of his denim vest are the red letters *MC* and *Oakland* in a familiar reverse arch near the bottom hem.

"Aw, hell." Taz whips around to stare at Chia. "He's a fuckin' H.A. prospect. You stupid—"

"Taz! Enough. What's done is done. Leave her be." Redd rolls the biker onto his back, lifts him by the front of the blood-stained vest, and props him to sit up against the wall. He holds his fingers beneath the prospect's nose a moment, then straightens.

"He's breathing okay. But he might have a few questions when he wakes up," he says, stepping away.

"That'll be his problem. I'm more worried about who might've seen him leave with Chia. Can't afford to stir up that hornet's nest—don't want anyone stickin' their nose into our business."

Taz's mouth presses into a thin line before continuing.

"Here's how this is gonna go down. Chi, you clean up your mess. Redd, you get your bike. When Chia's done, she'll meet you at the other end of the alley. Head to the Shell station next to the freeway—we'll meet you there."

"You sure? Not too fond of splittin' up, especially if any of the H.A. wander back here lookin' for their prospect."

Taz snorts.

"They see Chi come back by the bar without him, they're *gonna* come looking for him, and we'll get the blame when they find him. It's best if you two just vanish. Now get on with it, Chi." Taz looks pointedly at her.

She sighs and nods, then sidles past him. Squatting next to the biker, she slashes her fingertips with the dagger, then rubs them across the kid's neck. She watches a moment as his torn flesh heals, then stands.

"It's done." Chia licks her dagger and rejoins Redd, her expression pouty.

"All right." Redd drapes his arm over her shoulders. "See you in a few. Stay safe, bro."

Taz grunts and watches them make their way down the alley, then turns toward the unconscious biker sitting against the wall. Taz positions the dumpsters to better hide the kid and, shaking his head, walks toward me.

"I'm going to the liquor store across the street. You still need to keep him from being seen. I'll be back in minute."

I nod and stuff my hands in my pockets, then lean against the building, watching him walk away.

His long stride has an easy rhythm to it, like that of a cheetah strolling across the African plains. He baffles me. He'd been furious with Chia—enough so that Redd felt compelled to protect her. His insistence on saving the life of her human victim only provides further contradiction to the monster he appears to be. But I have no clue whether his actions were from the innate need to avoid exposure or some moral code to which he adheres.

Disgusted with my growing curiosity about him, I shift my focus to the music and talk and laughter drifting through the night air. A stray breeze sends plastic wrappers and bits of paper fluttering across the dirty asphalt, accompanied by the putrid scents of burning pot and cigarettes. A resounding burp from the back patio of the bar echoes down the alley, triggering loud cheers and jeers.

Sure glad we're leaving. I've had enough of humans—and Chosen—for one evening. A hunt before sunrise is quickly becoming mandatory.

Taz will have a real fight on his hands if he tries to stop me.

# CHAPTER 44

My confidence wilts as I watch the big Indian walk back across the street carrying a paper bag, his expression stern. When he reaches me, he pulls out a bottle of Captain Morgan rum and a black bandana.

"Clean up his face and neck, and make sure Chia got rid of her mark. Leave the rest—it's better if his friends believe the blood on his hands and clothes is someone else's."

Me? There's no way I can handle this. I'll probably bite the kid myself.

But the tone of Taz's voice tells me I better try.

Just wanting to get the hell out of here, I keep my mouth shut and take the bottle and bandana from his outstretched hand. I slip between the dumpsters and stare down at the biker, the bloodlust hovering on the edge of my senses. Opening the rum, I take a mouthful and hold it. The stinging liquid sears my gums and, with a big whiff of the clove necklace, I tip the bottle against the bandana and set to work wiping off the blood as fast as possible. The kid's chest rises and falls quietly, but other than that, he doesn't move.

As I shift him to clean up the back of his neck, I discover another set of fang marks.

The two ragged holes are still seeping and my fangs ache to make their own. I spit out the rum.

"Taz . . ."

He bends over me and touches the holes.

"Shit. Well, get rid of them." He straightens. "If you can."

His eyes narrow as he folds his arms and studies me.

If I can? Does that mean I might not be able to? Why doesn't he do it? I've never tried to heal a wound this way. In fact, I've never tried to heal anyone—other than Sandy—but I don't want to tell *him* that.

Jaw clenched, I use my nails to slice open the vein in my wrist and jam my fingertips into it. The laceration heals as I withdraw them, and I quickly dab my blood on the kid's wounds, remembering how Chia did it.

The blood-smeared holes appear to vibrate, then slowly start shrinking until their edges meet. They seal shut, and red fades to pink, then fades to . . . nothing. The marks vanish without a sign of ever being there.

Wow. That's pretty amazing.

"You done yet?"

"Yeah." I wipe the last trace of blood from the pale skin.

Taz leans over my shoulder and silently inspects my handiwork. He then stoops beside me, takes the rum, and sloshes it on the biker's clothes. Prying open the kid's mouth, he splashes a little inside, then sets the half-empty bottle next to the wall. He checks the kid's pulse and breathing, then stands.

"Let's go."

When I get to my feet and glance at him, he's staring at me, his expression speculative. He slowly reaches toward my chest. I hold my ground, ready to sink my claws into his face. But he only grabs my necklace. He leans in and smells it. His lip curls as he recoils, and with a grunt, Taz releases the silver chain.

"Who are you from?" he says, brow furrowed.

"I beg your pardon?"

"Who's your Maker?"

The age-old question. I shake my head and give him a bemused grin. But as I'm about to tell him that I don't know, Éva's warning from her "schooling" session rings in my head.

Never reveal your weaknesses.

And not knowing to whose lineage I belong is a definite disadvantage in this struggle for dominance that Chosen call The Game.

"It's not your business," I answer. Frowning, I walk past him and he latches onto my arm.

"I'm making it my business."

I wrench out of his grasp, stuff the bloody bandana into the dumpster, and start walking toward the sidewalk.

"Thought we needed to get out of here and meet up with Redd."

He mutters a curse, then his footsteps are beside mine.

"We'll settle this later."

Whatever.

We walk side by side, mute and angry. But before we reach the corner, he stops.

"Need you to do something."

Crossing my arms, I turn around to look at him.

"Sure seems like I'm doing a lot for you."

"Just shut up and listen. We're gonna walk by the front of that club, and I don't want anyone wondering if we had anything to do with that prospect when they find him. So I need you to do a little play acting." He holds out the paper bag from the liquor store and I take it.

Inside is a bottle of Jack Daniels black label whiskey.

"You want me to play drunk."

"No. But I do want you to act like my ol' lady who's walked down to the liquor store with me."

I think about it, then give him my conditions.

"As long as you keep your hands off my ass."

He smiles.

"And my breasts."

He chuckles then.

"Fair enough."

I uncross my arms and hold out my hand.

He snorts and, ignoring it, strides past me. I turn and catch up to him, and we're once again walking side by side.

But he startles me when he reaches across my upper back and gently rests his hand on my shoulder. Worse, after a moment, it almost feels natural there, like it belongs.

Get hold of yourself, girl. He's *not* Nicolas.

We turn the corner, thoughts pinging through my mind like a pinball. As we near the bar, I edge a little closer to Taz.

Just to make it look real.

"Hey, Taz! What's up, man?"

Taz slows, then turns us to face the door.

Three Hells Angels are smoking next to the entrance.

"Not much. How's things?"

"They're good." The speaker, a burly blond with a mustache and goatee, offers a friendly smile. "How ya been? Haven't seen you around much lately."

"Yeah. Been on the road a bit." Taz casually reaches across me, and taking the bag from my hand, offers it to the bikers. The blond accepts it, reaches in, and unscrews the cap. He tips his head back to take a drink, exposing his throat.

The veins beneath his jaw pulse as he swallows and my gums spasm.

We need to get out of here before I lose it.

"Hey, Taz, baby, I'm feeling kinda sick." I slur my words and weave a little beneath his grasp.

"Well, then, we better get on home. Can't have you passin' out just yet." Smirking, he nuzzles my ear. I grit my teeth and force myself to hold still.

He whispers, "You're gettin' smarter."

Asshole.

Turning back to the Angels, he points toward the bottle. "Keep it. She don't need no more."

They laugh and one of them raises it in salute.

"Later, man."

"Later." Taz gestures with his chin, then maneuvers us toward the bike. I continue with my drunken performance, but try not to look so smashed I can't ride.

Taz hands me my helmet, swings his leg over the seat, and starts the bike. Its throaty rumble drowns out the din from the bar, and as he kicks the stand up into place, I climb on and lean against his back.

"Nice ride," one of the bikers yells. "Both of them."

Taz nods to them and they laugh as we take off down the street.

~

We turn into the driveway beneath the bright lights of the Shell station. Redd is parked off to the side, half-hidden in the shadows. He's lounging against his bike, fingers tucked into his Levi pockets. Chia's sitting on a rock, flicking her dagger into the soil surrounding the meager landscaping. As we stop beside Redd, she gets up and dusts off the seat of her pants, the dagger now mysteriously hidden wherever she keeps it.

"Things go okay?" Redd yells over the thumping of Taz's engine.

Taz nods.

"Then let's hit it."

Chia climbs up behind Redd and shoves on her helmet while he starts the Harley. She avoids looking at us. We follow them out of the driveway, and I hang on to Taz as the two bikes roar together down the street, a matched set of steel demons screaming at the night.

In spite of everything that's happened, I can't deny the thrill shooting up my spine.

We pull slightly ahead and Redd glances over at me, his customary grin lighting up his face. I smile back, noticing that Chia's has lost its tension, her childlike features now smooth and serene in the caress of the rushing wind.

There is something cleansing about its embrace, a sense of security and isolation all at once, as though we're the only creatures in the middle of our own private storm. The motorcycle headlights stab the darkness like lightning, chased by Harley engine thunder.

I grip Taz's waist, my thoughts drifting to this enigma of a Chosen. There is too much about him that just doesn't make sense. The violence simmering beneath his skin contradicts his actions both in the bar and the alley. His motivations remain a complete mystery to me. Was his decision not to feed due to a preference for a different type of human prey? Does he have a relationship with a human woman? Or does he truly survive on game?

Like me.

But he is nothing like me. And he's nothing like Nicolas.

He's like nothing I've ever known.

# FRIDAY

## CHAPTER 45

It's late afternoon when my eyes drift open. I listen for movement from the bedrooms, but the house is silent.

We'd ridden until almost sunrise, wandering aimlessly it seemed. After we got back to the house, there'd been no further discussion—about Chia's escapade in the alley or my origins. In fact, the three of them sounded like some kind of creepy Walton family as they headed toward their bedrooms with comments of "'Til the morrow, Chi" and "Catch ya on the flip side, Redd."

Well, two of them, anyway. Taz's only input to the exchange was his customary grunt as he closed his door.

It was even weirder when Redd included me with a "Fare thee well, lass." It made me want to respond with, "Good night, John Boy." But, afraid they might not understand the reference to the old TV show, especially the volatile Chia, I kept my reply to a simple, "G'night."

I can be such a chicken sometimes.

However, this afternoon I feel brave enough to chance a shower. The bathroom cabinet reveals clean towels, and the well-stocked laundry room even includes enzyme cleaner—a Chosen staple for removing bloodstains.

Grabbing my shirt from the garage, I strip off the rest of my clothes and dump them in the washing machine. Though my black jeans don't show evidence of yesterday's hunt, one leg is stiff with dried blood and they stink of deer. The idea of putting them back on after my shower sounds disgusting.

I mull over last night's events beneath the cleansing spray, perplexed by Taz and his efforts to blend in with human society. Something, or someone, is obviously keeping him on his best behavior when around people, because I'm not sure he'd care otherwise. I finish up and get out, no closer to solving his puzzle.

With the towel tucked around me, I transfer my clothes to the dryer and head back to the bathroom. I'm picking the tangles from my wet hair when a bedroom door opens.

Taz pads into the bathroom, barefooted and shirtless, apparently not realizing it's occupied. He stops and steps back, nonplussed, then a smile creeps its way across his face. Slowly stretching his arms upward, he hooks his fingers on the top of the doorframe, his gaze traveling up and down my towel-wrapped body.

I focus on my image in the mirror and try not to look at his, at his washboard abs, his sculpted arms and shoulders. My hair snaps as I jerk on a stubborn knot.

"Nice. I like waking up to a naked woman."

I want to rip the smirk from his face, but instead, I clutch the towel, half-afraid he might yank it off. Before I can think of a retort, the dryer buzzes, giving me a reason to escape. Taz shows no sign of moving aside at first, but relents when I shoo him back with a wave of my hand. Grabbing the comb, I slip by him, holding on to the towel for dear life, and duck into the laundry room.

"Wanna come wash my back?" he calls from the bathroom. He waits a half moment, then laughs and shuts the door. The sound of the shower triggers an image of him beneath the water as I retrieve my still-damp clothes. I slam the dryer door in an attempt to chase him from my head and focus on getting dressed before anyone else catches me half-naked.

Taz is such a Jekyll-and-Hyde. I don't know which one is worse—the tortured, angry monster with violence in his veins, or the teasing schoolboy yanking on my braids. But both are beginning to get under my skin, and I don't like it.

I'm on the couch finishing my hair when the bathroom door opens. I resist looking in his direction and nearly fall out of my seat when he silently looms over me, wearing nothing but a towel wound around his powerful hips. Which happen to be at my eye level. I tear my gaze away from that towel and look up.

Two hundred-plus pounds of bare-chested, muscled Indian completely scrambles my brain. All I can do is stare.

The smirk returns to tap dance across his lips. Taz pushes back his wet, tangled hair, hanging nearly to his waist, and I open my mouth to say something, anything, but nothing comes out.

"Done with my comb?" he says, his voice low, seductive.

"Uh. Sure." I fumble for it on my lap, but end up knocking it onto the floor. It lands between my feet.

As I reach for it, so does he. I get a closeup of beefy shoulder and bicep as his hand darts to the floor between my knees. His clean, masculine scent fills the air around me, and if he were to grab me right now, I . . . I don't know what I'd do.

But he only grabs the comb. Then he looks up at me, just inches away. His golden eyes glowing, his eyebrows arch in invitation, then he smiles and stands up. Smug self-assurance drifts lazily across his face. He steps away and tosses his hair back, then with a quiet laugh, he leaves.

"Sonya."

It takes a second to register he's talking to me.

"Yeah," I croak.

"Close your mouth. You look like a baby bird waiting for a worm."

Mortified, I snap my jaw shut.

Asshole.

~

Taz re-emerges from his bedroom, but I ignore him, focusing instead on the biker magazine in my lap. Yet I can't help being interested when he leaves through the back door in the laundry room.

The musky smell of deer on him the night before last still has me reeling. An unwelcome thrill runs through me at the thought of hunting with him.

This has to stop. I need to get away from him and his damned animal magnetism.

A possible solution to my problem announces itself when a bedroom door opens and Redd shuffles into the room, his wild, coppery hair sticking out in all directions. He stops, looses a noisy yawn, then scratches his belly. He's still wearing the denim shirt with the pea-sized bloodstain from the bar last night, rumpled from his daytime slumber. A wide grin breaks through his beard.

Maybe Redd will give me a ride back to my hotel under the guise of picking up some clean clothes. If I can't convince him to take me to Alina, I'll ditch him and come up with a new game plan. But at least I'll have my car.

"Evenin', lass." He thumbs back down the hall. "Is Taz up?"

"He went out back."

Redd nods, but before I can propose my idea to him, he heads out the laundry room door.

Crap. Getting him alone might be difficult.

As usual, his diminutive sidekick isn't far behind him. Chia's door opens and, suppressing a groan, I brace myself.

"Shit. You still here? What the fuck is Taz thinking?" She glares at me, then an evil smile lightens up her face. "Oh, wait. That *is* what he's thinking. Fucking. You. Wish you two would get it over with so we can get rid of you."

"I'm not interested in—" I start to stand, the magazine crumpling in my fist.

"Eh, save it. I don't give a rat's ass. I just hope he lets me use you for target practice before he kills you."

Little bitch.

But before I can voice a response, she disappears into the garage.

I fling the magazine across the room. I have no idea why she's so hostile to me, but it's beginning to tick me off.

Following Redd's path into the laundry room, I step outside through the back door into near total darkness. A tall, wooden fence, its sun-bleached boards exposed between ragged patches of peeling brown paint, encloses the expansive yard. Rusty frames and parts reveal a motorcycle cemetery in the far left corner. A dead lawn, its pale brown grass dotted with dried weeds and patches of bare soil, occupies the central area. And to the right, what looks to be a small workshop, stray slivers of light escaping its blanket-covered windows. An older black pickup truck bearing South Dakota plates is parked beside the building, and next to it, a camper shell on extended legs and a motorcycle trailer.

Voices drift across the darkened yard from the shop. Curious as to what they might be talking about, I quietly close the door and step nearer to listen.

"Taz, we've wasted enough time tailing her. She seems harmless enough. Why don't we just take her in and be done with it? Get back to business as usual."

"I'll take her in when I'm damned good and ready. We still know nothin' about her. There's too much that doesn't add up, Redd. I'm not letting an assassin slip through on my watch."

"You sure that's all it is? I mean, who wouldn't want a taste of that?"

A deep growl, punctuated with the sound of something heavy crashing against the floor, jars me back from the door.

"Hey, bro. Calm down. She's all yours. Wouldn't touch something you already claimed. You know that."

His? He's *claimed* me?

I'm no one's property, least of all *his*.

Seething, I reach for the doorknob.

It starts to turn from the inside and I suddenly panic at being caught eavesdropping. I dart back to the house, then pivot as though I'm just coming outside.

The shop door opens and fluorescent light frames Redd's bulk in the doorway.

"Just be careful, bro. We got a good thing goin' here—don't mess it up."

He shuts the door and looks up as he heads in my direction.

"If you're lookin' for Taz, lass, he's in there. Knock before you go in—he's a bit testy tonight."

I nod. But as he starts to walk past me into the house, I touch his arm. After what I heard, it's doubtful that smoky seduction will work, but sweet and innocent might.

"Wait, Redd. There's something I want to ask you. A favor."

Copper eyebrows arch over his russet eyes as he stops.

"What is it, lass?"

"I'd like to pick up some clean clothes from my motel. Can you take me?"

His smile softens and a warm light shines from his eyes.

"As much as I'd like to, that's up to Taz. You'll have to ask him."

He pats my hand and heads into the house.

Shit.

Don't know if that line will work on Taz, but one thing's for sure.

I suspect getting away from that hawk-like bottled violence will be a lot harder than running from laid-back Redd.

Sounds of hammering from the shop disrupt my inner debate, and the chance to learn more about my captor—because it finally sinks in that's who he really is—puts my game plan on hold. I just hope what I learn will help in my escape.

I take Redd's advice and knock on the door first.

"Come in."

Lulled by the unkempt state of the backyard, I'm once again surprised to find a refuge for cleanliness and order. Yet that external order is belied by the internal chaos of emotions in his eyes when he looks up at me.

His jaw clenches and he turns back to the workbench in front of him. He adjusts a small silver ring around a conical form and begins hammering again with a leather-headed mallet, the silver cuff on his wrist flashing beneath the work light. Long braid bouncing against his back with each blow, his muscles ripple beneath his black tank top and my earlier indignation evaporates.

It occurs to me that perhaps he's having as difficult a time maintaining his distance as I am. Maybe anger helps him keep that distance.

I wander slowly around the shop, noting the bars covering the inside of all the blanketed windows. Music from the '60s band The Doors quietly drifts out from ceiling-mounted speakers. To my right, a small bookcase squats against the far wall in one corner, fronted by several large floor pillows on a dark brown fur rug similar to the one in his bedroom.

The titles focus on craftsmanship, like silversmithing, drum and flute making, and welding. One shelf is dedicated to books about various Native American tribes and their customs. Another is devoted to spiritual-based works, with subjects such as vision quests and shamanism. A lone book on dreamwalking lies on top of the bookcase.

Along the same wall, a second bookcase holds a collection of Native American flutes in all shapes and sizes, and in the other corner rest several hide-covered tribal drums and a short wooden stool.

The wall opposite the entrance is home to a shiny, blood-red Harley with a wide back tire and cannon-sized exhaust pipes. As I look closer, I realize the inky black frame forms a skeleton. Bony feet anchor the rear tire, and skeletal arms and hands hold the front. The red tank and single seat rests on the skeleton's back, and the headlight emerges from the fanged mouth of a grinning black skull.

It looks like something the Devil would ride.

Creeped out, I turn back to where Taz is working. Most of the wall is lined with a single long workbench and built-in cabinets beneath. Tools, many of which I don't recognize, occupy pegboard hooks between more cabinets above the bench. The end closest to the door seems to be devoted to leather working, and at the other end, near the bike, is a mechanic's wheeled tool chest.

As I survey the bench top around Taz, something shiny catches my eye. I glance at him and step over to get a better look at it.

It's a silver necklace. *My* necklace.

My hand flies to my throat, and of course the necklace is not there.

I remember taking it off before I got in the shower, and forgot about it when I fled the tiny bathroom filled with too much Indian.

"Why do you have this?" I pick it up by the chain. The filigree pendant flashes beneath an overhead work light.

"Here. Give me your right hand."

I hesitate, then tuck the necklace into my pocket and hold my hand out.

Taz slips the ring onto my middle finger. It catches on the knuckle and barely goes past it. It's really too tight, but before I can say anything or even get a good look at it, he tugs it back off. He slides it down a tapered metal rod, taps on it a few times, then grabs my hand again.

His total concentration on his project reminds me of how he was last night dealing with Chia's near-murder of the young biker.

When the ring fits perfectly the second time, he nods, then starts putting away his tools.

I take off the ring and examine it. The top, where stones would normally be mounted, is a round disk, about the size of a dime and slightly domed. A paw print of a mountain lion is cut out in the middle, the toes and central pad forming separate windows into the hollow, blackened interior of the ring. Engraved deer tracks lead halfway down the tapering sides of the band. The smooth, flat underside of the disc bears a capital T with two round dots below the base of the letter. Like fang marks.

When I look up, Taz is watching me. I need to be careful here—I'm not sure about the meaning of his gift, and I don't want to encourage him. I would like to keep my head attached, though, so refusing the ring is probably not a good idea. I opt for light-hearted sarcasm.

"Does this mean we're going steady?"

He snorts and takes the ring. Picking up a small amber vial topped by an eyedropper, he unscrews the lid and squeezes several golden drops into the interior of the ring, then hands both vial and ring back to me.

"This'll be easier than fishin' for that necklace."

Closer examination of the interior reveals a small piece of black suede covering the bottom. I take a quick whiff of the ring, expecting a noxious smell. But the earthy scent, with hints of sage and something else I can't identify, smells good. I hold it closer and breathe in deeply. An immediate sense of calm descends over me, releasing some of the tension that's been building since I hooked up with these three Chosen.

"What's *in* this?" I smell it again, and my muscles relax a little more.

"Desert herbs and oils. An old Hopi medicine man helped me with it."

"Wow. Thanks. It feels like it'll work way better than stinky clove oil." I slip the ring back on, then raise my knuckles to my nose several times. Taz is right. This will be much easier than dealing with the necklace. "The design style . . . it looks familiar."

Then I realize why. It's the same style as the wide silver cuffs encircling his wrists, though his designs are different. Eagles soar across his silver in various flight positions, alternating with jagged bolts of lightning on one arm and flat-bottomed clouds with slanting lines beneath them on the other. All are windowed cutouts above a black interior, like the paw print on my ring, and finely crafted. An image of Taz with his arms folded, a position he favors, suddenly takes on a different meaning. It would bring the cuffs with their calming scent that much closer to his nose.

"It's a Hopi technique that I adapted." His voice startles me and I look up into his sharp gaze.

"It's beautiful. Are you Hopi?"

"No." But he offers nothing further.

"Well, you do nice work. Thank you."

"Can't have you fangin' out like a newborn when things get a little tight." But his dismissive tone doesn't hide the pleased expression on his face, nor the confident pride in the set of his shoulders as he ushers me out the door.

My footsteps slow as a memory surfaces of the last time I was given jewelry. The images flip by like a slideshow, ending with round blue sapphires and petite white diamonds bouncing across a polished hardwood floor. Their brittle sound as each one hits echoes in my head.

Nicolas had given me that bracelet. He'd said the sapphires paled beside my eyes.

I broke it.

And then a bear broke me. And my life changed forever. Again.

"Sonya."

Caught up in the past, I look up to see Taz waiting at the open door into the house.

"You comin' in?" He's frowning, aggravation replacing his earlier pride.

"Uh, no. Not yet. I . . . I'll be in shortly."

His frown deepens and he shuts the door hard behind him.

The cool night breeze reminds me of Colorado and I hug myself.

Nicolas had the bracelet fixed, adding emeralds for his emerald green eyes. The precious gems nestled against one another.

Green emerald. Blue sapphire. Green. Blue. Him. Me.

I didn't break it.

I broke us.

*Nicolas . . .*

The slideshow continues, each image hinting at a future which I'd so carelessly thrown away. A future—though it bore its own set of challenges—in which I was not alone.

Fighting the pressure building in my eyes, I turn around and step back behind the shop, hoping no one's watching from the house. Silent sobs rack my body as I hug myself tighter and try to imagine his arms around me once again.

Though my mind aches from the memories of being loved by him, of loving and losing him, the empty place in my core no longer does. It no longer remembers his presence, his essence, and I feel a fresh sadness at the loss of that heart-wrenching pain. Because at least that pain was a reminder of our connection, and its absence means all our connections are truly lost.

The sorrow drains from me, spent and lifeless. It's been a long time since I gave in to those emotions—emotions that have been safely locked inside the black box where I store all of the memories that hurt too much.

But Taz, with his volatile moods, his masculine allure, his unexpected gift, has cracked open that box, and I suddenly feel weak and vulnerable at a time when I most need my strength.

Taking several deep breaths, I wipe away the bloodtears, scrub my hands against the dead brown grass, and prepare to face the new monster in my life.

# CHAPTER 46

The roar of a departing motorcycle vibrates the windows as I finish washing my face in the bathroom. No one seems to be in the house, so I head through the kitchen to the garage and venture in.

The main garage door is open and Redd's bike is gone. Taz, kneeling next to his, ignores me. He picks up a spray can and coats the front wheel with white foam, then stands and does the same to the back. Returning to the front with a rag in his hand, he crouches and starts wiping the rim between the spokes.

I move closer to watch, noting his meticulousness. The impatience he exhibits much of the time doesn't seem to extend to his work. Rather, I wonder if being engaged in detailed tasks brings him a serenity he might otherwise find difficult to achieve.

He glances up at me, then grabs another rag and tosses it in my direction. I catch it and he waves his hand toward the rear wheel, which is held up off the floor by some sort of special stand.

"Since you're just standing there . . ."

Unable to come up with a satisfying retort, I keep my mouth shut, kneel beside the tire, and start wiping.

"Be sure to get the spokes too."

I grit my teeth and focus on my work. But instead of it calming me, I feel myself growing more irritated. Questions start pounding my head, and I blurt out the first one.

"Whose pickup is parked out back?"

"Mine."

"Is that where you're from? South Dakota?"

"Lived there a bit."

Taz stands, watching me. Pretending not to see him, I scrub a little harder at a piece of grime, hoping he'll find another spot on the bike to clean.

And then he's squatting behind me, almost but not quite touching my back. I stiffen as his arm reaches alongside mine. His cool breath tickles my neck, sending electric tingles across my skin. He grabs the wheel and rotates it so the area blocked by the chain guard is now accessible.

His hand drifts to the floor, but he makes no other movement. I can only stare at it, at the long, surprisingly graceful fingers tipped with nails as sharp as my own. Tension coils and recoils in my chest, writhing like some poisonous snake.

His breath moves from my neck to linger on my hair. His hand clenches, the knuckles growing whiter and whiter.

And then he's gone.

Where his hand rested on the cement are four bright drops of blood.

~

I pick up the next motorcycle magazine from the small pile I'd placed beside me on the couch. There's nothing else out here in the common area of the house to read or do, and TV's as ridiculous as always, especially on a big screen. And I'm not about to finish cleaning the bike. Even if I felt so inclined, which I don't, I suspect that touching it without Taz's permission would be as big a trespass as snooping in his bedroom.

Fleeting thoughts of escape continue to tantalize me, but each one withers beneath the possibility that he is out there, somewhere in the dark, waiting for me to make a move.

The kitchen door slams. Taz strides past me without a word and heads straight into the bathroom. He's covered in blood and stinks of deer, which slaps awake my own hunger. After running the faucet for a few moments, he comes out of the bathroom, shirtless, only to disappear into his bedroom. He's still tugging a clean T-shirt over his head when he walks back out. I catch myself staring and jerk my gaze back to the page in my lap.

"Redd said you needed clothes. Don't know why you didn't ask *me*," he snarls as he tucks in his shirt.

I shrug, set the magazine aside, and stand to face him.

"I expected you to say no." I thrust my chin in the air, daring him to deny it.

"So you thought to go behind my back? How old are you—thirteen?"

"Screw you. I'm tired of being—"

"What? Told what to do?" Taz brushes past me into the kitchen. "How's this? Get your jacket. We're leaving." He opens the door to the garage.

"No." To hell with him. I'm done with this.

"You sure about that?"

"I'm not going anywhere with you until you start treating me with a little respect. Which includes—"

Taz stalks back into the room, all steely calm on the outside. But I can almost feel what's on the inside, and it suddenly scares me.

He shoves the dining room table to one side and flips back the area rug.

Beneath it is a trap door.

Pulling it up by a recessed handle, he gives me a hard stare. The black hole in the floor yawns like a hungry beast eager for its next meal.

Stark terror melts all traces of my resistance.

"Your choice. Go or stay."

Shit.

Head held high, I grab my jacket and march to the garage.

When we pull into the motel and park next to the BMW, I'm not sure what surprises me more—that my car is here, and not in the twenty-four-hour parking lot where I'd left it, or that *we* are here.

Guess Taz wasn't kidding when he said they'd been tracking me since my arrival in the city.

"How'd my car get here?"

"Chia lifted your keys outside the Cat Club."

"On Halloween?"

He nods, that maddening smirk lighting up his face.

She must've brought it over that night before she and Redd came home.

I hadn't even noticed my keys were missing. Not until last night, when we left for the biker bar and I discovered my pockets were empty.

Taz is right. I am *so* dumb.

I peek through the driver's window as I pass, hoping Chia didn't leave any spiteful mementos with her little dagger.

Taz fishes my motel key card from his pocket, opens the door, and follows me in. Stopping halfway across the room, the first thing I notice is a partially open drawer in the dresser. When I examine it further, it's obvious someone's been through my things.

"Is this your handiwork?"

"Not this time."

I just look at him, dumbfounded, then start pulling out tops and socks and underwear.

"There's not a lot of room on the bike, so pack light." He walks over to a small garbage can, yanks out the plastic bag, and offers it to me.

A garbage bag? Really?

I snatch it from him and set it on the bed along with my pile, then grab a dark red turtleneck and duck into the bathroom to change. Slamming the door feels so good I want to do it again, but that would only invite further comparison to teenagers.

When I come out, Taz is standing by the bed, a pair of my black lacey underwear in his hand.

"Now who's the thirteen-year-old?" I jerk the underwear away and drop them back on the bed. He smiles, not the least contrite.

But I catch a glint of embarrassment in his eyes, and it surprises me.

He acts like such a jerk, yet I'm beginning to suspect it's just a front.

I check the dresser to see if there's anything left that I can't do without for now and look up into the mirror as Taz steps behind me. He slowly raises his hand and brushes the faint scar on my cheek with the backs of his fingers.

"How did you get these scars, and the ones on your back and arm?" His tone is softer than usual, matching the look in his eyes. He's so close to me I can't think, except to wonder what it might be like to . . .

*No.*

I duck away from him.

"I, uh . . ." Taking a deep breath, I try to overcome the confusion racing through me. "It was a bear."

"A bear? A bear attacked you?"

"Sort of. It was pretty mutual. He tried to take something from me."

"Like what?"

Might as well say it. I'm sure he's already figured it out.

"My . . . my kill. A deer."

His breath catches and I glance over to see him staring at the far wall.

"So . . ." He clears his throat as he looks back at me. "You attacked him?"

I nod.

Taz lets out a roar of laughter, the first genuine laugh I've heard from him.

"Why does that not surprise me?" He beams me a broad grin and shakes his head. "And what kind of scars did you leave *him*?"

"He's dead."

Taz's amusement fades, his expression shifting to one of admiration. "Now that might be worth a little respect."

I pull open a dresser drawer, take out the bear claw necklace from Montana, and toss it across the room to him.

He snags it mid-air, then examines several claws and looks up at me, the question in his eyes.

"Yeah. That's what I prefer to eat, but there aren't many bears in this area."

He frowns and throws it back to me.

"Bears are sacred."

"Bears have caused me more heartache than you can imagine." I think of the days before I tasted human blood—carefree and innocent when compared with now—and of Sandy, lying crushed against a rock. My fist tightens around the necklace as I put it away.

"Something I don't understand." His frown deepens. "Were you human when you fought the bear?"

"No."

Well, partly. But he doesn't need to know that.

"And yet you were left with scars." Eyes narrowing, he takes a quiet breath. "Chosen don't scar."

Shrugging, I walk back over to the bed and finish packing the trash bag. I spin it to tie a knot in the end, but he takes the bag from me, then crushes it against his chest to squeeze out all the air.

I swallow and look away.

"What about the rest of my stuff? My room's only paid up through Sunday."

"Don't worry about it."

"What's that supposed to mean?"

"Exactly what I said. Don't worry about it. It's taken care of." He knots the end of the bag.

"Until when?"

"Until you don't need it no more."

That's reassuring. Does he mean the room or my stuff? The only way I wouldn't need my stuff is if I'm dead.

"Any chance I can get my car keys or wallet?"

Taz shoves the bag at me and leans in, his lips just inches from my ear.

"Not a single one," he whispers, then walks out the door.

# SATURDAY

## CHAPTER 47

As thrilled as I am to finally have clean clothes and toiletries of my own again, I can't help but wonder just how long Taz intends to keep me here. When I broached the subject this evening shortly after he woke, his only response was, "Depends on you."

My options seem pretty limited at the moment. I've thought about calling a taxi, grabbing my car, and getting the hell out of the area until I can figure out another approach. But because I stupidly left my jacket behind the other night to go hunting, I now have no cash or credit cards.

Though I have backup resources hidden in the BMW, getting to them could prove difficult, and would either involve stealing a car in Mill Valley or swimming across the Bay to San Francisco. I don't feel quite that desperate yet. For now, I'll continue to play Taz's game.

My musings come to a halt at the sound of Chia's bedroom door opening. She tends to wake up later than the guys, and I've wondered if she's a lot younger than them in Chosen years as well as human.

Whatever her age, she sure doesn't seem to like me, as evidenced by the scowl that creases her face when she spots me on the couch.

I decide maybe we just got off on the wrong foot that first night.

"If you're looking for Redd, he and Taz are in the garage."

"Like he'd be anyplace else?" She snorts, rolling her eyes like a pouty teenager, and continues toward the kitchen.

Setting down my book, I turn and face her over the back of the couch.

"Hey, look. I don't know what I've done to upset you, but I'd like to start over."

Chia stops and whirls back around, her tiny hands curling into fists.

"You wanna know what you've *done*?" she screams, her face twisting with fury. "You screwed up *everything*. We were all getting along just fine, just the three of us, until *you* decided to show up. Since the second you got into town, nothing's been the same. We don't hit the bars anymore, or bust heads like we used to, or party with the blood bags. I'm hungry all the time, and Taz . . ." Her shrill voice cracks. "All Taz does is follow your ass around like a damn dog. It's been even worse since he brought you home. It disgusts me."

By the time she's done, Chia's entire body is shaking, and bloodtears brimming in her hazel eyes only emphasize the crimson blazing from their pupils.

Taken aback by her outburst, I try to find the right words to say.

"Chia, I . . . I'm sorry—"

"Fuck. You. I don't need your goddamn pity. I just want you gone. And if Taz is too pussy-whipped to do it, I'll kill you myself. Only you won't see me coming. Just one quick swipe of my blade and our problems are solved."

And then she vanishes out the front door.

I slowly sink back down into the couch, stunned. Because what I saw in her eyes wasn't just anger. What I saw was jealous rage.

She's in love with Taz, and probably always has been. And the only time I've seen him acknowledge her existence was the night she nearly killed the biker.

Sadly, I think that was no accident.

~

She's been gone about a half hour when Redd opens the front door and steps partway in.

"Evening, lass. We're heading out for the night and need ye to come along."

I grab my jacket, slip past him, and wait while he locks the door.

Redd's silent during our walk to the garage.

Taz is sitting on his bike, dark glasses and helmet on, and obviously ready to go.

"We can't wait any longer," Taz says to Redd. He ignores me, other than to hold out my helmet.

"Just a few more minutes, bro. I don't like leaving her behind, especially now."

Taz just shakes his head.

The awkward silence weighs heavy in the air. They obviously heard Chia's explosive rant. After several long moments, Taz rises from the seat and violently shoves his foot down on the kickstarter. The engine sputters in protest, and he stomps down again. This time it responds, its thunder exploding from the garage. He glances at me and jerks his head, and with a sigh, I climb on behind him.

Redd's tight-lipped as he tugs his helmet on and straddles his bike, but then does nothing more.

The wheel beneath me suddenly spins for a split second before grabbing cement, and we shoot out of the bright garage and into the dark. Taz slows halfway up the driveway, his head slightly turned to one side. But no answering rumble breaks the silence behind us, and with a curse, he turns the throttle and we continue, though at a slower pace than before.

We reach the asphalt, and he pauses, then with another curse turns the bike onto the road. Our progress into town is a bit more leisurely than usual. Taz downshifts for the light at the freeway on-ramp.

Finally, in the distance behind us, the roar of a Harley rips through the night.

He pulls over at the base of the on-ramp, and within a minute, the orange bike flashes past, a tiny, leather-jacketed form tucked tight around Redd's back.

~

We blast south down Highway 101 in the darkness, weaving in and out of traffic. I don't know how fast we're going—not sure I want to know. But it's a lot faster than all the cars. At first I'm terrified, then slowly relax and marvel at how Taz and the metal monster beneath us function together as a single unit. I shift a little closer to him, concentrating on matching the subtle movements in his muscles as he leans the bike this way and that. I become part of the one and my fear of crashing dissipates.

The Golden Gate Bridge and the condensed traffic crossing it force us to slow our mad pace. A brief pause at the tollgate and we're on our way again, albeit at a much slower rate. Crossing San Francisco is never quick, with its endless hills, stoplights, and congested streets, and this time is no different. I fight the claustrophobia closing in on me, that feeling of trapped panic that arises every time I enter a big city.

After an eternity of stop-and-go, we finally get on the 101 Freeway south and resume our headlong rush through the night. I have no idea where we are, other than someplace on the long peninsula between San Francisco Bay and the Pacific Ocean. I taste the strange combination of seaside scents and urban odors and, closing my eyes, let the vibrations from the motorcycle lull me into a semi-hypnotic state.

The pungent reek of jet fuel invades my nose, and I open my eyes as we take the off-ramp for the San Francisco International Airport. Working our way through the airport complex to the private jet area, we stop at a security booth where we're asked to produce identification. Before I can say anything, Taz removes his sunglasses and hands over two ID cards. The guard's glance at me confirms the second one is mine.

I reach out to take it, but Taz's hand blocks mine, and the guard gives both IDs back to him.

Crap.

We continue on past parking lots and an array of different-sized hangars, our passage marked by the sudden brightness of motion-detecting spotlights.

The bike engines echo between the steel buildings, fading to a muted rumble as we pull in front of a hangar and coast to a stop in its shadows. Several other motorcycles—brightly colored crotch rockets—and a black SUV are parked together near the open bay door. A black Mercedes limousine sits apart from them, its dark windows concealing whoever might be inside.

A group of Chosen saunters out of the hangar as Taz and Redd shut off their engines. There are seven of them, all good-sized males. Three of them wear sport biker garb, but what gets my attention are the four military types carrying Uzis.

First a trashy biker bar. Now some sort of covert, and probably illegal, operation. Taz and his crew hang out with a real savory cast of characters.

The underbelly of Chosen existence is sure a far cry from Nicolas's elite lifestyle.

Taz pokes my leg and I follow his cue to get off. He dismounts and hangs his helmet from the handlebars, leaving on his sunglasses.

"Stay here with Chia. But keep your helmet on and be ready to go. Got it?"

I nod, wondering if he knows any other way to communicate besides giving orders, then carefully lean back against the seat of the Harley to watch whatever is about to unfold.

He and Redd stride over to the group. Greetings are exchanged, accompanied by tight smiles, but no handshaking. Apparently contact, either formal or casual, is something Chosen avoid with each other as well as with humans who aren't their meal of the day.

And these Chosen, wearing amber and violet auras like those at the club on Halloween night, all seem to be of Nicolas's descent. I can almost taste his stamp upon them.

I want to ask Chia what's happening, but we're not exactly on speaking terms. She's squatting motionless on the ground beside Redd's bike, and one look at the simmering anger creasing her face tells me we may never be.

The varying pitch of aircraft engines both in the air and on the ground deadens the quiet banter among the group of Chosen. Taz and Redd hold themselves a little apart from the others, and I sense an uneasy truce binding them all together.

All talk ceases as a white Lear jet, bearing no identifying marks other than a long number on its tail, taxis up to the hangar and stops.

It sits idling, the roar of its engines drowning out all other sounds. The blue-white strobe lights and flashing orange beacons pierce the darkness in and around the hangar like some sort of bizarre rock concert laser show. Movements within the group of waiting Chosen appear herky-jerky from the pulsing lights, shifting the tableau into a cheesy haunted house attraction as they ready their weapons and spread out. Their focus is not on the plane, but the area surrounding it.

The bright strobes cut off as the door opens and a stairway lowers to the tarmac. Two mountainous Chosen dressed in dark suits step down and look around. One of them speaks into a collar-mounted microphone. They move to either side of the stairway and stand, continuously scanning the area around the plane.

The presidential-level security means only one thing.

An Elder. Or maybe even . . . Nicolas.

*Nicolas.*

I ease to my feet, breath held tight, and watch the open doorway.

A tall figure in a tailored suit steps down the stairs.

The involuntary cry in my throat dies as the sharp edge of a dagger presses against the back of my neck.

"Don't you say a fucking word, bitch." Chia, perched on Taz's bike behind me, yanks my ponytail. "And don't fucking move, either, or you'll be wearing a backward smile—right before I slice off your head."

Her threat doesn't still the whirlwind of emotions churning inside me. I watch the well-guarded Chosen walk toward the waiting limousine, trailed by his bodyguards and several others from the plane, and Chia tugs again on my ponytail.

*No . . .*

But it's not Nicolas. Not his walk, not his grace, not his beautifully arrogant bearing.

It is, however, one of his Elders. Robert. From Los Angeles.

And as the recognition tenses my body, Chia's dagger bites deeper. Blood traces its way down my back and I resist the urge to twist around and tear her apart.

Robert pauses a moment, his nostrils flaring as he looks in our direction.

Not just our direction. He's looking at *me*. His aura, amber with yellow instead of violet, pulses several times. Dozens of threads in dozens of colors writhe through it like a nest of angry snakes.

Gaze hardening, he disappears into the limousine, followed by his retinue. The group near the hangar moves toward the SUV and sport bikes.

Taz and Redd waste no time returning to their own motorcycles, but both wear frowns as they approach. Chia says nothing more and releases me.

The harsh look Taz gives me indicates he missed none of my reaction to Robert, nor Robert's to me, and I steel myself for the interrogation he's sure to deliver later.

He tugs on his helmet, slides onto the seat, and starts the Harley, staring back over his shoulder at me as I climb on. Redd's bike fires up and we roll into position behind the black SUV as it takes off after the departing limo.

The sport bikes race ahead of the procession in a staggered formation and within minutes we're on the freeway heading north to San Francisco.

Our progress slows when we exit onto city streets I'm a little more familiar with. As we travel up and down the city's signature hills, the sport bikes in front of the SUV add a peculiar note to the echoes bouncing back at us from the Victorian row houses lining our route, which seems to be heading into the upscale neighborhoods of Pacific Heights.

The SUV turns a corner up yet another steep street. But instead of following, Taz pulls over to the curb and waves Redd on past. Redd and the SUV both disappear over the top of the hill. Taz keeps his bike idling. He makes no move to get off.

Rock-hard muscles in his back, along with a rigid silence, indicate the rest of our evening is about to get even worse than it began. I debate slipping off the bike and high-tailing it down the hill, but my thoughts of escape wither beneath the thunder of a Harley engine announcing Redd's return. Taz silently shifts into gear as Redd passes, only to shoot by the other bike in a mad race to the bottom of the hill. I cringe and hang on tight, suddenly terrified that Taz's rage is going to smear us all over the pavement.

We make it back to Mill Valley in what I'm sure is record time. But when Redd slows and turns into the driveway, Taz cranks the throttle. We roar past the house, leaning so far over in the curves my footpegs are nearly scraping.

Chosen or not, we are going to die.

I close my eyes and hang on.

# CHAPTER 48

But we don't crash. Taz finally slows and pulls off the road at a turnout overlooking a wild area I'm guessing is Mt. Tamalpais State Park.

He shuts off the bike. After several long moments of absolute stillness, he takes a deep breath.

"Get off."

I slowly swing my leg over, hand him my helmet, and take a stand near the edge of the slope. I don't know why we stopped here, but I'm sure I'm about to get an earful.

Taz dismounts, then pushes his bike into a gap between a large boulder and the brush on the edge of the hill so that it's hidden from anyone else who might pull in—though I don't know who else would be out here at two in the morning.

Glancing down the steep drop-off, I decide the terrain would be a tough area in which to hunt. The slope is a jumble of sandstone boulders and dense brush, and locating a deer in all that might be like finding a needle in the proverbial haystack.

I look back at Taz. He's walking toward me, eyes blazing red, an ugly curl to his lip. A low growl rumbles from his chest as his fingers arch and stiffen into dagger-like talons.

"I'm done playin' games. Who the *hell* are you? You're gonna tell me, or—"

Instinct takes hold, and with no further thoughts, I dive over the hill, aiming for a big rock about twenty feet below. My hands and feet touch down, and I push off for the next one, land, and launch again, then hit the ground running. Bushes and low-hanging branches snatch at my clothing as I half-run, half-slide down the steep slope.

The sounds of snapping brush and Taz's grunts tell me he's right behind me. I start zig-zagging, feeling like a rabbit with a mountain lion on its tail. Darting to the left, I catch sight of his big hand reaching for me and duck away to the right. A giant boulder looms ahead of me and I leap for its top, then leap again.

The breath explodes from my chest as Taz slams into me mid-air. A dense patch of brush breaks our fall, but gives way and we tumble down the slope in a tangle of arms and legs. I bite and kick and try to claw free, but can't dislodge his hold on me.

His weight pounds me into the ground over and over again as we roll and slide through the underbrush. I feel my ribs crack on a sharp rock.

On the next bounce, my left shoulder erupts into red hot coals of pain.

We smash to a stop against a boulder and his grip loosens. Wreathed in agony, I shove away from him and stagger to my feet, only to have them yanked out from under me.

I land on my shoulder. Molten spikes hammer into the joint and the shockwave races down my entire arm. Shrieks fill the air, and they're coming from me, and I can't stop them.

Like a demon rising from Satan's furnace, the healing hunger detonates through my veins, incinerating all thought and awareness.

~

Gentle hands roll me over onto my back and a sharp, indrawn breath breaks through the ringing in my ears.

"Aw, hell. Sonya . . . I'm sorry. I didn't . . ."

His voice guides me back from the brink of madness and I swallow back the sounds ripping from my chest. I force my eyes open to see Taz kneeling next to me, his face twisted in concern, his hands hovering over the jagged edges of bone poking through what used to be my shoulder. Blood is running from the slowly closing wound, but I don't know how it can heal with my bones sticking out. A glance down at my other side reveals a spreading red stain, meaning my ribs are more than just cracked.

A fresh wave of pain and burning hunger sends a shudder through my battered body.

I try to talk, to tell Taz to help me up, but all that comes out are ragged sobs.

He stands, swearing, then stalks away and stares out into the distance. A half moment later he returns and glowers down at me, a frown creasing his face. He presses his lips tight and shakes his head.

I grit my teeth around another agonized groan and try to get up.

But then he's kneeling next to me and pushing me back down.

"There's no other way. I don't know what else to do. Here, take this."

Taz slashes his wrist and jams his fingers into its ragged wound.

*No . . .*

He holds it to my mouth.

I try to turn away. I don't want his blood. Not *his.*

But the hunger spikes at the sight of it dripping from his fingers and my fangs descend, aching, eager. Against my will, they search out and sink into the bloody gash.

No. *No.*

*Oh, Nicolas . . .* Please forgive me.

My traitorous hands clutch his arm to my mouth and I draw deeply, again and again. But as Taz's healing blood moves through me, so do his emotions—raw with anger and regret and . . . yearning.

For me.

The horror of it frees me from the hunger's spell and I tear my mouth away.

"NO! Get away from me! I don't want . . ."

I push myself to my feet and glare at him as he stands. All I feel now is his hellish rage, his violence threatening to explode from my skin.

But there's something else, something lurking beneath his anger. It's pain, the pain of rejection and crushing disappointment, and as I look at him, I see it on his face.

His expression darkens. Resentment and fury boil through his blood in me, erasing all else.

Without saying a word, he reaches out and grabs my shoulder, then shoves the broken bones back inside.

I scream and everything goes black.

~

Blood. The smell of it, the taste of it, the feel of it. I dream of it filling my mouth—warm and thick with life—and I swallow and swallow. The musky scent of deer and coarse hair against my face seem so real, and I fight to stay in my dream world, to drown in red oblivion.

But the electric tingle of healing tissue, racing throughout my body to concentrate in my shoulder, drags me back to harsh reality.

I open my eyes and realize this isn't a dream. My fangs are buried in the throat of a doe wrapped in my arms, her cooling body lying in the dirt beside mine. Taz is sitting cross-legged just beyond the deer, his chin resting on folded hands, watching me.

It becomes harder to draw out the blood, and with a last few swallows, I release the carcass and shove it away. A second one flops its dead weight across my chest, and I gratefully accept the gift.

When I finally sit up to wipe my mouth, I realize the pain in my shoulder is a ghost of its former self. Frowning, I crane my neck back to check it out.

The sleeve has been cut from my T-shirt and the blood wiped off my skin. The injury is laced with a series of raised pink scars which are fading even as I watch. I move my arm, carefully at first, and though stiff and still sore, it seems to have regained most of its mobility. An examination of my ribs shows they are back in place as well, the skin almost completely healed.

I push myself to my feet, still aching all over from cartwheeling down the hill, and glare at Taz.

"I don't know if I should thank you—or rip out your throat."

Taz grunts, his features twitching as he gets to his feet. The turmoil in his blood enrages me even further and I quickly slam an internal barricade into place against his unwanted emotions.

But it's not only his perpetual anger that I seek to block. His attraction to me is much deeper than I'd imagined, and I . . . I'm scared to death of my own response to it.

I squeeze my throbbing shoulder, using its answering pain as an anchor.

"Why did you attack me?"

"Why did you run?"

"I thought you were going to kill me."

"If I wanted you dead . . . you'd be dead." He takes a deep breath, his gaze hard. "What I want are some answers."

My jaw clenches as he continues.

"How do you know that Elder from the airport? And Alina, for that matter? Who are you?"

I glance down to the canyon bottom below us, trying to decide how much to tell him. But I don't trust anyone where Nicolas is concerned. I'm not even sure I trust Alina.

"I met them . . . at a club in Colorado."

"Colorado." He frowns and rubs his jaw. "I don't get you. You feel old, like an Elder, but at the same time, you behave like a dumb newborn. And you still sleep." He gestures at my shoulder. "And that . . ."

"Yeah? It broke." Shattered, actually.

"It shouldn't have. Not that easily."

"Well, being steamrolled by a two-hundred-pound pissed-off Indian might do that to a gal."

"Two-seventy. And you still shouldn't be that fragile, especially if you're an Elder, or even close to it. Unless . . ." His frown deepens. "Unless you really are a newborn."

I shrug, not willing to give him any more info than I have to.

Taz gazes out into the distance, shaking his head, then looks back at me.

"Gonna be daylight soon. We can finish our talk later." Taz picks up the deer carcasses and quickly dismembers them, then flings the parts in different directions.

Smart. Bloodless deer, whose only injuries are torn throats, are best not left lying around for hikers or rangers to find.

However, I'm still hungry, and still hurt all over. I debate telling him to go on home without me so I can get in a hunt before sunrise. As for morning coma time—there are plenty of big oaks down near the canyon bottom. It wouldn't be the first time I've slept in a tree.

"Come on," he says.

But instead of hiking up the hill, Taz breaks into a jog heading downslope.

Staring at the natural way he navigates the sea of brush, I hesitate, then fall in behind him, hoping I'm not making another mistake with this big Chosen.

# CHAPTER 49

We're nearly at the bottom when Taz stops and scents the air.

It's so bizarre seeing him do something I've done thousands of times—it's like watching a distorted image of myself tasting the wind, seeking wild prey. The odor of deer drifts up the canyon, and I'm once again amazed that they seem to be a regular part of his diet. According to Nicolas, Chosen are generally disgusted by the idea of feeding on animals.

Taz goes still, then tips his head back and releases a blood-curdling coyote howl. The eerie call startles me, raising the hair all over my body—it sounds so real, I'm not surprised when he's answered by a chorus of identical howls in the distance.

He replies with a series of yips, then continues silently down the hill. Intrigued by his interchange with the coyotes, I follow him.

When Nicolas and I visited the zoo in Colorado Springs, the wolves, as well as the bears and apes, reacted violently to our presence. Though the big cats exhibited curiosity more than anything else, I had the distinct impression that the other predators considered us to be deadly enemies.

But it seems like Taz has a bond with these canines. I wonder if they help him hunt. The possibility boggles my mind.

We reach the canyon bottom and Taz veers downstream, following a dry creek bed. He glances at me, then lowers into a half crouch and, placing his feet carefully, weaves through the brush and rocks with no sound. The scent of deer is stronger now, and I creep along behind him, mimicking his careful movements.

I can't deny the thrill of hunting with another hunter. Though Nicolas accompanied me several times in the Colorado forests, he always gave me the lead, allowing me the pleasure of finding and taking down the quarry. And he never joined in for the kill, nor the feeding afterward.

Taz stops and motions me forward with a flick of his hand. Just up ahead is a small group of blacktails browsing along the streambed.

The anticipation and hunger flaring up in my veins is not all my own, and I fight to keep my head as every muscle tenses for the attack. A touch on my arm pulls my red gaze away from the deer, and when I look at Taz, his crimson eyes are shining above a feral smile. I can't help but grin back.

Moving only his finger, he points to himself and the uphill side of the herd, then signals me to take the downhill side. I give him a faint nod and watch him slip into stalking mode.

He drops low to the ground and inches his way up the hill. Even in boots and a leather jacket, Taz makes no sound as he edges closer to the unsuspecting deer. Mesmerized by his sinuous movements, I finally tear my eyes from him and focus on my own hunt.

I draw nearer to my quarry, a fat young buck in his third year, then freeze in preparation for my leap. Taz gives no outward sign, but his blood sends a jolt of electricity through me, signaling his charge at his selected target farther up the hill. I launch straight into the buck's legs and sweep them out from beneath him, then grab his antlers and pin him to the ground. My fangs find their home, and as I descend into the euphoria of feeding, I feel Taz's savage triumph adding to my own, and I joyfully embrace our twin ecstasies.

~

The bliss wrapping the inside of my body becomes warmer and warmer, and suddenly blossoms into the heat of desire. My eyes fly open to see Taz standing over me, his lips bloody, the lust in his eyes matching that building in my veins.

I slowly stand, wiping the blood from my own mouth, and shake my head. "No."

The smoldering look in his eyes shifts into anger. I can barely withstand his war with himself as I struggle to block him out.

Fear, all mine, urges me to run, but that did me no good last time. I brace myself for a fight.

The dark canyon around us is silent, like the calm on a battlefield before all hell breaks loose.

"You remind me of someone I used to know," he finally says, his voice husky. His swirling emotions inside me give way to sadness and loss. His gaze softens and he looks away, then starts walking back upstream.

Shaken, I watch his retreating back. His mystery deepens and I feel myself becoming trapped by this fierce Chosen.

"What . . . what about the carcasses?" I call after him.

Taz answers with several coyote yips, and a dozen grey shapes slink out of the surrounding brush. The sounds of snarling and snapping quickly fill the air as they fight over the meat we've left.

He's trained a cleanup crew. That's something I never thought of.

Huh.

~

Taz remains silent during our long hike back up to the road. When we reach the top, I can no longer contain my curiosity about his origins.

"Taz. Where are you from?"

"You first."

I press my lips tight.

"The sun's going to be up in less than half an hour. We gotta move." He steps into the brush where his bike is hidden and carefully backs it out, then tosses my helmet at me and straps on his own.

"Will you take me to see Alina tomorrow?"

He snorts.

"Not unless you give me some real answers." He glares, puts on his sunglasses, and straddles the Harley. "Now get your ass on this bike, or sleep here on the side of the road."

He stomps down on the kickstarter and the engine's answering thunder breaks the silence of the surrounding night.

"Go to hell." I slam my helmet to the ground. Screw this. I'll get to Alina another way.

I turn and start walking down the road. I don't make it two paces before he steps behind me and grabs my uninjured shoulder, stopping me mid-stride.

"By the way," he says quietly. "The other reason I brought you out here was to hunt. And just cuz we shared one doesn't mean things have changed. You're gonna have to share a lot more than that if you want anything from me."

"Oh, you mean, like my body? My blood? Is that what I have to do to see Alina?"

The desire in *his* blood surges through my barrier, and I quickly slam it back into place.

He laughs, then presses against my back.

"No, but that's not a bad idea. If you're offering, I might consider it."

I wrench out of his grasp and rake him across the cheek.

He sucks his breath in through his teeth.

"Not now, though. I like to take my time—which we're out of." He turns his back on me and walks over to the idling Harley. "Your choice. Couch or rocks. But I'm leaving."

Crossing my arms, I shake my head in refusal as he gets on the bike.

"Just for the record, you won't get to Alina unless it's through me. Any of the others *will* kill you on sight. I'm the only thing keeping you alive right now."

Shit.

I don't know whether to believe him or not, but suddenly I'm not sure I want to take any chances.

I grab my helmet from the ground and hop on behind him. We take off while I'm still fastening the strap.

The ride to the house is nearly as fast as the ride out, but now our speed is fueled by a sense of urgency rather than anger. The sky is grey as we roar into the garage and stagger off the bike. Taz is in his room before the garage door finishes closing. I gratefully collapse onto the couch and bury myself beneath the ragged blanket.

As grimy as it is, it's still way better than a tree.

*A gentle hand brushes the hair back from my brow.*

*I open my eyes and Taz is crouching beside me, wonder shining in his golden eyes. He looks different, almost transparent. His fingers shimmer like candlelight above my shoulder, sorrow whispering across his face, then he pulls back the blanket and helps me sit up. When I look down at my arms, my legs, they bear the same transparency as his.*

*He stands and reaches out a ghostly hand and I take it to stand beside him.*

*Taz pads barefooted across the room, wearing nothing more than his jeans, his ebony hair loose and flowing down his back. He leads me to the front door and then we're standing in the bright outside.*

*With a soft tug on my hand, he leaps into the air, and I follow.*

*We're flying through the morning sunlight now, over tall forest speckled with rooftops in reds and browns, and then with nothing more than the green of the trees. The landscape beneath us changes to the short, grey brush of chaparral-covered hills, and back to the deep green of the coastal redwood forest. Taz guides us downward and the ground rises to meet our bare feet, and we take off running.*

*He keeps firm hold of my hand as we weave through the redwoods and leap over downed limbs across the steep slope. Cool shadows and warm sunlight stream past us, adding depth to the kaleidoscope of rust-colored tree trunks, greens of every shade, and the browns of the forest floor skimming beneath our feet.*

*Low, grey-furred shapes join us in our run, their ears back and pointed muzzles silent as they flow around us. Our mad race flushes a small herd of blacktail deer and, with quick, bounding leaps, the deer scatter. The coyotes take off in pursuit, but we continue our run, now heading upslope.*

*A wide strip of asphalt greets us, its center lined with twin yellow ribbons, and we follow them, our ghostly feet barely touching the ground. Bright sky ahead signals the edge of the forest, and as we draw closer, the redwood curtain draws back, revealing the blue-green waters and white-topped waves of the Pacific Ocean far below.*

*We slow, then stop on an overlook beside the road. The sounds of the eternal battle between sea and land drift upward, crashing and splashing as the ever-shifting water eats away at stalwart rock.*

*Taz draws me close, his fingers still entwined in mine. He kisses our clasped hands and, facing us toward the ocean, moves behind me and pulls me against his chest. His chin resting light upon my head, he begins to softly sing in a language I do not know.*

*His song seems to tell a story, and I catch glimpses of an Indian village, running buffalo across a wide plain, majestic snow-capped peaks piercing a bright blue sky. A group of Indian boys sit in a half circle around a young Catholic priest, a book in his lap. A beautiful Indian maiden flashes a shy smile as she walks by with a basket of berries. Large, slim-fingered hands cradle a ragged piece of paper inked with the faded lines of a tiny sailing ship on an untamed sea.*

*His song dies, and he falls into silence. The sea below us continues its melody, and after a long moment, Taz kisses the top of my head, steps back, and with a tug on my hand, launches us into the bright air. We circle once over the restless waters below, then with the speed of an arrow, we're back at the house and I'm on the couch. Taz tucks the blanket around me, kisses our spectral hands once again, and releases me into oblivion.*

# SUNDAY

## CHAPTER 50

A hot shower usually gives me a clean outlook on things. Today all it does is wash off the dried blood and dirt.

I had awakened feeling unsettled, the taste of Taz's blood fresh in my mouth as if I'd just savored its wild energy. Worse, a vague memory of being elsewhere, the almost-remembering of a dream, had slipped away with my first breath, leaving me confused and longing for whatever it was.

Now I just feel frustrated and pissed off.

Residual healing hunger also still has me a bit on edge, but compounding it is the uncertainty about Taz and, to a lesser extent, what may happen if I keep refusing to answer his questions.

Yet my deepest instincts demand that I continue to guard both my origins and my connection to Nicolas.

Taz's blood in me stirs, signaling that he's beginning to awaken. I quickly shut him off, unable to deal with his complex emotions. Or mine.

I think back on our tumble down the hill last night and the severity of my injuries. Nicolas wasn't kidding when he said broken bones demand huge amounts of blood to heal. Though I went through three deer last night, I'm sure I could handle a couple more if given the chance.

Even more surprising is that I healed perfectly fine without human blood, and much faster than before. Though the speed of healing might be due to the fact that I'm now full-Chosen, it only reinforces what I'd suspected when recovering from the bear injuries—that what I'd really needed then was the blood of deer and elk. Not horse blood, and certainly not human blood. Maybe my healing would've taken a bit longer, but at least I wouldn't have bitten into the proverbial forbidden fruit and discovered a new kind of thirst that continues to plague me even now, more than six months later.

But this time around, the deer blood seems to have been enough. The stiffness in my shoulder is completely gone, and wiping down the mirror confirms what I'd already determined in the shower—no outward trace of injury remains to either my shoulder or my ribs.

Yet, though I have none from my human life, the spider's web of silvery scars from the bear attack in Colorado still crisscrosses my back, arm, and cheek. The antelope horn scar on my belly remains as well. Those events happened months ago, while I was still a half-Chosen. Before I made the final Change.

Wonder what Nicolas would make of that.

Or the fact that Taz's emotions are wreaking havoc within me. I felt none of Nicolas's after he gave me his blood to heal me from the bear. Perhaps he, as an Elder and Maker, had better control. Taz certainly seems to hover on the edge of losing it much of the time.

One thing's for sure.

I don't want to be in his path again when he does.

~

Tension fills the house as the others wake, one by one, and stumble from their respective bedrooms. Their wordless exchanges, accompanied by tight-set jaws and glowering expressions, only emphasize the disharmony I suspect is unusual in this household.

Even the normally jovial Redd says nothing as he fusses with motorcycle parts at the dining room table, his silent condemnation following Taz as the big Chosen returns from the garage and disappears into his bedroom. The odor of burning sage hovers outside the door, and I wonder if it brings him a sense of calm similar to the oils in the ring. But lowering my internal barrier to find out will expose me to his other emotions. I decide it's not worth the risk.

Chia's out in the backyard, her knife thumping into the side of the house over and over. Her words from last night ring in my head as though she just screamed them at me. I feel a twinge of guilt for disrupting what may have been a previously well-oiled machine.

But, I remind myself, I'm not the real culprit, though I may be getting the blame.

The holder of that responsibility re-emerges from his bedroom, shrugging on his leather jacket.

Taz stops and looks at me, questions shining in his golden eyes. His blood in me surges and I resolutely block whatever it is he's feeling.

"What?" I ask, puzzled by his expression, a mixture of curiosity and hopefulness.

"You don't remember, do you?"

"Remember what? You attacking me? Like I could ever forget that."

Dismay paints his features for a split second before flashing into raw anger.

"Aw, to hell with it."

He stomps across the kitchen toward the garage, ignoring Redd's inquisitive look.

"Let's go," Taz yells just before the door slams behind him.

I grab my jacket as Redd opens the window behind him and calls Chia. Within minutes we're leaving the still-closing garage door behind, the sound of Harley engines filling the painful void between the three Chosen.

~

It's nearly midnight. We've spent the evening in the East Bay, cruising from bar to bar in what must be an established route for Taz and his crew. We didn't stay long at any single place; rather, it seemed like they were searching for someone, though who remains a complete mystery to me. The terse communications between the three indicate they've resolved none of their issues, and I wonder how long this will go on before the backlash strikes out again.

And when it does, it will most likely be at me.

We pull into the parking lot at yet another seedy dive. But as I slide off the seat and remove my helmet, two Chosen emerge from a black Audi sedan parked a few spaces away.

I step away from the bike, instantly on guard. Taz and Redd didn't seem to care for the last Chosen we encountered—those of Nicolas's lineage at the airport—and I watch their reactions as these approach.

"Stay here." Taz hangs his helmet from the handlebars and takes off his sunglasses. Redd and Chia seem in no hurry as they dismount.

The Chosen stop about ten feet away.

One of them is dark haired and clean shaven; the other, a honey blond, sports a neatly trimmed beard. Dressed in tailored slacks and button-down shirts, the distinct scents of alcohol, cigarettes, and perfume cling to them as though they just stepped out of an upscale nightclub.

More notably, they do not bear the scent or any other sign of belonging to Nicolas's lineage. Like Taz and his crew, their single-colored auras, one a pale yellow, the other turquoise, are unique and unrelated to one another.

Taz walks toward them, his body loose and relaxed. They, on the other hand, seem to grow more tense as he nears.

"Evening, Taz." The clean-shaven one hesitates, then steps forward and nods.

"Haven't heard from you in awhile." Taz's gruff admonishment sends a flicker of fear across both of their faces.

"There's . . . there's been nothing to report."

"What about that new club in Oakland?"

"Oh. Well, we haven't been there yet. It just opened last week."

"Should've been there several times by now."

"Sorry. We'll go by there tonight."

Taz studies them a moment—a long moment in which I can almost feel them twitching beneath their manicured façades.

"Keep Redd updated. Nightly. Got it?"

"Will do." The Chosen nods. "Anything else?"

"No. We're finished."

The two visibly shaken Chosen offer half bows, then take several steps back before turning and heading for their car at a fast walk.

"Looks like they've been playing more than working," Redd says as Taz returns to the bikes.

Taz just nods.

"You want me to split 'em up?"

"No. Have Jansen and Twig check on them. If they didn't get the message, they're done." Taz puts on his helmet, and I take that as my cue to do the same.

"It's all clear inside," Chia announces, walking toward us from the direction of the bar. Redd holds out her tiny helmet and she tugs it onto her head.

"Let's roll then."

I climb on behind Taz, relieved to hear normal conversation happening once again between these three. As crude as they are, their little family's beginning to grow on me.

Because they have the one thing I don't.

Companionship.

And with that companionship, the trust that those guarding your back aren't going to stick a dagger in it.

# CHAPTER 51

Echoes from our engines bounce back at us as we cruise through one of the many warehouse districts that line the East Bay. Some of the areas near the docks are brightly lit, with towering cranes unloading massive container ships, like giant dinosaurs taking great bites from the swamp. Others are dark and silent, their sky-high steel monsters lying in wait for the next ship so they can pick at its flesh until it's nothing more than a stripped carcass, only to reload it again a short time later.

We pull up to a small warehouse on the waterfront and park. People are milling around outside drinking from bottles hidden within paper bags, smoking cigarettes, smoking other stuff.

But the huge bouncer at the entrance is one of Nicolas's Chosen—one who looks like a candidate for world-wide wrestling, though he's not as tall as Taz. He nods and opens the door.

Bon Jovi's "Wanted Dead or Alive" is screaming from the jukebox when we walk in. Glancing up at Taz, I chuckle. Someone must've expected him—they couldn't have picked a better song for his entrance. But my amusement dies as we get all the way inside.

Chosen scents and auras fill the air, but overriding it all is the coppery sweet smell of blood. Human blood. Taz pauses for a moment, his nostrils flaring.

My jaw spasms once and the fangs are down. Electric anxiety, both his and mine, pulses through my veins. I press Taz's ring against my nose and inhale, over and over.

Reeling, I try to understand what we've walked into. Square tables surround a small but crowded dance floor in the dimly lit bar. Most of the tables are taken, primarily by humans, but a few are exclusively

Chosen. And some are mixed, and no one's bothering to hide what they're doing. The bloodlust explodes as a female Chosen drinks from the wrist of a young man at one table, while at the next, two males are sharing a pretty brunette.

The dance floor is no better. Entwined limbs and mouths are all I see when I look at the couples swaying to the pounding music.

Chia quickly disappears into the mix.

"Taz."

"Hmm." He seems as mesmerized as I am. His blood hungers in my veins, adding to my own craving, and panic races through me.

"I can't be in here."

He doesn't answer.

"*Taz*. I need to leave. Now."

Confusion creases his brow as he looks down at me.

"I don't do this. Get me out of here. *Please*." I grip his upper arm and he tenses as my nails sink into his flesh. The ache in my mouth demands satisfaction, and I fight the urge to bite anything, anyone. Even him.

He looks at Redd. The big Scot sighs and nods.

"I'll be here, laddie."

"We're good?"

"Yeah. We're good, bro."

Without another word, Taz turns and escorts me outside.

I release him and walk ahead, not stopping until I reach the seawall on the other end of the parking lot. Below me, the water's black satin surface shimmers beneath the city lights. The smell of the harbor clears the other scent from my passages, and I gratefully breathe in the fishy stench.

Taz stops behind me. He brushes a wisp of hair back from my face and I resist the impulse to lean into him, to gain any comfort I can. But encouraging him won't do me any good—once I give in, there will be no going back.

And I'm not ready to give up Nicolas.

"You never feed on humans?"

"No," I whisper.

"That could be a problem."

"Sometimes it is."

The water laps gently against the seawall. The sounds of distant traffic and a helicopter across the harbor blend with laughter from outside the bar to form the nighttime voice of this city. I yearn once again for the quiet mountain forests of Colorado and Montana, and wonder what the hell I'm doing here.

Taz steps closer, close enough that I feel him against my back. His hand strokes the scar on my face, then he kisses my temple. His desire and bittersweet longing pulse through me, and my resistance begins to fail.

"Taz. No. Please."

His breath against my ear, he takes hold of my shoulders. Gently. His touch bears a lover's intimacy that somehow feels familiar, like it's caressed me before.

"Tell me you don't want this."

I nearly choke on my response.

"I . . . I don't. I can't." Bloodtears blur the restless water below me.

He goes very still. An eternity passes in a few short seconds.

"Someone else?"

I nod.

"Is that who you're looking for? Who you're *really* looking for?"

I nod again.

He's statue still for a long moment, then brushes his lips against my ear.

"I hope you don't find him."

And with that he steps away. I listen to his near silent footfalls as they cross the parking lot. His blood screams inside me, thick with unsatisfied need and pained rejection, and most shocking, deep self-disgust.

He'll never take me to Alina now.

Taz is leaning against his bike with his arms folded when I walk up. His expression is cold, distant.

"I need to go back inside, and you're not staying out here by yourself. So get your shit together. We might be in there a while."

"No. Don't make me . . ."

"I'm tired of hearing that word from you. You either walk in on your own or I'll throw you over my shoulder and carry you in."

Bastard.

"Just try it."

"Have it your way." He advances on me, crimson-eyed and fully fanged.

I back across the sidewalk and bump into someone. Someone big.

The bouncer.

His massive arms wrap around me. "I got her, Taz."

But apparently Taz doesn't hear him, and the big Indian roars and peels the skin from the bouncer's face with one swipe of his nails. The Chosen releases me as Taz throws him up against the wall. He rears his hand back again, this time aiming for the bouncer's throat.

The door bangs open.

"Hey, bro. Thought I heard you singing out here. Now what're you doing? Let the poor lad go. I'm sure whatever insult he gave you wasn't worth losing his head over." Redd eases in between Taz and the terrified bouncer.

Taz growls and gives the Scot a nasty look, then drops his hand and backs away.

"Watch her. Don't let her out of your sight." He storms into the bar.

"Well, lassie, you heard what he said. Inside. Now." Redd gestures with his bearded chin.

Taking a deep breath, I walk back into the bar, Redd trailing. I keep my gaze on the floor as he guides me to a table.

"Have a seat, lass."

I sit down, the ring plastered against my nose. A commotion on the dance floor is impossible to ignore, and I watch as Taz engages in a growling match with another Chosen over a tall, leggy brunette in a tight dress. A human.

"Ach. Gonna be one of those nights, is it?" But Redd makes no move to interfere this time.

The other Chosen backs down. Taz grabs the wrist of the brunette and tugs her along behind him across the dance floor. They disappear down a hallway at the back.

Redd looks sidelong at me.

"Don't know what you did to piss him off, lass. But I haven't seen *that* Taz in a very long time."

Taz's violence howls in my blood. I struggle to contain it and finally wall it off, along with all of his other wild emotions. The effort drains me, and I sag back against the chair for a moment, then turn to Redd.

"He's not going to kill her, is he?"

Please don't let him kill her over me.

I start to stand, but a heavy hand on my shoulder presses me back into my seat.

"No need to worry about her. She'll be fine."

"He won't—?"

"No, lass. He won't." He frowns. "At least, I don't think he will."

Worry for the girl slips just enough for the hunger to reclaim my attention. My hand trembles as I once again inhale the Hopi herbs in the silver ring. They seem to be working better now that the shock of this place has worn off, and I just keep breathing them in, over and over.

"You're a strange one, I'll give you that. Never seen anyone so concerned about killing before. Except maybe that big Indian." Redd laughs. "At least with humans. Chosen, on the other hand . . ."

"What do you mean?"

He takes in a breath to answer, but just then a waitress—human—walks up to the table, a bottle of what must be bloodwine on her tray along with several glasses.

Redd looks at me, his eyebrows raised in question, and I shake my head.

"Think we'll pass on that for now, missy. But *you* look mighty tasty." He smoothes the russet beard back from his mouth and smiles at the young woman, the tips of his fangs pressing against his lower lip.

I hug the ring to my nose.

She laughs, obviously used to such offers.

"You know the rules. Hands and teeth off the help." With a nod to me, she leaves.

Her uniform is similar to the other waitresses circling the bar—black high heels and skimpy black shorts, topped by a tuxedo-style white blouse with rolled up sleeves and a red bow tie at the throat. Nothing ever changes, not even in the world of the undead. Just like in the human world, women seem to be sex objects in this one as well.

I watch the waitresses hover around the tables, intent on keeping both Chosen and human well-supplied with drink. The humans all have small decanters of liqueur in front of them, and I suppose it's part of the waitresses' jobs to make sure each human patron consumes the alcohol laced with Chosen blood. That would be the only way to keep this place secret. Once bound by the blood, the humans would be physically unable to reveal the underground society's existence and would even go to great lengths to protect it.

But all my musings do little to blunt the impact of what's happening around me. Flashing fangs and the heady aroma of human red nectar has me nearly crawling out of my skin. I stare down at the table and wish I had the clove necklace as well as the ring to help keep me grounded.

A shadow falls over our table and I look up to see two Chosen in suits staring down at me.

They're of Nicolas's lineage, with his feel and characteristic amber-and-violet auras.

Redd slowly eases his chair back.

The shorter of the two leans toward the other as he gestures toward me. "That's her. She's got the scar on her face."

Instinct shifts my body into fight mode as it assesses the two Chosen. Medium in build and height, even together they are no match for the burly Scot beside me. He sits up, suddenly larger, more imposing than normal.

"Is there something I can do for you gents?"

"Where's your partner, Redd?" The taller one takes off his sunglasses. His eyes are deep brown, almost black.

"It's none of your business."

"Doesn't matter anyway." He turns his dark gaze on me. "We're here for her."

I'm not liking this. Something doesn't feel right.

"I don't think so, Johnny Boy." Redd's bearded mouth twitches, exposing a fang.

The other Chosen bristles. A third suit, taller and stockier than the other two, materializes behind them.

"It's Mr. Jonathon to you. And we're taking her." He motions to the others.

"She's not going anywhere," Taz growls from the other side of Redd. I didn't even see him cross the room.

"Nice of you to join us." The Chosen points toward me. "Mr. Isaac wants to know why you haven't brought her in yet."

"I don't answer to Isaac."

"You're overstepping your boundaries, Taz."

"You trying to tell me how to do my job?"

"Yeah. Right now I am. She's coming with us." He moves toward me, his hand reaching as though to grab my arm.

My growl is drowned out by Taz's as he shoves himself between me and the Chosen. The other two rush forward and Redd is out of his chair. Someone pushes someone else and the mass of Chosen explodes into fists, claws, and fangs.

I scramble backward out of the way and look toward the door. With the whole city in which to disappear, now might be my only chance.

But as I sidle away from the battle, I'm brought up short by Chia's dagger poking me in the belly.

"Going somewhere? You got a ringside seat to this little party you started. Sit down and enjoy it."

I feint to the left, then try to duck out to the right. But she's faster, and all I get for my efforts is a slash across the cheek.

"Sit your ass down, bitch. Or I'll take an eye. Or both. That'll keep you still for a while."

Growling, I sit. I look back at the fight, which is now over. Redd stands facing Taz, shaking his head, a thick-fingered hand against the Indian's chest. The three Chosen straighten their torn suits as the last of their injuries heal up on their faces. Other than a few strands of hair that escaped his black braid, Taz looks none the worse for wear.

The dark-eyed Chosen puts on his sunglasses and straightens his jacket, then sneers at the big Indian.

"Psychopathic unbound scum. You're nothing but an overpaid garbage collector. Bring the woman. Tonight." The three walk away, their confidence clearing a path before them.

The muscles across Taz's jaw flex and tension ripples down his neck and across his back. Fingers arched, a low snarl slips from his curled lips. Redd clamps an iron grip on Taz's shoulder.

"Easy now, bro. Save 'em for later, when there's less likely to be questions."

Taz nods and slowly relaxes. He turns to look at me, then at Chia behind me with her dagger resting on my shoulder. He looks back at me and shakes his head.

"Let's go."

~

I stand between the idling bikes, helmet on, and wait while Taz and Redd argue on the other side of the parking lot. Worms of worry crawl up my spine. I don't know who this Isaac is. As much as I want to be rid of Taz and the emotional turmoil that goes with him, I'm reluctant to leave his protection.

Better the enemy you know than the one you don't.

Robert's the only Chosen who's seen me and knows who I am. Worse, he didn't seem too pleased by my presence. I certainly don't know if I can trust him or not. My instincts tell me Alina's still my best bet.

If I can ever get to her.

For now, my fate rests in the big hands of the angry Indian striding toward me.

Taz climbs onto the rumbling motorcycle and I slide on behind him. The sound of the bikes bounces off each warehouse we pass and soon we're back on city streets.

But several blocks later, Redd waves and turns right while we continue straight. The last thing I see of him is Chia on the back of his bike, her middle finger stabbing the air above her head.

# CHAPTER 52

We grab the 880 Freeway north, then swing onto the 80 toward Sacramento. Considering what just happened in the club, the ensuing argument between Taz and Redd and his obvious displeasure at its outcome, I can only assume I'm being delivered to this Isaac—whoever he is.

I just hope he's the next stop on the road to Alina.

Once again I mentally kick myself for failing to use common sense on Halloween night. I never should've gotten on this damn bike, which is now taking me farther and farther from my car and everything I own.

Shit.

Our destination remains a mystery as Taz veers onto the 580 heading to San Rafael, and within a short time, we're crossing through one of the toll booths that accompany nearly every bridge in the area. Dark water flashes beneath us, and in the distant south, lights dot the Bay Bridge crossing from Oakland into San Francisco.

Lost in berating myself, I'm not paying attention to the signs and have no idea where we are when we exit the freeway.

Great. I'm such an idiot.

When we jump onto the 101 south to San Francisco, I'm even more puzzled. We've just gone in a big circle. Why didn't we just take the 80 to the Bay Bridge in the first place?

The answer becomes clear when Taz exits onto Highway 1.

He's not taking me to Isaac, nor to Alina. We're heading back to his place.

I don't know whether to be concerned or relieved.

However, confusion takes over as we blow past the turnoff for his house and begin winding up the steep Panoramic Highway and into the Mt. Tamalpais State Park.

The mood he's in, I'm not sure I want to go hunting with him—I just might be tonight's prey. In any number of ways.

One thing's for sure. The twisting road now heading down the densely forested mountain toward the sea wasn't built for the speed we're traveling, and I have no choice but to wrap myself tightly around him as we lean into tree-lined curve after curve.

Though I haven't been here before, the ocean view peeking through the trees looks familiar. But any appreciation I might have for the breathtaking scenery is quickly buried beneath the apprehension regarding my fate.

Dark sky opens up before us as we slow for a stop sign. Taz ignores it and we turn onto Highway 1 heading back toward San Francisco, the engine roaring its protest as he slams it back up through gear after gear. The winding road along the sea cliffs doesn't hamper our speed one bit, and I continue to cling to Taz, wondering at each turn if he intends to plunge us into the water far below.

But he doesn't. We fly along the road, leaning this way and that in the dance of the biker and his steel steed, and I begin to wonder if this is just his version of going for a run to blow off steam.

I finally relax and release my death grip on him when we turn onto the street for his house. We pull into the garage beside Redd's bike, the engine's thumping heartbeat drowning all thought as it's caged in by painted walls.

It continues to echo in my head after Taz shuts it off. I swing my leg over and step away, then remove my helmet and wait for him.

Not knowing what else to say, I decide a simple thanks might ease the tension between us.

"Thank you for the ride. It was, uh, beautiful." Terrifying, but beautiful.

He looks at me, pained regret flickering across his features a half second before the cold-eyed smirk slams down over his face like a mask.

His mouth twists to one side.

"Just wanted to feel you wrapped around me with those tits in my back one last time."

Then he turns and heads into the house, leaving me standing open-mouthed in the now-silent garage.

*Butterfly wings brush against my lips and I open my eyes to gaze into Taz's, hovering just inches away. Mouth curving into a soft smile, he rises, his hair falling forward around his bare shoulders.*

*Once again he's translucent, as am I, though we're a little fainter than before.*

*He takes my ghost-hand into his and we shoot straight up into a dove grey dawn. Our flight is swift and sure, down the mountain and out over the sea. We continue to descend until we're skimming the coastline just above the water, its silvery surface surging with the pulse of the earth. The sea cliffs follow our descent before falling away to a pale golden beach.*

*Our feet touch down upon the wet sand as gently as falling leaves. Spirit-Taz leads me up beyond the surf line, then motions me to sit with my back to the sea. He sits cross-legged facing me, never letting go of my hand, and then turns and points with his other up at the mountaintop behind him.*

*The grey dawn has melted into palest blue, and as I watch, it fades and begins to glow.*

*The glow brightens and turns to golden-white fire as the sharp edge of the sun peeks over the mountain.*

*Entranced, I watch as the shining disk creeps upward to claim the day.*

*Sunrise.*

*I haven't seen one in over five years.*

*My chest near-bursting with emotion, I look across at Taz. The soft smile lighting his face is as bright as the celestial body above him, and he reaches out to touch my lips with feather-light fingers. Peace and joyful calm blossom outward from him to gather me within their gentle folds, and a golden serenity I've never known settles over me like the warming rays of the morning sun.*

*He then shifts his body to sit beside mine. Together we watch the sun free itself from the mountain and take its place high in the sky.*

*After long breathless moments, Spirit-Taz helps me to my feet and we join it, circling once over the pale sand below, and in less than a heartbeat, we're back in the house. As he guides me to the couch, I'm surprised to see myself already there, deep in the sleep of the undead. I look back at Taz, puzzled, as he lays me down, then with a soft kiss on my brow, he releases my hand and the darkness rushes in.*

# MONDAY

## CHAPTER 53

For the second afternoon in a row, I awaken with a sense of restlessness and confusion, and a yearning for something I can't quite recall. The only thing I can attribute it to is Taz's blood. Thankfully its effect seems to be weakening, and I'll be glad when it wears off, which hopefully, will be sometime in the next couple days.

But from what he said last night, his blood might not be the only thing I'll soon be rid of.

I may soon be rid of him as well, and the thought of that distresses me much more than it should. Worse, I'm not sure if the source of that distress is him—or me.

It's shortly after sunset when Taz emerges from his bedroom, shrugging into his leather jacket.

He stops next to the couch and stares at me for a moment, his expression neutral.

I say nothing as I try to assess his mood.

A flicker of sadness darts across his face, then he shakes his head.

"Pack your stuff," he growls. Yanking his braid from beneath his collar, he heads toward the garage.

I quickly gather my things into the plastic bag, slip my jacket on, and follow him.

Must be taking me to Isaac after all. Unless . . . unless he's finally taking me to Alina.

And suddenly, I don't want to go.

Puzzled over my unexplained panic at the thought of leaving, I hesitate as I step into the garage.

Any further thoughts I have on my fate are drowned out by the roar of the sleek black machine, its chrome gleaming beneath the garage light as it warms up to a steady idle. Taz tosses my helmet at me and revs the engine several times, obviously impatient to get wherever it is we're going.

I hand him the plastic bag and he quickly bungees it to the handlebars while I fasten my helmet. I'm barely seated before he hits the throttle. The back tire screeches against the concrete floor as I desperately grab for him and hang on. When it hits the dew-slickened cement outside, the whole bike slews to one side and then the other, spitting tiny rocks in its wake.

But Taz keeps control of the wild, steel monster beneath us, only backing off the gas a fraction as we tear up the driveway toward the road.

I close my eyes and press against his back, positive that this time he's going to kill us both as we race toward town.

Wherever he's taking me, he sure isn't happy about it.

~

The tension rolling off him makes me feel as though my arms are wrapped around a nuclear bomb as we wait at the stoplight for the southbound 101 on-ramp. Red changes to green, then changes to red again. Still we sit here, the only ones on the road, the Harley idling impatiently. Taz revs it several times, then lets out the clutch at the next green light.

But instead of staying in the right lane to get on the freeway heading south, he veers the bike across the road and into the left lane and we take the northbound on-ramp.

Somehow, I have a feeling that him changing his mind is a not good thing.

And I have no choice but to hang on.

We aren't on the 101 for more than a few rushed moments when Taz exits onto Highway 37 heading east. Skirting the waters and wetlands of a small bay, we join up with Interstate 80 and continue east toward Sacramento.

The coiled steel beneath my arms slowly relaxes now that he's made whatever decision he was wrestling with. I loosen my hold slightly, take a deep breath, and let the roar of the motorcycle and rushing wind work their calming magic on me.

As we approach the outer limits of the city, my nerves ratchet up again in anticipation of our journey's end. But Taz doesn't slow, and the overhead freeway signs name a new eastbound destination—Reno and Lake Tahoe.

Unable to guess where we might actually be heading now, I close my eyes, lean against Taz's broad, leather-jacketed back, and give myself over to the rumbling serenity of the ride.

~

Crisp, mountain air and the smell of pines stir me from my semi-catatonic state. I open my eyes in time to see a green freeway sign flash by bearing the name Donner Pass. On either side of the split highway, trees and rock-studded road-cuts bear a thin blanket of white snow. The east- and westbound lanes weave along the pass like dance partners, drifting apart briefly over the steep terrain before once again reuniting to carry their precious steel cargoes side by side. When we reach the top of the pass and begin our descent toward the Nevada desert, the Truckee River teases us with peeks at its frothy skirt as it attempts to cut in on the asphalt couple.

Memories and their associated emotions suddenly assault me as the pine-covered mountains and their intoxicating scents whip past us. Yet, as much as I loved my time in the Colorado and Montana Rockies, I can no longer think of those places without feeling the pain that came with them.

And, as much as I yearn for Nicolas, I'm beginning to wish I'd never left the oak forests and rolling hills of California an eternity ago.

Because I'm no longer sure it was worth it. I'm no longer sure *he* was worth it.

I feel adrift, cut loose from my moorings as the current takes me wherever it wills. And the current right now deftly steers a big Harley through a series of descending curves, and I lean with it, and my rebellious body wants to keep leaning with it, to learn its song and its secrets and its joys.

Worse, the connection between us seems to be more than just through his blood, and though Taz has done nothing to deserve it, my growing attraction to him is becoming difficult to deny.

Shutting my eyes once again, I shift slightly to one side, away from the sheltering back, and allow the full force of the wind to rip away my thoughts.

~

A loud, popping backfire from the engine accompanies our final descent into Reno. The Nevada desert, though not as cold as the Sierra Nevada Mountains, still holds its own November chill. As we approach the bright lights of the state's second largest city-that-never-sleeps, I wonder how I'll cope with the bombardment of sights, sounds, and odors that go along with one of the West's premiere gambling centers.

That fear is allayed when Taz blows right through the city and toward the desert.

A very empty desert.

The new fear is much worse.

At the far edge of town, Taz turns off, and within a few blocks, pulls up to a storage facility gate, then jabs his fingers into the electronic code box. We roll through the opening and cruise past several aisles before turning down one and stopping midway in front of a garage-style door that looks just like all the other doors lining the way.

I slip off the bike and wait while he opens the padlock and lifts the door. A rugged but non-descript tan, hardtop Jeep outfitted for desert travel fills most of the small storage unit. Within minutes the Jeep is outside and the bike is inside.

"What about my stuff?" I point to the plastic bag tied to his handlebars.

"It's not going anywhere." Taz holds the passenger door open for me, his expression tight.

What's that supposed to mean?

Having no real alternative, I get in the Jeep.

Taz climbs in behind the wheel and we're off again, this time under 4x4 power.

Heading north, we're soon on a dirt road surrounded by nothing but passing desert scrub beside us and a glittering star blanket above. The moon hasn't risen yet, but my night-centric vision has no problems making out rock formations and small mountain ranges in both the near and far distance. We forge through the darkness with headlights off, the Jeep groaning and rattling in protest as we bounce down the washboard and pothole-pitted road.

Taz doesn't say a word to me the entire time.

My own brain fills the void with question after question. I don't know what to think. He was clearly against doing as Redd suggested, and his apparent relief in his decision at the freeway on-ramp in Mill Valley indicates that he's following his own game plan now—whatever that might be. I don't know if he's hiding me or planning to kill me. If it's the latter, why take me clear out into the desert to do it? He could do it anywhere in the Bay Area, where there's plenty of deep water in which to dispose of my body.

# CHAPTER 54

Our wild ride takes on the character of a whitewater rafting trip when he slows, veers off the road, and cuts across the raw desert, leaving dust and flying stones in our wake. I tighten my harness—simple seat belts would be a joke in this beast of a Jeep—and hang on to the inner roll bar as we careen madly through grasping brush and maneuver around crouching rocks.

He's gone from trying to kill us on two wheels to doing so on four, and somehow it's even more terrifying.

After a breathless airborne moment ends with a jaw-shattering impact that would've obliterated any lesser machine, I catch Taz stealing a sly glance in my direction and realize our mad dash may not be as fueled by rage as I thought. But his expression quickly shifts into his normal glare and leaves me wondering just who I'm dealing with tonight—monster or schoolboy.

As we approach the base of a small, flat-topped mountain range, he yanks the steering wheel to one side. We slide sideways in a flurry of dirt and debris and come to a sharp halt just a few feet from the edge of a steep drop into a ravine. As the dust cloud settles down around us, Taz looks over at me.

I just stare back, speechless that we're still in one piece.

He chuckles, releases his harness, and gets out.

Insane. Taz is one-hundred-percent, certifiably insane. And I had to be stupid enough to get on his bike the first time we met.

"You gonna to sit there all night?"

With a sigh, I unfasten my harness and climb out.

He balances on the rim of the gully. As I step beside him, he turns his head to study me a moment, then gestures across the thirty-foot gap.

"Ready?"

Without waiting for an answer, he grabs my wrist. When he pushes out into the air, I have no choice but to leap with him. It's that or have my arm torn off.

Taz releases me as we hit the ledge across from the Jeep and takes off in a steady jog toward the mountains. I run behind him, unable to ignore the way his long strides eat up the ground with a grace you wouldn't expect from someone so big. But he is a Chosen, I remind myself, and I haven't encountered one yet who lacked total mastery over their body.

Nearing the base of the mountain, we begin to ascend the lower slopes, continuing along the gully until it goes no farther. Without missing a beat, Taz darts up a game trail on the side of the formation and we keep climbing. The desert below us disappears as we head around a bend toward a hidden canyon.

Though I should be pretty worried about his plans for me, nothing in his demeanor indicates he intends any harm. In fact, the violence he wears as a second skin seems to slough off with each step he takes, revealing an inner calm I'd not thought possible for him.

The ravine far below ends in a box canyon. Ahead of us the terrain changes from steep, scree-filled slopes to a wall of vertical rock.

Taz doesn't even break stride as he shifts from sure-footed mountain goat to fearless desert lizard and heads straight up the wall. I try to use the same ledges and handholds, but his reach is much longer than mine and I slow to seek my own path.

At one point when I cannot find a good grip with which to pull myself up, his hand shoots down from above me. I glance at him as I take it and am surprised at the smiling light in his eyes and the soft, upward curve of his lips.

He slows his pace then, offering help even where not really needed, and together we make our way up the imposing face of the mountain.

When we reach the top, I'm amazed at the sweeping view of the desert in the distance, its flat terrain interrupted by long spines of mountain ranges running north and south. The stars above nearly outnumber the black spaces between them, and to the east the half-moon peers over the horizon. The cold air is still, the surrounding night silent, and I experience the strange sensation of being on an alien planet.

Taz's dark silhouette stands out against the starlight, a part of the landscape like one of the surrounding mountains, and my sense of otherworldliness increases.

How can something so unnatural fit so easily into a natural environment?

Waving me over, Taz starts walking toward the other side of the table-topped mountain. I catch up to him, only to be brought up short by a sudden drop-off that appears at my feet. A flash of imbalance is steadied by a strong arm blocking me from the edge and I hastily step back.

What appears to be part of the mountain we're on is actually a separate mesa, its wind-scoured top over sixty feet away. The black, yawning chasm between the two seems bottomless and I shudder at the thought of toppling over into it.

"Think you can make it?"

"What? Jump across *that*? Are you crazy?"

"Do it all the time."

"What—crazy? Yeah, that I can believe."

Taz snorts, takes a step back, and launches across the darkness, landing with at least ten feet to spare.

"Come on, newborn. You can do it. If you're worried, just get a running start."

He's nuts.

But I start sizing up the jump anyway. I haven't really tested my full-Chosen abilities, not like this, but I guess if he thought I couldn't make it, he wouldn't suggest it.

At least, I hope not.

With a sigh, I take several strides back, then take off into a dead run. At the edge I leap and feel myself soaring like a bird, only to find the opposite side rushing at me faster than I'd prepared. My landing collapses into a tumble across dirt and rock until I hit something solid and come to an abrupt stop.

I open my eyes to stare at a black boot and denim-covered leg just inches from my face. Disgusted with myself, I roll away and scramble to my feet, though not much more gracefully than I'd landed.

A deep laugh explodes from the broad chest behind me. I refuse to look at him as I brush the dirt from my clothes.

"Bear killer, huh? Did they die from laughing?"

Asshole.

But I hide my mortified smile as I think about how ridiculous I must've looked. And how much more I prefer the teasing schoolboy over the sullen monster.

Shaking his head, he turns and walks toward the other side. I fall in behind him, determined not to repeat my mistake. When we reach the edge, he stops.

Before us is another mesa, though much smaller. It can't be more than about a hundred feet wide, and stands out like a little thumb surrounded by the thicker fists of the tabletops around it. Rock and soil from the gap detaching it from our mesa litter the ground far below.

Taz stares across the opening, his cloak of serenity ruffled by what appears to be a momentary unease. He takes a deep breath, then another.

"Wait here," he finally says, and vanishes over the edge.

I peek over its lip to see him leap across the gap and land on a narrow ledge of the thumb-shaped mesa. He sidles toward a boulder as tall as he is and, pressing his back against it, shoves. It reluctantly gives ground, revealing a dark opening behind it. Taz reaches in, the entire upper half of his body disappearing into the rock, and emerges a moment later carrying a large, rolled-up fur and a smaller leather-wrapped bundle.

With both tucked beneath an arm, he works his way around the boulder and follows the ledge until he's lost to my view around a curve. I continue to watch the tiny trail, waiting for his signal to follow.

After several long moments, I dust away the rubble from beneath my feet, then take a seat on the rim and let my legs dangle out into space. A soft, cool breeze springs up and plays around my face, bringing desert scents unknown to me. In addition to the earthy smell of sand and soil, I catch fragments of the dried brush, rodent, and reptilian odors that make up the bulk of the life out here in this harsh environment.

Combined with the lack of cover, this is the last place someone like us would want to be, and I wonder at Taz's attraction to the area.

A new scent reaches me—burning sage. Movement, along with a soft, low singsong chant, pulls my attention from the trail on which Taz disappeared and to the top of the thumb across from me. Taz is once again framed by starlight, shirtless and barefoot now, with long hair unbound and waving in the breeze, and standing with his arms upraised in offering to the sky. He holds the ends of a flute between his hands—no, it's a long, Native American pipe—and turns toward the east. His muscular back to me, he repeats the chant, then faces south and again the soft words of an unknown language reach my ears.

Except—the rhythm of the words seems familiar, like I've heard it before.

When Taz turns in my direction, his gaze is far away, his face serene as he communes with his gods.

I feel embarrassed to be there, an intruder into his secret world, yet privileged to be allowed to witness it.

Because he's chosen to let me see this, to see a side of him I suspect he closely guards.

But why?

He finishes his song and reverently places the pipe onto a small, flat rock beside the fur. Picking up a smoldering bundle of sage, he waves it gently around his body before setting it back down next to the pipe.

Then raising his arms straight out at his sides, he closes his eyes and slowly begins to chant once again. His body seems to vibrate, as though seeking to break its earthly bonds and leap into the sky.

A strange vision of him, of feathers sprouting from his upraised arms, steps from his still form. The ghost of Taz moves out into an ancient dance that predates civilization, its feathered arms waving up and down in long, slow strokes. It begins slowly whirling around the perimeter of the fur in a series of graceful circles, a whispered song tumbling from its lips.

The translucent specter screeches its ownership of the sky as its dance speeds up, mimicking the steep dives of the falcon. Turning faster and faster, it wheels against the backdrop of the starlit night, long hair flying, until it's nothing more than a blur of untamed, carefree energy.

The breath catches in my throat as this magnificent Chosen unveils his true self to me, and a fear sharper than any he's struck before settles deep into my gut.

I don't know if what I'm witnessing is real or imagined, but this raw, violent force of nature, with his lightning-fast mood changes, his mastery over his environment, the sensitivity hidden beneath his harsh exterior, sends the wild part of me into a frenzy. Visions of us running together, hunting together, join his ghostly dance and I fight the heat building within my veins.

The whirlwind slows, mimicking the lazy drift of the eagle, then it rejoins its earthbound body. With a final shake of his hair, Taz lowers his arms, his profile stark against the rising moon.

I'm transfixed, waiting, dreading what might happen next.

The cliff upon which I now stand has nothing to do with the one at my feet.

Sharp pain in my fists shakes me from my stupor and I stare at the dripping blood, at the nails buried deep within my palms.

*Nicolas . . .*

I . . . I feel like he's slipping farther and farther away.

Swallowing, I open my hands and watch the wounds seal, then take a deep breath and look up.

Taz is staring in my direction, eyes reddened, his nostrils flared.

I crouch and scrub my palms against the rough ground, then stand.

"Want to show you something," he says, his voice barely above a whisper. "Take off your shoes and socks, but bring them with you."

The cliff beckons, and in a moment of feral abandon, before rational thought can intrude, I unzip my boots and slip them off, tuck them beneath my arm, and make the short leap across to the top of the thumb.

He meets me and takes my things.

"Wait here." Taz deposits them at the edge of the fur, beside his own huge biker boots. Though my feet are not tiny by any measure, my boots look as though they belong to a child next to his. His leather jacket and T-shirt lie neatly folded in a pile on the other side of his boots.

He rejoins me, then points at the ground.

"Stay on the trail."

A narrow path, its smooth surface in sharp contrast to the rough, desert-baked crust around it, winds its way back and forth along the rim of the thumb. Taz turns north, his bare feet padding softly ahead of me, then stops and gestures at the ground.

"These are some of the Western tribes—Chumash, Miwok, Modoc." He points to a set of primitive figures carved into the rocky soil, then moves farther north along the trail. "Northwestern," he says, waving at more figures etched into the desert varnish.

I try to ignore the physicality of his presence—the way he moves, the long black hair brushing against his coppery skin, his masculine scent—and force myself to focus on his words as we weave back and forth around the mesa.

Taz seems completely absorbed in revealing his desert canvas, which turns out to be a map of tribal nations as they existed before losing their homes and cultures to the gold miners, settlers, and city builders who saw nothing but an empty land rich with opportunity.

He talks about some of the tribes, how they lived and how they died, and I begin to understand a bit of the rage that lives deep within his bones. Others he mentions only by name, but the silence that accompanies each of these speaks louder than any words.

And then we're at the center of the mesa, beside the fur.

He turns to me and the histories filling his golden eyes slip away, and what's left behind makes my breath stop.

"Close your eyes." The quiet words carry a hint of his earlier song.

"I . . ."

"Just close them."

My throat tight, I close them.

*If he touches me, I . . . I'm out of here.*

I say it to myself again and again, knowing that it will make little difference.

"Relax. I'm not going to hurt you. I want you to feel something." A long moment goes by before he speaks again. "Stop thinking. Just feel the earth beneath your feet—really *feel* it."

Trying to ignore his body standing only a dozen inches from mine, I do as he says.

The ground is cold, and rough. Little grains of broken and wind-scoured rocks dig into my soles. I concentrate, trying to figure out what it is I'm supposed to be feeling.

"Become part of the earth. Listen to its heartbeat. *Feel* its heartbeat."

I focus on the bottoms of my feet, and what's beneath them. My other senses finally relax and step aside, and I scarcely breathe. Time loses meaning as I stand there for long minutes, or maybe it's hours. And then I feel . . . something.

A vibration. Like a low hum, pulsing against my feet, its heat and energy slowly rising up my legs.

My eyes fly open and I stare at Taz in amazement.

He steps closer, his normally harsh expression soft and filled with longing.

I should move away. But I don't.

"Feel it?" Taz reaches out, his rough fingers gentle against my face, his eagle eyes peering deep into mine.

All I can do is nod.

He takes my hand and places it on his chest. Over his heart.

"Then feel this. Know this." He steps closer. "I . . . I exchange blood with no one. But with you, I would."

As his words sink in, I again see a vision of us running and hunting together. Of us moving and loving together, and of an eternity spent gazing up at the stars and living close to the earth.

The familiar pain of myself splitting in half—the same pain I felt when I left Nicolas—rips through me head to toe.

*No . . .*

Please no. Not another choice.

Bloodtears blur my vision before I can stop them and I quickly shut my eyes, then turn away from him. Hugging myself, I open them to stare out at the pale eastern horizon as full-scale war erupts within me.

"Sonya . . ." Taz steps behind me. His hands caress my shoulders as his cool breath whispers across the top of my head.

He abruptly freezes.

"Aw, hell." His hands slide away as he steps back.

I inwardly cringe, fighting against the urge to turn around.

"We gotta go."

The urgency in his voice jars me back to the here and now, and frowning, I turn to see him gathering his clothes and boots.

And then it dawns on me. I spin back around to the east.

The dawn. And it's fast approaching, and we're in the middle of the desert with absolutely no cover for miles.

Though I no longer burn, the idea of baking all day, unconscious beneath the desert sun, still triggers an instinctive fear I cannot control.

As I turn back to Taz, he shoves my boots and socks at me, stuffs the pipe into its leather bag, and slips the strap up over his shoulder.

"What about the rest of your things?"

"Leave 'em. We'll put our boots on over there." He gestures toward the next mesa. "Let's go. And watch where you step," he cautions, and we take off for the western edge of the rim.

I'm not sure I've ever run, leapt, and scrambled so fast in my life, but I can barely keep up with him. He stops several times to wait, to help me, before once again leading our downward rush.

We reach the Jeep in a quarter of the time it took to climb to the thumb. He throws his gear into the back and we're bouncing across the desert before I'm even all the way in. I grab the swinging door and slam it, then fight the buckle in the harness as we careen across the brightening landscape. The sky begins to fade from grey to pale blue.

"Hell. We're not gonna make it. Shoulda stayed at the gully. Better hope no one finds us." Taz jams on the brakes and bails out of his seat. He opens the tailgate and I watch, fascinated, as he yanks hinged steel plates down from the ceiling to cover the windows. My view of him is cut off as he drops a third one down between the driver's compartment and the back.

Within seconds, he's opening my door.

"Come on," he says as he hits the lock.

I hesitate. I haven't burned since before completing the Change. Since Nicolas and I shared blood. My earlier panic was strictly left over instincts.

I think.

But before I can explain, Taz grabs me and propels me toward the rear of the Jeep.

"Get inside."

The storage area has barely enough room for one, let alone both of us.

"But—"

My legs are scooped out from under me as he picks me up and unceremoniously dumps me into the back of the Jeep. As I twist to fight my way out, the heavy weight of the sun bleeds all my strength from me.

Taz fills the opening at the back of the Jeep as the first rays break the eastern horizon behind us.

"Move over," he slurs as he yanks the tailgate shut and cranks up a steel plate covering the back window.

I try to squish myself against the far end, but there's just not enough room in here for two of us, and my muscles are no longer responding.

Fading fast, I feel myself pulled and turned and then enveloped by his huge body as he curls himself around me.

The last thing I hear as I drown in the sun's darkness are his words whispered into my ear.

"Don't worry. I'll never let anything hurt you."

*A soft, low chant caresses my ear. I wake to the cramped interior of the Jeep as Spirit-Taz runs his spectral fingers down my arm to lace them with mine. We take to the desert sky just as the sun bursts from the eastern horizon in a halo of soft coral and palest rose.*

*I want to swim in it, to bask in its beckoning rays and drink in the kiss of its warmth, but when I try to pull my hand free, Taz grips it tighter and shakes his head no.*

*Three mesas rise from the desert floor and we head for the smallest. As it appears below us, morning shadows etch an ancient map into its flat, wind-scoured surface. Drawn stick figures hunt and fish and camp amid forested mountains and scrub-covered deserts, along rivers and lakes and seas, their lives woven with buffalo, deer, and horses.*

*Taz heads us downward to the center of the world carved from stone and we come to a rest upon a dark-colored fur. A slight breeze whips his hair around his head as he turns to me.*

*He's even more translucent than I remember. An image of him appears in my mind, his hand outstretched to me as he slowly fades into nothingness. Sadness paints his ghostly face, and I have the sense this may be our last time together in these forms.*

*His sadness becomes mine as well. But he smiles and shakes his head no, and a song of joy flutters from his lips to drift and curl around our bodies. He reaches out and touches my hair and it falls free from the braid binding it. The breeze lifts it to join his, and the strands intertwine like lovers discovering one another for the first time.*

*Taz moves closer. He raises our clasped hands to his lips, and with his other hand, reaches up to my face and touches mine.*

*I lean into his fingers, gently kissing each one.*

*The soft fur is now beneath my naked body, and Taz's above.*

*We make gentle love under the rising sun as it climbs higher and higher into a bright turquoise sky.*

*Human love, for our spirit-selves are human.*

*No fangs, no blood, no violent taking from one another.*

*Just giving and touching and sharing, and we give and touch and share until the sun is falling into the western mountains.*

*Taz's song fills me with light and warmth, then fades away into peaceful silence with our last kiss. He stands, his hand still clasping mine, draws me to my feet, and faces us toward the setting sun.*

*Then we run, and when we reach the mesa's rim, we dive from its edge, two falcons in freefall, and the desert rushes to greet us. At the last possible moment, we pull up, our bodies arching to taste the sky one more time.*

*The Jeep's roof blossoms from the sand below. The mountains are devouring the sun when we finally slip inside.*

*As Taz settles me back into my sleeping body, I want to ask him something, but no words are able to escape my mouth. He sadly smiles and his lips touch mine, and his soft chant is the last thing I feel before the darkness swallows me whole.*

# TUESDAY

## CHAPTER 55

The sun slowly releases its grip on me and I try to take my first breath of the day, but my chest cannot rise against the cold weight clamped tightly around it. Vein-screaming panic arcs into every cell and I snap awake to find myself encased in darkness as black as a tomb. I shove arms and legs outward, only to meet solid resistance just inches away.

I *am* in a tomb.

Choking with fear, I try to claw through a network of webs entangling my fingers. It covers my face as well, and spitting, I fight free of it and seek to tear away the restraints holding me down. My hands encounter skin and muscle and . . . an arm.

Memory floods in as my brain fully engages.

*Taz.*

He's wrapped tightly around me, his hair covering me like a blanket. And as I struggle to get loose, he only hangs on tighter.

"Taz. Let go. You're going to break my ribs."

I stop fighting and wait a moment. His hold eases, just a little.

"Taz . . . Let go of me."

But nothing. No response. No movement, no whisper of breath, nothing.

He's dead to the world. Literally, I suppose.

I try to lift his arm, but it once again clamps around me and my ribs shift ever so slightly.

Crap. I'm stuck here until he wakes up. And based on the last couple days, that could be hours from now. All earlier attraction to him is now buried beneath seething resentment at finding myself trapped within his arms.

Yet, they feel familiar, like they've held me before. I can't seem to shake this feeling of knowing him in another time, another place.

Confusion swirls within me, as though the blood of Nicolas is at war with that of Taz's.

Once again, my body is a battleground.

Very carefully, so as not to trigger Taz to tighten his hold again, I brush his hair away from my face and settle in to wait, my conflicting emotions the weapons in a new campaign for my soul.

An eternity later, he takes a half breath and freezes. His stillness now is not one of the sleeping undead, but that of one awakening and assessing its surroundings before moving and revealing itself to potential danger. A few seconds pass, and then he groans and presses himself even closer to me, shifting his hips against mine.

I nearly explode from his arms when I feel a hardness I don't want, and where I don't want it.

"What the hell! Get off me!" I slam an elbow into his ribs and he releases me.

Silence fills the tiny area inside the Jeep, only to be broken by his bitter chuckle.

"That's not the reaction I usually get from women who share my bed."

I twist around and bare my fangs at him.

"Touch me again and you'll lose any reason a woman might have for sharing your bed."

"Like to see you try." The red flash in his pupils underscores the mocking challenge in his dark golden eyes, only inches from mine.

"Let me out. *Now*."

"Can't do that yet. Sun's not quite down. Don't want to blister that delicate white skin of yours."

"I don't burn. Let me out."

"You don't burn? But you sleep. I felt the sun take you away."

Tired of arguing, I try to reach over him and grab the latch on the tailgate. He knocks my arm aside.

"Well, *you* might not burn, but I do. We're staying put until I say it's time to go."

Fuming, I cross my arms and push away from him as far as the tiny compartment will let me—which is all of about six inches.

The smirk on his face slides away, and in its place rises a smoldering anger.

Taz takes a breath as though to snarl more words at me, then his jaw snaps shut and he rolls onto his back to stare at the ceiling. His bare chest rises and falls several times.

"Fuck this." He cranks down the steel covering the tailgate window, turns the latch, and kicks the tailgate open. He slides his half-naked body out into the fading light of early evening.

"You want out? Then get out."

I slip past him, shove my hands into my jacket pockets, and start walking west.

After several long moments, the Jeep's engine starts. Tires crunching against the rocky ground, it passes me on my left and stops. The passenger door flings open.

My hesitation only lasts a second or two before I climb in, fasten the harness, and once again clutch the roll bar.

~

Our trip back to town ends the way it began—in total silence. Only this silence is heavy and definitely laced with anger, and the drive back determined rather than exuberant.

I wait outside the storage unit while Taz parks the Jeep and pushes out his bike. He starts it and leaves it idling, then gathers his hair into a ponytail, quickly weaves it into a braid, and winds an elastic band around the end. When he's finished, he jerks a cell phone from inside his jacket and, moving away from the noise of the bike, thumbs the keypad and raises it to his ear.

"Where are you?" He nods. "Meet you at the office in a few hours."

I hand him his helmet when he returns to the bike, feeling guilty for the way I reacted after what he shared with me on the mountain last night.

But I didn't ask him for that. And yet, as I climb on behind him and grab on to his waist, I can't help but think about what might've happened on the mesa if the sun had been a little farther from making its morning appearance.

~

Some of the San Francisco streets seem familiar, and as we turn onto a particularly steep one, I recognize the corner where Taz and I waited for Redd after the airport. Halfway up the street, we stop at a pair of wrought-iron gates set within a stucco archway and a camera whirs awake, its shutter opening and closing as it focuses on us.

The gates hum and swing inward. We ride into a small courtyard surrounded by an elegant, early-1900s mansion. Taz parks in a shrub-bordered alcove off to the side, next to Redd's bike. We dismount and take off our helmets, then he loosens the bungee cord and hands me my bag of clothes. But he refuses to even look at me.

Taz stands next to the bike for a moment, staring out toward the street, then shrugs off his jacket and drapes it across the handlebars, his movements slow and deliberate. He starts toward the front door, and as I fall in beside him, he stops. With a deep breath, he turns and faces me. The shadow in his gaze doesn't mask the desperation building in the fading remnants of his blood.

"Sonya. I . . ." He reaches toward me.

"Don't."

Don't say it, because I can't handle it right now.

Sadness and regret flicker across his face, only to be replaced by a look of utter darkness. His jaw tightens, and fingers curling tight against his palm, his arm drops to hang stiffly by his side. His blood in my veins turns to ice.

Without another word, he heads toward the house, and I follow him.

We're greeted by what I can only describe as a butler—a human one. But as we walk into the chandeliered foyer, I noticed two brawny Chosen bodyguards armed with Uzis. Their auras mark them as Nicolas's. They study us with cold gazes, but make no other movement.

"I'll announce your presence." The butler's purposeful walk as he heads down the marble-lined hall makes me realize I've once again entered the formal world of sophisticated and highly manipulative Chosen—one in which I never felt at ease. In retrospect, Taz's crude environment doesn't seem so bad. I sense the hidden dangers here are much worse than the obvious ones in his social circle.

Taz stands near the door, his arms crossed and expression closed. His stillness matches that of the bodyguards, and I feel increasingly uncomfortable. I'm almost relieved when the butler returns, but the feeling is short-lived as I contemplate the impending meeting.

"Follow me, please." With a nod of his head, the butler turns and heads back the way he came. Taz falls in behind him, dwarfing the man. The black braid swings against the stiffness of his back in rhythm with his long and easy stride. His power and confidence wrap around him like a mantle, his pride glitters like a crown, and despite his savagery, he strikes me as though he could be a king among our kind if he wanted to.

I wonder what he'd have been like if we'd met under different circumstances.

But I'll never get to know that Taz, the one I glimpsed in quiet whispers and brief caresses, who blends with the wild even easier than I do and offered me the precious gift of acceptance of me as I am.

Regret twists within me. My goal of finding Nicolas—the one driving force that's kept me going—is now even more tainted with uncertainty and doubt.

ϰ

When we enter what looks to be a tastefully decorated waiting room, Redd leans forward in the deep seat of an upholstered antique chair. Thankfully, Chia's nowhere in sight.

"Had me a little worried, bro. Shit's been hittin' the fan, if you know what I mean."

Taz grunts and, without waiting for the butler, walks past and opens the ornate door at the end of the room. Frowning, the butler hastens to close it behind him.

I'm left standing in the middle of the waiting room, feeling a little lost. Spotting a gilded mirror on the wall across from Redd, I undo my braid and finger comb the hair the best I can, then re-braid it. I notice Redd watching me in the mirror.

"Redd. Can I ask you a question?"

"Sure, lassie."

"What is it you and Taz do? What's your job?"

Redd scratches his beard.

"We're Hunters. We patrol the territory and make sure no foreign Chosen come in unannounced." He fixes me with a curious stare.

"What do you do when you find them?"

He squirms in his chair.

"Well, lassie, here's the thing. When we find them, and we always do, no matter how clever they think they are . . ." Redd tips his head. "We kill them."

"You what?"

"We kill them. Maybe after a little interrogation first. But usually? No questions asked. It's territory law, and everyone knows it. Gotta ask permission to enter first; otherwise, it's a guaranteed form of suicide."

My hand flies to my mouth.

"Why . . . why didn't you kill me?"

"I've been asking myself that since Taz spotted you. You're not the first pretty thing that's snuck in without an invite, but you are the first to live to talk about it."

I swallow and think back over the last several days. Taz's voice rings through my ears as though he's standing right before me.

*Been tracking your every movement for weeks.*

The door opens. Taz emerges and strides right past me like I'm not even here.

*If I wanted you dead . . . you'd be dead.*

Doesn't say goodbye, doesn't look at me, nothing.

*I exchange blood with no one. But with you, I would.*

His boots echo against the marble floor, the sound receding with every step down the hallway, until I no longer hear them at all.

Like the ghostly remnants of a half-remembered dream, slipping further into oblivion with each waking breath, he fades from all my awareness of him.

# CHAPTER 56

Redd pauses beside me and pats my shoulder.

"Good luck to ye, lass." And then he's gone as well.

I'm still lost in my thoughts when a slender blonde human opens the door. I realize my life's about to change again.

"You may come in now," she says, holding the door.

Taking a deep breath, I tuck the clothes bag under my arm and walk across the room, nerves twitching beneath my skin. I knew my search for Nicolas was likely to result in me becoming a pawn for someone in the Game. Guess I'm about to find out who's next in line.

When I enter, the first thing I see is a huge, dark-skinned Chosen standing in front of a mahogany desk, his frame stark against the ivory draperies hanging from the back wall. An amber-and-violet aura marks him as a member of Nicolas's lineage, and a curious blend of power radiates from the space he occupies. His tailored suit and rigid stance belong to someone accustomed to command, and I shudder beneath his dissecting gaze. Feeling as though I'm approaching a coiled adder, I stop partway into the room and wait.

"Isaac." A woman's soft voice behind him breaks the tension.

His wide nostrils flare, then he steps to one side, revealing the diminutive Alina Dăneşti sitting behind the desk. A pale, jade-colored silk blouse accents her dark hair, which lies in gentle curls around her shoulders and frames her nearly lavender eyes. With her petite, straight nose above delicate lips, and a softly rounded jaw, Alina represents the embodiment of Chosen femininity.

The power signature dominating the room belongs to her.

Nicolas's aura, the amber and violet, floats about Alina, woven with numerous slender threads in a multitude of colors, similar to the colorful array in Robert's amber and yellow. But unlike Robert's, their slow and graceful movements radiate serenity and an air of welcome.

"Sunny. It is so good to see you." The genuine warmth in her tone surprises me. She rises and beckons to a pair of rose-hued upholstered chairs before the desk. "Please. Sit."

With a glance at the big Chosen, I take the one on the right, farthest from his looming presence.

"Sunny, this is Isaac. He's head of my internal security, and a little overprotective at times." Alina smiles at him and nods. "Everything's fine, Isaac. You may go."

He stiffens and seems about to argue, then with a critical look at me, leaves through a door near the rear of the room.

Alina settles back into her chair, her eyes sparkling with an ancient fire.

The same fire that Nicolas's held.

"How have you been, my dear?"

I don't even know how to answer that. Glancing down at my lap, I try to form a response that doesn't sound trite, and fail to find any words at all.

"I'm sorry. That was thoughtless of me." Sympathy colors her quiet tone. "Much has happened since we last saw one another."

That was at the club, the night Katerina slaughtered the donors and attempted to kill Nicolas. Before Éva ripped the lineage away from him.

I look up into the sorrow barely hidden in Alina's violet eyes and nod my agreement.

A soft knock on the door to the waiting area interrupts the pained silence.

"Come in, Karen."

The blonde woman enters carrying a tray with two bottles of wine and a pair of delicate long-stemmed glasses.

This might be awkward. Refusing a host's offer of refreshment is an insult in many cultures, and I can't imagine that the upper echelon of Chosen society is any different. But bloodwine, a favorite drink among Chosen, is heavily laced with human blood, and something I've sworn to avoid.

"The bloodwine is a sweet port, and the Pinot Noir is one you enjoyed the night of our Council meeting."

I'm surprised she remembered that. Though I'm grateful for her perception, I suspect this is also a test to see if my preferences have changed.

"The Pinot, please."

Alina nods, her expression thoughtful.

Karen pours a glass of bloodwine for Alina, then hands me one of Pinot.

"Thank you, Karen. You may go now."

Leaving the tray on the desk, the woman bows her head and exits the room.

We sip our wine in contemplative silence. Alina finally sets her glass on the desk and leans forward, her slender hands clasped. The sleeve on her left arm slides back, revealing a delicate silver bracelet, a thin band in Taz's distinctive style.

Huh. A gift for his Elder perhaps?

"So tell me, Sunny. What can I do for you?"

I take a deep breath. Everything for the last five months has led up to this moment.

"I'm hoping you can help me find Nicolas."

Staring at me, expressionless, Alina shakes her head, then slowly pushes her chair back and stands. She turns and pulls a drapery panel aside, just enough to peek out. The wedge of dark window reflects her face twisting in anguish. She stares into the night for several moments, then releases the draperies and slowly walks around the desk toward me, her expression once again schooled into neutrality.

She stops before my chair and leans back against the desk, her arms folded.

"Do you have any idea what your rejection of Nicolas did to this lineage?" Her voice is now brittle, all trace of gentleness gone.

I look down at my lap, tasting guilt and shame along with the ever-present remorse I feel whenever I think of him.

"Fortunately for you, I'm aware of the underlying circumstances, though I still hold you somewhat responsible." Her voice softens. "The others, though . . . it's good you not did approach any of them, as they would have likely destroyed you on the spot. The only reason Robert did not do so at the airport is because this is *my* territory, which now makes you *my* responsibility."

My instincts had been right. The little I'd been around Alina in Colorado had given me hope that she might be the most forgiving. But the look on her face right now is making me think otherwise.

"By coming to me, you've placed me in a precarious position. Éva's made it clear that you are not to be welcomed. And should you continue to venture into Chosen territory—*anyone's* territory—" She presses her lips together, then takes a deep breath. "You are to be terminated."

I stare at her, feeling as though I'm balancing on the edge of a knife.

"I just want to find Nicolas," I whisper.

"I'm sorry. Regret, especially in matters of the heart, can be quite unbearable." She shakes her head. "And I sense the main obstacle to your relationship with him is no longer a concern. You've completed the Change?"

"You knew that I wasn't . . . wasn't full-Chosen?"

"As I mentioned before, I'm well-acquainted with your unique situation. In fact, I probably know more about you than Éva does." Alina unfolds her arms and rests her hands against the edge of the desk. "Nicolas had me investigating your past."

Panic rises up in my throat at the thought she may have found Andrea. I try not to squirm beneath her penetrating gaze.

"So far, my inquiries have confirmed that you are nothing more than what you appear to be—an unbound Chosen who was abandoned by her Maker. I *am* concerned about who that was, however, and what they were doing in our territory." She pauses, looking thoughtful. "Although, why *you* were targeted is part of the mystery. It was not just any Chosen who Made you."

Alina pushes off from the desk and walks back around to her chair. She takes a sip of bloodwine and sits down.

Feeling a little less threatened, I lean forward.

"So do you know where Nicolas is?"

"No, I do not."

An upwelling of despair tightens my throat and I again study my lap, this time fighting back the bloodtears.

It all seems so pointless. All of it—meeting and falling in love with Nicolas, then rejecting him, only to realize I don't want to live without him.

"Though I may know someone who does."

Startled from my self-recrimination, I look up at her through tear-filled eyes.

"But I have to be very careful. Éva is now the head of our lineage, and unfortunately, is also now my Maker. I cannot do anything counter to her wishes, which includes assisting you." She tips her head, reminding me of Nicolas. A tiny smile plays about her lips. "However, there's nothing to prevent me from having a meeting with a mutual acquaintance about territory affairs. It's possible the topic of your Maker might arise, and subsequently, a conversation regarding you. Whether he chooses to help you or not is up to him, and certainly none of my business."

"Thank you."

She rises and presses a call button.

"For now, I'll consider you my prisoner until I decide what to do with you. Éva certainly can't object to that."

Prisoner? I stand, about to protest, when Isaac enters the room.

"Take her down to detainment," Alina says. "Be sure she has everything she needs."

Grim satisfaction painting his dark face, Isaac gestures me ahead of him.

"And Isaac . . . she is not to be harmed in any way. Make sure your staff members are clear on that."

~

When Isaac opens the door to my new—and hopefully temporary—home, I'm stunned.

Rather than the bleak cell I was expecting, I enter a luxurious suite rivaling that of a fine hotel. With a richly carpeted and furnished sitting area, a full wet bar, and, in a separate room, a king-sized bed that appears fit for a king, this looks more like quarters for a VIP than a prisoner.

The only thing missing is windows.

"If you need anything, you can reach someone on the house phone. Dial zero." Isaac indicates an old-fashioned dial phone on a desk against the wall.

"Thank you."

With no further word, he shuts the door—a very solid-sounding door, its apparent strength reinforced by the click of a stout deadbolt.

Despite the locked door, it sure beats the hell out of a bloodstained couch and a ratty blanket.

But as I wander through the rooms, I realize the luxury is only for appearances. There are no books or magazines, nor is there a TV. And I suspect since we're belowground, cell reception—if I even had my phone—isn't possible, leaving no way to contact the outside world.

This is more than just detainment—I'm in total isolation.

Being alone is something I should be used to. But after spending the past week with Taz's crew, their constant presence is something to which I've surprisingly grown accustomed.

As the evening wears on, I find myself wondering what they are up to. I miss Redd's light-hearted banter and Taz's gruff silence, and even Chia's snide remarks.

The hush in my lavish tomb deepens. The only sounds I can hear are in my mind, which slowly fills with regret piled upon regret.

And beneath those dismal thoughts echoes the memory of Taz's boots ringing out against the marble floor.

*I Remember*

*I remember*

*Nights of darkness*
*Darkness of the soul*

*I remember*

*Nights of frenzy*
*Frenzy beyond control*

*I remember*

*Nights of red thirst*
*Red thirst unending*

*I remember*

*Nights of death*
*Death unchanging*

*I also remember*

*Finding my love*
*Finding my self*

*But mostly*

*I remember*

*Losing my love*
*Losing my self*

*I once again remember*

*Nights of darkness*
*Darkness of my soul*

*- CN*

# PART IV

# THE CHAMELEON

# WEDNESDAY

## CHAPTER 57

I bolt awake to shrill alarms going off in my head. They stop, and as I sit up and take in my unfamiliar surroundings, the sound begins again. Beside me, not in my head.

The telephone.

Leaning over to the nightstand, I yank the receiver from its cradle.

"Hello?"

"Good evening, Miss Martin. Lady Dăneşti requests that you be available to meet with her at six o'clock. Do you need anything?" The voice belongs to Karen, Alina's secretary, or servant, or whatever she is.

I glance at the clock on the nightstand. It's 5:04.

"No, I'm fine. Tell her I'll be ready."

The line clicks into silence.

Studying the receiver, I try to recall the last time I spoke on a phone, and to whom. And then I remember.

It was to Danny, telling him Sandy wasn't coming back to him.

Another moment of heartache in my life—one that seems to be defined by continual loss—and what little shred of hope I held last night dissolves beneath its heavy weight. I climb wearily from the bed and head to the shower.

~

We step outside into the damp chill of the November night as tendrils of fog creep through the surrounding trees. The dark-haired Chosen ahead of me slows his stride and nods to Isaac standing on the covered porch that surrounds the house. The other one behind me pauses, then follows us down the back steps. Apparently they think I'm worth two guards, but I can't imagine why.

Our little procession passes through a gate into a large ornamental garden bordered by twenty-foot-tall hedges. Shorter hedges define gardens within the garden—roses grouped into different colors, hanging pots surrounding a birdbath, even an area devoted to unusual rocks. Small spotlights scatter light and shadow, providing accents throughout the landscape.

White pebbles crunch on the softly lit path beneath our feet as we wind our way through the maze of mini-gardens. The sound of running water accompanies us, growing louder the farther into the garden we go. When we walk through the opening in a wall of towering Italian cypresses, a huge fountain comes into view.

Playful stone cherubs, frozen in mid-frolic, splash and spit water upon one another around the pool forming its base. Soft pink-and-green lights cast an otherworldly glow upon the scene, which becomes even more surreal when one of the figures actually moves.

It's Alina. She's sitting on a large rock in the center of the pool, a book in her hands. Looking up at us, she closes it and stands, then gracefully steps onto the fountain's edge and down to the ground.

Both guards bow as she approaches.

"Mr. Isaac said he'll be right up there." The dark-haired Chosen gestures toward the house. Isaac, now on a second-floor balcony, tips his head in acknowledgement. "We'll be waiting just outside if you need anything."

"Thank you, Sean. But that's not necessary. You may return to the house."

"Yes, ma'am." With another bow, both guards spin on their heels and leave.

Alina, her petite figure accented by a lavender blouse and ivory slacks, strolls over to me and stops.

"Do you like poetry?" She tips her head as she looks up at me.

"I've never taken the time to study it."

"You should. It can provide a wonderful balm for the broken heart or tortured soul. Even better is to write it." She hands me the slender, leather-bound volume.

No title or author is printed on the elegant, mocha-colored cover. The front is embossed with a single rose painted in lavender, its petals edged in metallic gold. When I open the book, the pages are filled with a tiny, elegant handwriting. I slowly turn them, stopping at one with a bent corner. The poem is short, but its words resonate deep within me.

*The Chosen Lament*

*To love is to live*
*To see the world through another's eyes*
*To feel the world through another's joy.*
*But when time steals that love from you*
*And the world grows dark*
*And filled with pain,*
*Then perhaps it is better not to love at all.*

"Did you write this?" I ask, shaken by my selection.

"Yes. That is a rather morose piece. But writing it helped me during a particularly bleak period of my life."

She makes no move to take the book, so I turn to another bent corner. This handwriting is different, and a bolt of anguish lances through me as I recognize it.

*Oh Sweet Carpaţii*

*Oh sweet Carpaţii*
*With your cool gentle breezes*
*And star-dusted skies*

*Rocky peaks mantled*
*In shimmering silken snow*
*Made bright by moon's rise*

*Green velveteen flanks*
*Laced with crystal streams rushing*
*Trees dance, the wind sighs*

*Oh sweet Carpaţii*
*With your cool gentle breezes*
*And star-dusted skies*

*I long for your kiss*
*Your stone arms holding me tight*
*Safe from bright sun's rise*

*- CN*

I stare at the words on the page, *his* words, written in his precise hand, and find myself unable to breathe, unable to move. My throat tightens as I once again fight back the cursed bloodtears. When I feel under control, I look up at Alina.

"Nicolas wrote that for me when we first came to America. I missed my Carpathian mountains and Romanian homeland so much. That is one of the reasons he chose Colorado Springs as his base, because of the mountains there."

She reaches out for the book and I hand it to her.

"I want you to know that I understand your situation better than you might think. Nicolas and I were very close and I know how much he loved you. We . . . we've shared much through the years, he and I." Grief lines her face. "I do miss him and our long talks about both the past and the future. Did you know I was his first?"

Absorbing her words, I blink back my shock. *Another* ex?

Alina frowns, looking puzzled, and then she laughs.

"Oh, no, my dear. It's not what you think. Nicolas has always been more like a guardian to me. We've never been romantically involved."

I'm sure she can see the relief on my face. I don't seem to fare too well with Nicolas's ex-mates, and am glad Alina's not one.

Her smile fades.

"I met him the night . . . the night Tepes and his men stormed our castle and killed my father. When they attacked, I hid in the granary, crouching inside a half-empty bag of wheat, and listened to the servants scream as each one died . . ." She touches her lips, her expression grim.

How awful. I wonder about the rest of her family.

"Your mother?"

"It was just my father and me—my mother had died a few years before. In retrospect, it was a blessing, because at least she didn't have to suffer through the horror of that night . . ." Alina takes a deep breath.

"One of the raiders—Nicolas—found me, and though Tepes had ordered everyone killed, Nicolas warned me to stay quiet and did not reveal my presence. I did not know at the time—for I was unaware of The Chosen—but disobeying orders and lying to his Maker is almost impossible for an immature Chosen. Nicolas was strong, even then, and less ruled by bloodlust than the others."

Alina falls silent, her fingers tracing a pattern over and over on the cover of her book. I yearn to hear more, to catch a glimpse of Nicolas in his youth and likely filled with even more passion than he has now.

"Did he tell you why he didn't . . . ?"

"Kill me? He said it was because he was sick of Tepes and the endless slaughter, and that I was too beautiful to suffer such a violent end."

"But you said you were his first . . ."

"Yes. The next night several soldiers—human—discovered me hiding in the ruins of my home. I fought them off the best I could, until I was stabbed in the side. I lay there, bleeding, as one of them climbed on top of me . . ." Her breath catches and she stares down at the ground.

"And then suddenly, his weight was gone, and I heard the soldiers screaming. The handsome young man who'd spared me the night before had saved me once again. Or so I thought before I lost consciousness.

"I don't remember much after that. Nicolas later told me that I was dying, and the only way he knew to save me was to give me his blood, something forbidden for one so young to do. But he said when he held his arm to my mouth and I began to drink, he succumbed to the bloodlust and fed on me, nearly killing me. He stopped himself—which is extremely difficult for young Chosen—and gave me his blood once more, then departed before the thirst could take over again.

"I woke the next day, weak and very ill. Nicolas showed up after nightfall with food for me, but I was unable to keep it down. After staying with me most of the night, he left just before dawn. This went on for several evenings, and each time he brought food, and each time my body refused it. He finally broke down and confessed what had happened, that he'd saved me with his blood, but now feared that I was dying because of it, and that the only way to keep me alive was to give me more. He told me it would make me like him, but that seemed a far better choice than death."

Only one thought rings through my head.

"What about . . . what about a lifespark? I thought we had to have that to finalize the Change."

Because if that was another lie—if he lied to me about *that*—my search for Nicolas ends.

Right here, right now.

"Ah, well. That was not so difficult. He brought me the Tepes filth who had raped my handmaid and the cook in the kitchen near my hiding place. I'd listened as he brutalized and then killed them. I had little trouble returning the favor."

I can't help but shudder again at the vivid scene she's painted, yet at the same time, feel a profound sense of relief.

Alina wanders back to the fountain, saying no more.

"Do you ever wish you'd chosen differently?" I ask. The sadness in her voice, and her poetry, makes me think so.

"Oh, no. No. Nicolas not only delivered me from death, he gave me the tools to eventually exact my revenge. And I've had a good life, even with all of the pain and regrets that can accompany a Chosen existence." She looks at me curiously. "How do *you* feel about becoming a Chosen, now that you've completed the Change?"

"It's not a Choice I would've made had I been offered it originally."

"Hmm. Perhaps someday you'll wonder why you ever felt that way. You have many years ahead of you to learn new things, form new relationships, and experience new lands. Trust me, the benefits far outweigh the cost."

Maybe for her. She had no family to leave behind.

"But don't you ever get tired of it all?" I ask. "The hunger, the need to feed on people? The killing?"

Alina studies me, a frown creasing her face.

"I can see you've learned little of Chosen life, or the customs of our lineage. We are not in the habit of killing our donors. In fact, they become secondary family to us. We provide for them, they provide for us. Those in my circle have been with me for generations."

She paints a pretty picture, but I wonder if she knows how it really is for those in the rank and file—the ones who aren't rich and powerful Elders.

"Well, all I know is what I've seen in the clubs, and most of it isn't what I'd call family oriented."

"No, probably not. As with human society, there are always some who prefer a more sordid life. But killing those we feed upon is not allowed. That is one of the distinguishing features of our lineage. Or was until Éva took over. Now, I'm not so sure where we're headed, and it worries me." Alina shakes her head. "But this is not what I wished to speak with you about. Come, sit down with me."

She pats the edge of the fountain beside her. I take a seat on the cold stone, hoping she has good news for me about Nicolas.

"Your confidence has grown since the last time we met in Colorado. You seem more sure of yourself, in spite of your current situation. I can only attribute this to you making the final transition and your innate grasp of what it means to be a member of the most elite species in the world."

She makes it sounds like an honor. I've never viewed it as anything more than a curse.

"I do believe that you are better prepared to take your place by Nicolas's side. It's a pity it didn't happen sooner." Her voice is so low I can barely hear her over the gurgle of the cascading water behind us. "That being said, I have spoken with the acquaintance I mentioned."

A thousand needles prickle my skin as I hold my breath, waiting for her to continue.

"He has agreed to meet with you." Her gaze hardens. "But I'll permit it only under one condition."

Of course. There are always conditions.

"Go on." My gut twists as anticipation dissolves into dread.

"That you tell him as much about your initial Change as you can recall. Everything—when, where, how the attack occurred, as well as the details of your prior human life."

I swallow and turn away to stare across the garden.

*Andrea.*

"This is the only way I can justify allowing you to stay in Chosen territory. We need to find out who your Maker is, and whether or not there are any more like you. Do you understand?"

If I refuse, then it looks like I'm hiding something, and the only conclusion they'll reach is that I'm protecting my Maker.

And then they'll want answers I don't have. I can't imagine how many ways a Chosen can be tortured. Or for how long.

Forever, if they want.

A shudder ripples through me.

I reluctantly nod, then glance at Alina. Her narrowed eyes indicate she missed none of my reaction. She stands and looks down at me, her expression closed.

"Then it's settled. You will meet with him tomorrow night."

# CHAPTER 58

A knock on my door startles me to sharp awareness. I glance at the clock on the nightstand, surprised to see that it's already midnight. Several hours have passed since I returned from the meeting with Alina and lay down to stare at the ceiling, lost in my thoughts.

"Just a minute." I climb from the bed and glance in the mirror to smooth my hair. I wasn't asleep, but wasn't really all here, either. Shaking the fuzziness from my brain, I walk out into the sitting room.

"Come in."

One of the bodyguards from earlier—Sean, I think—carries in my suitcases and sets them in the middle of the floor. The other guard follows with my things from the hotel closet. He drapes them over the sofa, then heads back out the door, Sean on his heels.

The lock clicks before I can even ask about my car.

Since it appears I might be here awhile, I take my suitcases into the bedroom and begin unpacking. As I refold my things and tuck them into dresser drawers, I wonder who packed them.

It's a bit discomfiting to think about how many hands have pawed through my underwear.

Nothing seems to be missing, though, and as I add the clothing from the plastic garbage bag to the dresser, I feel relieved to be reunited with all of my belongings.

Except, of course, the little black BMW. But hopefully they brought it with my suitcases, and it's sitting safely somewhere inside the gates.

I don't need my keys—several spares are hidden in the underbody. The wallet and cell phone aren't really a problem, either. I have other IDs and cash squirreled away within the car as well as in several locations around the state. It's just a matter of finding the car and then I can get the hell out of here if necessary. I just hope it doesn't come to that.

And that Taz isn't the one they send after me.

A chill ripples across my skin. The cold, empty look on his face as he passed by me in the waiting room isn't anything I ever want to see again. I think back on what he said in the bar.

*We will hunt you down if you run. That's what we do, and we're very good at it.*

Redd's voice echoes in my head.

*We're Hunters. We kill them. No questions asked.*

I better make damn sure I have a good head start.

On that happy note, I grab one of the books I'd bought at one of San Francisco's many eclectic bookstores and settle into bed for a long night of reading.

# THURSDAY

## CHAPTER 59

I glance at the clock again as I make another circuit around the room. 8:01 PM. I've been awake for three hours, showered and ready to go for the last two-and-a-half. Reading is out of the question—the only thing I can do is pace while waiting to be summoned.

Alina said I would meet with him tonight. Whoever *he* is. She called him a "mutual acquaintance."

Mutual with whom? Nicolas? Is this mysterious acquaintance even a Chosen?

The same questions chase each other around and around in my head, matching the pattern I'm wearing into the carpet beneath my feet. Anxiety-triggered hunger is making the wait even more unbearable. It's been five nights since I last fed—the night Taz smashed me against the hill.

I suppress a growl and keep walking.

As much as I'm anticipating it, I nearly jump out of my skin when a knock sounds on my door a little after nine.

"Come in."

Sean enters, his expression impassive.

"Lady Dănești would like to know if you are ready."

"Yes." I resist adding that I've been ready for hours. I'm sure making me wait for something I'm bound to be anxious about is just part of The Game.

I straighten my sweater and follow Sean through the door. We make our way up the stairs, but instead of heading to Alina's office, Sean leads me out the front door and down the steps to a waiting Mercedes limousine, its windows as black as its paint. He opens the rear door, revealing Alina sitting on the far side. As usual, she looks stunning, her linen jacket and slacks in a dusky rose complementing the violet of her eyes. She smiles and gestures to the seat beside her, and I climb in, noting that the partition between driver and passenger compartments is up. The Mercedes pulls out into the street and toward the nighttime traffic of downtown San Francisco as I settle into the luxurious, ivory-toned leather.

"Good evening, Sunny. I trust you rested well?"

The way she says it reminds me of Nicolas, with a warm formality so like his, underscored by a similar accent. My irritation melts at the familiar feel.

"I did. Thank you."

She reaches out toward my hand resting on the seat and touches my ring.

"That's an interesting ring."

I almost didn't wear it. I don't want any reminders of Taz. He was nothing more than an unwelcome distraction in my search for Nicolas.

But the ring works so much better than the necklace.

At least, that's what I keep telling myself.

"It's an herb ring." I show her the windowed interior. "Taz made it. He thought it might help when I'm . . ."

What did he call it? Oh yeah.

"Having a moment," I finish lamely.

Alina smiles thoughtfully and nods.

"I see. Do you have many of those? Moments?"

"Not really." Not as long as I avoid humans, that is. "But a couple times when we were out, he thought I was having difficulty staying . . . focused."

Alina frowns.

"When you were out . . ." Her gaze hardens. "How long were you with him and his companions?"

"Since Halloween night. Guess it's been about a week or so."

"A week." She turns her head and stares out the window. "It must have been . . . difficult. He and his companions are rather crude, don't you think?"

I'm not sure how to answer. I'm a guest, and guests shouldn't whine to their hosts, no matter how trying the circumstances—but especially when the host holds the guest's fate in their hands.

"They treated me well enough. I have no complaints."

She nods, continuing to stare out the window.

I opt to do the same, wondering why she's suddenly become so distant.

After about ten minutes of strained silence, the car pulls to a stop in front of an office building. Alina's door opens and Isaac extends his hand to help her out. She ignores it and steps lightly onto the sidewalk. I join her as she turns to the hovering bodyguard.

"Please stay with the car, Isaac. I'll be fine."

"But Lady Dăneşti . . ."

"I said I'll be fine."

His eyes flicker at her sharp tone, but he says nothing more.

Alina glances at me, then turns and heads up the steps toward the front doors. As I fall in behind her, Isaac moves, fast, and has one open for her when she reaches it.

"Thank you, Isaac," she says, her voice softening as she passes him. I quickly follow her inside.

Alina remains silent while we wait for the elevator. When the doors open, we step inside and she hits the button for the third floor. The mechanisms whir and clank to a stop, but when the doors open, she presses another button, this one for the belowground parking garage. She turns, her eyes sparkling, and seems to be biting back a smile.

"Come," she said as the doors open, not bothering to hide the excitement now lighting up her face.

An electronic chirp and flashing lights from a sleek black Porsche beckon to us from a parking spot near the elevator. Alina smiles and waves toward the car as we near it, then opens the driver's door and climbs in. I follow suit, enjoying the soft German hum as she turns the ignition and the engine starts warming up.

She flashes me a conspiratorial smirk, shifts the car into gear, and backs out of the parking space.

"Poor Isaac. He will be furious with me once he realizes what I've done. He gets very upset whenever I slip my leash—the leash I allow him to maintain." She laughs and glances sidelong at me. "But he forgets how old I am, how strong I am, making the mistake most large men make when assuming someone smaller—or female—is less capable than they."

I nod, recalling making that mistake myself with Chia.

The Porsche slips out of the parking garage into the night, and the San Francisco streets become our own personal roller-coaster ride. I suck in my breath and Alina laughs as our tires momentarily part with the asphalt at the crest of a hill. But she'd taken it just right and the car lands as smooth as a cat and continues its headlong dash down the other side of the steep slope.

We cross the Bay Bridge and leave the city behind, heading toward Walnut Creek. After about fifteen minutes, Alina takes the Orinda off-ramp, then turns into the parking lot of a small shopping center. A grey car parked beneath a tree flashes its lights and we pull in beside it.

A male Chosen of an unfamiliar lineage, his aura a single shade of midnight blue, steps out of the car, which turns out to be an Aston Martin sedan. The dark grey wool of his finely tailored suit moves with him like a second skin—obviously not something off the rack. In contrast to his high-dollar clothing and well-bred car, he's rather ordinary looking—about five-ten, medium build, with dark blond hair and pale blue eyes. But those eyes light up when Alina gets out and steps into his embrace.

"Alina. It's so good to see you. It's been too long." His warm smile appears genuine as they hug.

She squeezes him, then shifts back, touching his face.

"It has been too long. How are you holding up?"

"As well as can be expected. I stay busy with my work. But it's difficult sometimes. After so many years of looking over my shoulder, of living every moment in pursuit of our goals and being so close to achieving them, to have it end so suddenly . . ." He shakes his head. "I miss him."

"Me too."

My throat tightens. Even though this Chosen is not of Nicolas's lineage, somehow I know that's who they're referring to. And they speak of him as though he were dead.

As they step apart, he glances at me, his expression unreadable.

Alina turns toward the Porsche and gestures for me to get out of the car.

If he was close to Nicolas, I can only guess how he feels about me. I take a deep breath, open the door, and walk around to where they stand.

I try to recall the brief protocol lessons Éva gave me in Colorado. But they were oriented toward my status as Nicolas's mate, one that evaporated when I rejected him. The only status I likely have among The Chosen now is that of Betrayer, or worse, Saboteur, so I have no idea how to proceed.

Alina and her associate watch me approach, remaining silent.

What the hell. Here goes nothing.

"Sunny. Sunny Martin." I bow my head, as Chosen seem to avoid shaking hands.

"Hello, Miss Martin. My name is Colin O'Neal." He offers me a smile—one that reaches his eyes, surprising me. "I've heard much about you."

"And probably little of it good." A rueful smile is all I can offer back.

"On the contrary. Nicolas spoke quite highly of you. It's such . . . an unfortunate turn of events."

That's the understatement of the year.

"Well, I must be off to my next appointment." Alina leans forward and kisses Colin lightly on the cheek. "You two have much to talk about. I'll see you in a few hours." He takes her hand and walks her to the Porsche, then opens her door. She turns to me as she climbs in.

"Sunny, since you have little experience with Chosen society, I asked Colin to instruct you in our basic social protocols. I hope you don't mind."

"Uh, no, I don't mind. Thank you."

Great. Now he can add Clueless to my list of titles.

I watch her pull out of the parking lot, feeling as though I'm a baton and have just been handed off to the next runner in my race to find Nicolas.

Colin clears his throat and I look over to see that he has the passenger door open and is waiting for me. With a quiet sigh, I walk over and get in.

# CHAPTER 60

The dove-grey leather interior absorbs all outside sound as we cruise along on the freeway, heading once again toward Walnut Creek. Speculations about this Chosen and his relationship to Nicolas war with questions about where we're going and what's going to happen to me next. My impatience with being kept in the dark finally gets the better of me.

"So. What's with the cloak-and-dagger?"

"Pardon me?"

"Alina leaves her security behind and meets you—a Chosen not of Nicolas's lineage—in a parking lot? That seems a little odd to me."

He's silent a moment before he answers.

"Two things you need to know if you are going to survive among The Chosen. One—most thoughts and observations are best kept to yourself. Everything you say gives your opponent one more piece to your puzzle, and they don't need many to figure out what's missing and how to use it against you. Two—we need to work on your expression and body language controls. Right now your eyes are a billboard, advertising your grief, regret, desperation, and fear. The lines around your mouth, the muscles in your jaw, the stiffness of your back and shoulders—all broadcast tension, and tension increases your opponent's confidence."

I swallow. Which probably told him how much he just freaked me out. I thought I *had* good control.

"Well, I'm willing to learn if you're willing to teach me."

"Good. Otherwise, all the rest of this is just a waste of time, and you will likely end up dead."

A chill runs up my spine and across my scalp, raising the fine little hairs on my neck and arms. I stare out the side window as we exit the freeway into Walnut Creek.

I knew going into this it would be dangerous, but imagination and reality can be worlds apart. Again, I wonder if I would just be better off forgetting Nicolas and retreating to the mountains, far from Chosen intrigues.

But that thought vanishes as quickly as it arises. I *can't* forget him. The need for him, for his quiet assurance and fiery passions, occupies every cell in my body. I'm not going to give up, no matter how difficult this is or how many Chosen try to kill me.

Or how many eagle-eyed Indians I run into.

I *will* find Nicolas.

Glancing over at Colin, I'm surprised to see the glint of approval in his pale eyes.

"Well that answers my question—how committed are you to your goal? At the moment, you are. But each day is a new one, and each day I will ask that question once again. And you better do the same."

He turns into the parking lot for a small office complex and shuts off the car. As we step out and into the open-air hallway between two tan stucco buildings, we pass a lit marquee listing several dozen suites, most occupied by attorneys.

Remembering what Colin said about body language, I study his as I follow him. Though he's not as tall as Nicolas, he has a similar build, with wide shoulders and an easy, purposeful stride. He's confident without the arrogance that seems to clothe most Chosen males, and I wonder if that's something he controls, or just his basic nature.

We stop outside an office bearing a sign stating C. W. O'Neill, Attorney-at-Law.

He's a bloodsucking lawyer. Literally.

I stifle a laugh.

Colin unlocks the door. He steps inside and taps in the code on a wall-mounted alarm, then gestures me inside.

I walk past him.

And then I'm slammed into from behind. The breath explodes from my chest at the impact and the floor rushes at me as I go down. My chin hits first. Pain lances through my tongue and I taste blood. Fear, quickly followed by rage, races through me as I spring up and whirl to face my attacker. But before I can even focus on him, Colin straight-arms me into the wall, then pins me there by the throat with one hand. Feeling the sting of his nails piercing my skin, I go immediately still in surrender.

He releases me and steps back.

"What the hell . . . ?" Rubbing my throat, I spit blood onto the polished wood floor and glare at him.

His eyes flicker down to the blood, then back up to meet mine.

"Your fighting skills need some serious work as well. But at least you had the sense to submit when you found yourself in an untenable position." He pulls a black silk handkerchief from a pocket inside his suit jacket and hands it to me. "Please, sit down."

Colin gestures me toward a chair in front of the desk at the far end of the room. I wipe my mouth and give him a wide berth as I pass, never taking my eyes from him as he trails off to one side and takes a seat opposite me at the elegant walnut desk. I perch on the edge of the offered chair, its brown leather upholstery softly creaking.

"Good. You learn quickly. Never turn your back on your enemy."

"I didn't think you were my enemy." I toss the bloody handkerchief onto the desk's gleaming wood surface in disgust.

"You must assume all Chosen are your enemies. *Especially* as an unbound."

"Unbound?"

"An unbound has no blood bonds to a Maker or a lineage. They are considered outcasts and viewed with suspicion by lineage members. In some communities where the Elder has declared them outlaws, they are hunted down and destroyed."

Unbound. Outcast. Outlaw.

As though I didn't have enough problems.

*Unbound scum.* That's what the suit called Taz the other night at the waterfront club. I suspect Redd and Chia are unbound as well. And yet they all work for Alina.

Colin is not of Nicolas's lineage, either.

"Are you unbound?"

Colin only smiles.

"Why do they hate . . . us?"

"Without a connection to the lineage, they cannot read us or sense our motives. Or our loyalties. Chosen have an inborn hatred against all those not of their lineage. Those who are not of any lineage, whose loyalties can be bought and sold by anyone, are especially detested."

He said "us." A roundabout way of answering my question, but an answer nonetheless.

"Alina doesn't seem to view unbound as outlaws. She has several working for her."

"There is some benefit to having Chosen in one's employ who are outside the lineage."

"Are you in her employ?"

"No. But we share enough of the same goals to be allies on occasion."

If Alina didn't trust Colin, then I doubt she would've handed me over to him. I finally relax, settle back in the chair, and take a look around to see what I can learn of this mysterious Chosen.

His office is decorated in the latest successful attorney style without being ostentatious. The subtle elegance of the room speaks of someone who pays special attention to details, a trait he's already revealed to me several times. Behind me on the other side of the room is a smaller desk—something a receptionist might use—and a door.

"So tell me, Sunny—how long ago did you complete the Change?"

"About . . . two-and-a-half months ago." It seems an entire lifetime.

Nothing in Colin's face registers his reaction.

"You seem to be functioning remarkably well for one so young. How long ago was the Change initiated?"

"Nearly six years ago."

I still can't read him. But his silence tells me that perhaps my answer surprises him, and he's choosing his next question with care.

"Nicolas had indicated it had been somewhat recent, but I had no idea that recent. He was quite intrigued by your circumstances." He leans back in his chair, his loosely curled fingers against his chin. "As am I."

Here it comes. The question I've been dreading.

But he says nothing for a moment as he studies me.

"Your jaw is clenched. Your body has shifted into a subtle but taut crouch. Your nails are likely near to drawing blood in your fists. You just shouted at me your discomfort with this line of questioning, and if I was your enemy, I'd be zeroing in on whatever it is you're hiding with the ferocity of a hungry shark."

Who *is* this guy? Just what did he do for Nicolas? Or are all Chosen this perceptive, and I've just been a blind, naïve fool?

He smiles. I swear he can read my mind.

"I wouldn't have needed anyone to tell me that you've had little to no training as a Chosen. It's apparent in your every expression and movement. You may have mastered enough control for the human world, but it won't fly here."

"Then help me."

"I am. Raising your awareness of your reactions is the first step in controlling them."

I nod.

"You're new to the Bay Area. How do you like it so far?" Colin tugs at the knot of his burgundy tie, loosening it.

"I don't."

"Why not?"

"It's too . . . chaotic. And—"

"And what?"

"And noisy. And—"

"Where would you rather be?"

"In the mountains. I—"

"Where were you Made?"

I snap my mouth shut.

My automatic responses to his harmless, rapid-fire questions nearly spilled the answer.

A look of satisfaction crosses his face.

"What did you just learn from our exchange?" he asks.

Frowning, I consider his question.

Colin sits back in his chair.

"You paused and are thinking," he says, pressing his fingertips together. "Good. That's what you should do every time you are asked a question, no matter how innocuous it appears, because when you are dealing with Chosen, most of the time the question is not. Whether the question is indirectly extracting information about you, or setting you up for an interrogative attack, pausing buys you time to consider its purpose and prevent you from blurting out things you'd rather not reveal."

I'm reminded of how on guard I had to be around former black ops Joe when I worked for him at the bar, and realize that even though I don't have to hide what I am when I'm among Chosen, I need to be every bit as vigilant. And apparently even more so.

"So let's begin again. You are new to the Bay Area. How do you like it so far?"

I stay silent.

"Ask yourself what I really want, besides just an inane exchange of pleasantries."

After several moments of contemplation, I offer my answer.

"You want to know if I've been here before, been here long enough to get acquainted with the city, relaxed enough to sightsee, if I'm comfortable in this environment, made any friends to enjoy it with."

"Good. And what did your original answer tell me?"

I think back. I'd said I didn't like the city.

"That I'm uncomfortable, likely alone, or had unpleasant experiences."

"It also revealed your instinctive level of honesty and a possible lack of adaptability, both traits which can be easily manipulated and used against you. Your facial expression and body language confirmed it."

Damn. It seemed like such an innocent question.

"The remainder of our conversation only served as a way to unbalance and prepare you to reveal the real information I was after." He pulls open a drawer and takes out a pad of paper. "Of course, my line of questioning was blunt and its delivery quite crude. Since most Chosen enjoy the verbal cat-and-mouse play that comprises The Game, you can be assured they will try to decipher you with much more finesse and sophistication."

The thought of engaging in meaningless talk with such calculating Chosen while having to maintain my guard beneath a façade of interest both exhausts and terrifies me.

Sympathy momentarily clouds Colin's eyes, then he bends over the pad of paper and begins writing.

The fountain pen scratches across the fine linen paper for several moments before he sets it down and tears the sheet from the pad.

"Here's a list of common questions you should be prepared for. Work on both an analysis of each question's purpose and your answer to it. Then rearrange the questions and do it again—you'll find their order changes the entire nature of the exchange. Do this several times and we'll discuss them the next time we meet."

I glance them over.

"You should also expect to answer any questions about your origins as per your agreement with Alina. I hope you understand I'll know if you are lying."

His delay in discussing my "origins" is almost as unsettling as the idea of answering his questions now.

A cell phone softly chimes and Colin withdraws it from an inner pocket.

"Yes." His gaze settles on me as he listens. "I believe so—with a little time." He pauses once more. "We'll see you then."

Colin slips the phone back inside his pocket.

I want to ask him if that was Alina, but he starts to speak before I can.

"Have you ever practiced meditation?"

Not sure where he's going with this new line of questioning, I answer cautiously.

"You mean like Buddhism?"

"Many cultures utilize meditation in their spiritual practices."

"Can't say that I have. I've not found religion to be particularly useful in my situation."

"Meditation isn't about religion. Its primary purpose is to raise awareness of self and one's interactions with the surrounding environment." His narrowed eyes and the slight edge to his words betrays the first sign of impatience I've detected. "Sit back in your chair and close your eyes."

"You're not going to attack me again, are you?"

"That depends upon whether or not you do as I ask." His gaze hardens. "I'm not here to play games."

I lean back and, closing my eyes, crank up my other senses. Just in case.

"Now focus on the space between your nose and upper lip. Think of nothing else. If a stray thought or image enters your mind, refocus on that space."

What the hell? My lip?

I touch it with my fingers.

"Not your lip. Just above it. And keep your hands in your lap."

I do as he says. After several minutes, I can feel a weird crawling sensation in that little area between my nose and upper lip.

"What do you feel?"

"A tingling there."

"Good. You can open your eyes."

When I do, I can't help but flinch. Colin is standing right in front of me, his arms folded.

"I want you to practice that for an hour—every other hour—until our next session."

He steps away and heads toward the door.

"It's time to meet Alina. Don't forget your homework questions."

I grab the paper and, rising from my chair, follow this strange and demanding Chosen—who's apparently my new teacher—out to his car.

~

Alina glances over at me as she maneuvers the shiny black Porsche out of the shopping center parking lot.

"Well? What do you think of Colin?"

"I . . . I'm not sure. He's hard to read. I can't tell where I stand with him."

Alina softly laughs.

"And you probably won't until he's ready to let you. In some circles, he's known only as *The Chameleon*—a title well-earned. I can't think of anyone better to introduce you to Chosen ways."

As long as he doesn't decide to kill me in the process.

She says nothing further, and after several moments, begins humming a quiet tune.

Surprised, I shift slightly so I can see her better without being obvious. I think back on some of Colin's instructions and note the air of relaxation that hovers about her. Her pale lavender eyes and rosy complexion indicate she's recently fed, but the soft smile playing about her lips and the way she's caressing the steering wheel lead me to believe that her donor may be more than just the meal of the evening.

My own hunger stirs, then something more awakens at the thought of Alina meeting a lover. I turn toward the window, trying to suppress the bitter loneliness in my throat as I recall being in Nicolas's arms, and wonder if I'll ever feel them around me again.

# SUNDAY

## CHAPTER 61

After several nights of practice interrogations by Colin, I feel better prepared to deal with Chosen inquiries, no matter how polite or direct. My meditations are going well—after the first session, he had me extend my concentration to my whole body until I now can almost feel my cells buzzing with electrical energy whenever I turn my focus inward.

But he hasn't asked me any more questions about my past.

He's in a rare mood tonight, seeming almost jovial. I'm not sure what's behind it—I still know nothing about him. But I like this easier-going Colin far better than the demanding taskmaster who's been drilling me in Chosen social behaviors.

Which is a good thing. Because even though I've made Alina aware of the fact that I need to feed, she hasn't made any provisions for me to go hunting. It's now been over a week since Taz and I fed after our tumble down the hill. And my increasing hunger has me irritable and on edge.

Colin walks back into his office from outside where he's been for the last ten minutes after answering a call on his cell phone. He settles into his chair across the desk from me.

"Now, where were we? Oh yes. I believe we were talking about the next phase of your training."

"Colin, before we do that, I need to ask a favor of you."

He leans forward and laces his fingers together on the desk, his expression friendly and open.

"Certainly, Sunny. Shoot."

"It's been awhile since my last meal. Would it be possible to take me out to hunt?"

He smiles.

"I don't see why not. Who's your Maker?"

I blink at the suddenness of the question, then focus on suppressing any further physical responses.

"I don't know."

"Hmm. You blinked and your fingers on your right hand twitched. You need further work on that question. Where were you when you were attacked?"

I have a little more trouble clamping down on my reaction this time. I focus inward and release the knots of tension threatening to work their way to the surface of my skin.

"Stockton."

"What were you doing?"

"Shopping." I ease out a smile, managing to keep the rest of my body stable.

"For whom?"

Andrea. Her birthday present.

My control shatters and I swallow.

Colin eases himself back in his chair, the satisfied expression on his face punctuated by an index finger resting against his lips.

"Hmm. I suspected as much. You're protecting someone. And it's not your Maker."

I retreat to that cold, detached place in the center of my core and, with my newfound awareness of my body, find that it's stronger than ever.

"I'm not protecting anyone. I was shopping for myself." I smile and tip my head.

Colin's eyebrows arch.

"Tell me about the attack."

I take a breath.

"I'd felt as though I was being watched for several weeks prior. The locations were random—work, school, my home. The night it happened, I had a feeling I was being followed, but couldn't spot anyone. Once I got into my car, I felt safe, but before I could leave, someone smashed in my window and grabbed me."

I keep my face neutral as I wait for the next question, monitoring all the fine muscles beneath the skin to erase any tension before it surfaces.

Colin studies me a moment.

"What happened next?" he asks.

"I'm not sure. I passed out. After that everything's a jumble. All I know is that I woke up at one point and broke out of an abandoned warehouse."

"Who were you shopping for?"

"I told you. Myself."

"Where did you live at the time of the attack?"

"Lodi." The lie I'd practiced over and over slides out easily.

"What kind of work did you do?"

"I was an administrative assistant."

"Who were you shopping for?"

"Myself."

Colin takes a slow breath.

"All right, we're done then. There will be no session tomorrow. Or the next night. Or any other night, for that matter." He stands, his expression ice cold.

"But—"

"But nothing. We had a deal. Your information in exchange for assistance in locating Nicolas."

"But I gave you—"

"Lies. I told you I would know if you were lying. Do you think a few nights of practice enables you to match wits with someone who's been practicing for well over a century?" His expression hardens as he moves out from behind the desk, heading toward the door.

"I don't want her hurt," I whisper, nearly choking on the fear rising up in my throat.

Colin stops as he passes my chair. He rests his hand on my shoulder, then touches my chin and raises it so he can look me in the eye.

"Oh, Sunny, Sunny. You gave in far too easily."

Bloodtears obscure my vision and I turn away. Colin strolls back to his seat.

"I assume you're protecting family?"

I nod.

"Well, if it's any consolation, I don't want to know anything more about them than is absolutely necessary." His voice softens. "I think we can discuss the circumstances of your change without involving them."

The years I've spent guarding the secret of Andrea's existence burst from my chest as an explosive breath I'd not been aware I was holding. A fresh wave of bloodtears threatens to spill from my eyes. Colin offers me a tissue which I gratefully accept.

"So now, tell me how it happened."

I tell him. Everything. My suspicions about my boss, the increasing sense of being watched, and where, the long sleepless nights filled with worry that I was losing my mind. But when I get to the attack itself, my memories blur into shadows and pain.

"Think, Sunny. What happened when you were pulled through the car window? Do you recall being bitten then?"

"I . . . I don't think so. All I remember is being crushed against someone's body, and being unable to breathe beneath the hand clamped over my mouth, and feeling so damned helpless as my strength and awareness slipped away."

Colin studies me a moment.

"From what you've said so far, this was not a random attack. You were targeted, and whoever snatched you from the car was not some revenant after his next meal. The question is—why you?"

I shrug, no nearer to the answer than I was six years ago, or any time since.

"You mentioned a warehouse. Do you know how long you were there?"

"No. It seemed like a long time. It could've been a week, or several weeks."

"How often did your captor visit you?"

"I . . . I don't know. It seemed like he was always there, but . . ."

"But what?"

"But I remember the door in the tiny room opening, and closing, a lot. Like someone was coming and going, yet he never left."

"Is it possible there was more than one?"

Was there? I try to think through the muddied haze of memories. Rising to my feet, I walk over to the window and stare out at the hallway, recalling the darkness of the room, and the darker shape of my captor. A shape that sometimes seemed to split in two.

"Do you remember what happened to you in that room?"

My mind recoils in horror as I try to force it to reveal the secrets it's kept hidden from me all these years. Secrets so terrifying I'd willed them to stay buried forever, far beyond my reach.

"No," I finally whisper, shaking my head.

And without warning, the fiery scourge of hunger sets my body aflame.

A small gasp slips out as I clamp my jaw, and clutching the window frame for support, I turn to look at Colin. Recognition flickers in his pale blue eyes and he gives me a sad smile.

"Come," he says, rising from his chair. "I believe I know how to help you remember. What we need is in the other room."

Trembling, my vision colored with the deep red of need, I trail him to the door behind the receptionist's desk. He opens it, ushers me past him, then follows me inside.

The windowless room is larger than his office and, in fact, likely takes up the rest of the building. We thread our way through a cluster of high-end workout equipment and past an area filled with boxing bags and other fighting gear, our heels ringing out against the tiled floor. At the far end of the room sits a lone chair.

But not just any chair.

This one is of steel, and has steel manacles attached to the arms and legs.

I spin around, but I'm too late. Colin's unyielding grip pins me by the shoulders against the wall.

His gaze bores into me.

"This is the only way. Your instincts will guard your memories unless the defense mechanism is completely broken down. And only one thing will do that."

I try to claw my way free, but his hands dart like lightning to my wrists.

"You lied to me, you son of a bitch! You said this was my choice!" My fangs descend, battle ready. His betrayal triggers something deep in me, and suddenly I'm back in the club with Nicolas, a dying man at my feet. Crimson rage erupts with a guttural roar and I head butt Colin, nearly stunning myself. I jerk my knee up, aiming for his crotch, but he twists and slams his hip against mine, now trapping me with his whole body against the wall.

"Stop," he says through gritted teeth. "Think about this. If I wanted to force the information from you, it would've already happened. The first day. I wouldn't have wasted my valuable time teaching you how to survive. I have better things to do than play nursemaid to someone who nearly destroyed all our lives."

He releases me.

Panting and rubbing my wrists, I glare at him, then start for the door.

"Sunny!"

I hesitate, then stop. If I take one more step, I have a feeling there's no turning back.

"You have two choices. You can either sit in that chair and do what needs to be done to learn who your Maker is and find Nicolas, or you can walk out the door. But I promise you this: if you leave, we are finished. I will not give you another second of my time." He takes a deep breath. "And furthermore, there will be a bounty on your head. That is not my doing. Alina is bound by blood to follow the wishes of her Maker, and the fact that you're still alive is a testament to her willpower, creativity, and loyalty to Nicolas."

The fight slowly drains out of me, leaving me limp and exhausted. And hungry.

I don't know what else to do. I want to know who Made me, but it's my need for Nicolas that drives me like a whip, and in spite of everything that's happened, I can't contemplate a future that doesn't have him in it.

"You'll take me to Nicolas?"

His expression softens.

"No. But I will point you in his direction. Finding him will be up to you."

Of course. It's never as simple as I think it's going to be. But it's all I have to go on.

Focusing on the chair, I stride over to it with as much dignity as I can muster, then plant my ass on the cold, steel seat and lay my arms into the waiting manacles. My instincts scream at me to run, to get the hell out of there and never look back. I struggle to remain still as Colin fastens the unforgiving metal around my forearms, then does the same with the ones at my ankles.

"How long has it been since you fed?" he asks, straightening.

"Eight nights."

He blinks.

"How long do you usually go between meals?"

"Five, maybe six nights."

Colin is silent as he studies me, his brow furrowed.

"Well," he says after a long moment. "That's a bit impressive, especially for one so young. Most can't go for more than a day or two. Have you thought about why you can do this?"

A fresh wave of hunger sears my throat and sends flickering tendrils along my veins. I suck in my breath and answer through throbbing gums.

"I never knew it was unusual until I met Nicolas. We think it's because my normal prey has a blood supply measured in gallons, not pints, and I consume as much as I can hold whenever I feed. Which seems to be more than the average Chosen, according to Nicolas."

Colin gazes down at me, his hands clasped behind his back.

"Fascinating. No wonder he was so intrigued by you when you first met. You're quite different from any Chosen I've ever known."

"So now what?" I pant, as the burning pulses through my body.

"So now we wait. And I ask you questions until you can no longer bear to answer. And then perhaps your mind will give way to your body's demands, and provide us access to the memories we need."

Oh God.

I stare at him through fear and pain.

"You can quit at any time. But remember what I said about you leaving without revealing your origins."

Biting back a sob, I nod and steel myself for what may be a very long night.

Or nights.

The prospect terrifies me.

"The room is soundproof, and no one is usually around here at night anyway. You'll be asleep during the day. Typically, one sleeps longer when weak from hunger."

Dawn is hours away. The thought of sitting here, helpless and starving until then, only turns up the flames.

I nod my agreement.

"Then let's begin. Tell me again about that night."

And so I do. Over and over, until the words no longer sound intelligible, even to me. And finally the unending night draws to a close, and I gratefully sink down into the darkness of the day.

# WEDNESDAY

## CHAPTER 62

Images rush at me, one after another, of flames and red eyes and fangs. My swollen tongue will no longer permit the screams to rip from my throat, and I choke on yet another as the agony of hunger pulses through my body.

"Do you want to keep going?" The voice echoes as though far away . . .

The sting of a slap against my face forces my eyes open, and Colin looms over me through a scarlet fog, backlit by the overhead spotlight.

"Yesss."

"Who do you see in the room with you? You said there were two. What are they doing?"

Terror overwhelms me as I slip back into the past. Fangs flash in the dark and a cold weight settles onto my chest. I scream through ragged vocal cords as the fangs disappear from view and a sharp pain pierces my throat.

"Biting," I rasp. "He's biting me, he's . . . he's *drinking* my blood. Oh God . . . someone help me . . . please . . ."

Red darkness rushes in, followed by the fires of hell.

A hand grabs my chin and raises it. I open my eyes to stare into Colin's blue ones, filled with frustration and sympathy. The light forms a halo around his face.

"Yes. This we know. But who? Who's biting you? What does he look like?"

Crimson eyes, glowing with madness. Sharp, dagger-like fangs, painted with blood. My blood.

Oh God. It *hurts*. He's sucking the life from me. I can feel it draining away with each moaning swallow, and it burns. My vision's speckled with tiny lights dancing to the ringing in my ears, and I cannot feel anything now . . .

Stabbing pain lances along my arm, bringing me back to the present. I look down to see my forearm bleeding from a gaping slash along its top, and a new panic takes hold when the wound fails to close. As the fires of healing add to those of my raging hunger, I lift my head to glare up at Colin. He's standing over me, a dripping knife in his hand.

"We're almost there, Sunny. Don't give up now."

I scream in answer.

Metal clatters against the tile floor and Colin cradles my head against his chest as I sob. I want to bite him, to consume every drop of his blood, but I'm too weak to move.

"I'm sorry," he whispers. "Keep going. You said there were two—a heavy-built one and a slender one. Which one is biting you?"

Their shadows hover over me in the darkness. The big one bites me again, and jerks my body against his, rough and insistent.

My mind shrieks as another layer peels away, and a new memory surfaces.

When he bites me this time, it doesn't hurt. It doesn't hurt at all.

In fact, it feels *good*, and I press my neck against his sharp teeth and cold lips. I want to pull him closer, but my arms are tied to the bed. He moans as he swallows, and my own cries of pleasure join his. As I sink into death once again, this time, to my horror, I welcome it . . .

"Sunny. Tell me what's happening now. What changed? What do you remember?"

"I . . . I like it. I want him to do it again."

My head is abruptly released, and I squint at the bright light as Colin's voice booms out from in front of me.

"So you must've drunk Chosen blood by this point. How? From whom? Think, Sunny."

I drank blood? I don't remember . . .

A pale arm looms over me in the black night and presses gently against my mouth.

"Drink, sweet daughter, drink." The quiet words embrace me in the tones of a cello, rich with a foreign-accented melody. A hand softly strokes my hair as a thick, metallic fluid fills my mouth. I try to turn away and can't, and choking, I finally swallow.

Liquid pleasure races down my belly and my body arches with a sudden yearning for sex. I want it, want it now. I want to drown in it, and in the blood that has become my entire existence.

Oh God.

The last barrier crumbles and the memories come flooding back. Memories of eagerly awaiting their visits—the one who violently brings me death, and the one who gently gives me life, each equally pleasurable in their own way.

Mortified at my own participation in my destruction, I understand now why my mind locked these memories away. After the initial assault, I no longer tried to escape and, in fact, was left loose in the pitch-black cell to anxiously pace from wall to wall until the moment I could throw my arms around whichever shadowy lover came through the door.

And I never once thought about Andrea.

"Sunny. What do you remember? Tell me."

"There . . . there are two," I gasp. "The burly one is cruel, and savages me each time he drains me to unconsciousness. The slender one, oh, the slender one, he's so gentle as he feeds me his blood, and pleasures me over and over . . ."

I can feel the bloodtears tracing their way down my cheeks as I speak, tears of embarrassment and shame.

"Does the slender one ever feed from you?"

"No. Yes. Once. In the beginning. I . . . I think the cruel one forces him to. They argue, and he tries to leave, but the cruel one is much stronger and makes the gentle one drink from my arm. He seems weak, and tries to resist, but I think he's giving in because he's hungry. His eyes, they're so sad as he drinks, and then he's yanked away. He falls to the floor . . ."

My words die beneath a fresh surge of agonizing fire racing through my body.

"Do you remember any others?"

Any others . . . any others . . . The words echo through my head, and I remember.

"Voices," I croak. "I can hear voices on the other side of the door, even when the two are with me . . ." The black pit of dawn begins to tug at me and I give in to it, seeking the peace that it brings.

"What else? What happens before you escape?" Colin squeezes my shoulder, bringing me out of my stupor. The memories well up once again, along with the crush of hunger. I struggle to get my words out.

"I'm alone. I wake to sounds of arguing, and growling, and crashing noises. I think they're fighting . . ."

"And then what? They're fighting and then what? Come on, stay with me!" Colin shakes me back from my hunger hell. I now try to resist the rising sun as I dig through the images and sounds stamped deep in my mind.

"And then nothing. I wait and wait and no one comes. I fall asleep, and when I wake, I'm *hungry*. So hungry. I break out of the room, smashing the door apart with a strength I've never had before . . ." Helpless against the day, I begin to sink into oblivion.

"Sunny!"

"I . . . I'm alone. No one is here. The warehouse is empty. *Run*, a gentle voice whispers in my head. *Run*. So I run . . ."

# THURSDAY

## CHAPTER 63

Blood.

Heartbeats.

My eyes snap open as my body leaves the ground. Fangs find their target upon impact and great, gasping swallows begin to quench the scorching fire. Too quickly there is no more, and I zero in on the heartbeats behind me. I launch, and the flames die back a little further as this new fount runs dry.

The heartbeats have moved again, and again one ceases beneath the deadly fangs. And so I continue, and pulses cease, one by one, and the inferno consuming me slowly diminishes.

I listen for more, but there are none. A musky scent filling the air matches the thick taste coating my tongue. I spit out bristly hair, wipe my mouth, and sit up.

Straw beneath me rustles as I peer through the surrounding dark. I'm in an unlit barn, cobwebs draping the wooden beams overhead. Scattered across the straw-covered floor are the bodies of what must be a dozen goats.

*Goats.* Disgusting.

But at least I'm no longer on fire, though a dull internal ache tells me I will need to feed again soon, preferably on something more palatable.

A movement to my left reveals Colin perched on a stack of hay, his scarlet eyes glittering in the darkness.

I slowly stand, brushing the straw and goat hair from my clothes. Spitting out a few more hairs, I head for the barn door.

"Sunny."

"What."

"You did it." He jumps down from the stack, flicking the hay from his slacks.

"*Screw. You.*" I continue on toward the door.

It's taking everything I have not to tear him into tiny pieces.

"Do you remember any of it?"

Pausing, I stare at the far wall.

"Yeah, I remember. I remember my screams, and the pain, and your relentless questions. I hope you're *satisfied*."

"Do you remember anything else? Do you remember your Change?"

I search my memory of that endless black night filled with fear and shadowy figures. And . . . nothing. Nothing more than that.

"No."

Heaving a sigh, I cross my arms and turn around.

"So it didn't work?"

"It worked."

"Did you get what you need?"

"As much as you had to give. And I commend you for your endurance." Colin runs a hand through his hair. "In fact, in all my years, I've seldom encountered anyone with such perseverance. Most other Chosen would have collapsed into a gibbering mess, but you kept your wits about you enough to push through the barrier and remember the details as you knew them."

"So who's my Maker?"

"That, unfortunately, you did not know. You knew there were two assailants, and one fed from you, and the other gave you his blood."

"Two? There were *two*? And we still don't know who Made me? Then I went through hell for *nothing*!" Blood runs from my fists as bitter anger boils up my throat.

"I didn't say you gave us nothing—only that you were unable to identify your Maker. We learned enough to conclude he was forced, and not of the same lineage as the others."

"Others. There were more than two?"

"Apparently so. We've not seen this before, but we believe the one who fed from you was to be your tracker, and there was something valuable about the lineage of the other—the one who gave you his blood. But we don't know what, nor how they intended to use you. I suspect your Maker might have been related to our lineage—Nicolas said there was something familiar about you. It's possible they planned to use you to infiltrate us, but that's just speculation at this point."

Great. It's all useless bullshit as far as I'm concerned.

"So are we done? Did I fulfill my end of the bargain? Cuz if you say I didn't, I'll tear your throat out right here, and *you* can become my next meal."

Colin laughs.

"In spite of the impressive and efficient way with which you—who should be completely incapacitated by hunger and blood loss—dispatched that herd of goats, I highly doubt you possess the skill to rip out my throat, or that of any other Chosen."

I glare at him, curling my lip to bare a fang.

But he's probably right. Katarina and Eva had both proven that to me with little effort.

"Sunny, I consider your part of the bargain complete. I still need to fulfill my end, which encompasses further instruction if you would like it. And that includes fight training."

That gets my attention.

"You would do this? Teach me to fight? How to kill you?"

He laughs again.

"Well, preferably not me." Blue eyes shining, his mouth curves into a half smile. "But yes, I will teach you how to defend yourself, and how to kill a Chosen if necessary."

I take a deep breath.

"Goats. Really?" I spit again in disgust.

"Gathering a herd of deer on such short notice wasn't really possible at the time." Colin slowly walks toward me. He's cautious, as though he's unsure whether or not I might attack.

Good.

"Where are we? Is this your barn?"

He waves me toward the door.

"No. It belongs to a friend of mine."

"And he let you have his goats, too, knowing they'd be killed?" I walk with my head half-turned, keeping him in my peripheral vision.

"I bought them at a livestock auction. They were destined for slaughter and seemed a better choice than a herd of sheep or a cow. I thought the taking of many small lives rather than a single large one might allow you to exorcise the violence that builds with extreme hunger as well as satisfy your body's need for blood."

He's probably right about that, though I still feel like ripping out another dozen throats, including his. And my need for blood is far from satisfied, but this should hold me.

For a little while.

"Well, I'm glad you didn't choose sheep. The wool . . ." I nearly gag at the thought.

Colin laughs.

"I considered that. They're all a bit loathsome for my taste. But the goats seemed more deerlike than the others, so . . ." He shrugs as he walks alongside me, yet still keeps some distance between us.

Colin opens the barn door and holds it. I stop and look back at the devastation I'd wrought, feeling a little bad about their violent end. At least it was quick, if nothing else.

"What about those?" I gesture toward the bodies.

"They'll be taken care of."

I walk past him through the door into the cool November night. Clouds drift overhead, obscuring both stars and moon. Unable to see what phase it's in, I have no idea how much time has passed since I first sat in the steel chair.

"What day is it?"

In spite of living my life by the night, I still can't break the human habit of referring to the days.

We stop next to Colin's car and he takes the keys from his pants pocket.

"Thursday." He glances at his watch. "A little before nine."

"And I went into the chair when?"

"Sunday, about midnight."

Sunday at midnight. Monday. Tuesday. Wednesday.

Three-and-a-half nights of being burned alive, of being bled, of being hounded. His voice will echo through my head for all eternity.

"You tortured me for *three-and-a-half nights*?"

Reddened vision and throbbing gums accompany the rage threatening to burst through my skin as I turn to look at Colin.

"Don't." His relaxed stance flows into something else, something lethal.

"Did you enjoy it?" I snarl. My fingers arch, ten tiny daggers needing a home.

"Did I enjoy it?" The careful mask he usually maintains fades into outrage. "Hell no, I didn't enjoy it. Not one single minute of it." Colin eases back, putting some much-needed space between us.

"From what I recall, you handled it like you've had lots of practice."

He snorts.

"I won't lie. I've done my fair share of interrogations."

"You mean torture."

"You can call it what you want, but I guarantee, what you experienced in that chair was nothing close to real torture, other than what your own body inflicted upon you." His blue eyes took on a scarlet hue. "I did what I had to do to help you remember, and I asked you over and over if you wanted to stop. And you said, 'Keep going.' So I did. And every time you screamed, I had to prevent myself from opening those restraints and offering you my arm. Don't think it was easy on me, because it most certainly was not!"

We glare at one another, both half-crouched and ready for the other to make a move.

Colin slowly straightens, flexing his fingers.

"Sunny, I like you. I admire your spirit and your determination. I will do everything I can to help you get what you want, even if it hurts me in the process. In fact, the truth is, I hope you find Nicolas. Not just for you, and not just for him. But for all of us. I hope you find him and bring him back, because I am unable to. I couldn't convince him to stay—I'm hoping you can convince him to come home."

By the time he's done, my indignation has melted away, leaving me ashamed of my reaction and accusations. A little spark of hope ignites at the thought that, with Colin's help, I actually have a real chance of finding Nicolas.

Taking a deep breath, I ease out of my crouch.

"I'm sorry." I bow my head.

Colin steps forward and gently grasps my shoulders. Sympathy and concern line his features.

"I understand your anger and frustration," he says quietly. "What you did was not easy. I kept waiting for you to break, to give up and put an end to it. But you kept digging through your memories, deeper and deeper, telling me every detail as you recalled it. Until you reached the bottom and there was nothing more to tell."

"Then why can't I remember any of them now?"

"Apparently the ordeal was so traumatic, you prefer not to remember it at all."

"Was there anything else? Besides the fact that there were two? Or more?"

Colin shakes his head, his blue eyes bright.

"No."

I nod.

"Well, then. I don't know about you, but I think I reek. I could really use a shower and some clean clothes."

"I believe I can arrange that." Colin smiles and gives my shoulders a gentle squeeze, then releases me.

"But first, is there anywhere around here I can hunt? I need to run, and I'd really like to get the taste of goat out of my mouth."

"I believe I can arrange that, too."

He walks toward the side of the barn, and I follow, wondering what he has up his sleeve now.

As we move into the open to the left of the barn, in the not-too-far distance is a hillside covered in a dense oak forest. Behind it, more such hills.

"I checked with my friend, and he said there are quite a number of deer in there."

This guy thinks of everything.

"I won't be gone long." Anticipation vibrates through my body. The red veil drops over my vision and my fangs descend, eager and ready. By my reckoning, it's been twelve days since I last hunted.

"Enjoy yourself. You deserve it." Colin smiles.

I'm sure the sound barrier breaks when I take off.

# TUESDAY

## CHAPTER 64

I arch my body, barely avoiding a kick in the ribs, only to open it up to a second one on the other side. It connects with a solid *thunk*, jarring the air from my lungs with a loud grunt. I wince and duck away from a third kick, then lash out with one of my own. Failing to land it, I throw up my hands in surrender and rub my freshly bruised side.

Damn, he's fast.

Colin never ceases to amaze me. Mister Mild-Mannered Attorney transforms into a lethal martial arts fighting machine during our training sessions. Though most would not consider him a big guy, he carries enough muscle mass to unleash a storm of hurt without being stocky. Instead, his taut physique—no doubt honed by the workout equipment at his office—combined with lightning-fast reflexes, ensures he can likely hold his own in any fight, no matter the size of his opponent.

"Let's take a break. You did well." Colin pads barefooted across the barn. In his white sleeveless T-shirt and karate pants, he certainly looks more like a professional fighter than a lawyer.

"What, by moving right into your last two kicks?"

He laughs.

"The last two of a series of nine. Your skills have greatly improved this past week."

"Thanks."

It's been three weeks since I woke up in the barn, killing everything that moved with no awareness of what it was. I once again shudder as I try not to imagine human bodies lying on the straw-covered floor.

As promised, Colin's been teaching me how to fight. We've set up the barn as a training center, complete with workout and martial arts equipment at one end, leaving the remaining area open for sparring.

The workout equipment surprised me when it first appeared here, just as it did when I saw it at Colin's offices. With our supernatural speed and strength, I wouldn't think working out would make any difference in our abilities. According to Colin, it doesn't. At least against humans. With Chosen, on the other hand, he says keeping the body fit with physical practice can make the difference between life and death.

What a lovely society I've entered.

Colin walks toward the door.

"I need to get a few things from my car. I'll meet you at the house."

The house.

That's been the best part yet. Apparently his friend only uses the Bear Creek property part-time, and was happy to rent it out for a few months. With Alina's approval, I moved in after she agreed that I'd held up my end of the deal. I live here alone, and am free to come and go as I please—Alina even returned my BMW—as long as I continue my training with Colin.

Heading to the rambling two-story, I wonder how much longer that'll last. I'm anxious to get started on my search for Nicolas.

The last time I asked Colin about it, he chided me for my impatience, reminding me that I'm learning in weeks what most Chosen take years to learn. He said he's taking as many shortcuts as he can, but there is much more I need to know before I venture off on my own.

And he's right. I still have some work to do on managing both my physical and emotional reactions. The nightly meditations are paying off—through an awareness of my body I've never had before, I've finally mastered control over the physical mechanism that releases the damn bloodtears. I won't miss them a bit.

The fang drop has proven a bit more difficult.

Stepping inside the house, I glance around, wondering if we're going to use my laptop that's set up in the small office next to the living room, or work at the dining room table.

My question is answered when Colin comes in the back door carrying several file boxes. Rolls of what look to be blueprints are tucked under one arm. He heads into the dining room, dumps the rolls on the table, and sets the boxes on the floor.

Curious, I watch as he slips the rubber band from one of the rolls and shoves the others down to the end of the table where they're trapped against a chair.

I reach down to hold one end of the paper as he unfurls it.

It's not a blueprint.

It's a map.

A giant map of Europe, with red and green markings inked on it, like something you'd see in a war room.

*Europe.*

Oh shit.

He starts talking as I stare at the map. Many of the major cities bear symbols in either red or green.

Rome. Moscow. Frankfurt. Paris.

*Paris.*

Where Gilles and Katarina are based.

Terror races up my spine and outward, immobilizing every muscle in its wake.

An eternity of training—let alone a few weeks or months—can't prepare me for *that*, for facing *them*.

"Sunny. Are you listening?"

"I . . . I'm sorry. What did you say?"

I can't stop staring at that word. It's such a simple word. Only five letters. The symbol next to it, one I don't recognize, is in red.

Fingers grip my chin and yank it to the side. Colin's gaze bores into me. "Get a hold of yourself. You can do this."

"No, I can't," I whisper.

All I can see in my mind is a head in a large, blood-filled jar, screaming soundlessly over and over.

Not just any head.

*My* head.

# SATURDAY

## CHAPTER 65

The San Francisco fog slithers and curls around us as we drive through dimly lit streets, its murky mood constantly shifting. Some nights it lies heavy, lazy, blanketing the whole city with sluggish mist that refuses to give way before even the brightest lights. Other nights, like tonight, it prowls, restless and secretive, hiding an entire block for long minutes before revealing its prize and slithering away to capture the next. At the moment, grey gloom clings to the warehouses we're passing along the waterfront, its fringes backlit with an eerie glow from the surrounding city lights.

Colin guides the Aston Martin into an alley between two graffiti-marked buildings and, after several turns, pulls into a nearly filled parking area protected by more buildings. Approaching headlights from several other alleys bounce through the fog, creating a crazy kaleidoscope of blue- and yellow-toned beams interlaced with black shadows. He parks next to a tan Maserati and, glancing at me, shuts off the ignition.

A uniformed security guard, toting an Uzi, nods his head to us as he strolls by. I note several others wandering the grounds, their watchful gazes roaming over the expensive steel-and-chrome under their care.

We watch for several moments as a steady stream of figures pass between the cars, heading toward a spotlighted warehouse to our left, their graceful strides labeling them as Chosen. Most are well-dressed, matching the shiny machines they arrived in. Others appear more working class, though none are shabby by middle-class standards.

Colin clears his throat.

"Shall we?" he asks, his eyebrows raised.

I nod and he exits the car, buttoning his tailored knee-length coat and adjusting the fedora perched on his head as he walks around to my side. He's looking pretty dapper himself tonight.

Opening my door, he reaches out to assist me and I accept, enjoying being treated like a lady for a change. As he closes it, I straighten the black cocktail dress he'd advised me to wear and smooth back the blonde strands of hair that have already managed to escape the low bun resting on the nape of my neck.

Blonde. Still kinda freaks me out when I spot it out of the corner of my eye. I never have liked myself as a blonde. But when Colin handed me the box of dye, I didn't argue. Disguises are something I understand.

Guess I look more like a Sunny now, though on his advice I'm going to stay Sonya for a while.

Offering his arm, he pauses as I take it, then guides me between the parked cars toward the warehouse. I keep an eye on the rough ground, trying to avoid catching a stiletto heel in one of the many cracks in the asphalt. But my attention is increasingly drawn to the door we're approaching. Varying tones of chatter and laughter, escorted by bright light, escape into the surrounding darkness each time the door opens to admit a Chosen. I try to catch a glimpse of how many might be inside the huge building, and feel a twinge of anxiety when we climb the concrete steps and it's our turn to enter.

Not unlike Nicolas, Colin has opted to keep me in the dark about our destination tonight. At first I thought we might be going to the theater, or even the opera, as he was fairly explicit on how I should dress. But our current surroundings in the warehouse district has me scratching my head over what the evening has in store for us.

The crowd noise grows louder as we cross the threshold onto a wide, concrete landing—noise that's coming from several hundred Chosen sitting in stadium-style seating all around the cavernous room. We've entered near the bottom, though there are a few tiers below us.

But what grabs my attention is the huge, steel-barred fight cage in the center of the floor.

This one's different from any I've seen on late-night TV when I was desperately seeking some relief from boredom. It seems to have more sides than a standard fight cage—I count nine rather than the normal eight. Narrowly spaced bars form the inner arena which is surrounded by an outer perimeter of plexiglass. It's also much bigger and the top is covered in bars as well, though they're more widely spaced. The two entrances at either side of the arena are boxed in by smaller, steel-barred holding cells.

The sturdiness of this cage indicates its fighters are not mere humans. I suspect they operate under a completely different set of rules as well.

I've never watched any kind of fight in its entirety. In the past, when the beast and the hunter still lurked in my head, I'd find myself growing hungry and agitated as they yearned to throw themselves through the TV screen and tangle with a prey that could potentially offer a satisfying struggle. I haven't bothered trying watch any since then.

"Our seats are on the other side." Colin ushers me ahead of him to a section with violet seats, then down to the sixth row from the bottom. "Pardon us," he says several times as we squeeze past bent knees, both cloth-covered and bare, and avoid stepping on polished wingtips and sandaled toes.

I focus on blocking out the sights and sounds, using my meditation skills to stay calm, as I've never been around so many Chosen. Hell, I haven't been around this many people of any kind since I was so roughly inducted into this life nearly six years ago.

"Here we are." Colin stops, waiting until I'm in my seat before taking his own.

We're sitting just above the cage top, giving us a perfect view down into the center of its rubber-matted floor.

"I thought it would be valuable to see how other Chosen fight. You're familiar with my style, but you need to learn how to analyze the techniques of different fighters so you can better defend yourself."

And here I thought we were taking a nice, quiet night off for the opera.

My gaze drifts around to examine the audience.

As I noted in the parking lot, most are well-dressed Chosen, both male and female. Their buzzing anticipation seems fueled in spots by the exchange of money. Empty seats are rare, and as I continue to survey the room, I realize the multi-tiered seating is arranged in triangular sections terminating at the cage in the center. Each section, including the seats and painted concrete floors, bears a unique color—a color also reflected in the auras of The Chosen seated within.

So many auras so close together creates a bizarre, unsettling shimmer over the whole crowd. I'm unable to distinguish the individual energy signatures any farther than about twenty feet away, and even trying to do so with those nearby makes my eyes and head hurt.

They all seem to bear the amber common to the lineage, but the second color varies by section. Bright yellow, coral, and brown, as well as several shades of blue and green create a haze around the seated Chosen. Violet seems to occur only in those Chosen in our area, which is painted violet as well.

The amber-colored section is more ornate than the others, constructed with several wide carpeted landings rather than rows of seats. Low tables surrounded by plush armchairs dot the landings; a bar inhabits the uppermost level. Although the section's décor is a little gaudy for Nicolas's standards, this is certainly where he would sit.

If he was here.

"What's the significance of the different section colors?" I ask.

"They represent the nine Elders. Audience members are seated in their Elder's section and the fighters wear shorts corresponding to their Elder's color. As you can see—"

The rest of his words fade away as a low hum fills the room, silencing the surrounding conversation and laughter. The hum grows louder, and beneath its vibration, a deep electronic thump-thump begins to build, dominating all other sound.

It sounds like a beating heart. A human heart.

The thump-thump increases in speed as red lasers shoot down from the ceiling, enclosing both audience and arena in twin curtains of tightly spaced beams. Crimson light pulses down the beams, mimicking the racing rhythm of human fear.

The mock rain of blood sends the crowd to their feet, roaring. I resist the impulse to join them as explosive violence surges within my veins.

The beat shifts into a drumroll, its hammering sound now joined by that of blaring trumpets and horns—traditional fanfare music. Spotlights shine onto a red-carpeted aisle leading from the arena to black draperies set within an opening in the concrete wall.

The draperies part, and two attractive human brunettes in short, red-sequined dresses enter with the exaggerated gaits of runway models. Glittering garnets encircle their throats and wrists. The women's images splash across giant ceiling-suspended flat-screens as the downpour of bloody light drains away to a trickle and disappears.

But instead of the catcalls and whistles I'd normally expect in such a testosterone-fueled setting, low growls and hisses rise from the watching crowd.

They don't want to screw the women. They want to *eat* them.

These are the only humans here, I realize. Nervous tension adds itself to the knots twisting my muscles.

I hope like hell the spectacle I'm about to witness doesn't include a human bloodbath.

"Breathe, Sunny. Calm yourself." Colin's stern voice brings me back to familiar ground and I focus on re-establishing control.

"Thanks. This is a bit . . . overwhelming."

"Adapting to unfamiliar situations is a critical survival skill. You need to assess rather than react. Not only will it make the difference between whether you live or die, it also allows you to maintain the detachment necessary to repress your reactions."

Nodding, I shift my attention back to the unfolding show.

The women, followed by the spotlights, head to a raised steel platform between the fight cage and the amber section. They climb the stairs and take positions at either end of a long table covered with a pristine white tablecloth. A microphone on a stand occupies the center of the platform

The spotlights over the entrance again flare to life and a new round of procession music fills the air. A stately Chosen male, in semi-formal black-tie wear and a top hat, walks through the curtain, followed by three more males in less formal dress. Each of the three assistants carries a silver tray supporting a massive gold award belt encrusted with bright-colored gems.

The procession makes its way to the platform. The lead Chosen stops at the microphone while the assistants arrange the belts on the table. When they're finished, the assistants head back down the stairs with their trays and disappear behind the black draperies.

"Good evening." The announcer's voice echoes over the loudspeakers and the audience responds with cheers and applause. "Welcome to the One-Hundred-and-Fiftieth Supreme Fighter Championships. Tonight's finals are the culmination of this year's series, a year in which we've witnessed some of the most exciting fights in our history.

"The fighters tonight are the Division One finalists in all three weight classes. Please join me in welcoming them to the West Coast and the NorCal SFC Arena."

As the crowd responds, Colin leans over to me.

"The divisions are by age," he says when the applause dies down. "The lower two divisions are under fifty years of age and fifty to one hundred fifty. Division One is for those over one hundred fifty years old."

"Are you saying that once someone has reached that age, their physical abilities no longer increase?"

"No. They do. But typically Chosen lose interest in such activities once they reach a certain age, viewing them as nothing more than pointless displays of juvenile aggression."

Peering around at the standing-room-only venue, I'd guess that either this would be considered a "young" crowd, or not all Chosen feel that way, no matter what their age.

The announcer continues with short biographies of each fighter, but they mean nothing to me. I'm more interested in what Colin has to say.

"So what prevents someone from claiming they're younger?"

"If they don't have documentation from their Maker, they're automatically placed in Division One. It's a risky venture—a fighter much younger than a hundred and fifty won't last long. The weight classes are more straightforward, though a fighter does have the option to move to a heavier class if he wishes. But once he does that, he cannot move back, so very few attempt to fight beyond their weight limit."

"Do females fight?"

"They do, but in a separate organization. Their pool of fighters is much smaller. As with human women, most females prefer to exert dominance by means other than physical. That's why they're so lethal when it comes to the Game."

Before I can ask more questions about the female fighters, a thunderous roar rises through the warehouse and the spotlights once again beam down onto the red-carpeted entrance to the arena.

The black curtains part. A Chosen male walks through, his build similar to Colin's but not as tall. He's barefoot and wears nothing more than a pair of tight, sky-blue shorts, like bicycle shorts. His pale skin gleams as though it's been oiled, as does his curly red hair. Faint freckles dust his arms, upper back, and shoulders, and his aura pulses in amber and pale blue, laced with a thin thread the color of rust. The caption below his image on the overhead flat-screens proclaims him as Mike "The Crazy Celt" Kelly.

He raises his fists to the crowd as he strides in, and they acknowledge him with both cheers and boos. He responds with a bare-fanged snarl and heads to the holding cell on the left of the fight cage.

The curtains open again, and this time the roar is even louder. Another Chosen enters, same size and build. This one, in pale-green shorts, appears to be half-Asian, and for him the cheers far outweigh the boos. Amber and light green, threaded with orange, hovers about his trim body. His name, Garry "The Ragin' Cajun" Cho, indicates he's likely from Geneviève d'Orléans's territory in Louisiana.

A flurry of hands exchanging cash in the audience accompanies his strut to the other holding cell. As he enters, the red-headed Crazy Celt growls and lowers himself into a crouch.

Colin once again leans over to me.

"Just to prepare you, there are no rules—except one. If a fighter signals submission, his opponent must honor the request."

"No rules. Does that mean—?"

The cage doors clang open. The two fighters launch through their doorways and the cage erupts into a snarling chaos of claws and fangs. Their bodies entwined in a writhing ball of fury, all I can see is flashes of color—the pale skin of the Celt, the darker skin of the Cajun, the sky-blue and pale-green fabric of their shorts. And red. Not red hair.

Red blood.

The rubber-matted floor slickens with it beneath them, and as they crash into the bars on one side of the cage, it splatters in an arcing

Rorschach inkblot across the plexiglass. The audience behind the glass recoils, the surprise on their faces quickly shifting to feral excitement.

The purpose of the glass suddenly becomes clear.

I'm struck by the savagery of the battle below us. There's nothing human about it. They look more like lions or tigers fighting, like something you'd see on a nature program on TV. The chilling growls and snarls only accent the horrific scene.

The fighters abruptly separate and move to opposite ends of the arena, the tension nearly vibrating the air surrounding them.

"Well. Now that they've gotten that out of their systems, perhaps they'll settle down and we'll see some real fighting."

I look at Colin in amazement.

"You don't call what they just did a fight?"

"No. They were just testing one another for strength, speed, and reaction time. Right now, they're gauging how quickly their opponent heals."

The fighters move toward the center and slowly begin circling one another. The Cajun flashes out with a lightning-quick kick, barely missing the leg of the Celt as the redhead whirls away.

"That was a Muay Thai kick—the most lethal in martial arts and, if it lands solidly, it will shatter bones, even those of a Chosen."

The fighters close again, unleashing a frenzy of punches upon one another before spinning apart. The Cajun continues his spin, converting it to a high kick. The Celt's head snaps back and he goes down. The Cajun's upon him with the speed of a rattlesnake, and the fight devolves once again into an animal battle of claw and fang.

Blood coats the mats, thicker than before. The seething motion slows, revealing the squirming Celt on his back, locked within a tangle of limbs by the Cajun above him. As the Cajun tightens his hold, panic darts across the redhead's face, and with a wild burst of energy, he frees himself and leaps to his feet.

But he doesn't take two steps before the Cajun has him down again, this time on his belly, and before he can twist onto his back, his limbs are once again trapped by the Cajun's.

The Cajun slips a hand free and grips the throat of the Chosen pinned beneath him. He waits a half moment, the Celt continuing to struggle beneath him, then slowly begins squeezing. Blood drips, then starts streaming past his buried fingers.

The crowd, so far silent, buzzes to life with muttered conversations. Here and there voices rise above the others.

They're chanting.

"Kill. Kill. Kill."

Horrified, I look at Colin.

"Is that legal? Can he do that?"

Colin's grim smile gives me all the answer I need. I find my gaze returning to the brutal exhibition below us.

"If Kelly signals his submission, then Cho must release him or forfeit the win."

"If he doesn't submit?"

"It's Cho's decision then. He can either show mercy or not. Most fighters at the lower levels choose not to kill their opponents—it's far more beneficial for future alliances. But at the championship level, it's anyone's guess what a fighter will do. Depends upon whether or not there's history between them."

I watch, fascinated, as the Cajun eases his grip, giving the Celt another opportunity to surrender. The Celt tries to yank himself loose and, as the grip around his neck tightens once again, goes completely limp.

The Cajun mutters something into the blood-slicked hair and the Celt nods. He then looks up at the crowd, whose chants to kill have become louder and louder.

He looks back down at the beaten Chosen, then abruptly releases him and leaps to his feet amid a cacophony of boos and cheers. As he parades around the arena's perimeter with a fist in the air, he smears the Celt's blood across his face and chest. The cheers of those collecting on their bets soon outweighs the disappointment of those anxious for a death to start their evening.

As the Cajun leaves the arena and heads toward the platform, several attendants move in and help the bloody Celt to his feet. Another two-man crew enters the arena, and pulling a hose from a recess hidden within the floor, begins washing down the mats and plexiglass.

"Well, Sunny—what did you think?" Colin looks at me curiously.

I snort.

"That was one of the most barbaric displays I've ever seen."

He laughs.

"I couldn't agree with you more. But we're not here for entertainment. What you just witnessed is typical of Chosen whose instincts overcome their training. I'm frankly surprised to see such a lack of discipline at this level. I suspect the Celt won his fight slot on a fluke. He seemed quite outmatched, and his opponent just waited for the right opportunity to exercise his superior skills. There is much you can learn from this fight. But we'll talk more about it once we have the others to compare it with."

I don't even want to see the other fights. I can't help but imagine myself in the Celt's place, panicked and begging for mercy as witnesses chant for my death.

# CHAPTER 66

Colin settles back into his seat as we wait for the next bout to start, which turns out to be no more than a few minutes. It features the middleweight finalists, Henry "The Clayman" Clayton and Steven "Double S" Sanderson. Their entry into the ring is more controlled, as is the rest of their fight. According to Colin, both are using various martial arts moves based in taekwando, kung fu, and karate. He keeps me engaged in analyzing their techniques, which provides a distraction from the sounds of breaking ribs and grunts of pain as the fighters trade solid strikes. The round comes to a sudden end when Double S delivers a bone-crunching kick to his opponent's thigh and it snaps, dropping the Clayman to the ground. He quickly signals his submission as Double S threatens to stomp the crippled Chosen's face.

Though I'm relieved when it's over, comments from the surrounding audience indicate their disappointment in both the shortness of the bout and its lack of blood.

That disappointment doesn't extend into the final round.

The heavyweights, Tom "The Battering Ram" Moore and Samuel "The Hurricane" Henderson, tear into one another like two grizzly bears, each using their weight to smash one another against the bars. Their battle has none of the finesse of the last bout, resembling a street brawl more than a championship fight. Blood splashes across the mat and up the plexiglass as the Ram pummels the Hurricane's face, who responds with a downward slash across the Ram's belly that nearly disembowels his opponent. They continue to inflict damage upon one another, then finally separate, each trying to buy time to heal.

Their temporary truce ends when, without any warning, they charge at each other like maddened bulls. Their impact knocks the Hurricane to the floor, and as he rolls away, the Ram leaps into the air and drives both feet down onto the fallen Chosen's back. The sound of the Hurricane's snapping spine is echoed by his scream. When the Ram jumps down onto the Hurricane's back a second time, the defeated Chosen passes out.

The crowd roars its approval as the Ram struts around the arena floor with both fists in the air. His voice joining theirs, he takes several laps while the unconscious Hurricane is carried out.

But when he heads toward the exit to claim his championship belt, the announcer shouts into the microphone.

"Ladies and gentlemen, this is unbelievable! Your evening's not over yet—I've just received word that a former champion has issued a challenge for this year's Heavyweight title!"

Already halfway out of his seat, Colin stops, then sits back down.

"Well, this should be interesting. Moore's suffered some fairly significant blood loss, and though he's one of the toughest fighters on the circuit, he's going to have his hands full with a fresh opponent. I wonder who his challenger is."

The Ram's only response to the announcement is the triumph on his face sliding away into a frown.

As the announcer prattles on about an unprecedented intermission, I turn to Colin.

"Is it really necessary to stay for this? I've seen enough."

"We should stay. This will give us the opportunity to analyze how a fighter changes his tactics when confronted with different fighting styles."

I have mixed emotions about this whole fighting thing. Though I know it's critical to have good defense skills, Colin's obsession with my training has me a bit worried about what I'm getting myself into once I embark on my search for Nicolas.

The entry music blares once again from the loudspeakers. The Ram makes his entrance into the arena amidst cheers and shouts of encouragement, his fist held high in the air, then grimly takes his place in one of the holding cells. He's been bathed, and wears a clean pair of shorts, and the faint color in his skin indicates he had enough time to feed and recharge his system.

I shudder to think how many humans it must take to support these fighters, and whether or not they do so willingly.

The shouting emcee and matching roar from the crowd announces the entry of the challenger. When I look up at the nearest flat-screen, it takes a moment for the image to register.

The Chosen walking through the curtains is tall and well-muscled, with reddish-brown skin and an angry glare. His fight shorts, similar to bicycle shorts like the others, are black, a color not represented by any of the nine sections.

The name emblazoned below his image declares him as The Tasmanian Devil.

It's Taz.

My ears ring with a sudden rush of emotion as I watch him stride down the red carpet and head to the holding cell.

I didn't think I'd ever see him again. I'd hoped he was out of my life for good.

"I'll be damned," Colin says. "Thought his arena days were over. He retired—undefeated—ten, maybe twelve years ago. Though I did hear he's been hanging around the scene lately. I just didn't think he was fighting." Colin scratches his chin as different sections of the audience begin chanting "Devil" and "Ram" in a verbal competition to outshout each other.

Taz ignores the crowd and enters his holding cell, his fierce gaze fixed upon the Ram across the arena. His black hair is oiled and pulled back tightly into a braided bun at the nape of his neck. His dark coppery skin shines with oil as well, a defensive measure which makes it difficult for an opponent to get a solid grip.

It also highlights his well-honed physique, which becomes the new topic of the night for the females in the seats behind us. So far, I've paid no mind to the running dialogue they've maintained all evening as they compared the fighters and whether or not they'd be worthy bedmates.

But it's Taz they're talking about now, and I can't help but feel a flash of jealousy as they discuss his potential as a lover and bloodsport playmate.

And the more I listen, the more I want to turn around and rip their heads off, and tell them he wouldn't waste his time on such empty-headed, shallow twits, let alone share blood with them.

"Are you all right?" Colin says quietly into my ear.

"I'm just fine," I snap. Then, recalling who I'm with and how perceptive he is, I apologize. "Sorry. I'm just hungry and want this to be over."

Colin nods, apparently accepting my lame excuse.

I focus inward and try to suppress the unwelcome turmoil Taz has triggered once again within me.

But all my thoughts fade as the cage doors slam open.

The Ram steps out warily, keeping his distance from Taz as the Indian saunters across the floor toward him. Taz is an inch or two taller, and though his muscles are more defined, he's not as stocky and thick-waisted as the Ram.

"I don't think Moore stands a chance," Colin says. "You're looking at the most lethal fighter to ever enter an arena. It's doubtful Moore will leave the cage alive, and I bet he's thinking the same thing. The Devil's already won this match before it really starts."

As much as I hate to see the Ram, or anyone, destroyed in the arena, I'm mesmerized by Taz and his catlike grace. He glides over the mat, his movements as smooth and oiled as his skin. His eagle-eyed glare gives no hint as to what his next move might be and the Ram continues to give the Indian a wide berth as they circle around the arena.

The air above Taz blurs as he leaps with no warning to crash feetfirst against the Ram's midsection. The Ram falls backward, twisting as he lands in an effort to regain his feet. Taz touches down beside him on all fours, like some big cat ready to pounce, and the snarling Ram scrambles to a stand. Taz's golden eyes gleam above a feral smile as he springs up from the mat and delivers a slashing blow across the Ram's chest, drawing the first blood of the match. The crowd shouts its approval.

The Ram staggers back then, true to his name, lowers his head and charges at the Indian. But as quick as he is, Taz is quicker. He dances to the side and, hooking the Ram's arm, spins his opponent around then pivots to drive his fist into the Ram's ear. Releasing him, Taz steps away and waits.

The Ram cradles his ear, then shakes his head. Enraged and likely in great pain, he turns and tackles Taz. It's almost as though the big Indian lets him, and just before they hit the mat, Taz flips their tangled bodies and winds up on top. He punches the Ram in the face, once, twice, three times in rapid succession with his right fist, then does the same with his left. The Ram squirms beneath him and raises his arms, attempting to block the punishing blows. Taz slams past them several more times, then shoves himself to his feet and walks away to the other end of the cage.

The Ram slowly stands and wipes the blood from his battered face. Hatred contorts his features as he spots Taz quietly waiting across the arena.

A hush settles over the warehouse as though everyone in the audience is holding their breath.

"Well, you gonna just stand there lookin' pretty or are you here to fight?" The Ram spits on the floor. "Mongrel outlaw son of a whore."

The last word is barely out of his mouth before he's slammed against the bars. Taz wraps his long fingers around the Ram's face and smashes his head against the steel bars several times, then grabs it with both hands and pulls it downward as he drives a knee upward again and again. Blood splatters across the mat with each impact, accompanied by the sickening sound of crunching bones.

Still gripping the Ram by his head, Taz flings him to the floor and places one foot on the fallen Chosen's back.

It's the same move Nicolas made just before he almost tore Katerina's head off.

Horrified, I can do nothing but watch.

And then Taz looks up.

He looks straight up at me, as though he knew I was there the whole time.

Without breaking eye contact, he twists his body and I cringe.

But when he stands, his hands are empty. The Ram, his head still attached, groans beneath him. Taz stares at me a half moment longer, then turns away and walks toward the exit.

The crowd goes insane. Outrage at being denied a kill saturates the air, accented with disbelief that Taz would leave an opponent alive. They're even more stunned when he passes the platform without collecting the championship belt.

"I do believe that's a first." Colin looks at me speculatively. "He always takes out his opponent. His nickname is The Executioner, and it's well-earned."

I keep my gaze fixed on the bloody arena floor below us.

Apparently, as much as Taz disturbs me, I disturb him. Enough to change his entire Game.

With a deep sigh, I finally glance over at Colin. He's still studying me, his expression unreadable.

"Well, then. Shall we?" He stands and offers his hand to help me up.

Other than a simple "good night" when he drops me off at the house, he says nothing more the rest of the evening.

# SUNDAY

## CHAPTER 67

Colin places a blank sticky note next to the word *Rome* on the European map, which is now mounted on the dining room wall.

"As with Paris, there are several factions operating in and around Rome." He prints their names on the note as precisely as he does everything else.

"What are their Elder colors?" Shifting in my chair, I copy the names into my reference journal, leaving space beneath each for important details.

"What?"

"Their auras. What colors are they?"

He turns around, looking as though I'd just asked why the sun and the moon exist.

"What are you talking about?"

"Their colors. Alina's is violet, Robert's yellow, and last night I saw the others belonging to Nicolas's lineage. His must be amber, because everyone carries that color."

Everyone except the independents. They seem to have only one color and, so far, none the same.

But my thoughts die as Colin shakes his head and frowns.

"Nicolas's is dark burgundy. The amber belongs to Éva."

"Oh."

This concrete proof of her takeover, evident in every bound Chosen I've seen, crushes the last of my denial.

Nicolas has truly lost the lineage.

And I caused it.

Sickened by my role in his downfall, I stare at my journal, the words blurring as bloodtears begin to fill my eyes.

"Sunny." Colin walks over to the table. "Don't go there. It doesn't do any good. It won't bring him back."

I nod as he leans down, placing his hands on the table.

"Now, center yourself and look at me," he quietly demands.

With a deep breath, I nod again and focus inward, leashing my emotions using the meditation techniques that he's been hammering into me daily. When I reach that place of absolute stillness, I look up at him.

"You said 'last night.'" Colin peers at me. "Do you mean the section colors in the fight stadium?"

"Well, yeah. Those too."

"But you used the word *auras*."

I lean back in my chair, at a bit of a loss.

"I don't know what else to call them. Do they have another name?"

Colin slowly takes a seat in the chair across from me, his eyes narrowing. "Explain what you mean by 'aura.'"

A chill ripples up my back as a disturbing thought begins to take hold.

Nicolas had said he'd sensed me the moment I entered Colorado Springs. And the power radiating from *him* nearly knocked me over the first few times we met—until I got used to it. Since then, I've always felt Chosen energy whenever they're near me, and assumed that all Chosen could do the same. Even Taz had indicated he knew exactly when I arrived in San Francisco.

It wasn't until I fully Changed that I could *see* the energy.

But maybe not all Chosen have the ability to sense one another.

Colin's palpable impatience spurs my explanation.

"The Chosen I've met all seem to have an energy field surrounding their bodies that I can feel."

"Yes, as you should. That energy signature, combined with scent, is how we identify one another, along with our level of maturation and to which lineage and sublineage we belong. We call it véren, which is derived from the Hungarian word for blood."

"Say it again?"

"Véren." He pronounces it *veeren*, with a rolling R.

I repeat it, trying not to sound like someone in a Dracula movie.

Colin studies me a moment, his piercing blue gaze that of the interrogator who'd drilled me so closely in our earlier days.

"Sunny . . . do you *see* the véren?"

My temporary relief at finding some token of normalcy in my Chosen life dissipates with his emphasis on the word "see."

Apparently that's *not* normal.

Why do I always have to be the odd one?

"Answer me."

Unable to extricate myself from Colin's line of inquiry, I can only nod.

"What do you see?"

"It's like a transparent veil of swirling colors that clings close to the body. It wasn't until last night, when I saw Chosen who belong to the other Elders, that I really understood the patterns."

"Explain."

"The auras, or véren, belonging to Alina's Chosen are amber and violet, just like hers. But her véren is brighter, more distinct, and she has multiple threads in different colors woven throughout. Her underlings only have a single thread, though their threads vary in color, shade, and thickness from Chosen to Chosen.

"Robert's véren was amber and *yellow*, and he also had threads of all colors rather than just one. I didn't see any other Elders last night at the fight, but most of The Chosen sat in sections matching their secondary color—the one that wasn't amber. Everyone has the amber, which I assume belongs to . . . Éva, along with a thread that seems to be unique to them. Except . . ." I glance away, suddenly uncomfortable, then peer back at Colin. "Except the Unbound. Their auras have only one color, and no thread."

His face has lost all expression, which tells me I just thoroughly rattled his cage. As pleasing as it feels to still be able to surprise him, I wish now I'd kept my mouth shut about colors. It would've been nice to have at least one thing he didn't know about.

"This . . . this is quite interesting. Normally, the only Chosen who can see véren are Makers, and Elders with sublineages."

Oh.

Great. Another mystery to add to my weird collection.

"So tell me, Sunny. What color is mine?"

Though his tone is neutral, something tells me this is important to him. The question hangs in the air a moment before I answer.

"It's primarily midnight blue. It pulses lighter and darker, but always shifts back to midnight blue. There's no other color with it."

A ghost of an emotion, possibly sorrow, flickers across his face and disappears.

"And yours?" he asks.

I shake my head.

"I can't see it. Not even in a mirror."

Colin nods, and I can almost hear the gears grinding in his head, reminding me of Nicolas and his reaction each time he attempted to fit another piece into the puzzle of my existence.

After a long silence, he settles back in his chair, his arms folded across his chest.

"Alina said it's strange, very pale, not like any she's seen before."

"She can see it?"

He nods again, his blue eyes bright with rekindled curiosity.

"What color is it?"

"A better question would be 'what colors.'"

"Colors? As in more than one?"

"Yes. More than one."

"But all the Unbound I've met only bore a single color. I don't understand." I stare at the far wall, thinking of the two shadowy figures who Made me. "Well? What colors are they? Do they reveal anything about my Makers?"

"That, they do not. As for what the colors are?" He shakes his head. "Your véren seems to carry all of them."

"All of them?"

"All of them. As in all the colors of every lineage across the world."

# MONDAY

## CHAPTER 68

I stare into the small wooden jewelry box I'd picked up during my first couple weeks in San Francisco. It doesn't hold much—just a few baubles I'd stumbled across in the odd boutiques scattered about the city. My clove oil necklace is coiled in one corner, its Celtic design traced in silver filigree.

In the other corner sits Taz's ring.

I'd taken it off after Alina's comment about it. Once I started working with Colin—and it seemed like humans were out of the equation, at least temporarily—I no longer really needed it.

But what I really didn't need was anything that reminded me of Taz.

I grab the necklace and shut the box.

Colin wants to take me shopping tonight. He said I need to practice my newfound meditation skills in different settings and that a crowded shopping mall would provide a wide variety of stressful inputs.

I suspect he just wants to see if I have an urge to eat people.

With a last-minute check of my makeup and hair, I shut off the bathroom light and finish dressing for my shopping date with Colin.

~

The one thing I'm not prepared for is my reaction when we walk into our first department store, a Penney's. It's not the people, or the bright lights, or the noise that triggers it.

It's the Christmas decorations.

The air in my chest suddenly rushes out, as though I'm being crushed by a boa constrictor. Ringing in my ears drowns out the holiday music drifting down from hidden speakers, and the urge to take flight is so overwhelming I nearly knock Colin over as I spin around to head back out the door.

He grabs me by the shoulders, frowning.

"Breathe. Center yourself."

"I can't . . . "

"Yes, you can. Cover your nose and mouth and take a breath."

"It's not—"

I can't even finish my sentence. Can't even tell him it's not the people or their blood scent that set me off.

It's the memories.

Memories of Christmases past, when my daughter was little and we had no money and made all of our decorations, and her bright smile when she gave me the sweet gifts she'd crafted in school. And later, when she saw her first bicycle parked next to our tiny tree, a bicycle I'd spent months saving for. Her proud expression when I untied the ribbon on the present she'd carefully wrapped and then held up the sweater she'd bought me with money she'd earned from babysitting.

All my weeks of training evaporate as the pressure builds within my eyes and the hated bloodtears threaten to spill down my cheeks.

Without another word, Colin turns and escorts me back outside to the car.

He offers me a handkerchief, his tacit permission to give in to the emotions nearly exploding from my skin.

I turn away and shake my head, and focus on that cold, still spot deep in my gut. Stuffing the images in my head back into the box from which they'd escaped, I visualize slamming its lid, wrapping steel chains around it, and clicking a padlock in place.

No more.

No more will I be ruled by that life, a life I cannot have. It's over and done with, and there's nothing I can do about it but bury it away in the darkest depths of my soul.

A quiet calm settles over me as I mentally restore order to my body. Tension fades first from my muscles, and then veins. My blood begins to circulate at its normal, sedate pace and air once again fills my lungs. Finally, the tear glands relax, allowing their cargo to flow back into my system.

Taking a deep breath, I look over at Colin.

"Let's do this."

# THURSDAY

## CHAPTER 69

Colin's kept me busy the last several nights. Each evening's been spent among crowds of people—shopping malls, movie theaters, and even a restaurant, which was absolutely disgusting. He said taking such trips on a regular basis are not only critical practice for maintaining control over the bloodlust, but necessary for learning how to better blend with the human population.

After my initial shock that first night, I've had little problem moving among people. The meditation training is beginning to pay off, and the clove oil necklace, though I haven't needed to use it, has been a reassuring backup.

Of course, my late afternoon hunts before Colin arrives haven't hurt, either.

Our nights on the town have been followed by workouts and sparring in the barn. Colin believes the body needs to be rewarded for behaving itself in stressful situations, and instilling the promise of an eventual release reinforces its cooperation with the mind. However one wants to look at it, it certainly does feel good to blow off a little steam after a night spent walking on a tightrope.

European geography lessons have wrapped up the last few hours before dawn. Colin's apparently spent a lot of time in Europe, though he avoids telling me doing what, other than to claim he ran an import-export business. I suspect it was more than that, but have been unable to pin him down.

Tonight, though, we're taking a break from our current routine.

Colin is bringing someone over to start teaching me French.

The idea I might need it terrifies me, but he says knowing your enemy is the most important step to survival. And that includes understanding what they're talking about, especially if you don't let on that you do.

One thing I can say about Colin. He's one of the most intelligent and observant beings I've ever encountered, and I can't help but wonder who his teacher was. However, as I've learned, inquiring about a Chosen's origins is highly personal and can be considered a grievous insult. I haven't found the nerve yet to ask him about his past.

When a Chosen freely offers such information, as Alina did, it should be taken as a sign of trust and respect—though I think it was done to gain mine as well as demonstrate hers. Nonetheless, that she chose to tell me her story is something I still marvel at.

Guess I'll have to wait to see if Colin chooses to tell me his. In the five weeks we've been working together, he's revealed little about himself, other than his extensive skills and knowledge on a wide variety of topics. I don't even know where he lives. He truly is a puzzle.

The doorbell rings, announcing their arrival. I brush back my hair and open the door.

I don't know what shocks me more.

That the beautiful brunette standing with Colin is human, or that her arm is tightly clasped about his, or that their body language screams out that they are a couple.

"Sunny, I'd like to introduce you to my wife, Jeanette."

Oh. *That* definitely shocks me the most.

"Hello." I bow my head and offer my hand. She tentatively smiles and takes it.

"It is nice to meet you, Sunny," she says in a strong French accent. "Colin speaks much of you."

"I can only imagine." I return her smile and step back, opening the door wider. "Please, come in."

Colin ushers Jeanette in, offering a nod as he passes me. The bright gleam in his eyes tells me he's enjoying my reaction.

"We can sit in the living room if you like." Gesturing across the entryway, I close the door and try to remember basic human etiquette.

"Jeanette, can I, uh, get you some tea, or maybe a glass of water? I'm afraid that's all I have."

"Water is good," she says with a nervous giggle.

Still reeling from Colin's little surprise, I head into the kitchen.

The analyst he's been training in me swings into full gear. I realize Colin's just offered me a greater sign of trust than a simple reveal of his origins.

He introduced me to his *wife*. A *human* wife.

And by his doting and protective expression, one he's deeply in love with.

He'd said that Chosen rarely engage in romantic liaisons with humans. That humans are too fragile both physically and psychologically to last long in a relationship with a Chosen. And the relationship almost never survives the transition to Chosen should the human partner wish it.

Our nights among the crowds of people take on a new meaning. He needed to make sure I was sufficiently stable to be around Jeanette.

I'm humbled that he trusts me enough to risk the safety of someone so precious to him.

Determined not to give him the slightest cause for doubt, I do a quick internal system check and center myself, then calmly walk back to the living room with Jeanette's water in hand.

~

"Sunny, are you happy about your new job in Colin's company? He says you do well in your training." Jeanette, sitting on the couch beside Colin, takes a sip of her water.

"Yes." I glance at Colin. I have no idea what she's talking about. "Yes, I am."

He only smiles, offering no help whatsoever.

Don't tell me this is another one of his tests.

"Have you traveled much to Europe?" she asks.

"No. I haven't ever been there."

"Oh, you will love it. Especially Paris. That is where I met my Colin." She smiles at him and pats his hand. "I should give you my sister's—"

"Jeanette, Sunny will only be in Paris a day or two, and will be too busy to do any visiting."

"Don't be silly, Colin. I am sure—"

"Actually, he's right, Jeanette." Following Colin's lead, I enhance the excuse. "I'm only spending one evening in Paris and my schedule's pretty filled with meetings. But I might have time in the future."

She nods. Not wanting to discuss a trip about which I know almost nothing, I change topics. The best defense in any game, or so I've been learning lately, is offense.

"You mentioned meeting Colin in Paris. How long have you known each other?" I glance at Colin. The sharp warning in his blue-eyed gaze bears the hint of approval as well.

"When did I come to work for you?" she asks Colin. "It was after Easter, *oui*?" Without waiting for his answer, she turns back to me. "About one-and-a-half years."

I smile.

"You must not have been married very long, then."

"No. It will be three months next week." She beams at Colin and squeezes his hand.

He coughs and leans forward.

"We should get started on Sunny's lessons, Jeanette. Perhaps we should move to the dining room table?" He looks at me, his eyebrows raised.

"Of course."

"May I use the *toilette* first?" Jeanette asks as we all stand.

It takes me a second to realize she means bathroom.

"Uh, yes. It's down the hall, first door on the left."

When the door closes, Colin gives me a tight-lipped smile.

"Nice redirect."

I assume he means my topic change.

"Thanks."

"But no more personal questions."

Nodding, I walk past him. He stops me with a hand on my arm.

"And Sunny. No one is to know about her."

I glance up. I've never seen a more dangerous expression on him, and a little flutter of fear tickles my scalp.

"No problem. You can trust me."

"I'm counting on it." Red flashes within his pupils.

He's the last Chosen I'd want as an enemy.

"I understand the chance you've taken bringing her here. Your secret's safe with me."

"I wouldn't have done so if I thought otherwise." He releases my arm as Jeanette opens the door, and turns to wait for her. I head into the dining room.

~

It's nearly eleven o'clock when we agree to quit for the evening. Jeanette has turned out to be a very patient teacher and I'm grateful Colin has decided to include her in my education.

She's also vivacious, filled with warm life and good humor. We'd laughed over and over at my pathetic attempts to mimic her pronunciations. I can't remember the last time I shared genuine laughter with someone.

I couldn't help but notice Colin's scrutiny as we worked together. I suspect he was monitoring my reactions to her and would've intervened if I'd shown any undue interest in her—or the blood pulsing through her body.

What I found interesting is that even though I was aware of her blood scent, Colin's was so thickly woven within it that it almost felt like a barrier. Perhaps that's how Chosen mark their donors—a clear biochemical signal stating "fangs off" to other Chosen. Whether it's for the donor's protection or a territorial thing, it seems to work. I had no real desire for her blood, which was a great relief to me, and I'm sure to Colin as well.

When I walk them to the door, Jeanette turns to me.

"I am very happy to know you. You will be good to run his European offices." She reaches out and takes both of my hands.

"Uh, thank you. It was nice meeting you, too."

"I had fun. We will have more lessons, oui? I teach you French and you teach me better English." She leans forward and lightly kisses me on each cheek.

Okay. That's a little too close.

I swallow as my gums twitch. I step back, but hopefully not so quick as to offend her.

"I look forward to it," I manage to stammer out.

Colin misses none of it. He moves in and takes her gently by the shoulders.

"Come, my darling. It's late. Let's get you home." He guides her outside. "I'll meet you in the car."

She nods and heads toward the Aston Martin.

I turn to Colin.

"I'm sorry—"

"Not to worry. Some reactions are instinctive. The important thing is not to act upon the impulse behind them." He smiles. "You did well."

"Thanks."

"We do need to discuss our schedule. I'm afraid that since I'll be bringing Jeanette over in the early evenings for your French lessons and she needs to go to bed at a reasonable hour, I won't be available for sparring practice. It's time you start working out with different partners anyway. I've been in contact with the local fight promoter, and he has several excellent female fighters who should be a good match for you."

Female fighters.

That'll be an interesting change. My skin ripples in anticipation of the fresh competition.

"He's sending one of them over tomorrow night around eight. I have an appointment in the city, but I'll stop by on my way in and make the necessary introductions."

"Do you know who he's sending?"

"No, not personally. But I know of them both and have seen them fight. They each have excellent form and technique, yet fight in a completely different style from one another. This will be good for you."

"All right. Then I guess I'll see you tomorrow night."

Colin nods and turns toward his car.

"And Colin—"

He pauses.

"You have a lovely wife. You're very lucky."

Nodding, he continues on to the car.

"I know."

I head back into the house, which suddenly seems very empty.

# FRIDAY

## CHAPTER 70

Colin and I are waiting in the barn when I hear the roar of an approaching motorcycle.

Electricity shoots through my veins at the sound.

But as I listen to it, I realize it's not an engine I recognize. This one sounds different, beats in a lower, deeper rhythm than either Taz's or Redd's bike.

I sigh in relief. And, to my chagrin, disappointment.

The rumbling sound shuts off outside the barn door.

When the door opens, the dark shape filling its frame is definitely not female. It is, however, a shape with which I'm intimately familiar. Too familiar.

Shit.

It's Taz.

"Heard you were lookin' for a fight trainer."

My jaw clenches at the sound of his voice.

I just can't seem to get away from him.

Colin steps forward.

"I thought Jeffers was sending Delilah or Carmen."

"They couldn't make it." Taz glances at me, his customary smirk hiding within those damn eagle eyes.

Colin stands his ground.

"This isn't going to work. She's not ready for someone of your size."

"I can make her ready," Taz slowly responds as he looks sidelong at me, the corner of his lip twitching.

Colin snarls at the innuendo. Taz looks down at him, red flashing in his pupils.

Oh crap.

I step between them and face Colin.

"I got this, Colin."

"Do you have any idea who—"

"Actually, I do. We . . . we've spent some time together. Unfortunately. But I can handle him."

Taz snorts.

Colin frowns, looks past me at Taz, then back at me. He places his hands on my shoulders.

"You're sure about this?"

I nod.

Colin takes a deep breath, his blue gaze searching mine.

"Just remember why you're here."

"I know. Trust me—I won't forget."

He looks back up at Taz. His expression darkens and his whole body radiates danger.

"If you hurt her," he says, his eyes flashing red. "I *will* kill you."

Taz's only answer is a rumbling growl.

Colin releases me and heads outside without another word.

As the barn door closes, I turn around to glare at Taz.

"What are you doing here?"

He folds his arms and returns my glare.

"I suppose that's who you've been lookin' for?"

"Who, Colin? No. He's just a friend. And it's not your business anyhow."

"He made it my business when he threatened to kill me."

"What do you want from me?"

"Thought I was pretty clear about that."

"Thought I was pretty clear every time I've said no."

"I don't know what you're talking about. I'm here to teach fight training." He leers at me. "You got something else in mind?"

Asshole.

Taz stares at me, the smirk briefly slipping away to reveal something else, something I'd rather not see. I glance away.

This is not going to work. I need to figure a way out of this.

"Blonde doesn't suit you. I like your real hair better."

"Is that what you call a compliment? You need to work on that."

"You're not wearing the ring."

I glance at my hand.

"I don't need it anymore."

He laughs.

"Look, Taz. I appreciate you coming out here, but your techniques just won't work for me. I don't have the body mass or reach you do. I really need to work with someone closer to my own size."

"Hit me."

"I mean it. And I was really looking forward to training with another female."

"Is that it? You prefer women?"

"No," I sputter. "That's not what I meant."

"Hit me."

"I'm not going to hit you."

Taz steps closer.

"Hit me." His tone takes on a threatening edge.

I shake my head no and start to turn away.

He reaches out toward me as though he's going to touch my breast.

I whirl and kick him in the gut.

There's no give at all. I might as well have kicked a steel beam.

"Again. Hit me."

I deliver several sharp jabs to his ribcage. He doesn't even grunt.

"You're right." Taz takes off his leather jacket and tosses it onto the incline bench. His black tank top only emphasizes our physical differences. "You can't fight like me."

He tenses, then lunges at me. I spin out of the way and leap across the barn.

"So you have to make me fight like you," he says. His body lowers into a crouch and he launches in my direction.

I dart to the side, easily avoiding him, and sprint for the other end.

Taz knocks me flat on my face before I take the third step.

I flip onto my back, claws and fangs ready. But all he does is offer me a hand up.

"What just happened?" he asks as he pulls me to my feet.

"What do you mean? You knocked me down. Isn't that obvious?" Disgusted, I brush the straw from my clothes.

"Before that."

"You leapt at me and I got out of the way."

"And how did you know which way to run?"

I think back.

"Because you came at me from the left."

"Which made you do what?"

"Move . . . to . . . the . . . right."

Taz smiles.

"So even though you *think* you got away several times, who was really in control?"

Apparently not me.

"What else did you see?" He studies me, his eyes flashing gold beneath the barn lights.

"What do you mean, what else?"

Impatience darkens his expression. He glances to my right, then lunges straight at me. When I spin away to the left, his fist is suddenly there, missing my cheek by a fraction of an inch.

"Why'd you move that direction?" he snaps at me.

"Because you looked toward the other."

He shakes his head.

"You always tell your kill which way you're movin'?"

My kill?

"I'm not out to kill anyone. I just want to save my own neck."

Taz looms over me, fangs bared. I step back.

"That's exactly what'll *get* you killed. Especially you." He jabs his finger at me. "*Every fight* is to the death—don't let anyone tell you otherwise."

Especially me? Great.

"What're you good at?" He crosses his arms.

"What am I good at? I don't know. Bartending. Staying alive. That's about it." Well, not quite alive. It's all rather sad, when I boil it down like that.

Taz rolls his eyes.

"Still pretty. Still dumb."

"Screw you." I wince as soon as the words leave my mouth.

"Like I've said, anytime." His slow, taunting smile just infuriates me more. "So how do you stay alive?"

"I feed on blood, like every other Chosen."

He raises his eyebrows.

"Okay," I admit. "So not like other Chosen."

"I'd guess if you've survived this long on nothin' but deer and bear, you know how to hunt."

I nod. That is something I know how to do, and do pretty well.

"You just need to train for a new quarry. Learn their body language, and how to move them wherever you want. Once you view every Chosen as nothing more than your next kill, you'll stay alive a whole lot longer."

That's a pretty vicious outlook on life.

"I'm sorry, but I don't hate the world. I'm not like you." I shake my head.

Taz's chest is pressing me against the wall before I can blink.

He breathes into my ear.

"You're exactly like me. I can sense the violence in your blood. You *love* to kill."

"Get off of me." I shove him back and he surprisingly gives ground.

Chuckling, he saunters over to the punching bags.

"Come over here. Let's see what else you got."

Fuming, I clench my fists and look toward the door.

"Running away won't help. It'll just delay the inevitable. Now get your ass over here if you want to learn how to fight someone like me."

Bastard.

With a deep sigh, I do as he says. Again.

~

It's about two a.m. when we quit for the evening. Except for his occasional rude comments, Taz behaved remarkably well. He kept his hands to himself, only touching my arms and legs to guide them in various trajectories when delivering punches and kicks.

Unfortunately, when he did so, it also meant that his body was close to mine. As the evening wore on, I found myself hoping he'd accidentally brush against me. The punching bag took an extra beating each time that happened, until the leather case finally split open beneath my last flurry of blows, ending that part of our training.

It was worse when he was demonstrating a new technique. His absolute concentration only enhanced the raw animal beauty of his movements, and at times like those, I'd find myself so mesmerized that I'd fail to hear either his explanations or his questions.

And unfortunately, he'd caught me several times, accusing me of daydreaming.

His secretive smirks told me that he knew exactly what I was daydreaming about.

Relieved that our session is finally over, I follow Taz across the barn.

"What time tomorrow?" he asks.

"I don't know. I need to check with Colin."

"Well, after you talk with your little boyfriend, you let me know."

"He's *not* my—" I glare up at him. "Oh, go to hell."

"I tell you what. You want me to come back, you call me."

Taz holds his left forearm out, the underside exposed. He jams his nails into a vein.

What the—?

Appalled, I watch as his dripping fingers paint the first part of his phone number onto the vinyl-covered incline bench. He punctures his arm a second time to finish it, then wipes his hand onto his jeans and picks up his jacket.

"That's twice I've given you my blood." Those eagle eyes fix me with their piercing stare. And then he stalks out the door.

Unable to stop myself, I follow him outside. I now see why I didn't recognize the sound of his motorcycle

He's riding the red devil bike, the one I saw in his shop.

The fanged skeleton frame takes on a new meaning in view of everything I've heard and learned about him lately.

The Executioner. Deliverer of the Final Death. Killer of Chosen.

The open-mouthed skull clenching the headlight between its fangs disappears behind the bright beam as Taz starts the engine. Its deep, throaty roar, like that of some beast from Hell, shatters the quiet country night.

It heads down the driveway and fades into the dark, leaving me as conflicted as ever about its ruthless rider.

# CHAPTER 71

I'm finishing another set of pull-ups when I hear the Aston Martin outside the barn. Colin had said he'd stop by around three a.m. on his way back from the city. That's the main reason I'm taking my frustrations out on the workout equipment instead of the deer I'd rather be hunting.

Colin's nose wrinkles as he steps inside. He glances around the barn, lingers over the punching bag with its guts spilling onto the floor, then settles his gaze on the bloody phone number painted on the incline bench.

"What a barbarian." He looks up at me. "Everything go okay?"

"Yeah."

"I can see that."

"He just irritates me."

"Is that all it is?"

Instant fury tenses my body at his implied accusation.

"Yeah. That's all it is. I just thought I was rid of him."

"You mentioned you'd spent time together."

"It's more like he held me prisoner."

"I'm surprised you agreed to train with him, then."

"We still had some unfinished business. And, it turns out, he knows what he's doing when it comes to fighting."

"Of that, I had no doubt. But nonetheless, I contacted Jeffers, the fight promoter, and requested he send someone else next Monday night."

I nod and glance at the incline bench.

Colin follows my look.

"Sunny. There's something you need to know about him."

"I don't need to know anything more about him. I'm done with him. We still on schedule for tomorrow night?"

Colin nods.

"Jeanette and I will be over around eight o'clock. I promised her a night on the coast, so that will give us a little more time for your lesson."

"All right. Well, if we have nothing more to talk about, I need to go hunt." I turn toward the barn door.

"Sunny. Be patient. You're almost ready."

I pause.

"Colin, all I can say is . . . the sooner, the better."

What I don't say is that the sooner I can put miles between me and that damned Indian, the better for all of us.

# SATURDAY

## CHAPTER 72

Learning a new language easily doesn't seem to be one of my talents. Understanding it isn't a problem. Speaking it, trying to roll my R's and twist my tongue around the foreign words, is another matter entirely.

Fortunately, Jeanette is endowed with an extra dose of patience, which makes me dig deeper for mine.

But by the time we're done for the evening, I'm all tapped out. I wave goodbye to Colin and Jeanette as they pull away from the house and gratefully shut the door.

I've just finished changing into my hunting blacks when I catch the distant sound of a motorcycle. It's growing louder and louder, until it's right outside the door.

You've got to be kidding me.

I'm tempted to slip out the back and avoid him altogether.

But I don't.

Instead, I head out the front to take the proverbial bull by the horns. I just hope he doesn't gore me in the process.

I wait with my arms folded while Taz shuts down the bike and climbs off. The fanged skull grins at me as the headlight winks out.

"Thought you were going to wait until I called."

"I don't wait for no one."

He stalks past me and into the barn, his braid snapping like a whip against his leather-covered back.

Walking over to the small pasture next to the barn, I stare out at the oak-covered hills in the near distance. But I have a feeling it wouldn't take him long to track me down, and that he'd be in quite a mood by the time he found me.

The sound of bumping and clanging metal from inside the barn ends my fanciful musings, and too curious for my own good, I head in to see what Taz is up to.

He's rearranged most of the exercise equipment, scattering it around the sparring area of the barn. He drags the cable machine out a little farther into the middle, then, with his hands on his hips, looks around, apparently satisfied with his redecorating job.

"What are you doing?"

"Building a new playground."

"Jeffers wasn't supposed to send anyone until Monday."

"I don't give a rat's ass what Jeffers does. I don't answer to him."

"Do you answer to anyone?"

An arrogant glare is his only response.

He walks over to his leather jacket hanging from a nail in the barn wall and reaches into a pocket. When he returns to where I'm standing, Taz holds out his hand.

In his palm is a slender dagger sheathed within a black leather case. The blade looks to be about six inches long, with another four for the handle. It's bigger than Chia's dagger, nearly the same size as Redd's, but more refined.

The handle appears to be made from polished antler, and has a silver cap on the end. The cap bears the same mountain lion paw print as the ring Taz made me.

"You ever use a knife?"

"No. Never really needed to." I hold my hand up, flexing my fingers with their sharp nails.

"Well, you can't throw your fingers."

He has a point.

His hand blurs and a *thunk* from across the barn tells me where the dagger landed.

"That won't slow down a Chosen."

Taz snorts as he walks over and pulls the blade from the wall.

"It will if you plant it in an eye."

Gross.

He hands me the knife hilt first.

"Grip it by the blade. Like this." He fits the steel between my thumb and forefinger. "Hold it, but not too tight. Now bring your arm back, snap it forward, and release the blade."

It hits the wall handle first and falls to the barn floor.

"Try it again."

And I do. Over and over. But soon, the blade is sticking into the wood more often than not.

Feeling a bit proud of myself, I look over where Taz is leaning against a cable machine, his arms folded.

His expression makes me wish I hadn't. The animal need on his face sends a jolt through me and I quickly look away.

"Enough with the blade," he says, his voice thick. His boots whisper through the straw as he approaches. "Let's see what you learned last night."

I turn toward him just as his fist shoots out, straight for my face. I duck beneath it, then dart to the left, toward the equipment rather than the open area. He swings around the other side, then hops onto the incline bench and leaps over the leg press. I dash through the narrow opening between two machines, barely ahead of his grasp.

Our cat-and-mouse game proceeds with me just one step ahead of him at every turn. His expression grows more feral with each near-miss. I fight the growing excitement in my veins and focus on eluding him.

Deciding to shift the game, I ignore an obvious escape, and instead twist to one side and deliver a glancing kick to his ribcage.

His elbow snaps back, just missing my face. I drop to the ground, intending to sweep his legs out from beneath him as I would an elk.

But he's not there, and I'm suddenly on the run again as he lands behind me. I manage to slip through several tight gaps between the equipment, gaps too small for him to follow.

Taz stops, peering at me through the bars and cables.

"Whose game we playin', Sonya? Yours or mine?"

"At the moment? Mine, I believe."

"Good. Cuz you know if I get you into the open, it'll be my game, right?"

I nod.

"You only have three weapons. Speed, agility, and, most important, your mind. Read your prey. Use their strengths and the environment against them. The rest is simple." His lip curls into a half smile. "Just pretend they're a bear."

His analogy makes sense. I'm not strong enough to defeat him or any other Chosen. Nor am I strong enough to kill a bear. Yet I have a bear-claw necklace that proves otherwise.

The tautness fades from Taz's body and he walks across the open area toward the dagger.

Disgusted with my mixed feelings over the end of our chase game, yet grateful for a break, I follow him. Knife throwing does seem a little safer at the moment. Anything is, as long as it maintains some distance between us.

A blur is all I see before my back hits the ground, hard. When I open my eyes, Taz is on his hands and knees over me, red flashing in his eyes.

A low, sensual growl slips from his chest.

My breath stops.

His nostrils flare and he slowly lowers his face toward mine.

And then he is on his feet, his eyes narrowing above a thin-lipped smile.

"Never fall for that trap. A fight isn't over until your enemy is dead."

Unnerved, I can only glare up at him.

Stupid me. He'd just lured me into the open with the same fake-out tactic I'd seen him use in the arena, not once but twice.

"Don't just read my body. Read my *mind.*" He jabs a forefinger at his temple.

I scramble to my feet, nodding and brushing the straw from my butt.

He stares at me, his gaze predatory.

"So what's it saying?" His voice is low, rough. "My mind. What's it saying?"

Something in his expression shifts.

"*Tell me*. What's it *saying*?" Raw hunger slowly creeps across his face. Tension ripples up his arms and across his chest, like a snake coiling just before it strikes.

His entire being is screaming only one thing.

*I . . . want . . . you.*

My throat tightens.

"*What's it saying?!*" Taz steps closer, a savage light flaring in his golden eyes.

Unable to answer, I slowly shake my head no and step back.

He follows, and just inches away now, he takes hold of my shoulders.

I can't move. My body's trapped by an internal battle between wanting to run and wanting to stay.

One hand slides up from my shoulder and grabs my hair.

Those eagle eyes bore into me as he slowly presses me against the wall.

"*What's your answer?*" he breathes.

I want to resist, but my body craves this. *Needs* this. Like the deer frozen by the gaze of the hunter, all I can do is helplessly wait.

His lips touch mine, gently at first, then with a crushing intensity that echoes through his whole body.

My mind shouts its protest as my mouth hungrily seeks his. Growling in response, he tightens the grip on my hair as he releases my shoulder. His hand drifts downward, touching, squeezing, and fear ripples across my skin at what I'm allowing to happen. I tense, trying to summon the will to struggle against both my body and his.

Taz growls again. His fangs graze my lips, and then he bites down, piercing my tongue. Blood fills our mouths—not just my blood, but his as well.

The desire within it consumes me.

Ghostly images flit through my mind—

—an endless blue-grey ocean beside a cool sandy beach

—the morning sun rising over a forest-covered mountain

—carvings on a mesa, viewed from high in the sky

He moans, pressing his body harder against mine, and instead of the wall behind my back, I feel soft fur beneath me, beneath us, as we make love beneath a sunlit sky.

My soul screams for more as I clutch him against me.

But my mind screams louder.

*No!*

This can't happen. I'm supposed to be with Nicolas.

This . . . this is *true* betrayal. I cannot do this.

Outrage—at myself, at Taz, at the whole screwed-up situation—explodes within me.

A deep roar bursts from my blood-filled throat as I rip my mouth away from his. Sinking claws into Taz's chest, I try to shove him away.

Violence explodes in the blood working its way through my system. I slash at his face and he grabs my hands and pins them against the wall.

"*Who is it?*" he snarls. "Who is it that you're choosing over *me*?"

I clamp my jaw shut.

"You owe me that much. Tell me his name. Tell me who he is!"

All my instincts, all my past teachers, scream out *No!*

But Taz is right. After all he's shared with me, I do owe him that much. Because if it wasn't for Nicolas . . .

"*Nicolas*," I whisper.

"Who?" Shock and disbelief slice across his features. "What did you say?"

"Nicolas."

He abruptly releases me and steps back, wiping his mouth. Fury now twists his face.

"As in . . . ?"

I nod.

"Who *are* you?"

"My name is Sunny. Sunny Martin."

With a heart-wrenching roar, he slams his fist into the barn wall. The wood explodes outward, and he slams the wall again and again. It disintegrates beneath his savage attack.

I back away. It's only a matter of seconds before he turns that rage on me.

I'm on the floor before I take another step. His heavy body pins me down as he snarls in my face.

"If I'd known you were *his*, I'd have destroyed you the instant you showed up. Take from him what he took from me."

His fist pounds the dirt beside my head, once, twice. Anguish flits across his face and he turns his sorrow-filled gaze back to me. Loss and loneliness echo through his blood, along with crushing regret. His expression softens.

He brushes the hair back from my face, then slowly lowers his mouth to mine. Before I can force myself to turn away, our lips touch, soft as a butterfly's kiss.

"I would've shared everything with you," he whispers. A fresh drop of blood hits my tongue, and then his weight is gone from me.

Bloodtears course down my temples as the roar of his motorcycle fades into the distance.

# CHAPTER 73

The chaparral tears at my bloody clothes as I race through the brush toward the reservoir.

Taz was right about one thing.

I do love to kill.

Especially at times like this, when my emotions turn me into a monster every bit as violent as him.

I did not lose the beast when I completed the Change.

I *became* the beast.

And my fight training has made me an even more efficient killer than I was before.

It's a good thing I don't feed on people.

A fresh scent drifts up from the ravine below me. Even though I've had more than my fill, the smell draws me like a magnet. I slow and shift into stalking mode.

Red ecstasy vaporizes all my thoughts as yet another unfortunate creature dies beneath my fangs.

When I regain my awareness, I'm so bloated I can barely move. The eastern sky is grey and the sun's tugging at me as I crawl up into the arms of a big oak tree. My thoughts still numb, I gratefully settle onto a well-hidden branch just as the red blood haze fades into dawn's darkness.

~

*A cool breeze tickles my cheek. When I open my eyes, Spirit-Taz's ghostly form hovers in the branches beside mine. Golden light from his eyes pierces the shadows drifting across his face, like that of the sunlight dancing through the surrounding leaves.*

*He's so transparent I can barely make him out. Sadness shrouds his spectral body and the pang of loss taints the air around us. He reaches out as though to take my hand, but instead of his ethereal touch, all I feel is the whisper of an ice-cold flame passing through my skin.*

*A crystal tear traces its way down his cheek. His lips form words, words I can no longer hear, and with a final sigh, he slowly disappears.*

# TUESDAY

## CHAPTER 74

The four-point buck within my arms kicks one last time as I dig my fangs in a little deeper. I want to drown myself in his blood, in any blood I can find. My veins hum with joy, yet the craving is still strong.

But it's not a craving for deer blood, or bear, or even human.

It's for *him*.

I can't forget the feeling of Taz wrapped around my body, the need in his blood interwoven with my own.

It's been three nights since I tasted it, since he tasted mine. I no longer feel him or his boiling emotions, but my mind still remembers. And no matter how much deer blood I drink, no matter how many deer I rip apart, I cannot erase his presence. Or my own longing for it.

A snarl behind me brings me back to the here and now. Growling, I release the carcass and stand up.

"Just wait your goddamn turn." I wipe my mouth and glare at the pack of coyotes skulking in the brush around me. One, a little braver than the rest, slinks forward and attempts to intimidate me with his bared teeth.

Before he even registers my movement, I have him in the air by the scruff of the neck, a hand clamped tightly around his muzzle. His muted whines as he twists in my grasp send the rest scurrying.

"I said, wait your turn." I toss him into the brush, not too hard, and tucking his tail, he vanishes into the woods.

Walking down to the lake to wash up, I smile at the snapping and yelping behind me as the pack moves in on my kill.

It's pretty handy having my own personal clean-up crew. I'd been training them over the past month or so, but the last three nights I haven't even needed to call them. They always seem to find me, and each afternoon when I wake in whatever tree I've chosen to sleep in, they're nearby, waiting for the hunt.

But they're going to be on their own tomorrow. I've been gone long enough, and I'm sure Colin is fit to be tied over my disappearance.

By my reckoning, it must be Tuesday. Dawn's not too far off, but I should have enough time to get home and take a proper shower before the sun comes up.

~

The yellow note taped to my front door contains only two words in Colin's neat script.

*Call me.*

I rip it down. He can wait one more night. I'm really not in the mood to answer his questions.

The dark bulk looming next to the house is something I can't ignore, though, as much as I want to. I look over at the barn, at its accusing visage, and find myself walking toward it.

From the doorway, the evidence is still there, as though lit with neon lights.

The dagger buried in the post.

The space on the wall where his body and his mouth pressed against mine, and mine pressed back against his.

The ruptured wood next to it, the victim of his rage and frustration.

And on the floor, there, where his heart broke. And mine.

# WEDNESDAY

## CHAPTER 75

I'm at the dining room table working my way through a book on Eastern Europe when the Aston Martin parks outside.

Taking a breath, I prepare myself. This is not going to be good. The only thing Colin had said when I called him shortly after sunset was, "Wait. There."

Colin walks in without bothering to knock. He comes into the dining room and sets a manila envelope onto the table, then pulls out a chair and sits across from me.

I lean back and fold my arms.

The ice-cold expression on Colin's face matches the tone I'd heard in his voice earlier.

"No phone call. No note. Nothing. You just disappeared for three nights without a word."

Any explanation I offer will only make things worse, so I opt for silence.

"I know he was here. There were fresh tire tracks at the barn. His scent wasn't a day old when we came by Sunday night."

Shit.

Nothing I say will fix this. All I can do is stare at him and wait for his verdict.

"What you do and who you do it with is your business. Except for one thing—you asked for help to find Nicolas. And now I'm wondering why. I know how he felt about you. I thought I understood how you felt about him."

I thought I did, too.

"I've invested nearly six weeks in you. Six weeks of missing nights home with my wife. Six weeks condensing decades of knowledge into enough concise elements to hopefully keep you from getting killed the moment you leave here. Six weeks of pinning all of our hopes onto the one Chosen who might be able to bring Nicolas home."

"Why?" I lean forward. "Why is it so important to you that Nicolas comes back? You're not even of his lineage."

Colin slowly rises, the red in his pupils only underscoring his anger.

"Nicolas is my Maker. When he needed me to step outside the lineage, I did so without question. Wherever he sent me, I went willingly. Whatever he asked me to do, I did it gladly. He is my lord, my commander, and my king. I would *die* for him."

In the face of such fierce loyalty, all I feel is soul-blackening shame.

"You *will* finish this. Or so help me God, I'll kill you myself."

Cold night air rushes in as the door opens and slams.

~

I finish washing the bloodtears from my face and look up into the mirror. Into the dark, hollow guilt shining from my eyes.

Guilt that I'm sure Colin didn't miss. Even though he didn't say so in plain terms, he pretty much accused me of betraying Nicolas with Taz. He was quite clear on how he felt about it, though.

I'd been so unprepared for the harshness of his judgment that any reassurance about my commitment to finding Nicolas would've sounded weak and pathetic.

And right now, I'm not sure how convincing it would've been.

Because I'm no longer sure about my feelings for him. Too much time has passed, too much has happened. I've changed, in more ways than the one. And I'm sure he's changed as well. There's no telling how having his lineage stripped away has affected him, and the Nicolas I find may not be the Nicolas I lost.

Not to mention the obstacles in my search that continue to haunt me, the biggest of which is a golden-eyed Indian who has somehow gotten so far under my skin that I cannot seem to shake him loose.

His words haunt me as well.

*Take from him what he took from me.*

What did he mean by that? What did Nicolas do to him?

I walk into my bedroom and stare at the pillow on my bed.

Beneath it is a small rectangular box wrapped in brown paper and twine. I found it there when I returned home and had no time to examine it before the sun shut my eyes.

I take it out from where it rests, from where a long-fingered hand had placed it one night while I was off rampaging in the hills.

It's still wrapped in its plain brown paper. *Sonya* is written on it in a barely legible scrawl, a scrawl I've seen before in a worn copy of an old travel book on Europe, its yellowed, dog-eared pages bearing tiny notes in the margins and a bitter poem about the city of Paris.

It's amazing how such a small package can be so frightening. Whatever's inside is only going to cause me pain, yet I can wait no longer to open it. With a deep breath, I take it out to the dining room table and set it next to the manila envelope left by Colin.

I stare down at the box and the envelope, unable to decide which one is more intimidating. I decide to open Taz's first and get the most damaging of the two out of the way.

After carefully peeling back the paper, I set the handmade wooden box on the table and take off the lid. The interior is covered with soft rabbit fur, and resting upon it is a miniature replica of a Native American flute carved from a smooth, ivory-colored deer antler. The finger holes are etched rather than cut all the way through, and a tiny bone feather on a leather lace is tied to the bottom end. The top end serves as a cap with a tight-fitting plug, though it's loosely inserted now. A long leather thong, woven through two holes in the cap, allows the flute to be worn as a necklace.

Picking up the flute, I pull the cap free and peer inside. Not understanding what I'm seeing, I dump the contents into my palm.

One of the items is a small, folded piece of paper.

The other is a clear glass vial with a rubber cap, like that used in a medical laboratory.

Clinging to the vial, and the precious red fluid within it, is Taz's scent.

The memory of his passion-filled blood—wild, exotic, tasting of redwoods and sky and sunlit beaches—fills my mouth as though it happened only moments ago.

Through the crimson blur of fresh tears, I unfold and read the note.

*Drink this, and no matter where you are, I will find you.*

The sketch of an eagle feather is his only signature.

Regret stains my cheeks as I clutch the vial and mourn the loss of a future that is not the one I've chosen.

~

After washing my face a second time, I return to the table and examine Taz's note.

I don't understand. How does drinking his blood allow him to find me? It should be the other way around, and even then, only if the distance isn't too great.

Unless Nicolas lied to me.

He'd said that me drinking his blood only allowed me to sense his emotions. He didn't say anything about *him* using it to *track* me. I thought he could only do that through *my* blood.

Nicolas.

I'd forgotten how manipulative he is, and that he's a Master of the Game for good reason.

Taz, on the other hand, uses brute force to get his way. In some respects, he's far more honest about what he wants and how he goes about getting it.

Damn them both.

Irritated, I put the vial back into the flute and cap it. It seals tightly, the seam hidden within a line etched into the flute body. To look at the flute now, you'd never know it's actually two separate pieces. Or bears a secret gift too heart-wrenching for words.

I place the flute and note back in the box, pick up the envelope, and open it.

All I can do is stare at the photographs in my hand.

I was wrong.

About everything.

*This* . . . this is the most painful.

And Taz is anything but honest. He's just as big a liar as Nicolas.

The photos, all taken at night, fall to the table, one by one—

—Taz's red bike parked outside a country estate, a vineyard in the foreground

—Taz walking out the front door

—Taz, half-turned around

—a women in a flowing, sheer robe, her arms reaching out to him
—the woman and Taz, wrapped in a lover's embrace
—the woman, a close-up of her face as she smiles up into his
I shut my eyes. I can't bear to look at it again.
But I have to.
The woman in the photograph is Alina.

# THURSDAY

## CHAPTER 76

*Thunk!*

I walk over and yank the dagger from the post, its wood riddled with narrow slices deep into its marrow.

*Thunk!*

There's something satisfying about the sound that follows the release of the blade, that solid, auditory proof that one has executed a move properly.

*Thunk!*

Especially when one imagines it sinking deep into a golden target, or a blue one, or a green one. Or even a violet one for that matter.

I'm pissed at all of them.

The Aston Martin pulls up outside. I listen as Colin gets out, my frustration eager for a fresh target.

He opens the barn door.

*Thunk!*

The dagger lands in a new post, just inches from Colin's blue eyes.

He ducks, then darts to the side. His growl is echoed by mine as I drop into a crouch.

But he's still faster than me. Part of me isn't surprised when he's gripping me from behind, the dagger against my throat.

"You should be thanking me," he scolds.

"For what? For sticking your nose into business that isn't yours?"

"It most certainly is mine." Colin releases me and I turn around to glare at him.

"Sunny, you're my student. And it's the job of any good instructor to keep their student focused on the work at hand."

"That's bullshit and you know it."

"You're behaving like a child. I tried to warn you about him."

"I don't care about him. I care that you took it upon yourself to play private investigator into my affairs."

"Is that what it was? An affair?"

"It wasn't anything. It was just another asshole Chosen trying to use me. Just like every single one I've met, including you and Alina."

Colin's expression grows cold.

"Get used to it. That's what Chosen do. And as I recall, *you* came to Alina for help. If you haven't figured out by now that nothing's free, then I've truly wasted my time."

I hate this life. Why anyone would ever choose it is beyond me.

Colin hands me back the dagger.

"Now, if you've finished with your little tantrum, we have a lot of work to do, starting with repairing that hole in the wall."

ϰ

It doesn't take long for us to fall back into our usual balance, with Colin instructing and me absorbing and mimicking. Pounding new boards into place is almost as satisfying as throwing the dagger, until I hit a nail so hard the hammer goes all the way through the wood. Colin just shakes his head and tells me to go get another board from the stack of lumber delivered earlier this morning.

We finish up the night with a workout and sparring session. He seems impressed with some of the new skills I'd gained working with Taz and mentions I'd probably hold my own in the arena against most Chosen in my age division and weight bracket.

That probably wouldn't be a good idea. The way I feel about Chosen right now would likely result in me being labeled the new Executioner.

Tomorrow Colin's bringing Jeanette over for another French lesson. I guess that means he's forgiven me for my perceived indiscretion. I haven't quite forgiven him for blindsiding me with those damn photos, but I suppose he did do me a favor.

Betrayal tastes bitter on both ends, and any feelings I thought I had for Taz are now sufficiently buried beneath its acrid taint.

I hope.

# MONDAY

## CHAPTER 77

It's Christmas Eve. I grimace at the lights and lawn decorations plastering the quiet Sacramento neighborhood and wish once again I'd had the guts to decline Jeanette's invitation.

But she was so excited when she'd asked me to spend the evening with her and Colin, I couldn't turn her down.

I curse Colin, though, for not giving me a heads up about her plan so I could prepare a logical excuse in advance. He probably just saw it as another training opportunity to practice my mental agility and emotional control.

Spotting the address, I pull into the driveway of a brown two-story and turn off the car. Blue and white icicle lights frame the eaves of the garage and house, and it makes me grin to think of Colin on a ladder putting them up while his neighbors peek through their curtained windows and wonder why he was doing so after dark.

My grin fades, though, when I recall hanging my own lights in the dark. That year, Andrea and I were both so busy with work and school, we agreed not to bother with outside decorations. And then, on Christmas Eve, unable to stand how forlorn our little house looked among its festive neighbors, we hauled out the ladder and hung lights until midnight. We were both so tired when we finished that we unplugged them after only five minutes and dragged ourselves to bed. It was our last Christmas together.

I take a deep breath and shove the memory away. Quickly centering myself, I grab Colin and Jeanette's gifts and head for the door.

A wreath occupies the center, its fresh pine branches accented in red ribbons and little white bells. The mountain scent takes me back to

Colorado, reminding me of Nicolas and, in spite of everything that's happened, how much I still miss him.

This promises to be a rough evening. Steeling myself once more, I knock on the door.

~

"You did well tonight," Colin says as he comes back downstairs and into the living room after seeing Jeanette off to bed.

"I think this was the cruelest thing you've done to me yet."

My body feels as though it's going to explode from the emotional pressure pulsing through my veins and muscles. I'm not sure which was worse—the whole Christmas thing or watching Jeanette and Colin function together as a couple. Their simple touches and knowing looks, the way she kissed him on the cheek when she excused herself for the evening, were all torturous reminders of my own loneliness.

"The best way to deal with painful memories is to build newer, happier ones." He stops before me, hands in the pockets of his grey slacks.

"That's easy for you to say."

"Do you really think that I've never suffered loss?" Colin asks quietly, a faint shadow flickering in his blue eyes. "That I didn't leave a family behind when I was faced with the Choice between death and life as a Chosen?"

I'd often wondered about his background, but he seems so secure in who he is that I'd never guessed he might bear his own emotional baggage.

Embarrassed by my self-absorption, I look away to stare at the hand-dyed silk scarf in pale rose and turquoise resting among the tissue paper in its gift box, my Christmas present from Jeanette and Colin.

He clears his throat.

"We should move to the study where our conversation will be less likely to disturb Jeanette."

His study is small, but adequately furnished with a modest oak desk, leather-upholstered chairs, and several bookcases. Colin gestures for me to take a seat and heads to a mini-bar at the other end of the room.

Pictures of him and Jeanette dot the desk and walls, along with a number of framed oil canvases bearing her signature. Most of the paintings are landscapes, but two contain children, and I wonder how hard it was for her to give up the idea having any of her own when she married Colin.

"Jeanette is not my first wife." He sets down two long-stemmed glasses and a small bottle of wine, then adds a corkscrew from his pocket. "But before meeting her, I spent many years unattached, mostly due to the demands of my work."

He's silent a moment as he takes the chair across from mine.

"Though it would seem logical for a competitive species like ours to be solitary, our survival rate is higher when we live within bloodline-based communities. Along with providing security and companionship, a lineage shares resources, which helps ensure its members will thrive among the dangers presented by both humans and other Chosen."

I wouldn't know. I was denied that benefit when this life was forced upon me.

"The need for connection is innate to Chosen," Colin continues. "Normally it's satisfied through renewal with one's Maker and bloodplay within the lineage—"

"Bloodplay?"

"Think of it as a Chosen one-night stand."

Huh. Is that what Taz was doing when he kissed me? Bloodplay?

But his words and the emotions in his blood claimed otherwise.

"As I was saying, for those outside a lineage, that unsatisfied need to connect can become all-consuming. And if too much time is spent estranged from others of our kind, Chosen can become quite antisocial and extremely violent."

Is he talking about Taz?

Or me . . .

Colin picks up the bottle of wine and studies the label.

"When Nicolas needed me to separate myself from the lineage, it was one of the most painful periods of my life." He pauses, pressing his lips tight. "You see, lineage members enjoy a special association with one another, through the blood of their Maker and Elders, that sustains and helps them to remain stable and in control. To relinquish that sense of family and belonging, as well as severing all connection to one's Maker, is akin to breaking a mate bond. Or so I've been told. Although I've experienced the one, I've never had the misfortune to suffer the other."

I inwardly cringe. Even though Nicolas and I had not quite bonded, the gaping hole he left in my core as his blood faded from my system was excruciating. I cannot imagine what it must be like to lose one's Maker, or entire lineage for that matter. I never knew mine, and what few memories I might have are locked away where I cannot reach them.

With a deep sigh, Colin pulls off the seal on the wine bottle. He picks up the opener and I'm surprised at the sorrow he allows to crease his features. He uncorks the bottle.

What the . . . ? No. *No* . . .

The blood scent escaping its glass prison sends a shockwave ripping through my entire body, ending with a gut-twisting spasm deep within my core. And another. And another.

The scent belongs to Nicolas.

Memories of us spin through my mind, a whirling montage of heart-wrenching images. The first time I saw him, standing across the street, watching me. Our first hunt together, and the way he flowed across the ground, a lean black leopard loping through the shadows of the pines. His first sharp caress on my throat, and the deep rumble of his impassioned growl. And our first sharing as we washed away the aftermath of Katarina's brutal massacre at his club, and the ecstasies of each fiery sharing thereafter.

My hand can't contain the ragged gasps tearing from my mouth and I look up at Colin through a haze of scarlet tears.

His own eyes reddening with emotion, he pours a small amount of the wine into a glass and offers it to me.

Horrified by the pain and longing it will bring, I shake my head no, even as the blood calls to me and triggers a yearning for Nicolas I haven't felt in months.

"I will not share blood with you," Colin says. "But I will share Nicolas's. Please, take it. It will provide some relief to the isolation to which you've been subjected these many months, and in fact, most of your Chosen life." He holds the glass out a moment longer, then sets it in front of me and pours more into the second glass.

"You see, I miss him, too. And now that I'm with Jeanette, I have no desire to share blood with anyone, even though my sense of alienation from our kind can be unbearable at times. So when I feel my breaking point approaching, I drink a little of Nicolas's special wine and remember what it was like to have my Maker's reassuring presence in my life."

I stare at my glass, at the crimson essence which seems to curl through the ruby wine like smoke from a lazy fire. Knowing it will only increase the renewed pain of separation, I pick it up anyway. My eyes close as I bring the glass nearer to my nose and slowly inhale. The scent molecules light up every surface as they stream by and a shudder ripples through me, ending in my gums as my fangs descend. I breathe in and out, immersing myself in his smell and my memories.

But it's not enough. I want more of him, *need* more of him.

When I open my eyes, Colin's watching me.

"You just erased any doubts I may have harbored about your motivation to find Nicolas." He leans back and, raising the glass to his nose, takes in the heady aroma. The muscles in his face twitch, the only evidence of the blood's effect upon him.

Wanting to delay the first sip as long as possible, to savor the anticipation beginning to overshadow the dread, I set down my glass.

"Why did Nicolas ask you to leave the lineage, knowing what it would cost you?"

"Our enemies were growing stronger. We needed to monitor their activities undetected. Apparently he felt I was the only one he could trust enough to release from the restraints of the lineage. Though he warned me of the price, I willingly accepted the assignment. As any good lieutenant would."

Lieutenant?

"How . . . how did you . . .?"

"Nicolas was the captain of my unit. When his personal assistant was killed in a skirmish with the rebels, he needed someone with an aptitude for maps. I volunteered."

"The rebels?"

"Lee's forces. In the War Between the States."

The Civil War. That was the 1860s. Nearly a hundred and fifty years ago.

"You're saying that Nicolas fought in the Civil War. I . . . I didn't think he was that involved in human affairs."

"Nicolas abhors slavery of any kind, no matter who the master. He not only led Union troops, he ran sabotage operations behind the lines."

"Did you know what he was?" I ask, trying to picture Nicolas on a human battlefield, surrounded by gunsmoke, bodies, and blood.

Colin frowns.

"Of course not. Though he had a habit of going for long walks during the night, and preferred to dine alone, I had no idea there was anything unusual about him. That is, until I was shot and lying on my deathbed. When he offered me the Choice, my only thought was getting well so I could continue to serve my captain and my country. I had no concept of how my life would change."

A hundred and fifty years. Because of my familiarity with him, and that era of American history, Colin's story resonates with me far more than Alina's did.

"I can't imagine knowing someone that long."

Chuckling, Colin shakes his head.

"I tend to forget how young you are sometimes. With your ability to move about during the day, and the remarkable control you maintain around humans, one could easily believe you're two to three hundred years old."

Colin has never met with me before dusk. That someone of his age and demeanor, let alone his experience, still cannot rise until after sunset seems very odd to me.

"So what is it you do for him that requires you to not be a member of his lineage?"

He smiles.

"Let's just say I keep an eye on things. Unbound are a little more difficult to track than those who belong to a lineage."

It all fits together now. Our clandestine meetings with Alina, my interrogation, his knowledge of European geography and impressive fighting skills, the quiet existence he leads in the human suburbs.

Though I'd had suspicions, I wasn't sure. Until now.

He's Nicolas's spy.

Alina called him The Chameleon.

With his nondescript appearance and bland mannerisms, I can see how he could lull anyone into not giving him a second glance. Yet his sharp intelligence and observation skills surpass anyone's I've ever met, with the possible exception of Nicolas himself.

Looking at Colin with newfound respect, I nod.

"Well, it's been a long evening." He picks up the bottle, uncorks it, and tops off his glass. "Thank you for spending it with us, even though I know it was difficult. You made Jeanette happy—this is our first Christmas together as husband and wife, and our first in the States. She's quite anxious to integrate into what she perceives as American life, and I do everything I can to enable that for her."

"She knows what you are, right?"

"Of course. But I prefer to keep Chosen life as far from her as possible. Other than Nicolas, you're the only one of our kind she's met."

"You told her about me?"

"Yes."

"Why? Why risk me knowing about her?"

He stands, holding his glass.

"Someday she may be ready to face the Choice. I want her to know that I'm not an exception to the legends, that our kind *can* exist peaceably among humans. You're a good example of a woman who's successfully made the transition."

I laugh.

Right. He should've brought her the night I woke up in the barn and ripped an entire herd of goats to pieces.

"You *want* this life for her?"

"I want whatever will make her happy. And whether she chooses to spend her life with me as a mortal or as an immortal is up to her. But it will be her Choice, not mine."

That's what Nicolas said to me. But he continually manipulated me to make the Choice *he* wanted. I wonder if that's what Colin is doing to Jeanette.

"I'm going to leave the bottle for you to enjoy in privacy. Please stay as long as you like. There's a spare bedroom down the hall should you wish to spend the day. But first—" Colin gestures with his glass. "I'd like to propose a toast."

Picking up my own, I stand.

"To the success of your journey." He raises his glass.

I touch mine to his and nod.

"To Nicolas," he adds.

"To Nicolas." I whisper.

"And a toast that he and I always shared." Colin's eyes redden as he raises his glass once again. "To the Blood."

Raising mine in a newfound understanding, I join him.

"To the Blood."

And with a final nod to me, he leaves the room.

❧

It's been several hours since Colin went upstairs.

The bottle still sits before me, still corked. The wine in the glass is as he poured it.

Every so often, I pick up the glass and inhale its alluring aroma. Several times I've touched the edge to my lips, then lowered it, the wine untasted.

Weary of my indecision, I open the bottle and pour the contents of the glass back inside, then recork it. I grab a pen and a pad of paper from Colin's desk, scribble a short thank you to him and Jeanette, and leave it next to the glass.

I stare at the bottle a moment, then tuck it beneath my arm, retrieve Jeanette's present, and head home.

The sun is still an hour away from making its appearance when I arrive. I swing by the kitchen for a glass on my way to the bedroom.

The white, fluffy down comforter and pillows are a stark reminder of my nights at Nicolas's estate. Though I'd splurged on them for the remembered comfort of those in his guest bedroom, tonight they take me back to my time there and all that took place.

Filling the glass with wine, I look at the bed, as pristine as newly fallen snow.

Screw that. I have a feeling this going to be messy.

I strip and head for the shower.

The water is steaming hot when I step in, glass and bottle in hand. I set the bottle on the shower shelf, move to the edge of the spray, and raise the glass.

Like it did at Colin's, the darker blood drifts and swirls through the ruby-colored wine as though it's a separate entity, almost as if it were alive.

Bringing the glass closer, I once again breathe in Nicolas's scent, savoring every molecule, and then, pressing the glass to my mouth, tip it up ever so slightly.

Vibrant liquid softly splashes against my lips, like fine silk sliding across my skin. I recall the first time his lips touched mine, and the fiery promise they held. I treasure the wine's caress a moment longer, then give way and allow it to enter.

The taste of him is almost more than I can bear. But worse is the feel of his blood as its fire dances across my tongue.

Steam fills the shower as aching memories of the first time Nicolas offered himself to me explode in my head, triggering the bloodtears the same as it did that night. I set the glass aside and, hugging myself, hold the wine in my mouth as I remember him slashing his upper arm, and me taking hold of him as he took hold of me, and the combined ecstasies as our blood became one.

The water beneath me turns pink as crimson tears stream down the drain. I finally give in to the craving within my body and swallow.

His blood etches its way down my throat, leaving an acid trail of desire in its wake. Its tendrils are entering my veins when I take another swallow.

Passion's hunger ignites within me.

Oh God. I miss him so much . . .

Draining the glass, I hurl it to the shower floor. It shatters into a thousand pieces against the tile as I grab the bottle and yank out the cork.

His essence electrifies my whole body as it knifes through every cell, tantalizing me with forgotten sensations and ghostly raptures. The bottle pours its precious gift down my throat and I swallow and swallow.

But all it really gives me is Nicolas's blood. None of his heat, his need, his love. Though it carries his vibration, it lacks his emotions and his body's intimate caress.

My knees give way beneath the crush of sorrow, and clutching the bottle, I slowly sink to the glass-covered tile, icy pink water running over my breasts and unfulfilled hunger coursing through my veins.

Why? Why did I ever leave him?

Embraced only by the stinging cold shower, I bleed the bottle dry as the sun's dark touch bleeds away the memories, and the longing and, finally, the bitter taste of soul-crushing regret.

# THURSDAY

## CHAPTER 78

I stare at the open suitcase stuffed to the brim with my belongings. Today is the fourteenth of February—Valentine's Day—and I wonder if it will be my last one alone.

Tomorrow I leave for Europe to find Nicolas.

Only two things remain to be packed.

One is my passport, which will go into my jacket pocket, along with my current ID.

The other is the small wooden box, with the miniature antler flute necklace and its hidden treasure—and Taz's ring, its shank bent and useless, the victim of my rage at his betrayal.

Since Christmas night when I woke up beneath an ice-cold shower, an empty wine bottle as my sole physical remnant of Nicolas clasped to my breast, I've thought several times that I should just throw Taz's blood away. Though Colin may gain some benefit from an occasional reminder of Nicolas, it did nothing for me except re-awaken my remorse and deepen my loneliness.

I never want to experience anything like that again.

But I can't quite bring myself to dispose of the wooden box, in spite of Taz's duplicity. Something within me clings to it, to some reminder of another possible future. Frustrated with my indecision, I shove the box into my carry-on bag, next to the satin pouch containing Nicolas's bracelet, and tug the zipper into place.

After closing up the suitcase, I grab the heavy postal tape to seal up the box I'm leaving with Colin. Inside it are a few unnecessary clothing items and some personal odds and ends, like my bear claw collection.

Beside it is the dagger Taz gave me. It won't pass through a security check, so I'm reluctantly leaving it behind, along with my .357 and ammo.

Colin thought the gun was quite amusing when I showed it to him—until I explained how I'd planned to use it against Éva. His expression grew thoughtful enough that it made me wonder if my plan would've actually worked.

The last thing I see as I close up the box is the little purple stuffed dragon whose twin is buried on a mountainside with the precious girl who made me whole.

Sandy. I don't think about her very often, yet whenever I do, I can hear her final whispered, "I love you," and it makes me want to be worthy of the admiration she had for me.

Thankfully she doesn't haunt me the way I feared she would. Chosen life would be that much more horrid if we were all haunted by the stolen souls of those we'd killed.

A glance at the clock reveals it's time to go—Alina wants to meet with me before I fly out. I grab my keys and the directions and head out to my car.

ઋ

As I turn onto Highway 12 for Napa, it begins to rain, and I think back over the last three months. Just when I'd thought Colin had taught me everything I'd need to survive, it turns out he still had a few tricks up his sleeve.

Including the carbon-fiber throwing knives that are now hidden up my own sleeve. He said they were far superior to the dagger, though I'm not sure about that. They work well enough, but lack that satisfying *thunk* of the metal blade. However, they will pass through security. The decorative carbon-fiber strips on my new jacket he'd had made offer the perfect decoy for the little knives, which are secreted within its hidden panels.

But the best trick revealed how Colin had earned his nickname, The Chameleon. Nicolas had taught it to him, and Colin said that in all of his years slipping through Chosen social circles, he'd never encountered another who could successfully pull it off.

Their secret weapon, and the key to their survival of many years among enemies, is the ability to mask their auras—the primary way Chosen identify one another and their lineages of origin. Though only able to mask for short periods of time, Colin credited the technique with saving his life on several occasions.

And when Colin passed the technique on to me, the reason behind my months of meditation practice became crystal clear. The exercises weren't just about learning how to manage my emotions and physical reactions, but were really preparation for suppressing the mechanism that emits my aura—that personal stamp which advertises my lack of lineage connection and level of Chosen maturity.

Colin was surprised at how quickly I picked it up. He speculated that my aptitude was due to Nicolas's blood influence on my half-Chosen state when we were together. That because Nicolas and I had shared so often and so deeply, nearly to the point of bonding several times, his potent essence was now tightly interwoven with my own.

Not to mention the impact of the night when Nicolas came close to killing me. Though I'd heaved up all of his blood I'd just taken in, the weeks of sharing left enough embedded within my system that it nearly usurped that of my unnamed Maker.

Nicolas almost re-Made me that night. He almost became my new Maker, which would have ruined any chance for us to have an equitable relationship. I would have forever been subject to his wishes, with no will of my own.

That was unacceptable to either of us.

Yet, I now wonder if the craving I feel for him is more than that for a lost mate. That my body is mourning the absence of its almost-Maker as well, and what drives me is a need to reconnect with both lover and lineage.

Is it possible that, despite my efforts to maintain my independence, Nicolas stole it anyway? That I'm bound to him in more ways than one?

The thought disturbs me beyond all reason.

I fight back the flash of rage surging through me. Whether or not it was his intention, the idea that he might control me even after our lengthy separation has rekindled the doubts that continually plagued me while we were together, and ultimately drove us apart.

But they make no difference. I have to find him. Not just for Colin and Alina and the lineage, but for myself.

Now that I'm completely Chosen, and have learned how to survive among others of my kind, I need to know if what we had is still possible.

And if I still truly want it.

I'm deep within vineyard country and the rain has faded to a light mist when I pull up to a white wrought-iron gate. A fence-mounted camera whirs to life when I press the call button, and after several seconds, the gate swings open. Rows of dormant grapes frame the wet driveway, their leafless canes tied neatly to the trellis wires as all await the first bloom of the approaching spring.

Lights up ahead indicate I'm nearing the house. As the sprawling, Spanish-style mansion comes into view, my suspicions are confirmed.

This is the house where Colin took the photographs of Taz and Alina.

But fortunately, the motorcycle is nowhere to be seen. Blocking the unwanted thoughts spurred by the months-old memories of those pictures, I park and get out.

The house is two stories in white stucco with a red-tiled roof. Traditional mission-style arches grace the front, centering on a pair of heavy, dark-stained oak doors carved with trailing vines and clusters of grapes. Lush foliage drips rainwater from hanging pots and flower beds lining the brick walkways.

Anxious to practice my new-found aura-cloaking skill on someone who knows me besides Colin, I do a quick internal check as I walk up to the entrance, then knock.

The door is opened by an attractive Hispanic woman in her late forties, her shoulder-length dark hair offset by a teal blue sweater and black slacks. She smiles and steps back.

She's human. The scent of the blood within her veins reaches me, and beneath it is Alina's. As with Jeanette, I feel no reaction to it.

She must be one of the donors of whom Alina spoke.

"Miss Martin? Please, come in."

The sound of trickling water from an Old World fountain greets me as my boot heels ring out against mahogany-colored ceramic tile. The fountain occupies the center of a high-ceilinged entryway, its white walls along the floor lined with large greenery-filled clay pots. A massive, black wrought-iron chandelier above sheds muted light from candle-flame-shaped bulbs. Arched doorways on either side admit glimpses of an elegant dining room and what appears to be a formal sitting area.

A huge portrait, painted in rich oils and mounted within an ornate gold-leaf frame, covers the wall at the end of the entryway. The subject, an aristocratic young noblewoman crowned with snowy lace in her Spanish-colonial wedding dress, is posed sitting against a waterfall of bougainvillea, its paperlike flowers in fuchsia, salmon, and pale coral. Petite hands resting in her lap, her violet eyes carry a spark of mischief above a delicate nose and lips curved into a knowing smile.

Alina made a beautiful bride, and I wonder how long ago the painting was done, and who her husband is. Or was.

"Isn't that a stunning portrait?" The woman turns to me, the flush of embarrassment spreading up her face. "I'm sorry. My name is Reina. I should've introduced myself when I answered the door."

"No problem. You can call me Sunny." I smile to put her at ease.

"We're in the parlor. If you'd like to come this way . . ." Reina gestures and I follow her lead through the archway.

Rather than the bright shades usually associated with Spanish mission décor, the muted tones in this room better reflect Alina's introspective nature. My boots sink into plush carpet the color of fresh milk, and floral patterns in pale blue, dove grey, and touches of soft taupe cover the sofas, chairs, and draperies. Potted plants dot shelves and small tables, and on the far wall, flames flicker and curl within a stately white brick fireplace, adding to the warmth and serenity of the room.

"I'll let Alina know you're here." Reina disappears into a hallway adjacent to the fireplace.

I wander about the room examining the various artwork on the walls and stop before a beautiful landscape above the fireplace. The scene is of a vineyard right before harvest, with plump clusters of purple grapes hanging from the vines, and golden California hills in the background. The work looks like Jeanette's, but it's unsigned.

"Hello, Sunny." Alina walks into the room through the archway, elegant as always. She's dressed in grey slacks and a lavender cashmere sweater, and her dark hair is loosely pulled back into a soft bun. Elder power emanates from her in gentle pulses through languid swirls of violet and amber.

Curiosity lights up her expression as she approaches me.

"Alina." I offer a half bow.

"I see that spending time with The Chameleon has been of great benefit to you. You've learned your lessons well."

Assuming she means my cloaked aura, I nod.

"Thank you."

"And the blonde is a nice touch. It certainly makes you less recognizable."

Not sure if that's a compliment, I just smile and nod.

Voices from the hallway into which Reina disappeared grow louder, then stop altogether as an older gentleman enters the room.

He's good looking, somewhere in his mid-fifties I guess. Sporting neatly groomed dark hair and a navy blue sweater over khakis, his confident air indicates he's someone who's accustomed to success.

"Ah. Charles. Thank you for joining us." Alina walks over to him and taking both his hands, tips her head as he bends to kiss her cheek.

The gesture of affection between them surprises me, and I study the man more closely.

"Did I hear Stephen and Carol?" she asks.

"They'll be down in a moment." He glances over at me.

"Come. Let me introduce you to my guest." Alina releases one hand and leads him toward me.

"Sunny, this is Charles, Reina's husband."

He bows.

"Welcome to our home, Sunny."

Like Reina, he carries Alina's blood scent, only stronger. Again, I feel no reaction to his presence.

Before I can respond to his greeting, feminine laughter, accompanied by a male voice, echoes from the hallway and a pretty redhead in her mid-thirties enters the room.

Bright blue eyes shine with curiosity above faint freckles and a petite, upturned nose. A broad smile lights up her face. Designer jeans and a frilly orange blouse accentuate a slender body, completing her youthful appearance.

Behind her is a younger version of the first man, early forties, with lighter hair and a more casual attitude, reinforced by a white polo shirt, simple jeans, and lime green Nike shoes.

"Hello. Sorry. Carol couldn't decide what to wear—" He grins.

"Stephen!" She playfully punches him in the shoulder. "Don't blame it on me. You were the one—"

Laughing, he draws her close and kisses the top of her head. With his arm around her waist, he guides her over to me.

"We're always the last ones to the party. Hi. I'm Stephen. And this is Carol."

Though they both bear Alina's blood scent, which has so far seemed to prevent any instinctive response within me, my gums twinge as Carol's scent drifts over me. Its exotic fragrance triggers a memory of a young man in Colorado who claimed his blood, like that of all redheads, was especially satisfying—a claim that proved to be quite true.

Clamping down on my body's reaction, I nod.

"Hello. I'm Sunny. Do you live here too?"

"Yeah. We all do, along with Tammy and Cherise. Just one big, happy family." Stephen grins and turns to Alina. "Isn't that right, Lina?"

Even though his tone carries no hint of sarcasm, the shadow that flits through Alina's violet eyes tells me all might not be well in paradise.

Charles coughs.

"Well, we really must be going or we'll be late for our dinner reservation." He squeezes Alina's hand, then releases it. "Has anyone seen Reina?"

"I'm right here." She enters carrying a wine tray with two bottles and glasses, then sets it on the long coffee table in front of the couch. Charles joins her at the table and opens both bottles, then pours a glass of each. He hands one to Alina and the other to me.

Though hers smells of the heavily spiced bloodwine favored by most Chosen, mine bears a simple Zinfandel with no trace of human blood. I murmur my thanks.

"Do you need anything else before we leave, Alina?" Charles asks.

"No, thank you. Are the girls joining you?"

Stephen snickers.

"They're meeting us at the theater. They just stepped into the shower. Finally. Those three have been going at it for hours."

"Thank you, Stephen." Alina shoots him an exasperated look before turning back to Charles. "I hope you enjoy your dinner and movie. We'll be fine here."

The four of them nod to me as they leave, their comments of "nice meeting you" and "have a good evening" fading into silence once they close the door.

"You have a nice . . ." I search for the right word. On the heels of Stephen's remarks, I'm not sure what fits.

"Family? Yes. Yes I do. And yes, that's what we are. With all of its ups and downs. Please, sit."

She gestures toward one of the upholstered chairs, then settles into a loveseat, curling her legs onto the cushion beside her. Raising the glass to her lips, she takes a mouthful of the bloodwine and holds it a moment before swallowing. The tiny lines of tension creasing her face disappear.

I follow suit, though I doubt I get the same pleasure from my glass that she does.

"Are they brothers? Charles and Stephen?"

"Yes, they are. As you witnessed, they have quite different personalities, and offer quite different delights."

Embarrassed yet fascinated by the glimpse into Alina's personal life, I offer a quick smile before continuing.

"Have they been with you long?"

"Let me see. Charles is turning eighty-one this year, and I believe Stephen will be seventy-two. So about thirty years, give or take a few."

I'm shocked.

As with Marie, these men appear far younger than their actual ages.

"And Reina?"

"Reina. What a lovely woman. So kind and generous. I'm glad Charles found her." Alina smiles and takes another sip of her bloodwine. "She's been with me about twenty-seven years. She and Charles just celebrated their twenty-fifth anniversary.

"Carol is the youngster of the group. She's only been with us a short while, and has completely rejuvenated Stephen. Of course, he's always been on the immature and playful side anyhow." Alina's eyes light up as she laughs. "He's quite fun—together they are a marvelous joy. And you haven't met Tammy and Cherise. They're also somewhat new to our family. They've been here about nine years. They tend to keep to themselves."

Feeling a bit like a voyeur, I can't help but want to know more about their intriguing arrangement.

"So they're all your donors?"

"Yes, along with several others that live elsewhere. I take it you've little experience with donor circles?"

"None. Only those in Nicolas's clubs."

"Ah. Well, those unfortunate individuals never experience the true intimacy and benefits of belonging to a donor family."

No. They're too busy hoping their pickup for the night doesn't kill them.

"You mentioned benefits." I try to focus on the positive. "Like not growing old?"

"Our blood offers resistance to disease and aging, though it's not a complete cure for either. It merely inhibits the process. Donors are more than willing to exchange a bit of their blood for such a blessing."

Blessing. That's not a word I'd use in an arrangement that so closely resembles a pact in which you sell your soul to the devil.

I avert my gaze and take a swallow of the wine, hoping my thoughts haven't broadcast themselves.

"Judgment is an unearned privilege for the young and inexperienced. Be careful."

Her neutral expression and tone emphasize my failure.

"My donors are healthy and happy and share a good life with me, as well as with each other. Do not presume they suffer by any means."

"What about children?"

"Children?" Alina frowns.

"Yeah. What if Stephen and Carol want children?"

"If you think I would feed on children, you can leave. Now." Though her voice is steady, an angry spark flares to life in her violet eyes.

"No. No, that's not what I meant." I swallow. "Children are curious and ask questions and talk about things they shouldn't with classmates . . ."

"Sunny. You seem to think that after five hundred years, I've learned nothing. Of course I wouldn't allow children in the household—for many reasons. That is why I do not accept donors who have any aspirations toward raising a family. The women who join me have either already done so, lack the desire, or are incapable. Carol herself is an example. Her ovarian cancer had rendered her sterile, and furthermore, she would have died without an infusion of my blood. I normally would not choose someone so young, someone who might still long for children, even through adoption. But Stephen had been seeing her for quite some time, and he begged me to save her. So I did. She understood the price, and the two of them are quite happy now."

Feeling like an idiot, I bow my head. I used to do the same thing to Nicolas—judge him, then discover all was not as it seemed.

"I'm sorry. I didn't mean to offend you."

She nods and drains her glass.

"I'm not offended. I can see that you still have much to learn of Chosen ways. Unfortunately, we are out of time."

"Out of time? Why? Can't we reschedule my flight?" As anxious as I am to start my search for Nicolas, I'd almost welcome any excuse to delay a little longer if it meant a better chance for my survival.

"Our lineage is moving in a direction that makes many of us uncomfortable. There is a relaxation of certain guidelines dictating our behavior that does not bode well for the future."

"What does that mean?"

"Éva's always been a bit more . . . traditional-minded. She doesn't hold humans in quite the same regard as Nicolas and I."

"What about the others?"

"They are divided. I fear if we don't split off, the entire lineage will become contaminated."

"Contaminated?"

"Once a Chosen becomes accustomed to killing humans, they develop a constant need for the lifespark. And when one is surrounded by Chosen who thrive on death, it is extremely difficult to resist that lifestyle. It spreads, like a disease. And the only way to eradicate it is to eliminate the host."

Eliminate the host.

"You're talking Chosen war."

"Yes. Unfortunately, I am."

"Here. In America."

"Yes. It will eventually spill over into Canada and South America. And in the meantime, our enemies are circling, waiting for the right moment to move in."

Holy crap.

"So, you see, your trip has more than one purpose. Whatever your personal reasons are, you need to find Nicolas and bring him back. Only he can restore the order. None of us are strong enough to wrest the lineage from Éva."

"I don't understand. How are you able to even talk about this? I thought the Maker bond prevented rebellion, or at least revealed it."

"Yes. That is the other reason why you must leave now. Éva's flying in at the end of the week."

Oh shit.

"She's realized how thin the bond has become, and will be here to renew it with me, as well as with Robert and Elizabeth."

"But can't you just leave? Go elsewhere? Split off, like you said?"

"We cannot just yet. Our numbers are too small, and we do not have enough resources to do so. We now must wait until Éva's attention lapses and she allows the bond to fade again. Perhaps then we'll be able to move against her."

"But isn't there *something* you can do?"

Alina smiles.

"Play the Game. That is all we can do for now. Just play the Game."

# CHAPTER 79

I mull over everything Alina said about Éva's impact on the lineage. There's no doubt about the change in tone I'd witnessed at Nicolas's club in the Springs after Leandro took it over.

And that was last June. I can't imagine what it might be like there now.

Suppressing a shudder, I turn as Alina comes back into the living room after excusing herself to take a phone call.

A door slams upstairs, accompanied by a woman's laugh.

"Well, now that they are out of the shower, perhaps you can meet Tammy and Cherise. They're both musicians and are quite a delight."

I nod, not knowing what else to say.

Alina pours herself another glass of bloodwine

"Would you like more wine, or perhaps a taste of this?" She holds up her glass.

"No, thank you. I'm fine."

She gracefully settles back into the loveseat, her legs once again tucked beside her.

"So. Are you ready for your trip? Do you have everything you need?"

"I think so."

"I trust that Colin would not send you unprepared."

"He's pretty thorough."

"Yes. Yes he is." She takes another sip of wine. "There is much about Europe that I miss. But I doubt you'll have time to enjoy its diverse cultures and scenery. I imagine attempting to pass unobserved and alone through our enemy's territory won't afford you many opportunities to relax."

"I'm going to Europe for only one thing. To find Nicolas."

A loud crash upstairs rattles the ceiling. Alina frowns.

Movement in the archway catches my attention and I glance in that direction.

I stop breathing.

The tall, bare-chested figure rooted there is one I know all too well, yet wish with every feral cell in my body to know better. His damp hair hangs loose over his shoulder, begging to be untangled, but the comb in his hand is crumpled beyond use.

Frozen disbelief on his face melts away, revealing anguished desire that quickly vanishes beneath an expression devoid of all emotion as he slowly looks over at Alina.

"Ah. I'd wondered." She sits up and puts her glass on the table.

The air itself suddenly feels as though it will explode.

"Do you two think to play me for a fool?" Her quiet voice cuts through me like a knife.

"Alina." I shove myself out of the chair. "No. There's nothing—"

"Do not lie to me. It's all over your face. All over both of your faces." She stands, her fists slowly clenching, the colors in her aura roiling faster and faster.

Violence knots his body as Taz snarls. Alina's violet eyes blossom into crimson.

They glare at one another, their unspoken words thundering throughout the room.

And then he's gone.

The slam of a door rattles the windows and I try not to look at the empty archway.

"Coward." She turns her burning red gaze on me.

"And you. I took you in at the risk of losing my place on the Council, of being stripped of my lineage, which would leave me powerless to prevent the oncoming war. I sheltered you and gave you the best training possible. And you do this to me? To Nicolas?" Rage contorts her delicate features for a brief second, then it quickly gives way to a stony stare. She crosses her arms as blood from her clenched fists stains the lavender cashmere.

"I didn't know . . . We haven't . . . Nothing's happened—"

"I should cancel the whole operation. It's pointless now."

"NOTHING HAPPENED!"

Alina takes a step toward me.

"Oh, something's happened all right. You can deny it all you want. But I can see it. He's been acting strange for months. Now I know why."

The sound of a departing motorcycle only emphasizes her words.

"In spite of what you say, Alina, I'm still going to look for Nicolas. I . . . I do love him. And I *will* find him. With or without anyone's help."

She just stares at me with empty eyes.

"As much as I need you to find him," she says, "I almost wish you don't. You do not deserve him. You walked out on him and left all of our lives in turmoil. And now this. You think Nicolas won't know there's someone else? That he won't taste your lack of total commitment to him in your blood? There's no way he'll come back now. He made it quite clear to me when he allowed Éva to take the lineage that without you by his side, he had no desire to continue leading us."

He *allowed* Éva to take the lineage?

Oh my God.

I block out her other words along with my reaction to them, though each one twists in my gut with the fire of a heated blade.

Screw her. Screw all of them.

I'll do this on my own.

"Goodbye, Alina. Thank you for everything you've done."

My back straight, I walk out the door and into the wet winter night.

# CHAPTER 80

I fight to keep the car at a reasonable speed as I head toward home, though the manic beat of the windshield wipers urges me on. The last thing I need is to get pulled over, because all I want to do right now is tear something apart. Thoughts and images chase each other around and around in my head, and I can hardly focus on the rain-slicked road in front of me. At last, the interminable drive ends as I turn onto the lane leading to the house.

But just as I thought things couldn't be worse, I spot Taz beneath the spotlight in front of the barn, leaning against his bike in the rain.

Hell. I'm not ready for this. I don't think I ever will be.

Still a quarter mile from the house, I stop the car. The windshield wipers mesmerize me as they go back and forth, back and forth. Falling raindrops slice through my headlight beams, their sound against my roof growing faint as they diminish.

If I turn around, he'll just follow me. I picture our high-speed chase ending only one way—in a fiery crash, with our bodies and machines strewn all over the highway.

And as much as I want to bolt into the woods, that too would end in a similar, and possibly even more devastating crash. Because I wouldn't be able to control the wild part of me that wants him—that wants him so badly I feel as though my body is exploding.

God damn him.

Why did he have to shove himself into my life? I didn't want this . . .

Using every bit of the skills Colin taught me, I suppress the cursed bloodtears and center myself, then shift the car into gear and finish the drive to the house as the rain dwindles to a heavy mist.

Taz, his arms folded as he leans against the bike, makes no movement when I pull up. He's soaked. Water coats his eyelashes and runs down his cheeks, and drips from his tangled hair onto his wet leather jacket and the bare chest beneath.

I get out and shut the door, then walk around to the other side of the car, soggy gravel squishing beneath my boots. Adopting his stance, I cross my arms and lean against the muddy car door.

"What are you doing here?"

"You can't go."

"You don't have any say in the matter."

He stands.

"I have plenty to say."

"I don't want to hear it."

The air sighs and he's standing a half-dozen feet in front of me.

"Europe's too dangerous. You have no business being there."

"My business is my own. I can take care of myself. In spite of what you think, I'm not completely helpless."

"No. You're not." He steps closer, smelling of wet hair and leather. "But as pretty as you are, if you think you can make it there alone, you haven't learned much."

I bristle at the familiar insult, and easing away from the car, I casually take a step to the side, needing to put some space between us.

"I've learned more than you think—"

And then I'm back against the car, his damp body pinning mine to the fender.

I want to struggle, but I don't, knowing it would do little good.

Or so I tell myself.

His lips touch my brow. Cool breath tickles my scalp as his fingers follow the line of my jaw.

He eases back, shrugs off his jacket, and lays it inside-up on the car's wet hood. Before I can protest, he grips my waist and, lifting me, sets me on the dry lining.

His eyes, a deep gold tinged with red, bore into mine as he cups my scarred cheek.

"I would go with you."

"I . . . I . . . no, you can't."

"You go to look for *him*."

I nod, fighting the tears that want to burst from my eyes.

"I would help you." The touch of his thumb on my lips is as feather-soft as his words.

Wanting nothing more than for him to take me in his arms and crush the life from me, I pull away from his gentle touch.

"Why? So you can kill him?"

He goes still, then lowers his hand to the car.

"Only if you'll let me."

I close my eyes as the bloodtears slip past my barrier.

His fingers follow the path of my tears, then trail away.

And the next touch on my lips is slick with blood.

But it's not mine.

His finger brushes my tongue, and his taste curls about it, bringing memories of blue skies and sunlit love.

Oh God.

I can't. I can't give in to this.

I try to push him away, but he only wraps his arms around me. My body trembles against his cold skin as I fight the sobs seeking to tear themselves free.

Images rip through my mind as full-scale war erupts between my past with Nicolas and my present with Taz. Twin futures enter the fray, then fragment into endless possibilities.

"Stay. Stay here with me."

Oh, how I want to. To run and hunt and fight and love—with *him*. With this wild, independent animal of a Chosen who's so like me in so many ways.

But I can't.

The blood in me that belongs to Nicolas won't allow it.

I have to go.

I have to find out if Nicolas and I truly belong together, and if not, to make my final peace with him.

Not for him. Not for the lineage.

For me.

This is something I must do, and I cannot move on with my life until it's done.

Summoning every last bit of my will, I tear myself away from that protective body I've grown to love so much.

"What about Alina?"

Taz shifts back.

"What about her?" The gentle tone is gone from his voice, replaced by a knife-sharp edge.

I slide off of his jacket, then swing my leg past his knees and push myself to the ground. Stuffing my hands into my pockets, I move farther away.

"It's obvious you and she are together."

"We're not—"

I raise my eyebrows.

"Looked and sounded like it to me. She certainly seems to think so."

"It's complicated."

I snort and lace my voice with as much scorn as I can muster.

"I'm sure it is."

"I do not share blood with her."

I laugh, to keep from crying.

"I do not share blood with anyone. Ever."

Except with me.

I turn to stare through the mist at the hills, unable to face him any longer, and think back on his teachings about using an enemy's strengths as well as their weaknesses against them. I can't best him physically, but now I know how to cripple him emotionally.

The truth will wound him deeply. The lies will scar *me* forever.

I feel as though I'm going to die as I force out my words.

"Well. I don't share blood either. Not *willingly*."

"What's that supposed to mean?"

"It means whatever blood of mine you've tasted—you *took*. It was not given."

His silence is his only reply.

"And whatever blood of yours I've *endured* was forced upon me. I did not ask for it. I did not want it."

Even though his gift healed me when I was broken.

Even though all I want now is to drink it with every bit of my soul.

Bloodtears sear my cheeks like acid as I steel myself for the killing blow.

And the sky itself begins to cry.

"I do not want you . . . not now . . . not ever."

The choking silence between us is broken only by the pitter-patter of falling rain. The sound grows louder and louder, pounding metallic against the car, then finally dies beneath that of the Harley engine rending the dark with its demonic roar.

I continue to stare out at the hills as pink rain streams down my face, wincing at the retreating crunch of gravel beneath his tires, at each answering rumble as he shifts gears, and at the fading thunder of Taz as he vanishes into the cold, wet February night.

# FRIDAY

## CHAPTER 81

Once again I'm on the road, though this one ends at the edge of the runway. The engines of the Lear jet grow louder as the small plane Colin chartered backs away from the hangar. I'm the only passenger. Which is good, because I can't stop crying.

A dream that once filled me with so much hope has crashed and burned, leaving only bitter ashes in my mouth.

I thought finding Nicolas was the answer. I thought that might repair the hole in my core, one that's ached with emptiness since the night I left him.

Now, I'm not so sure.

Because now there are two of them.

I stare out the window as we taxi down the runway. The loud engine roar and shuddering through the cabin makes me think of my last ride with Taz—the cold wind tearing at my face, the growl and vibration of the bike beneath me, the broad back before me.

Clutching the little ceramic tile of the Golden Gate Bridge that Jeanette gave me, I can't believe I've done it again.

I can't believe I walked away from another possible shot at ending the loneliness that guards me with such fierce jealousy.

Stars peer through the clouds dotting the dark night sky, forming a backdrop for the vision that's driven me these many months—fierce emerald eyes staring into my very soul.

But now the green keeps fading, shifting, turning.

To gold.

The engines scream louder, and the vibration increases, and then the Lear tilts sharply upward and we're airborne.

As the landing gear rumbles back into the belly of the plane, I watch the earth fall away.

The last thing I see down there, on an empty road across a field from the runway's end, is a lonely, amber-lit streetlight.

And parked beneath it, staring upward, a tall figure sitting on a motorcycle.

# EPILOGUE

The brittle wind snatches at me as I crest the mountain peak and stare down into the snow-blanketed crevasses below. In the distance, the tortured path of a frozen stream winds its way around broken boulders and disappears in a steep mountain divide.

Nothing down there is moving, except dead windblown grasses and shrubs clinging to tiny patches of soil between the icy rocks.

I've grown fond of this rugged, bleak terrain. Surviving its challenges is the only thing that keeps me sane, that keeps me from re-living the horrific nightmare I walked into when I arrived at Nicolas's castle and found a monster far worse than any I could've imagined.

Shrugging off his sinuous whispers that continually slither through my mind, I start working my way down yet another cliff.

It's been many nights since my last meal, a scrawny hare plucked from the mouth of his den. It wasn't even enough to bring a moment's relief to my shriveled tongue and parched throat. Burning hunger is my constant companion now, but I welcome its distraction—anything to hold my memories at bay.

Neither time nor distance has meaning out here. I just keep moving, night after night, pulled by some instinct I do not understand.

Movement above the streambed far ahead freezes me in my tracks. I wait, senses straining.

There.

A small herd of the wild, goat-like creatures inhabiting these heights is bedded down on the steep slope, their tawny coats blending with the rocks on which they perch. I steal forward, step by step, fighting to keep my impatience under control.

I'm within a quarter mile, almost striking distance, when they bolt to their feet and run straight up the slope, leaping from rock to rock. I take off after them, but they have too much of a head start, and by the time I reach the point I'd last seen them, they've vanished.

I yowl my rage and hunger to the surrounding peaks, and the sound echoes back at me, a too-vivid reminder of the nights I spent screaming in the dungeon. Clamping my hands over my ears, I crouch among the rocks until my trembling fit passes.

When I feel steady enough, I move downslope, back toward the twisting streambed.

Fighting off the hopelessness that swoops in with every failure, I focus on making my way through the endless rocks and boulders, drawn by what, I do not know.

And then I feel it.

Something, or someone, is watching me.

I look upslope ahead of me, and there, on a broad ledge, a snow leopard crouches, its furry tail lashing back and forth.

We stare at one another a long moment, and then it hisses and disappears into a cave at the back of the ledge.

A memory surfaces, a pleasant one, of a day spent at the zoo with Nicolas and the beautiful snow leopard there, and his story of spending time with one when he was on the run from his Maker.

*Nicolas.*

The lash on my back, the spur in my side. The need to find him drives me ever onward, giving way only to the incessant hunger that rules every painful breath.

Movement on the ledge vanquishes the gloom beginning to descend over me, that descends every time I think of him, and I look back up.

And I see someone standing there.

Standing on the ledge, looking down at me.

A brown fur covers him, protecting him against the wind whipping through his long black hair. His sharp features and sharper eyes bear little resemblance to their former selves, and I inwardly cringe at the changes wrought in him.

Changes, I fear, that were caused by *me.*

Breath held tight, I scramble up the slope.

He steps back as I pull myself onto the ledge and get to my feet.

Time freezes as the moment I've long dreaded, the same moment for which I've long yearned, arrives with a chill that sinks into the marrow of every bone in my body.

His eyes search mine and I want to shrink away from their cold, distant gaze.

I struggle to formulate words, to use a language almost forgotten.

"Hello, Nicolas."

He stares at me, his emerald gaze now curious as he tips his head and answers.

"Who are you?"

# ACKNOWLEDGMENTS

This journey started eight years ago with a vision of a lonely vampire woman lamenting her existence. Her compelling story unfolded like a movie, and her demands that it be told resulted in the crafting of this series.

I'm deeply indebted to the family and friends, and the writers and readers, who supported my efforts to bring her story to life. Without their encouragement, feedback, and enthusiasm, these books would never have seen the light of day.

To paraphrase a famous saying, it takes a village to publish a book—at least a book that readers will enjoy. In a village, inhabitants cluster around a central square—in this case, the book—and contribute to its development as the heart of the community.

Beta readers are essential members of that community, providing insight and suggestions to help an author shape their story into one with a universal appeal.

My beta readers, many of whom were instrumental in the honing of *Watcher*, were invaluable with this book as well. A big thank you to Lex, Janine, Mellie, Ed, Earl, Vanessa, Odette, Jeannie, Danielle, Tirzah, Amanda, Ayesha, and Kirsten. Their in-depth comments on *Runner* helped me identify problems and bring clarity to the story. Though I may not have addressed all of their concerns to their satisfaction, I hope they like the final version.

The medical scenes in *Runner* presented a unique obstacle. As with all of my works, I endeavor to keep as much realism in the fantasy as possible and devote much time to extensive research. But these scenes needed the guidance of experts, and I'm grateful to Janeane Stover and Gazelle Sexton for providing their medical advice. Any errors in the portrayal of the depicted procedures are entirely the fault of the author.

Kirsten Starkweather played in integral role in the final stages of this book. Her viewpoint as a voracious and discerning reader of many genres gave me a better understanding of the reading audience and the reassurance that this book stays on track as a sequel. I appreciate the long hours she spent on the phone with me discussing everything from reader expectations to pop culture, and am especially grateful for her input on the book covers for the series.

The appearance of the central square in a village is the responsibility of the landscape designer. In our village, that task belongs to the cover designer, and I believe Milo, Kim, and Darja at Deranged Doctor Design have served the village well with their beautiful covers for *Watcher* and *Runner*. My thanks to them, and to Lex, Kirsten, Jodi, and Vicky for their valuable feedback during the development process.

One of the key figures in the publishing village is the editor, and it took me some time find the right one for The Chosen series. My deepest thanks to Jodi Renée Lester for her editorial skills, her unflagging commitment to Sunny's story, and her partnership in bringing these books up to their full potential. And most of all, her friendship.

None of this would have been possible without the primary residents of our village—the readers. I'm sincerely humbled by the devotion of those who've been on this journey with me since the beginning, and their continuing support for Sunny's story. Many of these folks were fellow members of the Fresno Scifi & Fantasy Writers and were the first to read my work outside of family and close friends; others I met through shared interests in pop culture. A few I've never met, nor spoken with, but their appreciation for *Watcher* and anticipation for *Runner* kept me working through those dark times when I wondered if it would ever be published.

To those who've waited patiently for this book, I offer my humblest thanks.

And last, but never least, I want to thank my parents, my children, and especially my husband for everything they do to encourage and support my writing. Without them, there would be no village at all.

# MUSIC PLAYLIST

Music plays an important role in my life, and that includes my writing as well. It provides a sound buffer, preventing the outer world from intruding into my inner one. It helps me to feel the emotions of the story inhabitants and bring those emotions to the page.

Some songs on this list belong to a specific character; others to a scene. For me, the most important part of a song is the mood it creates and enhances, whether it does that through the melody, the rhythm, or the tone. The lyrics may or may not have anything to do the scene, but the emotion with which they are sung does. And when the words in the song align with the words on the page, the effect is magnified.

Sunny's emotions are all over the map in this book, and the songs for her vary, from quiet laments to proclamations of strength. Sandy is epitomized with Leona Lewis's "I See You." Taz's old-school biker attitude harkens back to The Allman Brothers and The Doors. And Chia—poor Chia—gives her frustration and outrage a voice in Skrillex's "First of the Year." Though the words don't quite fit, the tone most certainly does.

Colin continues to slip through these stories with honor and elegance, belying the steel beneath, and in the process, winning the hearts of more than a few readers. The Italian composer Ludovico Einaudi best captures Colin's essence in "Life" and "Two Trees."

Enjoy.

PROLOGUE

* Closer – Kings of Leon

PART I – THE HITCHHIKER

* And All That Could Have Been – Nine Inch Nails
* Lament of a Lost Soul – Brigitte Handley and the Dark Shadows
* Bring Me to Life – Evanescence
* Into Dust – Mazzy Star
* Comfort Zone – General Fuzz
* Casualty – Kopecky Family Band

PART II – THE CATALYST

* Let Me Go – Avril Lavigne & Chad Kroeger
* Dark Undercoat – Emily Jane White
* The Winter – Balmorhea

* Silver Coin – Angus & Julia Stonex
* I See You (Theme from Avatar) – Leona Lewis
* Mad World (Instrumental) – Jennifer Ann

PART III – THE DEVIL

* Keep the Streets Empty for Me – Fever Ray
* Blood Like Lemonade – Morcheeba
* Stranglehold – Ted Nugent
* Whipping Post – The Allman Brothers
* Keep Me – The Black Keys
* People Are Strange – The Doors
* Riders on the Storm – The Doors
* The End – The Doors
* First Of The Year (Equinox) – Skrillex
* Nobody But You – The Black Keys
* Have Mercy on Me – The Black Keys
* In Memory of Elizabeth Reed – The Allman Brothers
* The Flame – The Black Keys
* Dreams – The Allman Brothers
* The Crystal Ship – The Doors
* The One That Got Away – The Civil Wars

PART IV – THE CHAMELEON

* Metal Heart – Cat Power
* Life – Ludovico Einaudi
* Experience – Ludovico Einaudi
* The Sound of Winter – Bush
* Stand Up – Bush
* Iris – Goo Goo Dolls
* Two Trees – Ludovico Einaudi
* Slow – Fuel
* Innocent – Fuel
* Hemorrhage (In My Hands) – Fuel
* Wicked Game – Emika
* Wicked Game – Chris Isaak
* Intro – Alt-J

EPILOGUE

* In The End – Linkin Park/Piano Tribute Players

# ABOUT THE AUTHOR

Roh Morgon discovered the magic in stories at an early age, both in books and in those she made up in her head. As a child growing up in a remote Southern California canyon, she explored the wild hills barefoot with her brothers and rode her horse bareback at top speed. A wicked youth spent hitchhiking across the West and perched on the backs of Harleys eventually gave way to soccer mom duties and full-time college studies—at the same time. In her spare moments, she learned how to herd cattle, swordfight, and plant an arrow or a knife in a target—not necessarily at the same time.

Her years spent in the lofty mountains of Colorado and the stark plains of Wyoming, the red canyons of central Arizona and the rolling hills of California, provide some of the diverse stages upon which her characters re-enact their lives.

Roh currently shares her home in the Sierra Nevada foothills with three mustang horses, two crazy herding dogs, and a very patient husband who reminds her of the need to eat and sleep. She writes fantasy and urban fantasy for middle grade, young adult, and adult readers.

If you would like to read other works by this author or be kept up to date on new releases, please visit her website at www.rohmorgon.com.

And if you enjoyed *Runner: Book II of The Chosen*, please feel free to leave a review on Amazon.

# BOOKS BY ROH MORGON
# THE CHOSEN SERIES

## WATCHER
### BOOK I OF THE CHOSEN

Sunny Martin's been a monster—or so she thinks—since the night she was drained of her blood and left for dead, but when she falls in love with Nicolas, the mysterious leader of The Chosen, she discovers a startling truth behind her savage nature which may force her to choose between her heart and the last remnant of her human soul.

## RUNNER
### BOOK II OF THE CHOSEN

Sunny Martin is on the run from a monster—the monster within herself. When murder and betrayal end her affair with the mysterious leader of The Chosen, Sunny must face the death of someone she loves, and face the love of someone she fears—an outlaw Chosen even more dangerous than the one who broke her heart.

## THE GAMES MONSTERS PLAY
### A NOVELETTE OF THE CHOSEN

When corporate spy Colin O'Neill receives a personal invitation from Katarina Habsburg to join an elite high-stakes game, he fears his cover blown. With his time running out, Colin must choose between finishing his mission and making his escape before the game's end in this chilling tale of industrial espionage with a bite.

## THE LAST TRACE
### A NOVELLA OF THE CHOSEN

Trace Pierre Tasman's simple life as a mountain man in 1842 Montana turns into a living nightmare when a beautiful but vicious she-demon begins stalking him. This is the beginning of Taz's story.

# MONSTERS IN THE MACHINES
## SHORT STORY COLLECTION

### THE SEDUCTION

The first time Erica saw the black, low-slung sports car, she felt its sensual pull deep within her soul—but when she began succumbing to its whispered promises, she didn't suspect she might be losing much more than her mind.

### THE MONSTER'S GROWL

The stakes of the game in the small-town bar are higher than Carly and her friends realize when a mysterious biker puts his quarter on their pool table.

### HELLBOUND TRAIN

(coming soon)

A gambler's winning hand in a high-stakes game may cost him more than he's willing to pay.

Book III of The Chosen

# SEEKER

Coming Soon

www.darkdreamspublishing.com